DEDICATIONS

To Carolyn, my best friend and partner of more than fifty years. With patience, love and skill she has accompanied me on this writing journey—unafraid to comment, edit and propose improvements—always cheering me on and giving comfort.

To my parents and grandparents for leaving me so many tangible memories of their lives, and for making sure I was safe in the early days.

To my two sons, Elliot and Matthew and their families who have supported my efforts with encouragement and love. I hope my novels provide a solid connection to their European past.

Map shows locations of Kohut family members in Great Britain during WWII.

First Printing: 2019
Cover Design by Marlin Greene / 3hats.com
ISBN 978-0-9993631-4-0
Published by Kurti Publishing, Seattle
www.petercurtisauthor.com
© 2019 Peter Curtis

KURTI
PUBLISHING

PAVEL'S WAR

Peter Curtis

The Kohut Trilogy:

THE DRAGONTAIL BUTTONHOLE

CAFE BUDAPEST

PAVEL'S WAR

For background information on these books please visit:
www.petercurtisauthor.com

PART ONE :: THE BLITZ

1.5 million incendiary bombs were dropped on London between Sept. 1940 and May 1941—10,000 per air raid. Photo: Wikipedia

You can never tell whether bad luck may not after all turn out to be good luck.

Winston Churchill

CHAPTER ONE
42 Hampstead High Street,
London
September 1940

Sophie woke to the banshee B flat wail of the air raid siren. Panic and fear flooded her body. She dragged herself off the rug where she had been sleeping, and prodded her four-year old Pavel. Her mouth was dry, heart pounding. "We get dressed, *Pavelku.*"

Rubbing sleep from his eyes, he gave her his reproachful where-am-I, what's-going-on look.

Judit Kohut, Sophie's diminutive fifty-five year old mother in law, a light sleeper and already in her overcoat and slippers, was banging a metal dustpan. "*Schnell! Schnell, meine kinder!* Get ready."

Proboha … for God's sake! Wasn't a siren enough noise without also thumping a dustpan? Sophie suppressed a yell. Better to be diplomatic and silent. She and Pavel, recent arrivals off the refugee boat, were grateful for a roof over their heads.

Sophie knew it would be another twenty-five minutes or so before the German bomber squadrons reached London. She put on her shoes, a coat over her nightdress, and placed two empty chamber pots within easy reach of the kitchen table. She slipped a coat over Pavel's pajamas, and on hands and knees they followed Judit under the kitchen table where they positioned walls of cushions and pillows … protection against flying glass, wood splinters and shrapnel.

Huddled under the table, Sophie knew exactly what her stout and bald-headed father-in-law Emil would be doing: checking that the black-out curtain was closed tight, and stashing his precious family documents inside the cooking stove. As soon as he was done, he put on two pairs of trousers and a jacket and joined them under the table, clutching a paper bag filled with slices of bread, hard-boiled eggs, apple quarters, a glass jar of cold tea, and a flashlight.

"Be patient, my dears," he said before offering them cotton wool to stuff in their ears. "An hour or two and it will be over, and we can go back to sleep."

His calm deliberate words always reassured Sophie, helping her prepare for the barrage of sound that would sweep over them.

By the time the drone of the German squadrons had swollen to a full-throated roar, the nearby Ack-Ack batteries were firing continuously. Explosions of bombs and artillery fire, closer than usual, merged into an ear-splitting cacophony. Sophie held Pavel close, cupping her hands over his ears.

The old building shook violently, and there was a crash … inside the flat.

Emil peered out between the cushions. "*Mein Gott*. The drying rack … from the ceiling. Someone did not fasten it properly."

"Aie, aie, "Judit wailed. "The clean clothes and linens."

Pavel huddled and shivered against Sophie's breast. He cried tears into her nightdress. Strangely enough, having his curly head nestled in the crook of her neck was a great comfort, even when she was most afraid.

This raid seemed never-ending, and she did her best to show a brave face. Being cooped up in her in-laws' flat was bad enough, but stuck under the kitchen table with them every night made her want to scream.

When dawn came, Sophie was the first one up and brewed the tea. She wrapped a blanket around her flimsy nightdress, unclipped the black-out drapes, and pulled up a chair. She liked to sit at the window overlooking the street, her teacup perched on a ledge, peering down at the English housewives, pushing and shoving as they waited for the shops to open.

Lucky women. They have homes and a country.

This morning, instead of women waiting in line with shopping baskets, people crowded the street, talking and gesturing, pointing upwards.

Sophie edged forward for a better look. On the third floor of the opposite building, black smoke drifted from charred window frames, surrounded by blackened bricks. Higher up, thin gray wisps spiraled from a jumble of smashed roof tiles. For a moment she closed her eyes. Yesterday, those windows had glass in them and were capped by graceful white pediments.

What a terrible thing. That could have been us. Those poor people.

She opened the window and stood barefoot on the cold linoleum to get a better view. Home Guard men were sweeping and shoveling broken glass into buckets. A rope with red tags had been set up as a barrier along the pavement. She shuddered at the stench of burned wood and paint and closed the window. But it was reassuring to see all those people milling about in the street. It must be safe now. Perhaps later on, it would be safe to go outside and take a walk with Pavel.

Sophie felt a hand on her shoulder—Emil ... unshaven, thick-lensed glasses, gray hair uncombed, and in his dressing-gown. Back in Lučenec, first thing in the morning and not so long ago, Mr. Emil Kohut would have been clean-shaven and ready for work at his fabric store. Everything about his present shabbiness, the fallout of two years of dispossession and exile, made Sophie feel sad and sorry for him.

He gave her a puzzled smile. "Why do you always watch those English wives in the street, fighting over food?" he asked her in Czech.

"Free entertainment," she said matter-of-factly. "I imagine them at home, cooking for their families, and talking to their husbands, like I might talk to Willy." She looked across the street. "I think that place burned from the inside. But then, maybe it was some kind of bomb."

Emil looked out the window over her shoulder, scratching at his unkempt hair. "A bomb for sure. When I went down for the milk, Mr. Hardy, the shop owner from downstairs told me the tile-breakers started the fire. You see that hole in the roof? *Wir hatten Glück.* Lucky it was not us."

"Tile-breakers?" Sophie was trying to cope with a whole new lexicon of air raid terminology.

"Phosphorus bombs. Incendiaries. Long and thin. They smash through roof tiles and make a big fire inside."

Sophie's stomach tightened. If their flat had been hit by those tile-breakers they would be dead now … burned alive. Her hands began to shake. Why, for God's sake, was she still like this so long after the air raid was over? During their escape through Germany and France she experienced violence many times: Gestapo searches, their ship being machine-gunned and people drowning. She had often tried to hide, even fight back. But … how could she defend herself against faceless evil from the sky.

"Did this Mr. Hardy say what happened to the people inside?"

Emil shrugged. *"Ich weiss nicht genau.* Not sure. He thinks they saved everyone. "

Relieved, Sophie drank down the rest of her tea just as Pavel shuffled up to the window, barefoot and wearing pajamas. He held his only toy, Furry Lion, tight against his narrow chest.

She smiled then rubbed and kissed his back. "Hello my darling. Did Furry Lion have a good sleep?" Delicately, she touched the pink scar on his neck and tousled his hair. He batted her hand away. After an interrupted night, he was often in a bad mood, and sometimes she found it hard not to give him a warning slap. He was not the only one chronically short of sleep.

"Don't let the poor little thing run around like this," Judit scolded, as she joined them at the window, covering Pavel's shoulders with a thick towel. "He's so thin, he'll catch cold. And he needs socks." Ever the *hausfrau*, she was fully dressed; her sparse hair neatly curled and brushed into a bun, her face the color of old speckled ivory. Judit prepared the meals, cleaned the flat, washed and ironed, repaired old clothes, knitted and darned. She liked to wear a Slovak apron embroidered with blue and red flowers; a treasured memento of the old days. She tapped Sophie's shoulder. "Enough window-gazing, my dear. Time you got Pavel washed and dressed."

Sophie sighed. No good to protest or argue with this woman who had provided her and Pavel a home when there was nowhere else to go. "All right, Mother, but first let him have a look at how nice the weather is." She helped Pavel onto her lap and kissed his shoulder, pointing up at the slate-blue sky and the street facades awash with sunlight. She hoped he wouldn't notice the blackened windows. "Today, Pavel darling, the sun is shining. What do you think we should do, you and me?"

"Don't know, Maman." He looked upwards, out the window. "Furry Lion wants to know. Why is there smoke?"

Sophie was silent for a moment. At times, Pavel came up with questions that led to more questions, and then more questions. Now was the moment to distract him. "I'm not sure, darling." She turned him around. "What do you say we find a place outside where you can run and play?"

His face lit up.

That was exactly what she wanted; to be outside, away from the cramped apartment, stretching her legs. She wanted to forget the anxieties that dogged her day and night. *How much more bombing? Will we even survive? We have nowhere else to go.* Pavel, with his bed-wetting, disturbed nights and tantrums, needed to let off steam. Sunshine and a walk were definitely on the day's menu.

Pavel pointed again and turned to look at her with his grave blue eyes. "Was it a bomb?"

She rubbed his neck with her fingers. "I don't really know, darling. Some kind of fire."

His eyes widened and he squeezed her hand. "We go see it?"

"Not possible," said Emil sternly, coming up behind them, holding a steaming mug of tea. "Look down in the street. They have closed the entrance to that building. Nobody can go inside."

Pavel pouted. "I want to."

Sophie hugged him. Children in London had to be kept on a tight leash these days. Such a pity. "We'll look at it from the outside when we go for our walk," she murmured.

He smacked at her knuckles and squirmed away.

After breakfast, she put on a worn summer dress, a green wool cardigan and her only pair of shoes. She dressed Pavel in a shirt, shorts, socks and sandals; clothes donated three weeks earlier when they arrived at the Liverpool refugee center.

She presented her plan. "After lunch and his nap, Pavel and I will go up the hill to the big park you told me about. We need to be outside in the fresh air." She smiled at the idea of exploring Hampstead Heath—Emil had described it as a sort of natural park of grass, woods and ponds. He had even offered to take them, but she wanted some respite from her in-laws. She would find the park with Pavel and immerse herself in nature … try to forget London and the air raids.

"Don't be foolish, girl," said Judit as she peeled carrots at the tiny kitchen sink, her face a canvas of wrinkles and worry. "You will get lost in that big park." She wiped her hands and tugged on her husband's arm. "*Apa*, say something to her. Sophie is only twenty-two. She has no residence permit."

Groaning inwardly, Sophie ran angry fingers through her thick black hair. "We will be fine. Pavel needs to have some fun."

Judit faced Sophie, hands on hips. "Hampstead Heath is a wild place. People do bad things there. The boy must stay here with us."

"I *want* to go." Pavel had a determined look.

Sophie stared at Judit, itching to fight back. "I don't believe you. Why do you always invent reasons to stop me doing what I want?"

Judit's shoulders twitched. "How will you know when it is time to come home?"

"I can tell from the sun. Or, I will ask someone."

"Ha!" Judit exclaimed, raising her hands as if in justification. "You don't speak enough English to ask."

Sophie glared, pointing a finger to her wrist where her Longines, confiscated at the French frontier, had once been strapped. "I don't have to speak. What do you think I did in France? And, by the way, I'm twenty-four, not twenty-two!"

Emil, in a woolen undershirt, suspenders, and baggy brown corduroy pants, stood beside his wife, tying lengths of old string into neat bundles and putting them into a tin box.

Judit tipped her carrot peelings into a small saucepan, the basis of the concoction she called "my peelings *suppe*". She looked up. "Emil, did you not hear? She speaks no English. If she goes, you have to go with her."

Judit's fussing and warnings about dangerous streets made Sophie nervous. She was afraid of asking directions. Would people be helpful, rude or angry, even ignore her? It had been the same in France, but there she had learned to get along fine.

Emil snapped his tin box shut. "Leave Sophie in peace, woman. No one will ask her for identification. Many mothers and children walk on the Heath with no fear. She has to learn to manage."

Sophie flashed him a grateful smile. It was good to have him on her side for a change.

Judit positioned herself in front of Emil, palms together as if she was praying or begging. "What if an air raid starts when they are out—and something bad happens? I will never forgive you."

Emil put his hands on her shoulders. "Enough of this "what if" talk! The Nazis want us to act like little mice hiding in our holes. We refugees must be more like the Londoners who just carry on. Let the girl make up her own mind."

Later, Sophie, carrying her study workbook and two precious apples in a canvas bag, started Pavel down two floors of worn stairs to the street door. Emil called from the landing. "Turn left, daughter. Bear right past the Tube station and follow Heath Street up to the Whitestone Pond. There will be foot paths to the left. Twenty minutes, maybe thirty minutes' walk."

They set out along the High Street, Pavel twisting his head to peek at the blackened windows. Sophie grabbed his hand. "Come on, *miláčku*, darling. It's not far." She lengthened her stride happy to be out in the sunshine and ready to explore Hampstead Heath. Living with Emil and Judit had not turned out as she imagined. It was a cramped and hemmed-in prison run by over-solicitous relatives who expected obedience and gratitude. What she wanted most was to have her own place, with husband Willy at her side helping her learn the English ways. She knew he was with the Czechoslovak Army in England. But where?

CHAPTER TWO
Hampstead Heath, London

Sophie and Pavel passed the underground station and walked steadily up Heath Street, lined on either side by three story houses as solid and elegant, Sophie thought, as those of the Nové Mešto district in Prague. Wrought iron gates offered glimpses of neat gardens. Pavel skipped along holding his toy lion, asking questions in a mixture of French and Czech. Their year in Paris had given him a refugee child's fluency, dotted with grammatical errors. Later, in the south of France, he acquired a mellifluous *Midi* accent.

They paused at the top of the hill to watch an old man in rubber boots, kneeling at the edge of a shallow pond. He was using a long, thin pole to guide a little sailboat. Sophie presumed this was the Whitestone Pond Emil had mentioned. Pavel looked on wistfully as the yacht, flying British colors, heeled in the breeze. The man gave him a friendly wave.

"Maman, will Papa buy me a boat?"

Sophie sighed. "One day, perhaps, darling." For the time being she had no money, not even a shilling or two to buy Pavel a simple toy. It had been the same when they had arrived Paris a year earlier after being stripped and robbed by the German border guards. She could not let Emil go on paying for everything. She was counting on Willy, wherever he was, to earn money—army pay. Maybe soon, when he surfaced, he would send some to Emil.

As Emil had directed, they took a path crossing a daisy-filled meadow. A few other people, mostly gray-haired men, were walking their dogs. They nodded greetings, and a small group of soldiers, sprawled on the grass, whistled at her.

Drinking in the sunshine, Sophie watched patiently as Pavel chased butterflies, kicked at stones, and made his Furry Lion pick wildflowers. Emil was right. This heath was a lovely place and she was in no hurry—happy to see how much Pavel enjoyed himself. Intrigued by a shaded narrow side-path, she led him through a line of hazel thickets and beech trees. Their progress slowed to a standstill when Pavel stopped to poke and look at insects and grubs on the path. Then he was off again, foraging for sticks, using them to whack seed heads and splinter them on tree-trunks.

After a while Sophie called him back. "Isn't it wonderful here, *miláčku*?" she said, stroking his cheeks, still tanned from their recent sea voyage from Gibraltar. "So nice to be completely alone. Let's go on a bit farther." A swell of calm and pleasure swept over her. She put a finger to her lips. "Can you hear the birds, darling? It's just like…" She wanted to say "home" but couldn't. "Come on, we'll find a place where you can play and I can study my English."

In a few minutes, the winding path led to a clearing, shaded by a massive tree covered with coppery leaves. Rabbit burrows peppered the earth between its gnarled roots. They glimpsed the sudden movement of long ears and a white tail disappearing into one of the tunnels.

Pavel grabbed a pebble and threw it. "Rabbit! I want that rabbit, Maman," he shouted, grabbing at the folds of her dress. "Can I dig for one? We'll eat him for supper like we used to with Madame Esco."

After a short search, he found a stick. Dropping to his knees, he thrust it deep into a rabbit burrow … in and out, again and again. He looked at her with enthusiastic eyes. "*Je veux un gros.* I want a big one."

"*Oui, mon petit.* Dig as much as you like."

Sophie noticed a wide flat stone across the clearing. It was edged by grass, clover and buttercups—the perfect spot to rest and study. *With luck, I'll get some peace before Pavel gets bored.*

She untied her headscarf, spread it out and settled down. The first three pages of the exercise book she drew from her bag contained a list of English words and their Czechoslovak meanings. She began spelling and saying the English words aloud, pleased that there no one was around to witness her distorted articulations.

On the SS Neuralia, sailing from Gibraltar, she had mastered a few English phrases: *I am forener, spik slow, excuse me, sory to truble you, wat is time, whair is toilette*—and recently a new important one: *my 'ome is forty too 'Ampstead 'igh street.* Making herself understood was the first step she needed to take on the daunting task of adapting to England. She had set herself a challenge. *To speak English fluently in three months.*

Sophie's other ambition, even more important, was to find Willy. Shortly after she and Pavel had arrived by train from Liverpool, Emil received a telegram from Gibraltar. Her husband was on a troopship with his Czechoslovak regiment headed for England. It was only after Emil took Sophie to the Czechoslovak Provisional Government in Grosvenor Place that she learned that her husband's ship had berthed in Plymouth on the south coast.

"The Czechoslovak Army has set up camp near the town of Malpas," said the red-faced Czechoslovak official, clearly embarrassed by her copious tears. He glanced at some ink notations on his blotting pad. "Malpas is a town in the county of Cheshire. Anyway, it is long way from here. I can't tell you anything more and—I regret that you are not allowed to send any letters."

"She has been separated from her husband many times since they left Prague," said Emil with a sad smile, handing her a handkerchief as they rose to leave.

Sophie turned another page of her exercise book and gave up in frustration. The charm of the wooded clearing, spiced with green scents and the hum of insects ruined her concentration. It was easier to ponder the events of the last two weeks, rather than stumble through strange English words.

"This is your home now" Judit had said as she embraced them when they arrived from Liverpool. Their first few days at 42 Hampstead High Street were full of joy, and they told stories of their respective and dangerous escapes from Slovakia and Prague. Sophie was so happy to be with her loving relatives again. That bond, at least, was rock solid.

The London Blitz started five weeks after they arrived, and fear and strain replaced Sophie's happiness. There was hardly room to move around in the tiny flat: a tiled alcove housed a "kitchen" counter, the galvanized sink, and a four legged gas stove with two burners. There was only one window, the one overlooking the street. The rest of the space held an iron bedstead, an armchair and a wobbly clothes cupboard next to the scarred table, three chairs and a stool. On the landing outside, they shared a communal toilet with the downstairs tenants.

She and Pavel slept on the floor, wrapped in a rug. They had to wait their turn to wash in the sink. Judit, who had once been the mistress of a spick and span house in Lučenec, dried washing from the ceiling rack, or if she was in a hurry, in front of the coin-fed gas fire. She cooked for everyone, bristling at Sophie's offer of help. "I have some pride left, daughter!"

Here in London, Pavel, who on the sea voyage had been dry at night, started to wet himself again. He was a paradox, often sweet and amusing, yet subject to the same tantrums and night fears he had suffered in Paris. Sometimes he refused to go out into the street with Sophie. "*Il pleut. Sâle et mauvais,*" was his reasoning. "Rain, dirty, and nasty." When Sophie told him to behave and be quiet he just stared and cursed at her in the slang he had learned from the village children. He spoke French more fluently now than his native Czech.

After Sophie and Pavel arrived in London, her father-in-law took charge of her acclimation to British ways. Always a gruff, unemotional man, Emil made demands with little consideration for what she had been through. She had to admit that, a year earlier, he had been through his own hardships: imprisoned by the Hungarians who confiscated everything including his house. Here in London, he was adrift, unemployed and bitter. He spent his days, reading, standing in line for food and walking the streets. She felt sorry for him. He clearly relished teaching her about England but his authoritarian ways were irritating and aggressive.

He would waggle a lecturing finger. "So, daughter, when you speak to English people, always add *please* and *thank you* to every sentence. Also, when you meet an English person, do not shake hands unless they do so first. Just say, "How do you do?" And NEVER kiss the cheek, even of a woman. Keep at a distance, about a meter. And no smiling at people you do not know in the street, or at a shopkeeper, unless you know them very well—and they smile at you. If they ask where you come from, just say Central Europe. Most people do not know where is Czechoslovakia. If possible, no one should find out that you are a Jew. Many here do not like us, and they say there are fifty thousand Jewish refugees in London. Too many. Better to stay silent and be safe."

By now, Sophie realized that her in-laws had changed from the old days in Lučenec. They had lost their pride, confidence, and the sense of who they were. Unless he took a job as a servant or farmworker, Emil could not be employed, even by Kindell and Rivett, the English firm he had done business with for years. He had no friends and just a few acquaintances he had made at a refugee haven, the Cosmo café which he visited once a week. It was a place to discuss the war, play dominoes, drink weak tea, and share memories.

Even though British Jewish organizations and the Women's

International Zionist Organization welcomed refugees to meetings and promoted events and talks, Judit held back and kept to herself; she spoke so little English.

Here in London, Sophie had come to the conclusion that her once prosperous and affectionate in-laws were in charge of nothing but their own meager possessions. And for some reason they did not understand that what she had been through over the past year or so had matured her, made her resilient. To them she was still an inexperienced young girl married to their cosmopolitan son. Except that now, they had been given something good to focus on: an unruly but lovable grandson and a soldier son embedded in the remnants of the Czechoslovak Army, somewhere in the county of Cheshire, England.

Distracted by a soft breeze and sunshine glinting through the trees, Sophie looked around, sighing with pleasure. Saplings and shrubs surrounded her with whispering leaves. Birds pipped and chattered. This place was, tranquil and charming—almost as beautiful as the Divoká Šárka Park she loved to visit on the outskirts of Prague.

She closed her eyes, inhaling the soft smell of grass. Poor Pavel missed his father terribly. She did too, especially the warmth and vigor of his body at night. Tears came, as they did so easily these days, and she blinked at the exercise book. An errant tear smudged the English word THROUGH halfway down her list. *Get back to your studies, girl. Say it aloud.* "Thrruuh," she said, squeezing her tongue between her teeth and then flicking it back, as Emil had instructed. She flinched at her own strangled grunt and amused, glanced across at Pavel, still digging, wondering if he had heard her ruining Shakespeare's mother tongue.

A whomping noise blasted her ears. Tall wildflowers and grass seed-heads in the clearing swayed violently. Shrubs shook and rattled.

The workbook book fell from her knees. In a panic, she raced across the clearing to Pavel. His face, open-mouthed, was tilted up at the sky.

Then she saw them: three fighter planes in tight formation, zooming away over the tree tops. Their upswept wings and sleek bodies banked to the right. Relief sluiced over her when she recognized the rings on the plane's wings and fuselages … Royal Air Force. They dwindled into black dots and disappeared into puffy clouds. She wiped the sweat off her face with the hem of her dress and bent down. "*Ça va, chéri?*" These days she was never certain how Pavel would react.

Still on his knees, Pavel gave her a starry smile—dazzling white teeth in a tanned face. He ran earth-stained fingers through his blonde curls. "*Jolis avions*," he said, his face alight. He moved his stuffed lion to the edge of the rabbit hole. "Watch, Maman. He'll smell a big one out for me."

Sophie went back to her flat stone and, with a smile at his enthusiasm, retrieved the fallen exercise book. No danger. But her memory bank forced open by terrifying noise, replayed their arrival in London from the Liverpool docks. Emil took her to register as a Czechoslovak alien, after which she had to check-in at the Heath Street police station three times a week. Travel outside the city was forbidden. Refugees like her, with no money or sponsors, went straight to internment camps. Thank God for Willy's parents. She owed them so much, yet they were stifling her.

Sophie pushed the workbook into her purse, suddenly worried that they had been out too long. She had no watch and clouds obscured the sun. Cursing herself for not paying attention, Sophie brushed grass off her dress and ran to Pavel who was still crawling on his knees, plunging his stick in and out of rabbit holes. "Stop digging, *miláčku*. We must get home."

Pavel stuck out his tongue, an irritating trick he'd learned from the children in the French village where she and Willy had been billeted. "*Non*," he said with a sullen look, "*je ne veux pas*. Don't want to go. Want to stay and get rabbit."

"This is not France. The English don't eat rabbits." Sophie grasped his arm to pull him upright. "Get up now. Don't be naughty."

He arched backward and went limp: another French trick. Gritting her teeth, her temper on a hair trigger, she peeled Pavel off the ground, and for the first fifty meters half-carried him, legs kicking, along the woodland path. If they were late, Emil and Judit would be furious.

With a huff, Sophie set Pavel forcefully onto his feet. "For God's sake, child, obey me and walk—or there'll be a smack." For the past few months, she had found it difficult to control her temper when Pavel provoked her: it had almost turned into a smacking festival. Both she and Willy had grown up in homes where physical punishment for being naughty was normal practice, usually a cuff or two. Most people thought nothing of it, though she could tell from their faces that Judit and Emil disapproved.

Tears coursed down Pavel's dirty cheeks, revealing tracks of clear skin until he rubbed them into brown smudges. "No more smacks, Maman."

His abject look stabbed at her heart. She had handed out too much punishment during the hard months in Paris. A friend had told her it was because she was *malade*, depressed. Sophie grabbed Pavel's arm again and pulled him along. Children don't remember smacks, she reasoned. That's what everyone said. How often, over the past months, had Sophie wished Willy were there to help discipline Pavel? She firmly believed that Willy's place was with his family now, here in London—and certainly not in the Czechoslovak Army that had been involved in France's shameful defeat. Emil said the Allies were already losing the war, so why did Willy still want to fight? She sighed, knowing what her husband's reply would be. "I'm a Jew. If we don't join in the war, we lose and they will finish us off like they did in Poland."

Twice she and Pavel took the wrong path and had to double back on their route. It took much longer than she expected to make their way back to the Whitestone Pond. She guessed it was late afternoon. She saw a policeman and wanted to ask the time but she was afraid: her new identity card had not arrived. Without that she could be arrested. Judit had been right about that problem.

Passing the pond with its tall flagpole flying a St. George Cross, Sophie guided reluctant, whiny Pavel down the slope of Heath Street. Earlier, Judit had given her strict instructions. "Get here before dusk. Remember, daughter, we eat early today. It's chicken soup and dumplings. And don't talk to strangers."

Sophie was afraid she was late and dreaded the prospect of Emil's withering look. And, no doubt Judit would unleash one of her pull-yourself-together glares and say something mean. Sophie's stomach began its familiar gurgling. Tension, anxiety, fears … refugee emotions.

"Look, *Maminko*," said Pavel. Floating high above the city, a group of silver balloons with flaps at the rear, tethered to long ropes, swayed with silky luminescence. "What are those?"

She laughed. "Barrage balloons—they look like flying elephants, don't they?"

Pavel scratched at his blonde tangles, a gesture that meant he was thinking hard. "Why?"

Sophie dismissed the question with a shrug. Too complicated and no time to explain. "Come on, *miláčku*, it's late. We must hurry." She shivered. The threadbare clothes she'd been given at the refugee center were no match for the coolness of a late summer day. She had misjudged the day's early sunshine.

"I'm cold, *Maminko*," Pavel whined. He had goose-bumps on his legs.

As they descended Heath Street, an air-raid siren began its crescendo, reverberating off the houses. She held Pavel's hand more tightly. This was the first time she had been out in the streets when the siren went off … and it was still daylight! She pulled Pavel close, covering his ears with her hands.

He looked up with blue, knowing eyes. "*Les bombiers arrivent*," he mouthed as the wail died away. Sophie nodded.

"Come on, *Pavličku*, everything will be all right." She was surprised by his apparent lack of fear. "We'll be home in a few minutes."

"*Je suis fatigué*. Carry me," he beseeched with piteous eyes.

Sophie shook her head and then gasped at the familiar droning sound—*impossible; here already?* Her heart gave a jolt, fear cramped her legs. She heard her own voice, harsh and panicky. "Hurry now, *Pavlik*."

Within a couple of minutes, the droning changed to the roar of aero engines. Like skeins of migrating geese, silver-winged machines crawled across the sky. Flak mushroomed around them. Sophie couldn't stop herself from pausing to look up. Tracer fire slashed up from the ground toward the bomber formations and the staccato, head-hammering noise of anti-aircraft batteries came from the direction where they had just been walking. The noise was deafening. Tiny fragments, shrapnel, skittered on the street. On top of a strange burning smell, she tasted dust and her eyes felt gritty.

Pavel start to cough. He looked at her wide-eyed, trembling, and stretched out his arms.

She crouched, hugged him tightly and wound her scarf over his head, hoping that this might give him some protection. It was only then she realized that not a single bomb had fallen. No explosions. Her heart leaped with joy. Those Stukas, Heinkels and Messerschmitts—she knew the names well enough by now—were going somewhere else to drop their bombs. "It's all right, *miláčku,* darling," she shouted almost joyfully above the din. "No bombs. Come on."

When they got as far as Hampstead Tube station, its entrance protected by stacked sandbags, a crowd of people were scrambling and pushing to get inside. She started to walk past but a stout man in a white helmet, an ARP band on his arm, stopped her. "Wait a sec, lady. You orter be dahn the Tube like everyone else. An' where the 'ell's your gas mask?" His voice was harsh and accusatory.

Pavel clung to his mother's coat, his eyes glued to the short axe hanging from the man's belt.

Sophie cupped a protective hand round her boy's forehead. *Who is this angry man? A policeman?*

The air raid warden came close, his eyes glinting. Sophie smelled beer and tobacco. "Didn't you 'ear wot I said?" he shouted above the din. "Get dahn the Tube." With a cold shiver, Sophie wondered whether he was a special kind of policeman, like the ones in Prague who arrested Jews. She remembered Emil's warning that the underground would be a death-trap if a bomb fell on it, and Judit's description of hundreds of smelly, dirty people scrunched up on the platforms or lying between the de-activated rails.

She shook her head. "No understand, you spik slow. I sank you." She began to shake, afraid of being arrested.

He shrugged. "Bloody foreigners are yer, then?"

She willed herself to remain calm. "No Tube. We go home. Forty-two 'Ampstead 'Igh Street. Sank you." She pointed upward, stumbling out the words. "It is safe? I not see bombs."

The warden shrugged his shoulders. "Suit yerself then. I've got enough to do besides coddlin' foreigners." He spat on the ground and turned away.

"We must be quick now, *Pavlik*," said Sophie, taking her boy's hand. Smaller airplanes had appeared in the sky, swarming round the bomber formations, red dots flickering on their wings. She tightened her grip on Pavel's hand and increased her pace.

"Come on." They were only a few yards away from her in-laws' flat.

Damn, where is it. She pushed Pavel against the brick wall and dug deep into her purse for the front door key. "Don't move."

At that moment, an ear-splitting whine drowned everything.

Pavel's mouth sagged open.

A fighter plane, smoke streaming from its nose, spiraled from the heavens toward the ground. She saw the circle targets on its wings. "English," she whispered as her fingers found the key. *One of ours.* Knees shaking, she inserted the key in the lock and used her hip to push open the warped door. As she reached back to grab Pavel, she saw the airplane disappear behind some houses. A sheet of flame shot skyward.

"Is it a bomb, *maminko?*"

She slammed the door shut, her mind in a panic. "Upstairs, *now*." Her fingers tightened around his shirt collar and she dragged him up the stairs, her feet slipping on the worn linoleum, her body weak with fear and exhaustion.

Pavel clawed and kicked at her with renewed energy. "Let me go, let me *GO*." His knees and feet caught the wooden edges of the steps and he shrieked and struggled to get away from her.

Half way up the three flights of stairs, Sophie slapped him hard. "I've had enough of you. When *Táta* comes home I'll tell him you were a horrible boy."

He kicked her—hammer blows on her shins. "I hate you,

Maminko. I hate you, and I hate Papa too…" She held his forearm arm tight until they reached the landing on the top floor. With one hand she hauled him upright. With the other, she banged on the door of the flat. "Emil, Judit, help me—please. Open the door."

Something sharp dug into her wrist. Pain lanced up her arm. Pavel had bitten her. She jerked away, her knuckles striking the side of his face.

"*Maminko,*" he screamed as he lost his footing.

He fell backwards, thudding and bouncing down the flight of stairs between the wall and the banisters until he lay on the lower landing, sprawled and inert.

Sophie froze.

CHAPTER THREE
Broken Bone
London, September 1940

A strong hand gripped her shoulder, held her back. Emil's eyes were enormous behind the thick lenses of his glasses, swiveling this way and that. "What is this *meshuganah* door-banging?" he snarled. "The boy, where is he?"

Sophie's words almost died in her throat. "He fell … I …" She pried Emil's hand away from her shoulder.

A cry of pain floated up from the landing. One of Pavel's legs jerked. He rolled sideways and moaned. Sophie clutched at the bannister. *He's alive. Thank God.*

"*Gott in Himmel.*" Emil pushed her aside, losing his slippers as he half-stumbled down the stairs, hands brushing the wall and the bannister.

Sophie, hating him, followed, trying to slip past his lumbering frame.

At the foot of the stairs, Emil sank to his knees beside the boy. Whimpering, Pavel swung his head from side to side, bending his knees and shifting his feet. He opened his eyes and moved his left hand, pointing to his right shoulder. "Maman," he whispered.

Sophie knelt next to Emil.

The old man pushed her away. "I will see to him," he growled. "I know first aid."

Sophie pulled on his arm. "For God's sake, I'm his mother. Let me look."

Emil shook her off. He curled his lip. "Daughter, I know what to do."

Leaning forward, he positioned adroit fingertips on the side of the boy's neck. "His heart beats fast but steady," he muttered. "Normal breathing. It could have been worse."

"What do you think is wrong with him, *Apa*?" she whispered. Her words sounded weak and helpless. She closed her eyes and took a deep breath—at least her father-in-law knew what to do.

He grunted. "Pavel recognizes you. That is excellent. He had a big shock from tumbling down. I see he holds his right shoulder in a strange way. I have to make sure nothing is broken."

Sophie knelt beside Pavel whose eyes were fluttering. She did not dare touch him. "*Apa*, will he be…?"

Emil jabbed her with an elbow. "Silence, girl. Let me check him before anything else." Starting at the boy's feet, he began to probe and squeeze, watching for some reaction.

Pavel's face was chalk-white. Blinking tears, he looked at Emil and reached for Sophie with his left hand. "It hurts."

Her heart twisted in anguish. His voice sounded hollow, as if he was speaking from a deep tunnel, but the fact that he spoke and sought her touch gave her hope. *Maybe, it's not so bad.*

"What … where does it hurt, *Pavlik* darling?" she asked, taking the fingers of his left hand gently and kissing them. She heard noises in the street—shouting and fire engine bells.

The boy pulled his hand away and again pointed to his right shoulder. He started to breathe more quickly and met her eyes directly for the first time. His cheeks were wet and he licked at the tears sliding off his nose.

Sophie patted them dry with the hem of her dress.

"Do you have pain anywhere else?" Emil asked, gently running his hands over Pavel's belly, chest, head, and neck. He flexed the boy's neck and checked the movement of all the other joints, except for his right shoulder.

"No, Grandpa."

Emil sighed, then, leaning on Sophie's shoulder for purchase, stood up with a groan. He gave her a wry smile and stretched his back. "Hunh … this old Slovak man has no business running down even older stairs," he said—then patted her arm reassuringly. "Our boy has done something to his right shoulder. Maybe a broken bone."

Gently, he bent to touch Pavel's blonde thatch. "Now, listen to your *Děda*. I am going to carry you upstairs. It might hurt, so you must be a brave fellow. Then I can decide what needs to be done."

Sophie's heart turned over. What did Emil mean by "maybe a broken bone?" She squeezed her eyes shut. "Perhaps we shouldn't move him? Get help?"

Emil raised an eyebrow. "*Gott in Himmel*, girl, from where should we get help? Can you not hear the *megillah* outside? Guns firing, ambulances, fire engines? On the other side of our front door, the world is busy with its chaos. There is no one to help us."

"But the planes did not drop any bombs."

"That was very fortunate for us, young woman. So from now on … you do exactly what I say. First, support Pavel's right hand and arm and then slowly move it inward, so it rests on his belly. Good. Now hook his fingers into to the waist band of his shorts, there."

Pavel cried out.

"Do the same for the left arm. This stabilizes the shoulders. Fine. Now I lift him and take him upstairs." Emil slid an arm under the boy's upper back and the other behind his knees. He started to climb the creaking stairs and gave Pavel a reassuring smile. "I see your fingers and knees are dirty. What were you doing in the park?"

"Rabbits," Pavel said weakly. "I was digging."

"We were on the Heath," said Sophie. "He was… " Tears ran down her cheeks—it was clever of Emil to distract the boy with questions.

Judit waited on the landing, pale and rigid, twisting a dish cloth. "Heaven be merciful, what is this *mishegoss*? The poor child looks terrible." Her face dissolved into anguish when she saw Pavel up close. "What happened? Emil."

Sophie held the door open so that Emil could step sideways into the dimly-lit flat. He rested Pavel on the bed as delicately as if he were an injured bird. Judit hovered behind him. "What happened, *Apa*? Please, tell me. Is it serious?"

"He fell down the stairs, woman. Now, for heaven's sake, give me room to move. It's not so bad. Just bring me your nail scissors. *Schnell*."

Pavel whimpered. The only other sounds came from the street: police whistles and clanging ambulance bells.

Pavel's breathing stuttered as he watched Emil cut his shirt away, revealing his small, thin chest.

Sophie's heart raced. His skin was the color of weak tea and the scar on the right side of his neck, red and puckered, was more obvious. He looked terribly fragile. She could not hold back a sob. "How do you know so much, Emil?"

"*Ach so,* I understand now..." Emil pushed his spectacles up on to his forehead and pointed to the bluish lump that obscured the shape of Pavel's shoulder. "That is a big bruise, and underneath it the collar bone is not straight like on the left." He smiled benevolently at Sophie. "I learned first aid in the Polish trenches, long ago. Luckily, God gave us nearly two of everything. So we can see which one is not normal. I'm sure his collar bone is broken, or dislocated. I must test it." He bent forward to kiss the boy's head. "Be brave. It will hurt."

Sophie held her breath as the old man rotated Pavel's forearm very slightly and gently. The boy gasped and screamed "*Non.*" His voice was like a rasping saw and unable to watch, Sophie covered her face. "Stop, *Apa.* Please stop."

"Oh, my precious Pavel," Judit muttered, twisting her fingers and looking away. "Please ... Emil, be gentle."

Emil grunted. "I do what is best for the boy."

Judit glanced from Pavel to Sophie and back. Her voice quavered. "What happened on the stairs?"

"Cover him with a blanket," ordered Emil as if he hadn't heard her. "He needs a doctor. I will get dressed. We'll take him to the hospital at the bottom of the hill when the All-Clear sounds."

"*Maminko* pushed me," the boy whispered, eyelids fluttering again.

Sophie groaned and shook her head violently, touching the bite marks on her wrist. How could Pavel say such a horrible thing? She glanced at Emil with pleading eyes. "He tripped and fell backward. An accident. That's the truth."

Judit rose to her feet, her cheeks crimson. A fold of flesh quivered under her chin. "Why should Pavel tell lies? He says *she* pushed him." She tugged at Emil's sleeve. "Go out to a telephone box. Call an ambulance."

"This is an air raid, woman," Emil growled. "The ambulances are busy. Even if we called 999 we would have to wait a long time. This is no great emergency, but he cannot walk to the Royal Free Hospital, even part of the way."

Judit put on an apron, tying the strings with agitated fingers. "We *must* find an ambulance," she insisted. "Even an expensive taxi. I can't bear to watch him suffer. Do something, *Apushkam*. I beg you."

Emil shook his head. "Useless. We wait till the All-Clear sounds."

"Father," Sophie begged, "he needs a doctor. Something for pain. How do we get him to the hospital? Look how pale he is."

Emil straightened, arching his shoulder blades as if to ease his muscles. He sat down and pulled on his shoes. "Sophie will come with me to the hospital. It is on Haverstock Hill, not more than a kilometer. I will carry him. The boy does not weigh much."

"*Apa*, you are too old to carry him so far," Judit interjected, her face as taut as her apron strings.

"I will carry him," Sophie said.

Emil waved away her offer. "He has to be carried in a special way. Get the flashlight from Judit in case it is dark on the way back. If I get tired, then you take over. When we get there, I will help you speak to the doctors. We will learn something from this crisis."

He turned to Judit. "Please get my identity card and our alien certificates from the kitchen drawer."

"Do as *Apa* tells you … and come back soon," said Judit handing the documents to Sophie, her eyes searching her daughter-in-law's face, as if she hoped to uncover there the secret of the staircase accident. She stroked Pavel's cheeks with her fingertips and kissed his forehead. "See you soon, *malinký*, my little one," she murmured.

As they waited for the All-Clear to sound, Emil and Judit carefully wrapped a blanket around Pavel and stood watching him.

"I want Furry Lion," Pavel whispered.

"I think he's at the bottom of the stairs. We'll pick him up when we go out." Sophie put on her coat trying to untangle her thoughts and emotions. She was partly responsible for Pavel's fall. Who would not panic in an air raid? But why were Emil and Judit treating her as if she were irresponsible? Admittedly, she had only been in England a short time and hardly spoke English. Her in-laws had no idea what she had been through and what she was capable of.

The quicker she and Pavel found Willy, the better.

CHAPTER FOUR

Royal Free Hospital. London
Early August 1940

The drawn out note of the All-Clear vibrated through the thin walls of the flat. Sophie let out a deep sigh of relief as Emil got up from his chair and put on his hat and overcoat.

He looked at his watch. "Time to go."

She sat on the bed beside Pavel and kissed his forehead. His pale face had regained color. He gave her a brief smile and winced as he moved his arm. "Air raid gone, Maman?"

"Yes, my darling. We can get ready now." As she turned to lift him, she felt Emil's hand on her shoulder.

"No, daughter. I carry him. You get the flashlight for when we come back—and my umbrella. I saw rain on the bathroom window. Hold the umbrella over the boy when I carry him down the street. It is not so far."

Thinking that it would have been so much easier with Willy there, she watched Emil gently scoop Pavel into his arms and nod to Judit who was sniffling into a handkerchief.

"And you, wife, have some hot soup and bread ready for when we get back. This is only a small injury. Things can only get better."

Outside, in the street, the once-clear sky was blanketed with low clouds. They made their way down the unlit High Street in a fine drizzle, passing a blue police box with an air raid siren fixed atop. Sophie walked beside Emil, doing her best to keep the open umbrella over Pavel. The neighborhood was uncannily quiet, as if everyone wanted to stay home after the raid and soothe their shattered nerves.

In the white-tiled accident room, smelling heavily of carbolic, Sophie and Emil lifted Pavel onto a wooden examination table where he sat dangling his legs, his face creased in pain.

Sophie could see that his sandals and socks were damp from the rain; luckily the blanket had kept the rest of his clothes dry. He looked so small and vulnerable to her, with a far off look as if all he wanted was to be magically transported to a place where no pain or harm was possible.

Clutching the stuffed lion with his left hand, Pavel kept the injured arm resting on his lap. His eyes flickered anxiously around the room.

"Have you got the lad's identity card," said a fair-haired nurse as she inspected their documents and wrote down the details.

"Sorry, please," said Emil, digging into his wallet and handing her a ragged card. "He only has this French document. He does not speak English."

She peered into Pavel's face. "Dearie me! Things are so complicated with you refugees. Sorry, I don't know French." She drew wheeled curtain screens around them to form a temporary cubicle and then patted Pavel's knee. "Not to worry, lovey, we'll look after you. Hurt your arm, did you? The doctor'll be along soon." She handed Sophie a towel. "Take off his wet things—get him dry." She gave a little giggle. "I could do with some of those gold curls he's got."

Sophie nodded. "Sank you." She breathed a sigh of relief. At last, here was someone who was kind.

"My arm hurts," Pavel whispered in Czech, with a pleading look at Emil. "Make it better, Grandpa."

Emil placed a fingertip on the boy's nose. "I know it hurts. Be patient till the doctor comes."

A few minutes later, a young man in a white coat swept the screen aside and graced the Kohuts with a brief smile. He held a buff colored folder.

Sophie thought the doctor handsome—in the English way she

recognized from the movies: chiseled face, blue eyes, and straight straw-colored hair—a contrast to the seductively bronzed Dr. Mallamet who had operated on Pavel's abscess in Paris. She wondered whether handsome doctors were better or worse at their job than ugly ones. Instinctively, she pushed wayward strands of her dark hair off her forehead. She wanted to look more presentable—a neat, attractive and reliable mother.

"Hello, I'm Dr. Haynes," he said, pulling the stethoscope from round his neck. He stuffed it into a side pocket of his coat and flipped open the folder. "Ah, yes. Pavel Kohut. Name suggests a refugee child. An accident, huh. I see you're from just up the road—Hampstead High Street?" His eyes lingered on Sophie and he gave her an appreciative smile. "Very nice," he murmured. "Are you the boy's sister or his mother? And where are you people from?" He raised his eyebrows.

Sophie rubbed her forehead in frustration. He talked too fast, but she recognized the word "mother."

"She is the mother," said Emil quickly, giving Sophie a look that she read as a signal to be quiet. "We are from Czechoslovakia. The father is a soldier. He is in a camp here in England."

"Czechoslovakia, eh? Then I expect you're Jewish."

"We are *not* Jews."

Sophie caught her breath. She knew enough English to understand that Emil had just lied. She remembered how in the old days, when he was running his business, her father-in-law had no compunction about browbeating, bluffing, and sometimes deceiving suppliers and customers, but he had never denied his origins. His son Willy was more of a fixer and persuader; his lying when they escaped through Germany, had only been the result of fear and desperation— anything to escape arrest. But this was England. Why did Emil hide the fact that he was a Jew, here in England?

The nurse smiled. "So, how did the accident happen?"

Sophie felt reassured by the sympathetic way she looked at Pavel.

"My grandson fell down the stairs," said Emil bluntly, straightening his shoulders. "He has a broken collarbone. I knew what it was immediately. I was a medical aide in the Great War. In Poland."

The doctor chuckled. "Good heavens! You fought in *that* war?"

Emil nodded and looked away. "*Ja*, in those days I was on the German side."

"Golly! I bet you could tell a few good stories."

"Please to examine my grandson. This is no time to go over bad memories."

The doctor compressed his lips. "All right then. We'll take a peek at this little chap. Might *hurt* him a bit." He has a pleasant sing-song voice, Sophie thought, wishing she understood what he was saying.

When the doctor approached him, Pavel shrank back. Sophie and the nurse held him firmly. The doctor, seemingly oblivious to the boy's moaning and his occasional shriek of pain checked the swelling and shoulder movement. He looked at Emil approvingly. "Spot-on. A broken clavicle. Outer third." He prodded the puckered skin on the right side of Pavel's neck. "And what's this scar? Looks fairly new."

"He have tuberculosis in Paris," said Sophie as she watched the doctor running his hands over Pavel's ribs and belly. "Better now, after operation." She smiled, proud that he seemed to understand her.

"I see. Well now ... the fracture is near the shoulder joint. Nothing too serious, I'd say. We'll take an X-ray to make sure it's a clean break and then fix him up with a brace." Using his bent knee as a surface, he scribbled something on a sheet of paper and gave it to the nurse. "Here's the X-ray request."

Emil signaled to Sophie to get ready to accompany Pavel. But when he stood, holding his hat and coat, the doctor put a hand on the old man's chest and eased him back into his seat.

"You must stay here and wait. Shouldn't take long. Family's not allowed, y'see."

Emil's face went purple. "In my country, the family always stays with a sick child."

"Pavel. That's a funny name," said the nurse patting Pavel's head, ignoring Emil's anger. "But then you're foreign, aren't you?" She took his good arm and pointed to a nearby wheelchair. "Upsy-daisy, now and get in. I push and you get a nice free ride. It'll be fun. We'll take X-rays of your shoulder. Your mummy has to stay here."

Emil turned to Sophie. "Did you understand her?" he said in Czech. "What did she say?"

Sophie shot him a resentful glance. He had to make a lesson out of everything. "Yes father. Some of it. He is to have an X-ray." She kissed Pavel's forehead and stroked his face. "I'm sorry, darling," she whispered, "we cannot come with you. They will take you in this wheelchair to make pictures of your shoulder—so the doctor can see the bones. It will not take long. Now be brave and good, for Maman."

Pavel grabbed her with his left hand. "What pictures?"

"An X-ray takes pictures, like a camera," said Emil. "It shows what is inside your body. Then we will know exactly where the bone is broken." He nodded approval at Sophie. "Good. You understood the nurse well."

Pavel's eye widened. "What is a broken bone?"

The nurse and an aide wrapped a fluffy white blanket around Pavel's shoulders and rolled him away. Along the corridor, he kept twisting his head, trying to look back at his family.

Sophie wiped her eyes.

They settled on a bench to wait.

"Read me the words up there," said Emil after a few minutes. He pointed to several posters taped to the waiting room walls. "You might as well practice some English while we wait. Try that one."

Sophie peered at the picture of a well-dressed woman in feathered hat, with spray coming out of her mouth. "Coogs and Sneezes Spred Diz-eazes," Sophie mumbled. She pointed to a third poster showing a giant syringe and needle plunging through two huge black capital letters. "What is VD, father?"

"Sexual infection. Very dangerous for soldiers and their women." He waved an approving finger. "You are improving in your English. But now, we must talk—about why Judit was so angry with you."

Sophie's lip quivered and she looked away. "She accused me of pushing Pavel down the stairs. She has been unkind to me almost from the moment we arrived. Why? We got on so well in Lučenec."

"Try to understand, daughter. She suffered a shock. The boy is our treasure and our future. She is very protective—sometimes she can be like a tigress."

"The way she looked at me…"

"She is different since we came to London. Don't forget that in Lučenec Judit had a busy life. She managed our home, helped organize community events and musical evenings. She was secretary to the Women's Zionist Association. She went to the synagogue without me." He took a deep nostalgic breath. "How beautiful it was there: hot summers and winter snow. And those Tatra mountain streams, full of trout."

From his furtive sidelong glance, Sophie guessed he was embarrassed at revealing so much nostalgia. "Here we are poor and Judit has no one else except me—a grumpy husband who lost his country and his business. I cannot bring back her happiness, I think no one can."

Believing that under the grumpy carapace lurked a good-hearted man, Sophie put a hand on his arm. "Thank you for being so honest, Father. I'm also sad and unsettled—when we got off the boat in Liverpool I thought we would be safe with you. We arrived in time for the bombing to start. Most of all, I miss Willy. I need him to be with me." Her cheeks tightened, tears threatening.

Emil shook his head. "The war is hard on everyone. *Ach, mein Gott.*" He slapped his knee. "Pavel's accident made me forget. While you were walking with the boy on the Heath, a letter came." He pulled a crumpled envelope from his pocket. "It is addressed to me, sent a week ago."

Sophie nodded, eyes gleaming, breaths coming fast. "Open it now, Father."

Emil ran a finger under the envelope flap and pulled out a sheet of flimsy paper. "It has a postmark from Cheshire, but no return address. I wanted to open it when we were all together." He tilted his thick spectacles. "Very short … in English. So, I read it for you."

"From Willy. He is well and in a big camp. They live in tents. Hard conditions with good Czechoslovak cooking. But there have have been serious discipline problems between the men and the officers. A protest was being organized by one of the communist leaders, a man he knew in France, Povídka. "

Sophie pulled at Emil's arm. "Povídka? Ugh, I remember him from France. Why didn't Willy write sooner? Is there an address so we can write back? I want to visit him. I…"

Emil sighed. "Not so fast. He hopes you and Pavel are with us and says he sent this letter secretly, without permission." He smiled at her. "Good news, eh? Now we know where he is."

Sophie took the flimsy paper and looked at her husband's writing, tears in her eyes. "I want to visit him. We must tell him about Pavel's arm."

Emil sighed as he stood. "Daughter, we don't know where he is exactly—and if we did, we would need permits to travel. For us, that is not allowed." He walked to the entrance of the corridor through which the nurse had wheeled Pavel. "Not a soul," he grumbled. "Where is everybody?"

Emil returned and stood in front of her. "There's still something I want to know, daughter. The truth. What happened with Pavel on the stairs?"

Sophie gave a little gasp. "Please, father, I did not *push* him as Judit said. I wanted him inside the flat, away from danger. He had a tantrum. He bit me. See, here, on my wrist. "

"I understand," said Emil, carefully inspecting the bite marks. "Just broken skin. I hope you washed it carefully. As for Pavel, I think no one is to blame. An accident. Bad luck."

Sophie grasped his arm. "father, please. Why did you tell the young doctor you were not Jewish?"

Emil grunted. "To avoid trouble." He pulled a newspaper from his pocket and waved it at her. "I read *The News Chronicle* every day. It is socialist and gives money to the Czechoslovak Refugee Fund. But every day I read in it the bad things that happen to Jews here in England."

"It cannot be as bad as it was in France."

Emil took her hand. "I will happily deny facts and tell lies if it saves our skin. Whatever pride you have about your origins, do not speak of it in public."

Sophie's face reddened. Her father-in-law gave directives just like Willy.

"I don't want to discuss this anymore." Turning away from her, he picked up a half-folded *Daily News* lying on the bench and dropped it on Sophie's lap. "Here is a newspaper. While we wait, you can practice a little more. Go on, read me the headline. Aloud."

Sophie pointed to the date. "Why bother to read such an old thing."

"Do as I say, daughter."

Sophie dabbed her eyes dry and scanned the torn front page. She nudged him, pointing to a column just below the headlines. "Look Father ... something about Czechoslovak soldiers in England."

Emil grabbed the paper. *Gotteniu.* You are right. Czechoslovak soldiers mutiny in Cheshire. The date ... July 27. Show me the postmark on Willy's letter."

Sophie pulled out the letter and showed him the postmark.

Emil nodded. "Malpas. I think this is his camp ... the same place. I will read and explain to you."

Sophie felt a warming flow of relief. At last, news about Willy. Finding out this way was like reading a clue from a detective story. "What is this mutiny? Is it a problem?"

Nodding, Emil resumed reading. "You know, *Vzpoura*—when the soldiers refuse to obey orders. It says here that two thousand Czechoslovak troops are billeted in that camp, under the command of the British Army."

Sophie nodded enthusiastically. "I am sure Willy is there."

"Don't interrupt. It says President Beneš visited the camp from London to make a reassuring speech. There was a parade. Four battalions of Czechoslovak troops and officers marched under Colonel Kratochvil. The parade was interrupted by mutineers, *Vzbouřenci.* You understand?"

Sophie pulled at the corner of the newspaper to get a better look. "Maybe this is why we heard nothing from him?"

Emil continued. "The unarmed mutineers, marching in their own column, presented to President Beneš a list of complaints of unfair treatment, physical abuse and ethnic discrimination."

He looked at Sophie, crestfallen. "This report makes me very ashamed. Czechoslovak soldiers should not behave like this in a foreign country that has welcomed them. When you were in France, did Willy say anything about such problems among his comrades?"

She remembered Willy's anger when he described the insults and humiliations. "Well … he did say there was a lot of victimization, especially against the Jewish volunteers like him. His superior officer was horrible. A man called Rudček."

Emil slapped the newspaper against his leg and stared angrily at the cobwebbed ceiling. "*Idioten.* I hope to God, Willy is not one of those traitors." He began to read the rest of the newspaper.

Sophie squeezed her hands together, still tense. "I must be alone for a while," she said, "to digest this news."

Emil waved her away. "As you wish."

She got up, took off her coat, and found a reasonably clean seat against the opposite wall. She closed her eyes, hoping desperately that the nurse would bring Pavel back soon. Half-dozing, she remembered Willy describing how badly the Czechoslovak officers treated the volunteers and the Jews at the camp in France. Even then, he had predicted some kind of revolt. What if Willy *was* a mutineer and they kicked him out of the army?

She sighed. That would be wonderful. Then he would have to live at home.

The doctor returned and cleared his throat. "Look here, Mrs.…er…Mr. Kohut. The X-ray machine is on the blink. I'm sorry, can't be helped. But, as it's obvious your child broke his clavicle, we'll just go ahead with treatment."

Sophie, not understanding, looked away—acutely aware of how intently he was looking at her—the usual hungry male look. Despite her shabby clothes, she knew she was still attractive with a good figure, high cheekbones and striking dark hair. She wondered whether this would help or hinder the way he treated her child. "What did he say, Father?"

Frowning Emil leaned toward her, not angrily, but to get her attention. "*Krýt vaše prsa!* Cover yourself."

Sophie blushed and fastened the upper button of her blouse.

Emil looked up at the doctor. "What is this treatment?"

The doctor swung his stethoscope to and fro in his hand. "We'll use a hot compress to reduce the swelling. Then we wind an elastic bandage tightly round his shoulders and his back to hold the broken bone in position till it heals. A bandage brace, we call it. You will have to keep it on him for a few weeks, even when he sleeps."

Emil translated for Sophie and turned to the doctor. "If you do this, the boy needs something for the pain."

"It *will* hurt him a bit," said the doctor, whose gaze had switched back to Sophie. "I only have pethidine or morphine by injection. Far too strong for this little fellow. He'll just have to do the best he can with aspirin or codeine."

Emil clutched at the doctor's elbow. "The boy should not be on his own when you put on this brace. He is afraid. We want to be with him."

Dr. Haynes frowned as he shook off Emil's hand. "Families are not allowed during procedures: too much screaming and yelling. It's better this way. So, please, just *wait*." He walked off down the corridor.

Emil translated for Sophie again. "He says we cannot stay with Pavel. I don't know if he tells the truth. I'm nervous about insisting or complaining. We are refugees with no rights. They might throw us out—or get the police." He shrugged. "We must wait some more."

Sophie glared at him. Separating a child from his family like this would be considered cruelty in Prague. In Paris, when Pavel had his surgery she had even watched the operation on his neck. These English were a cold people, unfeeling. She imagined how frightened and in pain Pavel would be, manhandled by people who spoke a strange language. Her heart raced. She wanted to run down the corridor to look for him.

Emil looked down at his newspaper and muttered, almost to himself. "What can we do? We are helpless." He abruptly turned a page, tearing part of it. He looked at his watch "*Mein Gott*, we have been here nearly two hours. Judit will already be very nervous. She should not be alone so long. It will be dark soon."

He stood and buttoned up his raincoat. "I must go home and tell her what is happening."

Sophie grabbed his arm. "Father, you can't leave me here on my own."

"Yes, I can. I cannot look out for you all the time. But I will come back to help you get the boy home."

"I don't understand half of what they say," she said, almost in tears.

"Come daughter, you have more than sauerkraut for brains", he snapped. "If you ask them to speak slowly, you will understand. It is time to be independent. Just be polite."

Sophie put a pleading hand on his arm. "Don't you want to make sure Pavel has good treatment? *Tante* Judit is safe inside the flat. She will understand."

Emil studied her face for a few moments, then took her hand and stroked it gently. "I am sorry, daughter. I will stay. I am not used to choosing between what the two women in my family need."

Relieved, Sophie slumped against the wall wondering why they were taking so long with Pavel.

Faint shrieks echoed down the corridor. She jerked upright. It was a child's cry—a mixture of fear, protest, and panic. She shifted in her seat, uncertain what to do. There it was again. Ignoring Emil's restraining hand, she gathered up her things, ran down the corridor, and pushed through swinging doors.

A hand stopped her in her tracks, gripping her elbow. She was aware of the overpowering smell of tobacco. "Hold on, missus. You're not supposed to be wanderin' around the hospital on your own." A burly man in a rumpled, blue work coat turned her round and smiled, showing chapped lips and yellow, gapped teeth. "Whatyer lookin' fer?"

"My Pavel? I hear bad sound. He have broken shoulder. What is wrong?"

"You 'eard bad sounds?" he grunted with a twisted smile. "Then he'll be with the *young* doctor. There's always bad sounds when that bloke's seeing patients."

Sophie stared at him, terrified and trembling. Perhaps, English doctors were like the Nazis, experimenting on patients. "Pliss, help me."

The orderly offered her an apologetic smile. She tried not to shudder at the smell of his tobacco breath.

"Sorry, missus. Just a joke on the doc, y'know. A foreign lady are you?" He guided her back through the doors. "Don't worry yourself none. It'll be alright. C'mon, I'll take you back to yer seat."

Sophie sat down again and took Emil's hand. "I'm sure Pavel was crying out. He must be so frightened." She felt her face flush, a heavy stone of guilt filling her heart. His broken bone was her fault.

Emil looked at her, sympathy in his eyes. He patted her knee.

Half an hour later, the nurse returned. "Your nipper'll be ready soon." She blushed as if she was holding something back. "He made ever such a fuss with the hot compress. Anyway, Dr. Haynes says to take the dressing off tomorrow and keep the bandage on."

Emil nodded. "Thank you. Where is Pavel?"

"Coming, luv." She handed him a bottle and pointed to the label.

"Codeine syrup—for the pain—just follow the instructions."

Emil stood. "We need taxi."

"Of course, dear. I'll get the orderly to call one for you. It might take a while."

"Please, I pay you?"

The nurse shook her head. "Don't worry, lovey. We'll sort that out later. I've got your identity card and address."

Emil touched Sophie's shoulder. "The treatment is done. We can leave."

Pavel was still pale when they brought him into the waiting room. A flesh-colored, elastic bandage had been affixed and wound firmly around his chest and shoulders, like a two sided bandolier. Sophie stroked his cheeks and kissed him. "Does it still hurt a lot, darling?"

He nodded. "I want to go home, Maman. Doctor hurt me."

"Where is that doctor?" said Emil, frowning. "He must explain how we care for the boy."

The nurse smiled. "Sorry, he's busy on another case. I'll tell you how to look after your boy."

Emil, his frown deepening, pulled a pencil and a piece of cardboard from his coat pocket "Please tell. I write. But I prefer to speak to the doctor. "

The nurse patted Pavel gently on the head. "He was such brave little soul. The bandage—we call it a figure-of-eight brace—must be kept tight. And make sure his shoulders and upper arms are kept pressed backwards. Always put it on the same way and keep it on all the time, otherwise the bone won't heal straight. No bath, Use a sponge for washing. "

"Also in bed? How does he sleep?"

"On his back, dear. Keep a rolled up towel between his shoulders. And go to see your local doctor once a week. You know, your GP."

"We have no such doctor."

The nurse shrugged. "The police will tell you where there is one near you."

Sophie stared at the nurse, desperately wanting to understand the instructions. She watched Emil write his notes. "When will Pavel be healed, Father? What did she say?"

"Six weeks to get better," he grunted, shaking his head as he looked at her. "A long time. We did not need this trouble. And what will Willy say when he finds out what happened?"

CHAPTER FIVE

Complications

September 1940

That night, after the visit to the hospital, Pavel woke several times crying that his shoulder hurt. Twice, Sophie gave him codeine syrup and some bromide tincture, as advised by the nurse. But the boy was inconsolable. Sophie curled around him on the floor rug, wakeful and sensitive to his every twist and turn.

Early the next morning, she unwound Pavel's figure-of-eight bandage and slowly peeled off the shoulder dressing. He whimpered and shrank back as it came off. "*Christus,*" she screamed, starting to tremble.

She couldn't stop Pavel twisting to look at his shoulder.

"Maman. What's the matter?" He seemed more curious than frightened or in pain.

Judit rushed over. "*Emil, komm schnell*—quick," she called, her voice urgent and angry.

The skin on Pavel's shoulder was mottled scarlet, with tinges of blue and yellow, a moonscape of bulging blisters from which seeped yellow fluid. Sophie shuddered.

Emil gasped as he inspected Pavel's shoulder without touching anything. "*Oy vay, was für a Shandeh*—a scandal. This is not from the fall. This they did to him at that hospital." Crestfallen, he touched Sophie's arm. "The doctor prescribed a hot compress. This was a scalding. I should have watched. Poor boy."

"They tortured him," Judit cried out, tears starting down her cheeks. She covered her face with her apron and turned away.

"Scalded?" Sophie whispered. "Then they hid it with the bandage. That nurse and that doctor." She watched the muscles in Emil's flushed face clench and twitch. She had never seen him like this.

"Do not touch anything, daughter."

Sophie watched apprehensively as Emil rolled up his sleeves and filled a cooking pan with hot water from the Ascot heater. He scrubbed and dried his hands, and then with the end of a stubby finger delicately touched one of the largest blisters.

Pavel gave his grandpa a beseeching look. "Don't … don't."

Emil stopped. "All right, I stop." With a reassuring smile, he squeezed Pavel's nose gently between thumb and finger, the gesture of affection he had always used on Willy when he was little. "I'm sorry, *Pavelko*, you will have pain for a few days."

Judit's lips twitched, her fingers braiding loose apron strings round her waist. "For this, we go to the police."

Emil frowned. "A correct but useless suggestion," he grunted. "We are refugees. No one will pay attention, or if they do, then they think we make unnecessary trouble. This injury is nothing compared to what happens to London people every night after the bombing." He shrugged. "One look at that doctor's face and I knew he was incompetent."

Sophie looked from Judit to Emil, her face etched with misery. "What can we do?

Emil sat down by the small table. "He stays here. In the Great War, in the trenches, I helped care for phosphorus burns. We will do the same here." For a few moments, he rubbed and squeezed his nose as though digging out old memories. "Ah, now a little comes back to me. We need to dab the skin with diluted iodine to prevent infection. We must release the blisters but leave the covering skin. Vaseline will help healing and also stop the gauze dressings sticking. Then we put the big bandage back like before. I will get what we need from Mr. Hardy's chemist shop downstairs. He opens at nine. I'm sure he also has good advice."

Sophie stroked Pavel's face. Her head swam—events and wrongs were piling up. "Would you like something to eat, *miláčku?* It will help take the pain away." She kissed his cheek gently.

He shook his head.

Judit, mopping her tears with a handkerchief, gave Sophie a withering look. "Food and kisses won't do anything for the boy's pain. He fell because of you. That is what he said. I find it difficult to believe you and Willy were able to bring Pavel safely through Germany and France."

Sophie could not control her words. "But we did it. And mostly it was thanks to me. Willy was too busy training as a soldier; he was hardly ever at home."

Crack! Judit slapped her thigh, her face a mask of fury. "The sooner he gets here the better for all of us,"

"Leave me alone," Sophie shouted.

Pavel jerked his face up in surprise and began to cry.

Sophie slammed her hand on the table; the breakfast teacups jumped in their saucers. Judit was unbearable. What made her like this?

"What do you want from me, *Tante?* Unending gratitude for letting us live here with you? Why is it that you don't like me anymore? Because now I'm different from the respectful and obedient girl who married Willy? I've changed—just like you. We survived—in spite of Nazis, hunger, fear, and never knowing what was coming next. Isn't that something to be proud of?" She showed Judit a tiny gap between the ends of her right thumb and forefinger. "We were *this* close to the end of everything at the German frontier," she said with a half-sob. "You should be happy and thankful, not mean."

Judit took a step back, open-mouthed. She glanced at her husband as if it was his duty to defend her. "Say something, Emil."

Sophie continued more calmly. "People in the same family do not own each other. There should be give and take, and understanding. You won't even let me help with the cooking or cleaning. To reward yourself, you behave like a martyr. If it were possible Pavel and I would leave immediately and leave you alone. Please, I have had enough of the bad atmosphere here."

Emil slipped on his dressing gown and polished his glasses before replacing them on his nose. He frowned. "Sophie has a justified complaint. I want no more bickering. Because we live like rats in a box does not mean we should *behave* like rats, tearing at each other's throats."

"What is to be done, Emil?" said Judit, hands on hips, feet apart. "We do not have enough space. She has no money and nowhere to go."

His shoulders heaved. He set his jaw. "Simple. We will find something bigger. But first, with Sophie's help I will dress Pavel's shoulder and re-apply the bandage. After, I will go to Rosenheim, the rental man on Finchley Road. I know him from the Cosmo café. He will help us find somewhere. Perhaps it will be near a strong shelter where we can hide from the bombs without being surrounded by dirty people."

Sophie smiled inwardly at Emil's description of the people who sheltered in the underground stations. He and Willy were similar in some ways: blunt, often intolerant but also goodhearted. And when they met a problem they went into action.

"If we move, don't forget we have to make sure Willy has our new address," she said, "He has to know what happened about Pavel's shoulder."

Emil looked at her. "Our only way to locate him is to go back to the Czechoslovak Legation … beg them to send him a telegram."

CHAPTER SIX
The Mutineers
Malpas, Cheshire
September1940

The imposing battlements and turrets of 19th century Cholmondeley Castle had never been designed to witness a mutiny. Its clipped hedges, sweeping lawns and flowering borders surrounded an island set in the center of sumptuous water gardens and crowned by a small Greek-style temple. Groves of oaks, chestnuts, and cedars adorned the woodlands beyond. The British Ministry of Defense had requisitioned the estate from the Marquis of Cholmondeley—to house the Czechoslovak Army-in-Exile. More than three thousand soldiers, still in French uniforms, occupied canvas bell-tents that criss-crossed the lawns with geometric precision.

One third of the mutineers were Czech communists—volunteers from the Spanish Civil war who now refused to fight against Germany because of Stalin and Hitler's non-aggression pact. The rest were Jews, civilians who had volunteered in France.

Shortly before the mutiny, a communist member of the exiled Czechoslovak parliament in London, Anežka Hodinová, had visited the camp and encouraged the volunteers to stand down in an imperialist-capitalist war and leave the army. It was the duty of communists throughout the world, she said, to block the allied war effort. Now, stirred up by communist agitators, they had finally refused to obey orders after suffering discrimination from their own officers. On July 27, by order of exiled President Beneš, all were stripped of their rank and a section of the camp between the castle and the edge of the woods had been cordoned off, keeping the 539 mutineers separate from loyal troops. Willy Kohut was one of them. Their fate was uncertain.

Willy was by his tent, washing socks and underwear in a zinc tub when Sergeant Březinka, grabbed his arm. "You, Kohut. Come with me. Captain Rudček wants you." Březinka was grizzled and heavy shouldered, one of the hard-boiled professionals of the second Artillery unit.

"What for?" Willy saw distaste on the sergeant's face. Was it because he was Jewish, or just one of the mutineers? Probably both.

"How the hell should I know? And for Christ's sake smarten yourself up. Look like a soldier."

What did Rudček want, Willy wondered as he buttoned his army blouse … to deliver another dose of viciousness? In France, he had worked under Rudček in the provisioning section at Czechoslovak army headquarters in Narbonne—accompanying his superior to buy food at local farms. There had been instant mutual dislike followed by a string of humiliations.

Willy had to march through the fenced-in crowd of detainees who had stopped chatting and smoking to watch him cross the castle's forecourt. Sergeant Březinka pushed him through a studded side door of the castle. "Good luck, Kohut," someone shouted. "Shove it up their arse!"

A few minutes later, Willy and Březinka entered a large room where a handful of Czechoslovak officers were busy at what looked like school desks. Most wore wool caps, greatcoats, scarves and gloves. The Czechoslovak Army could not afford to heat the place.

The two soldiers removed their caps and stood at attention in front of Captain Rudček's desk. "Detainee Kohut, as ordered, sir," the sergeant said.

"At ease," the captain said, not looking up. He wore a military tunic, as well as the usual silk scarf and white gloves that covered up his unsightly psoriasis. He skimmed a couple of typed pages pulled from a buff colored file.

From a radio somewhere in the room Willy recognized the creamy sounds of Benny Goodman's clarinet, playing "How High the Moon". The music boosted his gloomy spirits.

Rudček raised his head and gave him a cold stare. "There's a rule for you mutineers, *Vojin* Kohut," he said, irritably tapping a forefinger on the desk. "No mail allowed in or out—except for emergencies." He pointed to a torn yellow envelope lying in front of him. "This fucking telegram arrived from the Czech Legation in London. It concerns you."

Willy tensed. It had to be from his family. Had Sophie and Pavel arrived in London? "May I read it, sir?"

Rudček slammed his hand on the desk. "Insolent as usual, Kohut."

Willy clenched his teeth. He could tell the other officers were watching with interest. He clicked his heels, tense with anger. "Permission to pick up *my* telegram, sir."

Rudcek crumpled it in his fist. "This is not *your* telegram, Kohut; it comes from the Czechoslovak Legation and is addressed to the attention of the Commanding Officer, Third Artillery Battalion."

Willy gave his escort sergeant a sideways glance, hoping for some sign of sympathy. Seeing none, he turned back to the officer, wanting to fight back in the subtle way that he knew Rudček detested. "I don't understand, Captain. You summoned me regarding an urgent telegram that concerns me. Now you say it's not my telegram. I'm not sure of the next step, sir."

Rudček thwacked his swagger stick on the table. "You're an insolent little yid, Kohut. There is no regulation that requires me to give you this telegram," he said, "but I *will* tell you what it says. It is in English and signed by some official in London. The text reads—Pavel fell on stairs. Stop. Broken shoulder. Stop. Can you come? Stop. Emil. Stop."

Rudček tossed the balled telegram into a waste basket and leaned his chair back on two legs. "So, *vojín*." He picked up his cigarette and blew a smoke ring. "You Yids shouldn't have teamed up with the communist bastards and turned into mutineers. However, I will inform the Legation in London that you received the telegram. You see, I can be generous, even to a traitor."

Behind his back, Willy clenched his fists, desperately hoping he could persuade Rudček to dredge up some shreds of sympathy. "I respectfully request permission to take some leave, sir," he said, his words coming out in a choked rush. "My injured child, my wife, my parents … they need me." His voice trailed off.

Rudček stood, looking Willy up and down with contempt. "Why in hell should I let you to sneak away to London? Anyway, there's no time. You yids and commies are to be shifted to another camp where the Brits will decide what to do with you. And, by God, I don't want you to miss that." He looked down at his file. "Take him back to the detention area, Sergeant."

Willy spread his arms wide, pleading. "I beg you, Captain Rudček; my family is alone in London. My boy must be in a lot of pain. At least, let me make a telephone call, to a friend who can help them—or let me send a message."

"Mother of God, Kohut, stop whining. You're confined to camp. No other options. Get that into your thick skull. Dismiss."

Willy bit his lip. He saluted. "Thank you, sir," he said, miserably.

Sergeant Březinka swung him round and marched him out along the broad terrace that overlooked the castle's parkland. Willy and the sergeant passed a handful of armed guards relaxing against an armored car and were admitted through a barred gate back into the fenced compound that included the castle's circular driveway and an area of trimmed lawn.

Březinka stopped suddenly and pulled Willy into the shadow of a nearby oak tree, its gnarled branches hanging low. The sergeant took an envelope from his blouse pocket and pulled out a handful of beige cards. He gave one to Willy and handed him a pencil. "These just came in. Field Post has been given permission to allow for soldiers to contact their families or friends. Mutineers excluded, of course. Fill one out quick and I'll make sure it gets mailed. Your family deserves to get something from you."

Willy looked down at the card. His heart jumped. Better than nothing. "Thanks, friend."

Nothing is to be written on this side except the date, signature and address of the sender. **If anything else is added the card will be destroyed.**

I am (ill) well.......

I have been admitted to hospital and am getting on well

I am being transferred to another camp

I have received your letter dated ....

Signature...

 Camp Address..

(1007) Demand 2023

Date.......................

Resting the card against the bark of the tree trunk, he filled out his father's address, wrote that he received the telegram, that he was well and being transferred to another camp. He signed and dated it and handed it back. "I'm grateful—you're a good man."

Willy walked toward his tent, elated, but also aware that his card might get lost or delayed. He had to come up with a backup way to contact Sophie or his father before he was transferred to the British camp Rudček had just mentioned.

But there was another way to get help for his family, if he could figure it out. There was George Kindell, a business acquaintance from before the war. George had succeeded his father as managing director of Kindell and Rivett, the London firm that supplied British fabrics to the Kohut textile stores in Czechoslovakia. Somewhere in his tent, Willy had a small notebook with George's home telephone number. If he was stuck in Cholmondeley, George was the only person he could ask for help.

Inside the tent, Willy threw himself on his cot and closed his eyes. He pictured Pavel with his arm and shoulder in a plaster cast, sobbing with pain. Sophie would be in shock, his mother Judit would be in a high state of anxiety while his father would be calm and practical but probably a little short on sympathy.

He lit a cigarette, hoping to calm his jitters. The desire to see his family, and the challenge of achieving it, drove other thoughts from his mind. The seeds of a plan germinated. He would telephone George Kindell and… get him to… do what? No, first, he had to *find* a damned telephone. It would be impossible for a mutineer to get at a telephone inside the castle but there had to be one outside, probably in some nearby village.

Among the mutineers, Willy knew of two unsavory characters; fixers who might find him a working telephone. Corporal Povídka and Private Bohomir Serbin…in France, they had been billeted with Willy in the same village. They were part of a cadre of hardened communist fighters—known as *Španiěláci*—who had battled Franco's troops in Spain. With Franco victorious, two thousand of them fled across the Pyrenees and joined the Czechoslovak Army-in-Exile. After the armistice was signed, fifteen hundred of them stayed on in France.

Willy was aware that Boho Serbin, even while in detention, still managed to smuggle in cigarettes and booze from a village pub, using a secret route through the estate's woods. He sold them to the other soldiers at double the price. Where there was a pub, Willy concluded, there had to be a telephone.

He left the tent and, after some reconnoitering, eventually spotted Boho's scarred face and squat body in the middle of a group of mutineers. He was selling individual smokes out of a knapsack. Willy pushed his way into the circle. "Glad, I found you, Boho," he exclaimed throwing a friendly arm round the private's solid shoulders; a risky move because the man sometimes acted reflexively with his fists. "This is an emergency, my friend. You're the only bastard in this camp who can help me. Can we talk somewhere alone? I have a deal for you."

Boho glared. "Fuck off, Kohut. I'm busy, see. Why should I help a pitiful Jew?" He pulled out his knife, sliced off a plug of tobacco and stuck it into his mouth. He turned back to selling cigarettes.

Willy wasn't put off. He knew that Boho, with his muscles, battle scars, shaved head, and foul language was only open to persuasion if he got something substantial in return. Besides, they all had common cause against Captain Rudček and the other officers.

"Listen comrade. Rudček just pulled me in and showed me a telegram … from my father in London. My son broke his shoulder. If you help me, there's money in it."

Boho didn't take the bait. "Your family ain't my business. And you don't have any money."

"Do me a favor, comrade. Show me how to get to the village. I need a telephone."

Boho grimaced. "I've a mind to chop off your Jewish pecker. Piss off, you're ruining my business. I've got to sell off my supplies, double quick. Didn't you know we're to be transferred out of here? Some dump in Scotland."

Willy recognized the dry scratchy sound behind his right ear. It was Corporal Leo Povídka, laughing.

"What do you want, Kohut?" Boho's superior said with a sneer. His hoarse, sometimes hesitant voice was the result of a botched Republican attempt to string him up in Alicante. He kept his sentences clipped and brief.

Willy knew a great deal about Leo Povídka: he had been a brigade commissar in Spain, an avid fan of Stalin. In contrast to Boho Serbin's refrigerator shape, Povídka was tall and gaunt, with a hawkish profile topped by sparse gray hair and pale eyes. If aroused, the strong but simple-minded Boho could be erratic and violent, but Willy feared Povídka. The commissar was intelligent, mean, and ruthless. He held sway over most of the communist volunteers who had mutinied. One dark word from Comrade Commissar and you could get a knife in your guts.

"I'm glad you're here, Leo. I have an emergency," Willy said, injecting sincere respect into his voice. "My four-year old kid in London broke his shoulder. All I need is an hour or so to get outside to make a telephone call to my family and get back to camp. Boho knows how to get outside the camp, but he's being sticky about it. Will you help me?"

Povídka rolled and clicked his neck, a quirk that frequently introduced his sentences. "Don't worry, little Kohut," he said patting Willy's cheek, "The telephone you want is at Bickerton." He turned and gave Boho's shoulder an affectionate punch. "My sturdy comrade has a woman in Bickerton. He's often at the pub there."

"Kohut's picked a fuckin' bad time to do this," Boho grunted in disgust. "And I don't like the idea of him knowin' my route."

Povídka pulled out his pipe and stuffed it with tobacco. "Come now, Boho, despite our reservations regarding his Jewish race, Kohut deserves our help with this one. His boy's been injured." He sucked in the match flame and puffed. "In return, he will pay you a route guidance fee of shall we say ... two pounds? I know he'll be grateful and work with us in the future, won't you, comrade?"

Willy winced at the cost—two week's wages. He nodded agreement. He knew that "working" with Commissar Povídka could land him in dark and dangerous waters. Couldn't be helped. Not if he wanted to get hold of George Kindell.

"All right, all right," said Boho, clearly irritated. "I'll show you some of the way. After that, you're on your own. Tell no one about my way through the woods. There's a telephone box next to the pub. But if you go in there and put a spell on the barmaid, I'll slit your throat."

Boho took Willy behind a tent and went over the details. Willy made notes on a scrap of torn newspaper. He handed over the two pound notes. "Thanks, Boho. Do you happen to have any change for the telephone box?"

Boho punched Willy in the chest, making him wince. "*Sakra*, you Jews never stop whining for handouts. Go find some other fool."

*   *   *

That evening, just after roll call Willy, using a flashlight covered with a sock, stumbled through the dark woods. He followed a trail marked by strips of torn sheets hanging from branches. He was still in his French army gear over which he wore a rain cape. "Stay on the path," Boho had said with a grin, "they've got fox and badger traps all over the place. I'll have a good laugh if you come back with your toes chopped off."

After being spooked by an owl, Willy found Boho's opening in the stone wall and eased himself through. As a car approached with dimmed headlights, he drew back into the shadows —he guessed he was on the Bickerton road.

After a twenty minute walk, he entered the village. He passed picket fences and front gardens shining in the moon. A dog barked, and drawn by distant laughter he found a telephone booth at the back of the Flying Dove, a rambling, Tudor-style, one story pub. From the rancid stink, Willy guessed the latrine was close by. He shrank against the wall as a man wearing boots—maybe a soldier—clomped past, fiddled with the latch and mumbling curses, stumbled in.

Inside the booth, Willy switched on the flashlight and placed four shilling coins on top of the telephone box, hoping it would be enough to get the job done. He found George Kindell's number in his address book and dialed the exchange.

"Number please."

He gave it to the operator.

"That'll be a shilling for three minutes. Please hold."

He put the silver coin into the slot.

"You're through, sir," she said.

He pushed the A button and heard a click.

After several rings, a throaty voice answered. "Hello, Kindell residence."

Willy took a breath. Was this George's mother? Willy remembered her—tall, flat-chested with a little too much powder and rouge on her face: a woman who knew almost nothing about Europe or Hitler. "Good evening, this is Willy Kohut … a friend of young Mr. George. We met three or four years ago when I visited from Czechoslovakia. Can I speak to George, please?"

"From Czechoslovakia, you say? Well, we're all in the middle of supper. We don't like phone calls during supper. Can you call later?"

"No, no, please, don't hang up. I can't call again. I'm in a phone box. Long distance. This is very, very important. Are you Mrs. Kindell?"

There was a silence as if she was weighing up what to do or say. Willy heard her cough and clear her throat. He tightened his grip on the receiver praying she would not hang up. He shivered. How could a telephone booth be so cold in September? What a country!

"I *am* George's mother. You know, young man, calling at this hour is rather impertinent, but I'll see if he'll talk to you. Wait a minute. "

A minute passed. Willy's teeth were on edge. Was he coming or not?

"George Kindell here. This is a super-inconvenient time. Who are you? We didn't get your name."

"For God's sake, don't hang up, George; it's Willy Kohut from Prague. Remember? My father Emil was your central European Finetex agent before the war started. We had dinner at your house before we went touring the woolen mills up north."

There was a long pause. "Oh, my God, yes. *Now,* I remember. Amazing how time flies and memories fade. Willy—I can picture you now ... a smallish chap with glasses. Always impeccable. You liked a good joke ... a super pianist. You played romantic stuff, Liszt, Chopin and all that. My mother adored it. Where are you? How on earth did you get to Britain?"

Willy heard a beeping noise and it took him a few seconds to realize that the telephone slot was hungry for money. He punched in another shilling.

"Good memory, George. Look, I have to be quick. I'm a soldier stuck in a Czechoslovak army camp near Malpas in Cheshire. I need your help. My family in London is in trouble. My four year-old broke his shoulder. I'm not allowed to get in touch with them, or visit them."

Willy heard beeping on the line again. He inserted his last shilling.

"You there, Willy?"

"Okay, just fed the phone again."

"Terribly rotten luck. What can I do?"

"Visit them and make sure my boy's all right."

George sighed. "Why don't you telephone them? Or write?"

"My father has no phone. The public box I'm calling from is outside the camp. I can't telephone from the camp and we can't send mail."

"I see. Well, let me think. Today's Sunday. I suppose I could manage to visit your father. I'll just have to turn up there. I've got a pencil. What's the address?"

"Forty-two Hampstead High Street, top floor, above a chemist shop. My wife, Sophie will be there … and my boy, Pavel. Got it?"

"That will be interesting. I'll meet her for the first time. My dad once said she was a stunner. Why don't you call me Thursday, after dinner, about eight and…" George's mellifluous voice was overwhelmed by beeps and then silence. More shillings were needed. For once, Willy was out of luck.

Forty minutes later, Willy greeted his tent mates with a gloomy face. There was no need for them to know where he had been or what he had done. "Took a walk round the camp. I got some bad news. My boy's been injured in London. I'm not sure how bad it is."

He clambered onto his cot and, to keep his mind from overheating, read a page of the three day-old *Daily Mail* newspaper that circulated interminably round the camp. The news fitted his mood of despondency and anger over Pavel's injury and Rudček's intransigence. All over the south of England, the Luftwaffe was bombing airfields, a new strategy interpreted by pundits as a preliminary to a Nazi invasion. Russia had annexed Latvia and Estonia and the Vichy regime in France had sentenced De Gaulle to death—*in absentia*.

Boho's ugly head poked in between the entrance flaps. Everyone turned to look at his shaved rectangular head and lopsided grin. "All smooth, Kohut? How did it go?"

Willy nodded, surprised at the man's thoughtfulness. "It was fine—thanks. You were a great help." The words stuck in his throat but then, in wartime, even unpleasant alliances were necessary. All he could do now was wait and wonder about poor Pavel, until he talked with George again.

CHAPTER SEVEN
60 Northways
September, 1940

Ten days after Pavel's fall on the stairs, Judit and Emil waited impatiently for the rental agent in the entrance hall of a substantial block of flats built in the 1920's, not far from Hampstead. Northways, as it was called, towered over Finchley Road, the main thoroughfare linking the northwest suburbs to central London. The sky was cloudless and heat radiated off the brick and stone walls.

Emil looked at his pocket watch. "Twenty past eleven already. I hate being kept waiting."

Judit fanned herself with a piece of folded paper. "Who is it this time? I am worn out with looking and it is too hot."

Emil tilted his glasses, peering at the note in his hand. "A Mr. Rudman is to show us the flat. Don't start complaining about what is wrong with it until we have seen everything. We are in a weak bargaining position ... almost homeless. And please, do not speak to me in German or Czech when the agent is with us. The English get annoyed if they cannot understand. We do not want him annoyed."

Alex Rudman looked to be in his fifties, with a pear-shaped belly, trim pepper and salt hair, and a jaunty, fixed smile. The right sleeve of his worn tweed jacket was pinned up on his shoulder and he walked with a limp. "Number 60 is on the third floor. Good condition, with a balcony and a nice view of the traffic on Finchley Road," he said as they stepped into the elevator. He put down his briefcase and punched the floor button with his left hand.

Judit glanced at the scratches and curses scrawled on the metal walls and pointed at the cigarette butts strewn over the floor. "It is a disgrace. I will not like it here."

Mr. Rudman lost his grin. "Sorry 'bout that, but that's how things are these days."

Emil nudged Judit. He wanted to keep her on a tight leash. "Be patient with your remarks, wife," he muttered in Czech. "How can I negotiate favorable terms with a man whose elevator you just insulted? Wait till we finish seeing the flat."

The agent led them along a dark corridor. A bucket of sand and a stirrup pump stood at each doorway. Half way down, he unlocked the door of # 60 and let them in. Unlike their gloomy, battered coop above Hardy's chemist shop, the flat had an airy feel: high ceilings with pastel blue walls. There were two small bedrooms with built-in closets and, off the living room, an alcove that housed the cooker, sink and worktop. The bathroom had a gas hot water heater with a long arm that swung from the hand basin to a small sit-up bathtub.

In the living room, which had French doors leading to a low-walled brick balcony, Emil pointed to the gas wall heater. "I smell gas. Are you sure it is turned off?"

"Of course, Mr. Kohut. I'm almost certain that smell comes from cleaning fluid. "

"Such a pleasure, *Apa*," Judit exclaimed repeatedly as she examined the bedroom cupboards and pulled the lavatory chain to check the flush. "Very good space, a nice kitchen and we can take a real bath. But I do not like the linoleum floor … it is old and cracked in many places."

Watching her inspect the rooms, Emil felt a surge of pleasure at her optimism. A good sign.

She looked at him with a sudden frown. "You say they cleaned this place but already I see plenty of dust and dirt. We will have work to do here."

"I know the place needs smartening up a bit," Rudman said, lighting a cigarette as he watched her face. "We've almost no staff y'see.

They're all in uniform or in the factories. But if you take the flat, I might find a way to get it cleaned up before you move in—cost you a bit extra."

"Not necessary," Emil said quickly, loath to spend what he guessed might be the equivalent of two week's rent, especially if he couldn't be certain of a job well done.

"Gas." Judit's voice echoed from the kitchen alcove. She was hovering over the cooker. She opened the oven door, recoiled, and pointed a finger. "Gas come from here, yes?"

"Ah, you've got a good nose, missus." Mr. Rudman's face was beet red. "I'll ask the gas people to fix it, but that usually takes a few days. If you want to speed things up—that would cost a couple of extra quid." He nodded at the window. "Hear that? Fire engines. Last night's raid. Two houses still burning in St. John's Wood. I expect the gas repair people will be there—standing by. They say more than fifty thousand Londoners have lost their homes since those Jerry bastards started in on us."

Emil's face was pale. "This leak could explode. We cannot move in."

Mr. Rudman patted him on the back. "I can get it fixed. With the bombing, we often get small gas leaks. A 500 pound DA went off across the road two nights ago and shook this place up somethin' awful."

"DA." Judit's face was a question mark.

"Delayed action bomb, missus. Now, if you've finished the tour, I'll take you down to the locker space and the underground garage. That's where the tenants go when the air raids are on."

Mr. Rudman took them down in the elevator to the basement garage. "There's the stairs as well," he said, deftly lighting a cigarette with one hand. "When the siren goes, there's always a rush."

The dimly-lit basement was empty apart from four cars parked in one corner. Emil nodded his approval. "Yes, this is good construction. Strong concrete." With a satisfied grunt he patted one of the massive pillars. "We will be safe here."

Judit looked around, frowning. She sniffed. "It's so dark. It smells also … cigarettes, and maybe vermin. You say this place is where we hide from the air raids?"

With a flourish worthy of a ballet dancer, Rudman spun around, throwing his one arm up in the air. "It's better than a bank vault down here, completely bomb proof—guaranteed. We can squeeze five hundred people in, though usually it's more like three hundred—tenants and neighbors."

Judit shook her head disapprovingly. "For this basement and the flat we pay twenty-three shillings a week? That is too much, *miláčku*. What is so good about living here that we must pay so much?"

Emil gave her a disparaging look. It was too easy for her to become obsessed with details and not see the big picture. "Think, Judit," he said switching from English to Czech "We must have more space and this basement means real safety. There is no time to waste. Give up your high standards for once. For Pavel's sake, it is worth twenty shillings a week to stay alive." He turned to Mr. Rudman and handed him an envelope. "No more talk. Here is the deposit. We take the flat. When can we move in?"

Mr. Rudman checked the envelope's contents and nodded. "Five quid. Righty-ho, then. How about next Friday?" Awkwardly, he held out his left hand for Emil to shake.

Four days later, after another air-raid on central London, the Kohut family moved to 60 Northways. The gas leak had been repaired, and with Pavel helping and hindering, Judit and Sophie spent two days cleaning. They hand-carried as many small items as they could, taking short trips by bus. Mr. Hardy, owner of the chemist shop, offered the use of his van. His son's strong arms helped with the transfer of the few pieces of furniture they owned. In spite of drizzle and slippery pavements, the move was completed in a few hours.

The day after the move, they ate lunch before noon: scrambled eggs made from American egg powder on pumpernickel bread from Grodzinski's Bakery on Finchley Road. Real eggs were now as rare as gold. Pavel, still wearing the shoulder brace and with his arm stabilized in a sling, ate with his left hand—with Judit helping to cut up his bread and spooning stewed apple into his mouth. After Emil finished his tea, he stood at the table with a thumb tucked into his waistcoat, clearing his throat. "Dear family, I am most happy we have a new home. I hope this means we can get along better."

Judit smiled agreement. "And now we can furnish it with things from the Lučenec crate."

Sophie's fork stopped in mid-air. "You sent a crate? We did too. When was yours shipped?"

Emil looked pleased. "A year ago and just in time; a few days before the Hungarians arrested me. We packed clothes, silverware, bed-linens and documents, all hidden inside rolls and bundles of fabric. Also, one or two small pieces of furniture."

"What about the police and customs?" Sophie helped Pavel spoon up the last of his egg.

Judit's eyes sparkled. A smile split her face. "We fooled them. Our bills of lading said we were returning damaged goods to the manufacturer—Kindell and Rivett. I sewed *Apa's* business documents and money into the eiderdowns. There were no problems."

Emil sighed. "There was a small fortune in there. Hungarian *Pengö* and bonds ... Czech *korun* banknotes—all worthless now."

Judit set two apples on a plate. "One half each. *Apa* will cut them for us." With a smile, she turned to Sophie. "At last, you and Pavel can sleep in a proper bed. I will be happier now with some of my old things around me."

Emil patted the top of Pavel's head. "Maybe you and your mama would like to come with me to the Kindell and Rivett warehouse this afternoon. I want to ask them to bring our crate here. On the way we can sit at the top of the bus and see what the driver sees."

Pavel pushed his spoon away. He had egg on his nose and upper lip. "Don't want the bus. I want to walk with Maman in the park. Dig for rabbits like before."

"How can you dig with only one arm working," said Judit, getting up from the table. "Anyway, we still have work to do. Sophie, please, clear and wash the dishes and then clean the toilet. Your boy made a mess in there." She bent down and kissed Pavel's nose. "I know you will be happy here, sweetheart. Now you have space to play with your toys."

Pavel's face brightened. "I only have Furry Lion. Please, you buy me a new toy?"

Emil laughed. "A *new* toy? I'm not even sure they make such things these days." He pushed back his chair and looked out of the window. "*Ach*, another gray day and much to do." He looked at Judit. "Now that we're settled, I must take Sophie to the police station for our check-in and to get her registered … and then we'll go to the Food Office for her ration books."

He glanced at the old fob-watch that hung from his waistcoat and turned to Sophie. "Soon we go. But also today, I'll show you how to use the ration books. We'll go shopping together. Then I want you to carry the food home while I take the bus to Kindell's about the crate."

Judit shook her head. "I want Sophie to help me clean here."

Emil shook a finger at her. "Not today. She has to learn how to buy food and fend for herself. Pavel will help you with the cleaning." He smiled at the boy.

Sophie got up from the table. She hadn't expected this: a whole afternoon speaking English with officials, shopkeepers, and even the police. The English policemen—tall with calm, serious faces, their eyes nearly hidden by pointy helmets—were nothing like the French gendarmes who smoked, were rude and patrolled café terraces, drinking beer and ogling young women. Refugees and police were … oil and water.

Judit squeezed a wet cloth into a bucket of soapy water. She looked up at Sophie. "I expect your refugee registration will be category C, like ours."

"What is Category C?"

"Category C, Category C," sang Pavel, swinging Furry Lion around his head with his healthy left arm. "Category ABC, ABCDEFG. What is category C, Judit?" he called out, mimicking his mother's voice.

Emil laughed. "Category C is for a refugee who does not need special surveillance, but cannot stay outside in the blackout. And you are forbidden to ride a bicycle or own a map."

"I read that German, Hungarian or Austrian, people in the C Category are often sent to a camp," said Judit as she began to mop the drain board in the kitchen alcove. She looked at Sophie, then at Emil. "Her family is Hungarian. What is to be done?"

"She has a child and a Czechoslovak passport. I hope that will be enough, "said Emil. "Anyway, we have to go to the police station every week to prove who we are, say where we live, and show we have enough money to live on. This I understand. A bureaucracy must keep track of so many refugees."

While Judit reset Pavel's shoulder brace, Sophie got ready to go out. Since the flare-up between them, she had brokered an uneasy truce. Under Emil's prodding, they had agreed to alternate the tasks of preparing food, cleaning the flat, and looking after Pavel, including re-dressing the loosening scabs from the poultice burns on his shoulder—a task that needed careful work with tweezers and antiseptic.

As Emil and Sophie were about to leave, Judit opened a cupboard and passed Pavel a square tin decorated with pictures of chocolates.

"It's heavy," he squeaked, almost dropping it. Cross-legged on the floor, he pulled off the lid. "Ooh," he said, tipping a mass of colored buttons onto the floor. He stared at them, then scattered them with a sweep of his fingers. "I like these buttons."

He sat quiet for a moment then began to place the buttons in lines along the floor. "I'll make a road of buttons. When she comes back, I want to see Maman walk on my road."

Passing by the Olde Swiss Chalet pub on Finchley Road with Emil, Sophie wondered how long it would take her to get used to her new neighborhood. Swiss Cottage was livelier than Hampstead: more shops, an underground tube station, Lefstein's delicatessen, two nice cafés, the Cosmo and the Dorice, two bus lines, and a department store farther down Finchley Road.

She would miss Hampstead Heath—her daily walk there had given her the salve of trees, grass, solitude and reflection. Over the past two years, her life had been in continuous flux: from Prague to Paris and the Café Budapest, to the village of Sillat in southern France—then the sea journey from Gibraltar to England, the cramped flat in Hampstead, and now this Swiss Cottage neighborhood. All through that time, Willy had appeared and disappeared from her side, like an affectionate puppet attached by an elastic band to its real owner … the Czechoslovak army.

All this time she had wanted him back, but now she was no

longer so sure. At the moment her marriage felt more like an arrangement between friends.

After they bought bread at Grodszinski's bakery, Sophie took Emil's arm. "Father, you are paying seven extra shillings a week rent for this new flat. Where does the extra money come from? "

Emil gave her an amused look "That is a nosy question, Daughter. I hope you are not complaining."

She shook her head wondering whether he would answer her question. "I'm just curious."

He took a deep breath. "It is best for us refugees to be discreet about what money we have—and better still that our women know as little as possible." There was no hostility in his voice. Just patience. He halted and drew her closer. His breath smelled sweet, from the mint pastilles he often sucked.

"This one time I will explain it to you. We receive one pound a week living expenses from the Czechoslovak Refugee Center. That is not enough for four people to live on, pay rent, and stay out of an internment camp. So—I tell you a secret. I have a bank account—at an English bank ... the Westminster Bank."

Sophie gasped. "*Jóság engem,* goodness me, father—a *bank* account? Willy never said we had money in London. I thought we were penniless."

Emil glared. "Hunh—Willy never told you that, because *I'm* the one who has money. He is the penniless one. No doubt, before the Nazis came, he was too busy with his *Anglotex* venture in Prague to listen to my advice. He and you were having too a good time to see what was coming."

Sophie put a hand on his arm. "Father, don't be so bitter. We worked hard and led a respectable life. We even went to *Shabbat* services once a month, for a while. You have the wrong impression of our life."

Emil knitted his eyebrows into a flat gray hedge. "You attended *Shabbat* services? Pfui! Ridiculous. Why would Willy bother to bow and scrape in a synagogue? My family never believed in that stuff. What hypocrisy. I believe only in the laws of nature." He looked up at the low gray clouds and shook his head. "*Verdammte regen*," he muttered pulling up the collar of his raincoat.

"We went to synagogue to help our business grow," said Sophie in a conciliatory tone. "To meet people and make friends. Willy always wore his best suits to show off the English fabrics. He was like a fashion show at the Synagogue. A different suit and tie each time. It worked. Congregation members came to our shop."

"Hunh! Interesting idea—using religion for business purposes. I never thought of anything like that in Lučenec."

Sophie sighed. "I know Judit isn't against Judaism like you. I get the feeling she would like to attend services here. Why don't you let her?"

"Because all religion is rubbish—and dangerous. People who believe in a God are fools."

Sophie did not like the way her father-in-law denigrated religion so viciously. In Berlin, she had been raised to respect and celebrate the Jewish traditions, and she knew that her in-laws had been through an arranged marriage, presided over by a rabbi. When Emil ranted like this, she wanted to argue with him but was afraid he would end up in one of his rare black rages. "Maybe Judit just wants to have a social time with other Jewish women? I think she needs friends."

Emil opened his umbrella. With a grunt, he batted away a broken strut and they resumed their pace. "No more religious talk, daughter. But as I said, I *will* explain to you about my English bank account. In 1938, in Lučenec, I saw what was coming—the fascist regime in Slovakia, and then the Sudetenland annexation by Hitler. I devised a scheme to hide our money in a safe country."

"The scheme was against regulations, of course—but nothing obvious. By then, we were not allowed to transfer funds abroad. So, when I ordered fabrics from my British suppliers, Kindell and Rivett, I overpaid them by ten percent. Old Mr. Kindell placed that ten percent in a special account for me at London's Westminster Bank. Ever since, it has been gathering interest—seven per cent at the moment."

Sophie smiled back at him, thinking about the handful of impromptu strategies Willy had devised to get them safely from Prague through Germany to Paris. "So, father, it seems you are a *macher* like Willy. Does he know about your bank account? "

Emil coughed assent, a smile on his lips. "That is enough talk about money," he said as they negotiated puddles in the increasingly heavy rain. "After we finish shopping, I will take the bus to Golden Square to ask old Mr. Kindell if he will arrange to have our crate moved to the Northways basement. He might even offer me a job. I feel almost useless now. My expertise in the textile trade feels like precious water draining into sand."

Sophie wondered if he needed cheering up. "Do you want me to accompany you? We could talk on the way."

Emil shook his head. "I'll go there on my own, daughter. In any case, I think you will be standing in the shopping line for a long time … in the rain."

*   *   *

They spent an hour at the police station. The policeman they dealt with was polite with warm, dark eyes and a luxuriant mustache. He spoke slowly and praised Sophie for the way she was learning English. She felt her apprehension drain away. Emil presented blurred photocopies of his and Judit's birth certificates, and their marriage certificate. All Sophie had was a copy of Pavel's birth certificate from Košice, and her passport from the Czechoslovak Legation in Paris. The policeman seemed satisfied and issued temporary identity cards.

The rain stopped and they set off to get ration books at the local Ministry of Food office. In a large room, full of war posters and empty shelves, she and Emil waited a few minutes on a long bench until a tall official wearing wire-rimmed glasses called them up to his desk.

Emil explained that she and Pavel were refugees from Czechoslovakia. He pulled out their new registration cards and wrote down their names and address. Sophie noticed that whenever she looked at him, the official's face went red. He kept his eyes averted and fixed on the documents. But with Emil, he talked quite naturally. She wondered if this was the usual way English officials behaved toward women.

"Everything is in order," the man said, rubbing at his mustache and blinking rapidly. "I ... I know these ration books are confusing for strangers like you. If you will allow me, I'll show you how they work." He spread a sheaf of soft-backed colored booklets out on the desk and sat back, as if waiting.

"Not necessary," said Emil. "I will explain to her. Thank you. We must go."

"Well, don't let these ration books out of your sight. Keep your handbag closed at all times. Ration books get pinched, and we don't replace them."

Outside, Emil took Sophie's arm. "We must hurry to the shops. I want you to learn to use the ration books before I take the bus. First, we go to the fishmonger." With a wry smile he handed her an empty string bag. "Back in our country, shopping was always a woman's affair." He looked away, as if unwilling to meet her questioning stare. "Shopping here makes me ashamed. I hate gossip and I hate to beg favors from the shopkeepers."

"What about Judit? She could do it."

"Ha! Shopping is like war for her. She says the other women are rude and say bad things about refugees. She does not have the *chutzpah* to get what she wants. She is very shy with English people." He smiled sadly. "Of course, she behaves quite differently with you."

Sophie inclined her head. "Emil, I have the impression you and Judit don't like the English. But I find they say please and thank you all the time. That is very nice, I think."

Emil shrugged. "English politeness is a custom. No one really means what they say. Shopkeepers show no pleasure in serving you. It's not like Lučenec or Prague where the tradesmen smiled and asked after your health and family."

Evans Bros, Fishmongers had a striped awning over an outside display of different kinds of fish, layered on ice chips. When Emil and Sophie reached the shop, the cheap herring that Emil usually bought, were sold out.

Emil pointed at the price list and shook his head. "Everything is too expensive today. Where is the cheap fish you always have?"

Sophie was impressed by his canny firmness.

"I've got only fish 'eads, today. You've 'ad 'em 'ere before," growled the jowly-faced, rubber-aproned owner. Sophie could tell he recognized Emil. She had the impression that the fishmonger no longer enjoyed his work, if he ever had.

Emil nodded. Sophie recognized his school-teacher look. He spoke Czech. "You see, Daughter, fish heads are not even on his price list. Now, listen how I ask." He turned back to the counter and asked in English, "How old are these fish heads? Are the eyes clear?"

"Not sure, mate," the fishmonger said with a weary expression. "Not more than a couple of days old. People round 'ere don't eat fish'eads. They're for pet cats. Tell you what though! I'll give yer a couple of pounds for free." Using a hand shovel, he dug into an enameled bin and, without weighing them, wrapped a pile of fish heads in layers of newspaper.

Emil sniffed the fish parcel. "Not too bad," he said grudgingly, looking sideways at Sophie. "Judit cooks them with onions and carrots to make a good soup."

Sophie put the wrapped fish in the string bag, nostalgic for the fresh mollusks, sardines, mackerel and striped mullet that Monsieur Pinchon, the singing fishmonger of Agde, brought to Sillat in his van every Friday. That had been in France, only a few weeks ago.

They crossed Finchley Road. At least eight women, dressed in dark coats and paisley-patterned headscarves, stood chatting on the pavement outside Worthington's Butcher Shoppe. Baskets and bags dangled from their elbows. The line continued inside. Emil lifted his hat politely as he and Sophie joined them. The women took no notice.

"I don't like this shop," said Emil, keeping his voice low. "But my ration book is registered with him. Look through the window. Chickens and rabbits hanging on the walls. I think they hang there all night!"

Sophie did not say anything when she saw the flies crawling and buzzing around the cuts of beef and lamb suspended on steel hooks from the ceiling. Her stomach flipped.

After the line moved forward a few paces, Emil pointed through the window at the butcher in his striped apron. He was cutting pork chops. "That man is not properly trained. He's never even heard of smoked sausage or salami, and he has no idea how to prepare meat." Emil shrugged hopelessly. "And he has sawdust and I don't know what else on the floor. Don't tell Judit. She would explode."

When it was Emil's turn at the counter, he asked for chicken livers. He had told Sophie that this was another thing the English did not eat. In England it was called offal.

The weasel-faced butcher flicked his cigarette butt on to the floor. "Chicken livers, mister? For your dog is it?"

"No, it is for us." Emil smiled. "We fry them with paprika."

There was a moment of shocked silence in the shop.

Sophie noticed that the butcher had dried blood under his nails. Even in her French village they did not handle food this way. Still, she knew that just like the Londoners, she would have to get used to the local way of doing things and negotiate the best deal for mediocre or scarce food. She would take the strangeness and unpleasantness of wartime shopping in her stride and help the Kohut household stay fed and healthy.

*   *   *

After she watched Emil leave on the #13 bus to Oxford Circus, Sophie carried the food home—she was no longer gloomy, but proud and content. Mission accomplished. She had registered as an alien, she and Pavel owned vital ration books, and she had just overcome the challenge of buying a pound of runner beans, four carrots, two eggs, and two rashers of bacon.

Just before the six o'clock BBC news, Emil returned. As Judit busied herself at the stove and Sophie set the supper table, he made a great show of walking along some of Pavel's button roads before he sat in his armchair. Judit handed him a steaming cup of tea.

Pavel looked up at him, a pleased look on his face. "You like my roads?"

Emil laughed. "Excellent design and construction, Master Pavel—but please do not build any more in here. We might have a traffic accident when your granny brings the supper." With a loud sucking noise, he drank the tea from his saucer.

Judit stood watching him hands on her hips. "So, *Apa*. Did you talk with them about giving you some work?"

He gave her a wry smile. "I completed an excellently useful visit to Kindell and Rivett. Old Mr. Kindell was most hospitable. He looked nearly the same as seven years ago. I asked if they might have a position for me, someone who knew the business inside-out. He said no. Their export business to Europe has vanished. Now, they make and sell fabrics only for the British military and anyway, hiring refugees is too complicated. Too much bureaucracy."

Sophie pulled Pavel on to her lap and started playing cat's cradle with him using some of Emil's saved string. She felt sorry for her father-in-law. His years of expertise had no value anymore. She guessed he was deeply disappointed, but she could not think of what to say without making him even more miserable.

Judit wiped her hands on a towel. "Not so good news about a job, *Apa*. What about the crate?"

"It's coming, wife. Day after tomorrow. They will help us unpack in the basement."

Judit clapped her hands. "Wonderful. We might even find a toy in there for Pavel." She smiled at Sophie. "Now you can tell Emil about Willy's card."

Sophie disentangled the cat's cradle and, with a big smile, pulled a small beige card from her apron pocket. She handed it to Emil. "It came in the mail, father," she said, a catch in her voice. "Just a form, really. It doesn't say much. He's well and going to another camp. It's as if I will never get the chance to see him, he's always being moved."

"Already, you are out of date," said Emil with an unusually cheery smile. "At the head office I met Kindell's son, George—elegant and most helpful. Willy's age. He said he was planning to visit us here, because … well, he talked to Willy on the telephone, four days ago. Willy wanted him to check on Pavel."

Sophie jerked upright, eyes glistening. She clapped her hands. "What! Go on, tell us, what did George say?"

Judit kneeling down to take off Emil's shoes, rocked back on her haunches, startled.

With a satisfied nod, Emil slipped his feet into slippers. "He said Willy has been moved to another camp, near Birmingham. It seems he is still a mutineer in detention. He cannot travel. But we can write to him, George gave me the postal address."

"So is young George Kindell coming to visit us? Yes or no?" Judit looked anxiously around the flat.

Emil dismissed her words with a wave. "He is too busy, and he already told me everything important. I told him Pavel had only a small bone fracture. No need to visit us."

Sophie's face crumpled. "Didn't Willy say anything about us? Me and Pavel?"

Emil nodded wearily. "Of course. He sent love and kisses. And now you can write to him."

CHAPTER EIGHT
Air Raid Precautions
October 1940

With the Luftwaffe air raids in full swing, Emil rushed to get his family settled at #60 Northways. He borrowed tools from Mr. Denby, a neighbor along the corridor, and with two of Mr. Denby's friends dismantled the crate in the basement. They worked only in the mornings, well before the sirens started up. The men carried the crate's heavier contents up to the flat. In addition to two of Emil's fly rods, Sophie ferried boxes of ornaments, silverware, books and paintings.

In the flat, Judit directed the placement of an easy chair with tasseled cushions, the footstool she embroidered as a young girl, a wicker couch, and two faded but valuable Persian carpets. Pavel helped Judit transfer bundles of clothes and the bedding: pillows, sheets, blankets, and two eiderdowns—one double, one single. He had fun rolling on to the billowy eiderdowns and watching them slowly fill back to their original shape

"What makes them do that, *Babička?*"

"Inside are thousands of beautiful soft feathers, taken from the breasts of Eider ducks. They keep your body warm even in the coldest cold of winter."

Ignoring Northways regulations, Emil and Pavel—who was "helping"—stored the crate's rough planks in a dark corner of the garage far from the parked cars. "Never throw anything out that might one day prove useful," Emil told Pavel as they lifted the planks, one by one,

In the flat, when Judit and Sophie started unwinding and unwrapping smaller packages and boxes, Pavel   launched into questions about what lay inside them. He was rewarded by stories:

about Judit's framed needlepoint tapestries woven when she was a young woman, the inlaid lime-wood box presented to Emil by the Lučenec Chamber of Commerce, a wedding set of silver cutlery with EK engraved on the handles, three small oils of Tatra mountain scenes and a sheaf of concert programs in which Willy had been a solo pianist.

*   *   *

The flat was almost a new world for Pavel. The walls, the furniture, and the toilet were bright and clean. There was a big gas fire that made the sitting room cozy. So much space! He and Maman even had their own small room. At night, he slept on a thick rug laid on top of a rubber sheet; Maman lay beside him on a proper second-hand bed that Emil got from Mr. Denby. Whenever the rug stayed dry, which was not often, Maman would smile at him. But his night-time wetting was often discussed at breakfast. He hated them talking about it, because waking up all stinky and wet was horrible. He didn't know why it happened. He felt sad about the way *Babička* spoke to Maman, as if his wetting came from something she had done. When he saw other children in the street, he hoped they were bed-wetters too. He couldn't be the only one. That made him feel better, not so bad or alone.

Pavel was much happier about his shoulder. He stopped wearing the sling but still wore the bandage brace around his chest and back. He could sleep on his side and move his arm side to side and back to front with only the occasional twinge. Often Grandpa watched and offered advice as Maman inspected and cleaned the scabs from his scalded shoulder.

Pavel, Maman and Granny, as he called Judit now, were still frightened by the air raids but they didn't frown or look so angry anymore. Some things were the same. Granny kissed him too much—big trembly kisses. He put up with it because she cooked nice food: chicken soup, cakes, scrambled eggs, and apple sauce.

When Grandpa was in the flat, Pavel felt even more safe and happy, because the old man knew so much about how to do everything, like shopping for food, putting hooks into the wall and how to polish shoes.

Pavel loved the radio. Grandpa said he bought it from one of the refugees at a place he called the Dorice Café. But even when he turned it on and Pavel danced about and marched to music, Grandpa never kissed or hugged him, and hardly ever smiled. It was a shiny, beehive-shaped four-legged monster with a patterned round celluloid face in the middle, and knobs on either side. Grandpa called it Signor Marconi in honor of the inventor, and said it was made of Bakelite. He had placed it by the gas fire so all he had to do was reach over from his armchair to turn the knobs.

When Signor Marconi was first delivered to the flat, Grandpa made a ponderous announcement. "This is the rule. Only the *men* of this family are allowed to switch on the radio." And from then on, every day, just before lunch he would—for perhaps the only time that day—smile and say, "Pavel, switch on Signor Marconi. It is time for the news and music. *Salute, Italia!*"

After a satisfying click of the on dial, Pavel would listen for a hum and watch a red glow spread across its celluloid face. It was magic. He asked how people's voices came out of the radio.

"Ooh … um … radio waves. You are too young to understand," Grandpa said, a pink flush to his cheeks.

So now, every day, the family ate lunch silently to the sound of Worker's Playtime. Grandpa explained that in Worker's Playtime, people sent messages to the radio announcer, asking for music and songs to be played for soldiers like Papa, who lived in camps or were fighting. He said the radio was also a wonderful way to learn English and understand the English people. He often made Maman sit at the table with her exercise book, writing down new words she heard on the radio.

There was a routine. Late in the afternoon, Pavel would sit by the armchair and watch Grandpa twiddle the radio dial looking for what he said were important European stations. Shrill, moaning whistles and grumblings would come from Signor Marconi, until Grandpa finally pinpointed a clear signal and announced the name of the source. "It is like finding an oasis in the desert," Grandpa would say triumphantly. This way, Pavel learned some of the station names: Radio Hilversum, Radio Bucharest, and Radio Berlin.

Pavel assumed that everyone in the family loved the radio because it brought news about the war, and music, and Children's Hour at five. His favorites were the Just-So stories and music. But one day, at tea-time, Sophie banged her hand on the table, rattling the dishes and making water spill from a glass. "Emil," she shouted above the buzzing and crackling, "please stop that horrible noise. Half an hour you have been torturing Signor Marconi. I can't stand it."

Granny nodded. "This habit is getting worse, *Apa*. You're glued to that Marconi creature like flypaper. You love it more than us. You even listen after nine on Sundays to that clever ... Priestley man. Pavel can't go to sleep. We women need quiet and rest for a change."

Pavel was surprised when Granny agreed with his mother. That was something new.

Grandpa's face went crimson. He levered himself out of his chair. "What is this women's criticism? What counts is that Pavel and I like it. Signor Marconi is my only way to learn the truth about the war. Long before it was on BBC or in the newspaper, I knew that Italy had invaded Greece. The moment Hungary joined the Axis powers I heard it on Radio Budapest, not BBC. The *Weltkronik* program from

Geneva was the only one reporting that thousands of French Jews were sent to camps in Germany. If you don't like the noise go to your room or stay outside on the balcony."

Pavel didn't understand what this argument was about except that Grandpa usually got what he wanted even though Granny argued with him. He wanted to be like Grandpa.

Pavel loved the new flat most of all, because the living room's French doors opened on to a balcony—as long and wide as Maman's bed and surrounded by a brick wall topped by a ledge of white stone. He was not sure why, but Grandpa had agreed that he could do anything he wanted on this balcony—even something messy and dirty. Grandpa usually loved everything to be just right. *Alles in Ordnung* ... that's what he always said. Everything in the flat had to be neat and in its place ... except for the balcony where Pavel could be alone. He made up songs, acted out adventures of fighting scary animals, being a soldier and discovering hidden treasure. He built little castles from string, sticks, and pieces of wood that Grandpa found for him in the ruins of bombed houses. If it didn't rain, he liked to sit out there on an old embroidered cushion with ragged tassels, holding Furry Lion and looking at comics and picture books that Maman and Granny brought home from the library.

In Pavel's heart, the balcony replaced Hampstead Heath as a safe, secret world where he was in charge. He could be a sailor looking out to sea, a soldier scouting on horseback, or a Spitfire pilot shooting down a Dornier 109. He could be anything he wanted.

Because the bandage round his shoulders looked so strange and he hardly knew English, Pavel felt shy whenever they walked in the streets. And he was afraid people might laugh at the way he spoke. It had happened in France. On the balcony, he had friends he could talk to ... pigeons. They strutted on the ledge, fluffing dust from their feathers and eating breadcrumbs he brought from the kitchen. They'd tell him what a good boy he was and that they were sorry he'd wet the bed again and made Maman angry. They promised to fly to Papa's camp and bring him back home, so he could stay forever and Pavel wouldn't have to try and remember what his face looked like.

Every so often, Grandpa brought a brush and pan, soapy water, and a sponge and cleaned up pigeon mess from the ledge. When he had finished, he would pull down his spectacles and say "*Alles in Ordnung,* Pavel. You have made the balcony into a very interesting place." He never said anything about it being dirty.

Pavel discovered that by standing on tiptoes, on stacked planks from Grandpa's crate, he could poke his head over the ledge and see a circular driveway far below. Something was always happening down there, even though it seemed very small, like a doll's house. Little people walked in and out of the Northways entrance and sometimes one of them would get out of a taxi—or a miniature horse and cart would wait while a man with a cap and apron stacked milk crates in the back. When he was sure Maman or Granny weren't checking on him through the French doors, Pavel would push dry pigeon droppings over the sill and then crouch down so that no-one knew where the little green bombs came from. He imagined that the bomber pilots got the same thrill during the air raids.

Pavel hated the days when the weather was cold or rainy or both. Grandpa would send him and Sophie to do the shopping. She often borrowed Granny's fur-lined overcoat and Pavel wore an oversized raincoat and knitted balaclava he was given at the Red Cross Center. They wore gloves and scarves that Granny knitted from unraveled pullovers.

By now, Pavel knew the shops: Chisholm's Meats, Dearlove the Grocer, Grodszinski's Bakery, and Evans Fishmongers. Maman sometimes forgot or took the wrong ration books; which meant they had to go back home to get them. Granny or Grandpa got cross and there would be an argument. Then out they went again. The shopping and the waiting in line seemed to go on forever.

But shopping could be fun—especially if there was a newly damaged house or shop close by. Pavel would beg Maman to let him go look, promising not to go anywhere else. He knew other children would be at the bomb site looking for treasures, watching the salvage crews pull down the walls with long hooked poles, pickaxes, and shovels. Children weren't supposed to do this, but most of the time no one seemed to care. One day, after he and Maman had seen an upstairs bathtub sticking out of the side of a blasted house, he asked Grandpa why the Germans did not drop their bombs in the daytime when it was easier to take aim.

"They come at night, so our pilots and the anti-aircraft guns cannot see them easily. That's why, when the siren goes, we go into the basement and miss our sleep."

The day after a bomb fell near Grodzinski's, the partly damaged bakery stayed open. While Sophie queued for bread, Pavel and a couple of other children poked about in the bakery's rubble looking for bomb or artillery shell fragments. The real treasure was a piece of shrapnel stamped with numbers or words. Pavel found one piece stamped with letters *and* numbers. At home, he showed it to Grandpa.

"This is very special," said Grandpa in a grave voice, peering through a magnifying glass he pulled out of a drawer. "Here it says: Wolfsburg, then the code EDA18t43. Wolfsburg is in Saxony. So this is from a German bomb. I write the code down for you. Next time you do it. It is high time you learned to read."

At night, Pavel often had dreams. When he woke in the morning, his sheets were usually wet and warm. There was one night-time dream that seemed so real he often wondered if he had been awake or asleep:

it was always about the same place and the same people.

In the dream, Pavel hears the siren wailing and Maman is bending over him when he opens his eyes. Half-awake, he stuffs Furry Lion into a bag. Grandpa and Granny, with gas masks over their shoulders, push water bottles, candles, and food into a shopping bag. They hurry down the stairs overloaded with pillows, blankets, and an eiderdown.

In the dark basement, they always sit in the same spot. There are people on either side of them. Mr. Denby is fat and jolly and guzzles a beer bottle, wiping his chin with a rag. He is bald and tells stories. Pavel knows they are funny because Sheryl, Mr. Denby's raggedy-haired daughter giggles behind her fingers. She teaches Pavel to play cards.

On the other side, sit two old people, much older than Grandpa and Granny. The old man sits in a deck chair and smokes a smelly pipe. He always looks at postcards he takes out of a cardboard box. He never says anything. The old woman is as thin as a stick and her face has more wrinkles than Grandpa and Granny put together. She trembles when the explosions start.

Granny tells Pavel how much she hates being down there. She pulls him on to her lap and kisses his face. "Don't you hate the smell of cigarettes and pipes, *Pavelko*? Now, if you need pee-pee, Maman will take you over to the buckets near where the cars are parked."

Often the dream is more like an indoor playground with people having picnics. Pavel follows other children who skip from one family to the next, asking for food. Sometimes they want him to play. He doesn't understand what they say but they show him how to "swop" shrapnel and play marbles. This is the best dream. It's like when he played with the village children when Maman and Papa lived in France.

He wakes and Maman is snoring. He sits up and sees daylight

filtering through the cracks of the door. Granny and Grandpa are on the other side, talking.

*   *   *

During the boring hours spent in the bomb shelter, Sophie had time to think about herself and the future. She hated being a refugee, subject to the whims of circumstance and other people's decisions—she resented being beholden to her in-laws for shelter, suffocated by their demanding ways. War had changed everything.

Urged on by Emil to improve her English, she laboriously read small sections of the newspaper to him. She learned that divorce rates had doubled, the black market was flourishing, workers sometimes went on strike, and even rich people made sacrifices. Women took men's jobs in factories, ran shops and businesses, and helped build planes and ships.

Sophie was impressed by how things were changing so much and so fast for women. Women were being cut free from kitchen and children. A seed of hope took root. She wanted to live the new way. How would Willy take it if she started to shape her own life?

One way to escape from her in-laws would be to find a job. But with no training, she had only her youth and a pretty face to offer—except that, in Paris, she had learned to cook: soups, frites, cheese soufflé, beef ragout, stuffed cauliflower, and rabbit stew with mushrooms … those were her favorite recipes. Judit told her that the Women's Zionist Organization in London was helping Jewish refugee women find jobs as maids and nannies. If Willy was going to be away all the time, fighting the Germans, Sophie was ready to go it alone. But what would she do with Pavel?

At about two in the morning, on the night of October 24, the two minute "All-Clear" blasted in Emil's eardrums. That night's raid had been particularly intense and close. In the basement garage, he and Pavel helped Sophie and Judit gather up their possessions. A mostly silent crowd halted at the exit staircase facing a heavy-shouldered ARP warden who held a sheet of paper. The usual post-raid report.

He held up his arms for silence. "QUIET, everyone. I've got news about last night's raid. Been a bad night."

"'Urry up, mister," someone said. "We're short of kip."

"Anything bad happen around here?" a woman shouted.

The ARP warden nodded gravely. "Incendiaries was dropped all over. And a five hundred pounder flattened two shops up on Child's Hill. Several people hurt, two dead. That's about it."

As people filed out, they nodded or gestured their thanks to him. Some shook the warden's hand. Emil smiled at him. "Thank you, please."

It took some time for the laden Kohuts to clamber up the stairs to their flat. On the fourth floor Pavel ran ahead, along the corridor. He reappeared, hopping from one leg to the other, gesturing frantically. "Come quick, Grandpa."

It was then that Emil smelled the burned wood and paint. He pointed to a flat hose snaked through puddles of water on the floor. "Fire brigade is here," he shouted back to Judit. "Be careful." A cluster of neighbors with anxious faces stood at the far end of the corridor.

Emil restrained Pavel by his pajama collar. "Stay back," he said, "don't touch anything."

Three men in helmets, wet slickers and Wellington boots stood at the open doorway of Number 60. The door was black and smoke drifted out from the top edge.

Relinquishing Pavel to Judit, Emil hurried up to the firemen. "We live here. What happened?"

"Sorry about the mess, mate," said the tallest man, whose wet slicker was stained with soot. "Looks like an incendiary blew in your winders—burned a lot of stuff. One of your neighbors called the ARP. We got here as soon as we could. Climbed in through the balcony window."

Emil caught his breath and groaned as he stepped warily across the threshold, barely registering the details. He shivered, feeling his stomach heave and churn as if he had eaten something tainted. A wave of panic followed, then rage and bitterness swamped his mind; the country whose music, science and literature he had once worshipped had done this. It was worse than betrayal. It was evil.

"Bad luck, mate. The Jerries've got a wicked new combination. Thermite and phosphorus in one little bomb. They call 'em "flying terrors." They hit the ground, bounce a few feet sideways and explode. The phosphorus burns whatever it touches."

Judit called from over the top of the eiderdown and blankets she was carrying. "*Apuskam*, Father," she said in strangled voice. "What are these men? The terrible smell. Was it the gas?"

Emil silenced her with a frown.

"Could 'ave been worse," said the fireman, shaking his head. "Bloody lucky, I'd say. Bedrooms are intact, but they're bit damp. A volunteer rescue squad will come in the mornin' to help clear up. Think you can cope for the rest of the night? We've got to go."

Judit burst into tears. Pavel moved silently to Sophie, reaching for her hand. The firemen rolled up the hose and began to pack their gear. Emil edged past them through the doorway and gazed at the destruction. Sophie, Judit and Pavel, stepping carefully, followed.

"Everything burned," said Pavel, his eyes big as walnuts.

Emil swiveled slowly, fists tight and jaw set as he assessed the damage. The stink of vaporized chemicals, burned fabric and charred wood made his eyes sting. His nose began to run. He didn't bother to wipe it. The floorboards and the old Persian carpet nearest the French doors were black. All the oil paintings, the Herend china set and Judit's Bohemian glass vases were gone. Their antique silverware lay half-melted on the charred shelves.

The Czechoslovak art deco furniture was scorched. Emil's beloved Bokhara carpet was only just recognizable. Among the glass splinters on the floor, Emil recognized the remnants of his precious lime wood box. *Sakra!* Inside he had kept birth, marriage and death certificates, official name changes from Cohen to Kohn to Kohut, and, saddest of all, Latin and Hebrew family documents from the early 1800s: all gone. He remembered the intriguing, spidery, illegible writings. He had always wanted to find some expert to decipher them.

Judit, white-faced, returned from the bathroom, her eyes red-rimmed. She wiped her mouth with her apron. "Are you all right, dear?" Emil stuttered. He had never seen her look as ill as this.

While Judit, Sophie and Pavel huddled in the middle of the sitting room gazing helplessly at the damage, Emil checked the two bedrooms, one on each side of the entrance. "The beds and cupboards are intact but very damp," he called out. "The firemen saved them. And we have our clothes."

Tears trickled down Sophie's face. "*Hovno bastardský,*" she said in a fierce voice.

Pavel looked up at her. "What did you say, Maman?"

Judit took hold of her daughter-in-law's arm. "Please, don't say such things in front of the boy."

"I agree with Sophie's sentiment." Emil's tone was bitter. "Not in a thousand years will I forgive the so-called civilized German nation for what they are doing."

"We'll be off now," one of the firemen called out, looking in at them through the burned entry door. He winked sympathetically at Sophie. "We've other fish to fry." The two other men laughed as they splashed off through the corridor puddles. Emil looked perplexed.

"English joke, I think," said Sophie shrugging her shoulders. "Perhaps they think our flat was fried."

Like automatons, Emil and Judit started to sweep up broken glass and pile it into a corner. With a long-handled broom, Sophie chivvied the wet ashes into a heap but stopped to rest and wipe away her tears. In the middle of the sitting room, they stacked every item that was damaged beyond redemption: glass, wood, china, leather and fabric.

Two hours later, Emil hurled his brush and pan through the fractured window on to the balcony, breaking more glass. The others stopped what they were doing and looked at him. "This is impossible," he said, looking at his watch with a scowl. "I am dog-tired. We go to bed."

Judit nodded. "I agree. But if the gas is still working, why can't we turn the stove on, to keep warm/"

Emil scowled. "Too risky. I will be afraid to sleep and we need sleep more than anything … even if we and the beds are wet. Come."

*   *   *

In their bedroom, while Sophie reapplied Pavel's shoulder bandage, she saw the bewilderment in his eyes.

"Why did everything burn, Maman? The bed is wet? It wasn't me did it."

She wrapped her arms around him. "Shush, *Pavlik* and listen. A bomb came through the window. The firemen put it out with water. That's why not everything burned but everything is wet. We'll talk more about it later. Time to sleep now."

Without undressing, she spread out the dry eiderdown they brought back from the basement. She lay beside him and pulled it over both of them. He soon fell asleep. It was amazing, she pondered, that they were all safe. Luckily, under her bed she had kept Willy's letters, a few clothes, their identity cards and ration books, and her exercise book of English words. It was obvious from the damage that they would have to move out ... another crisis for the family.

Unable to sleep, Sophie sat up in the dark and shivered, feeling the cold breeze blowing through the broken windows—she could still smell smoke in the air and it irritated her breathing. Beside her, Pavel was fast asleep, sometimes tossing from side to side, coughing and wheezing, his thin elbows protruding over the eiderdown. She counted the good things. They were alive. They had food and half a flat for shelter. And they were in England. Maybe there was a God keeping an eye on them.

Her thoughts jumped to Willy. If ever there was a time they needed him, it was now. Somehow, she had to let him know what had happened. All this time, she had stayed loyal to him, through all the separations. She had even kept her promise not to talk to Emil and Judit about Willy's terrible time in Pancrác prison—until he could tell them himself. When was the last time they had kissed? Sometime in June, before the evacuation from France.

Four hours later, Emil woke to the powerful smell of carbonized wood and sneezed several time. He looked at Judit still asleep beside him and covered her with the bath towel he had used as a blanket. He shivered as he put on his oldest clothes over his pajamas. He wound a scarf around his neck and slipped on galoshes to protect his feet from glass splinters. Quietly, he put the kettle on for tea and thanked the God he'd never believed in, for keeping the gas stove working. At least they could cook.

Early morning light outlined the burned frames and jagged glass holes in the French doors. They would have to be careful not to get cut when they cleaned up, especially little Pavel. And Emil would have to get something to keep out the cold: cardboard or brown paper. Those crate planks stored in the basement would now fulfill their purpose.

Out of habit, Emil went to turn on the news, but Signor Marconi was covered in soot, the tuning dials twisted and flattened by heat. He clicked the charred ON knob. There was a faint hum and a light glowed behind the dial. His heart leaped at the familiar sound of a piano: the final notes of Beethoven's sonata in C minor … he smiled. With such music there was still resilience and beauty in the world. And with music came hope.

Hot tea calmed Emil's thoughts as he carried his mug out to the balcony, wondering whether any of the other Northways flats had been hit. The balcony was covered with broken glass, blackened wood fragments, and stone chips. He looked over the wall. Theirs was the only damaged flat.

He felt a pull on his leg. Pavel, in pajamas and sandals, had tears rolling down his face. He looked up at Emil. "My treasures have gone, Grandpa."

A couple of pigeons fluttered down on to the chipped ledge, cocking their heads expectantly for Pavel's regular gift of early-morning crumbs.

"I'm sorry, *Pavlik*," Emil muttered drawing the boy's head against his thigh. He lifted him up and kissed his forehead.

Pavel wiped his eyes with the back of a hand. "Are we going to clean this mess, again?"

"We have to. In any case, it is time for us to move … live somewhere else until they repair this place. You must be very careful now." Emil picked up a dagger of glass and angled it against the window frame, carving out a sliver of charred wood. "See how sharp this is. So don't rush or grab anything until we have cleared up properly."

Pavel pointed to one corner of the balcony. "What's that funny green thing on the floor, Grandpa?"

"Oh, you mean that?" Emil stepped forward and retrieved a twisted metal object with fins, about the size of his hand. He showed it to Pavel. "I think it may be part of the bomb that ruined our flat. We'll take a closer look inside. It's too cold to stay out here."

Emil took the boy into the kitchen, stood him at the sink on one of the surviving chairs. Together they washed the soot and burn marks off the metal. He showed the boy a black mark on one of the fins. "Do you know what this is, Pavlik?"

"A swastika."

"Correct. And look here. Do you know your numbers and alphabet yet?"

Pavel hesitated. "JDEL…um…11056." His eyes widened with excitement. "Grandpa, this *is* treasure—isn't it?"

"Yes, sort of. Better to call it a memento, not a treasure."

"What is a memnito?"

Emil smiled. "Something that makes you remember. Like a photograph."

Pavel cradled the bomb casing in his hands. "Why can't this be a treasure?"

"I suppose it can. Anyway, we'll dry it off and I'll keep it safe. When you grow up, you can show it to your own children."

Pavel sniffed at the metal. "Grandpa. Can I show it to the other children when we go down into the shelter?"

Emil drained his cup. This bomb was a terrible warning. He wondered whether Pavel would ever get to have children. The boy had to survive this war … and the prospect of victory over the Germans was very dim at the moment. "We'll see. For the time being I'll look after it."

The kettle whistled again. Judit, in her flowery dressing gown, had poured herself some tea. She gave Emil a resigned smile. Realizing how much he respected and needed her, he folded his arms around her, resting his unshaven cheek against hers. "Thank God, we're still alive, my dearest," he murmured. "My heart is broken. For the moment, only my head works, and it is filled with anger."

She kissed him with quivering lips. "*Apa*, you have not called me dearest for many years."

Emil's face was grim. "It is because, if this *blitzkrieg* continues, the British will be forced to ask Hitler for peace. The Nazis will march through London—and that will be the end of you and me ... all of us."

He sighed. He hardly had the energy to think or act. They were trapped, and misfortune was their destiny. He remembered his own father's words. "When you're out of luck, Emil, even drinking water gets stuck between your teeth."

Emil picked up the cup of tea Judit had refilled for him. As he drank he looked at Pavel crouched among the debris, picking over bits and pieces. For this boy there had to be hope. Surely Britain was not finished. The British could still teach the Nazis a thing or two about ingenuity, toughness, and power. They were stubborn and proud. They had started the industrial revolution, built an empire ... and for years he had done business with them. They were clever, principled and tolerant people.

His family had also survived bad times before. Hatred and discrimination in Slovakia, ethnic riots after the First World War, and the recent Nazi invasion. This Blitz was just another crisis to be endured.

Emil smiled at Pavel. "Well, my grandson. We've had a lucky escape. Maybe this fire is a sign that we must find somewhere safe outside London, and as soon as possible. I will go to the Czech

Legation later this morning and ask them to send an urgent telegram to your papa's camp. This time, he *must* come and help us."

CHAPTER NINE
The Prodigal Soldier
October 1940

The Commandant at the Pioneer Corps camp in Sutton Coldfield was surprisingly sympathetic. "Telegrams," he said to Willy who stood to attention, "usually represent panic, not reality. However this one from the Czech Legation is urgent, clear and sensible. You've got three days to sort your family's problem."

The following day, Willy hitched a van ride to Birmingham's main station—the uniform made it easy. He spent a precious fifteen shillings on a round trip ticket to London. The train was crowded with uniformed men and women, many standing for the entire trip. After a couple of hours he could no longer tolerate a full bladder, and went to the washroom. When he got back, a curly-haired, blue-skirted-WAAF was ensconced in his seat, her feet resting on his travel bag. "Hope you don't mind," she said with a toothy smile.

After that, Willy stood in the corridor, looking out the window, half-dozing, and thinking about Sophie and his parents. What would he find at the flat? Fire damage to be sure but was anyone hurt? He had sent a telegram to say he was coming but wasn't able to give a specific day or time. He rejoiced at being able to see them, but doubted he could do much to help in just a couple of days.

Willy turned for distraction to the used newspapers that were being passed up and down the corridor. Depressing headlines: British factories bombed and hundreds of civilian casualties. He scanned gloomy editorials on the flailing dipping economy and the reasons why Britain needed Roosevelt's help—if he was re-elected. The President had already promised fifty out-of-date American destroyers in exchange for commercial access to the Commonwealth's ports, but Britain also needed food and heavy military equipment. Meanwhile the Nazis were doing well. They had overrun Romania and, in France they were massing troops at ports along the northern coast. One newspaper headlined the Sword of Damocles question in big black letters: **Will Hitler Invade Britain? When?** The sense of gloom that the national press portrayed, depressed him.

And how was Sophie coping, holed up with his parents? Before the emergency evacuation from France last July, she had accepted the primitive conditions in the French village with little complaint. But even then, he felt that a distance was growing between them. Endearments were few, and their love-making had been perfunctory. She often talked about the endless disruptions to their lives and his long absences at the nearby artillery unit. Their arguments had grown noisier and more frequent.

Willy was aware that his separation from Sophie and Pavel would continue—he had already made that decision. On this visit home he would explain his position. He was no longer a rogue mutineer. He was a Czechoslovak soldier about to enlist in a British regiment that would soon tangle with the Germans. As far as explaining how his right little finger came to be crushed, Willy decided to save his parents the anguish and say that it was an accident, not torture.

But he was cock-a-hoop about a possible solution to his family's impending homelessness; he had fixed up a meeting with George Kindell at the Finetex offices, for all of them. George had agreed to help them find a place to stay, if possible, outside London. It was a hopeful step in the right direction.

In London, before knocking on the sooty door of the Northways apartment building, Willy paused, preparing to play the role of a son who hadn't seen his parents in nearly two years. It brought back nostalgia for his previous life in Prague; the memory was so sad, strong and immediate that he teared up. He wiped his eyes and rapped out the let-me-in schoolboy code he had always used at home in Lučenec: three hard taps on the door, a pause, then two more.

Judit, wearing a floral apron, opened the door. She seemed not to recognize the smiling man in a jaunty field cap and military battledress.

A moment of shocked silence.

"Didn't you recognize my knock, Mother?"

"*Willy*," she screamed. "Your face is so thin. I did not… recog…"

He folded her into his arms and kissed her hair, avoiding the places where she had installed curlers. "It's Willy," she yelled. "*Gott sei dank.*"

Judit pulled him through the doorway in to the flat. Somehow, his mother seemed smaller and rounder than he remembered.

He stopped in his tracks, shocked by the damage. He looked hard at the blackened walls and broken windows covered over with cardboard. "My God, this is terrible." he muttered as Judit led him past a kerosene heater placed on bricks in the middle of the floor.

Emil got up from a chair, a newspaper dangling from his hand. "I'm very glad you are here, Willy. We have been three days like this and the landlord wants us to leave."

Willy winced at the way his father's shoulders drooped, the slow way he moved and the misery on his face … and hugged him.

Sophie erupted from her room holding her hands out to him. Her joyous laughter and tears mingled with kisses as he stroked her soft cheeks. Along with her unkempt dark curls and worn hands, Sophie was thinner than in France but still beautiful: her face the same lovely oval he knew so well. She seemed happy to see him. The urgent warmth of her body when she kissed him fuelled his hope that they would soon be making love; he didn't care where.

Pavel quietly stood his ground, picking his nose, looking down at his feet.

Willy felt a catch in his throat. Had Pavel forgotten him? Was he afraid of … a stranger? Smiling, he held out his arms. "Come; give your Papa a kiss. You remember Papa. Don't you?"

Pavel hid behind Sophie's legs, his lips moving soundlessly.

Willy gave Sophie an apologetic look. So Pavel *had* forgotten him. He sighed … to be expected perhaps, after six months of absence. Or maybe, the boy had turned shy because he was older.

When the hubbub died down, they celebrated with tea and *kolache* pastries that Judit had been hoarding in a tin for such an event—interrupting and talking over one another—commenting on how everyone looked, how they had changed: battered, thinner, older, and certainly much poorer.

The single ceiling pendant didn't cast much light. "We lost our lamps," Judit said with a shrug as she lit two candles and put them on the table.

Pavel stood by his mother's knee and shot glances at the man his mother was kissing so often.

Sophie pushed him forward. "Come now Pavel, this is *Táta* … Oh, I mean your Papa. He's come from a soldier's camp far away. He loves you. Give him a kiss."

Willy gently pulled the reluctant boy towards him. "Let's take this slowly," he said hoping to avoid a scene. In France, Pavel had been prone to tantrums. "He has to get used to me." He turned Pavel around, inspecting him with a pleased smile. "How quickly you have grown." He ruffled the boy's hair, approvingly. "Same curls but aren't they going dark." He looked at Sophie for confirmation.

Beaming, she nodded. Pavel stood there, silent.

Willy lifted Pavel's chin and laughed. "He still has his nursery blue eyes and charming nose." He pulled a bar of chocolate from his blouse pocket and broke off a piece for Pavel. "I've been saving this for you. Tell me something. What is this bandage round your chest and shoulders?"

"I—I fell on the stairs," Pavel finally whispered. He reached out and touched the scar on Willy's cheekbone, wrinkling his eyebrows as if he wasn't sure he remembered it.

"Let me see it."

Sophie unwound the bandage and undid Pavel's shirt to show where the hot compress had scarred his shoulder. Her face crumpled. "See how they damaged him at the hospital?"

"A schoolboy doctor," Emil snarled. "Criminal mistreatment. But now, Pavel is healed. In two days' time, no more bandages. "

Willy kissed Pavel's shoulder and tweaked his nose in fun. "I'm sure you were very brave, Pavel." Anger at Pavel's unnecessary suffering flooded his mind; and shame that he had not been there to help. And he was shocked by the damage to his parents' flat. As for the details of Pavel's accident, he would find out more when he and Sophie were alone. He knew his parents too well to allow them to participate in a general family discussion about the incident.

"He's on the mend," Emil sighed, getting up. "Most important is that I show you what happened in the fire. The landlord says we have to leave quickly so they can start repairs. It will take a long time. The incendiary landed on the balcony and shattered the windows."

After a thorough inspection of the fire damage, Emil showed Willy the incendiary casing.

"It must have been a shock when the landlord said you had to leave," Willy said, turning it over in his hands. He tried to suppress his rising anger at what the Blitz had done to his family. They were at the table again, drinking tea and eating crackers while Emil cut slices of apple for Pavel. "What are you going to do?"

"Get out of London," said Emil curtly. "We have lost most of our possessions but, thank God, not our passports. During the air raids I always put them with the documents in the kitchen oven. We had a routine. If they had burned, we could never prove our identity to the British. That would mean a god-forsaken camp somewhere in the countryside. Luckily, I still have some proof of what I owned in Lučenec. One day, I will go back and reclaim what is mine."

"You can't stay here, that's obvious, and I agree that getting out of London would be best." Willy rubbed his chin thoughtfully. "But it will be hard getting travel permissions, and dealing with the police. The big question is where will you go?"

Emil heaved his shoulders and glanced resignedly at Judit. He rubbed the prominent veins on the backs of his hands. "I don't know. I will go to the Czechoslovak Legation or get advice from the Jewish Refugee Council. "

"Just as well I came," said Willy. He was sad to see his once-resourceful father's spirit so battered. "I have some good news. After the Legation telegram came, I telephoned George Kindell. He promised to help find you a place to live. I've arranged a meeting at his office, tomorrow at two. All of us. If anyone can help us find somewhere to live, he can."

Emil started walking around the room, hands locked behind his back. "I am embarrassed," he said. "The Kindell family has already done us many favors." He shrugged despondently. "All we do is say thank you. We offer nothing in return. What you did was resourceful but it makes me feel useless. These days, everything moves too fast for me."

Willy unbuttoned his tunic and leaned back in his chair. Trust the old man to look at the dark side, he thought. "Don't be a *kvetcher*, Father. This flat is unlivable, and you say there is nothing available in the rest of the building. We have to move quickly. I have only tomorrow to spend in London. George will help us. We'll all go to see him. That will save discussion time."

"Yes, *Apa*, Willy is right," Judit said forcefully. "We must act."

She looked round the burned flat. "Get out of this hell."

"What about Pavel?" Willy continued. "I don't want him to disrupt our meeting with George. It's too important."

"Take him with us, of course" Judit said abruptly. "I'll bring a snack and the button box, and maybe we can find somewhere in the Kindell offices where he can have his nap."

"Forget about our London worries for a minute," said Emil, attempting a smile. "We want to hear about your escape through Germany to France and the evacuation by sea. All we got were a few postcards—just a sentence or two—saying you were well and still traveling. Sophie told us very little. She said she wanted you to be here to tell us the full story."

Emil reached over and grabbed his son's right wrist. "But first, what about this ... this *verkakte* little finger! What happened to the musician for God's sake?" He raised it for everyone to see—as if offering it for sale. Willy didn't resist but shared a conspiratorial look with Sophie. Emil, like a judge in a courtroom, glared over the rim of his glasses and let go of Willy's wrist. "Obviously, your piano days are over. How did this happen?"

Judit turned her head away, wringing her hands. "*Was für eine shandeh*," she murmured. "Such a tragedy." She looked back at Willy with melting eyes and stroked his hand. "All that care we took of your beautiful hands when you were a boy—and you repaid us with love and wonderful music. This breaks my heart."

Sophie was silent, her eyes downcast.

Emil's face was taut, insistent. "So ... how did it happen?"

"An accident in France. I was in a unit rehabilitating old weapons—in fact, Father, it could have been worse. After it healed, I managed to adapt my technique. Now I can play a few sonatas, slow

Chopin pieces and Mozart—easy stuff. The petty details of how, why, and where this happened are unimportant. No going back, no regrets."

Emil shrugged. "Very well, but I still want to know how you got away from France."

All through the talking, weak tea, and snacks, Willy studied his parents. He was saddened by their glum faces and bent shoulders. His father had aged: purple bags under his eyes, deep lines scored his cheeks, and age spots on his hands and forearms. Was this what despair, hardship, and alienation did to you in so short a time?

Apart from the problem with his shoulder, Pavel was the only one who had visibly changed for the better. He looked alert and solid. His face and jaw showed almost no puppy fat. He still spoke Czech and French but was threading a few English words together. Willy was proud of him.

Emil looked his watch. "Enough stories for today," he grunted. "My head is swimming. What time is supper, Judit? "

"Seven."

"Will we have enough food? We weren't expecting a hungry soldier for dinner."

On the six o'clock BBC evening news, Alvar Liddell—Sophie liked to pronounce his name over and over because it sounded so melodious—announced that Roosevelt had been re-elected president of the United States. She knew who Roosevelt was—a good, strong man—but nothing about how he was helping the British fight the Germans.

Emil levered himself out of his easy chair, rubbing his hands. "Excellent. America will come into the war now. Roosevelt is a clever man. And you heard the weather forecast. Heavy rain storms in London tonight. So … a ninety percent chance of *no* air raid."

Smiling, he patted the balding patch on the back of Willy's head. "It seems you will miss the pleasure of sitting in our cold basement listening to sirens and bombs exploding."

Emil walked to the front door and unhooked his raincoat. "Come, Pavel. We go out for a few minutes to see a house that was bombed last night." He nodded to Sophie as he helped Pavel into a small rain jacket. "While Judit prepares supper, take your man somewhere and talk privately."

Even though it was drizzling, Sophie took Willy up to Hampstead village. Arm in arm, umbrellas unfurled, they strolled up the hill to where she pointed out their old flat above Mr. Hardy's chemist shop and explained how Pavel had fallen down the stairs. Wiping tears from her cheeks, she described Pavel's visit to the hospital: the sloppy doctor and how they scalded him with the poultice.

Willy listened carefully offering kisses and comfort.

"You're lucky to be far from the bombing in that camp," she said. "Isn't it strange? I imagined we would be safe in England. Not true in London." Her lower lip trembled. "I don't want to die. Every night here terrifies me." She took out her handkerchief.

Willy pulled her into his arms. "Don't worry, dear. George will help us find a place."

"I don't know much about him. He seems so willing to help us."

"His family did business with Father and me for many years. Long before I met you, we came here once to inspect their weaving mills. They were very hospitable. George and I became friends. He's a very elegant fellow so make sure you dress nicely tomorrow." Willy chucked her under chin. "I don't want us to look like beggars."

Sophie gave him a weak smile. "I have nothing nice to wear."

Willy took her hand and kissed it. "I brought all my savings. We'll go shopping in the morning, and buy something you like."

Dinner that evening was goulash and noodles. Pavel was allowed to stay up late as a treat. Sophie sat next to Willy at the table. Every so often she smiled and touched him: his hand, his arm, his cheek, or his knee. It was as if the return of the prodigal soldier had washed away her unhappiness.

As they ate, she kept quiet while Emil gave Willy a detailed account of how he and Judit had arrived in London a year and a half earlier—with a crate of belongings, but little else. "We focused on survival. Day to day penny-pinching in a tiny rented flat above the chemist shop."

"We were on our own until the Blitz started," Judit added with a quick smile. "That was when Sophie arrived with Pavel from Liverpool. We were so happy."

"So, Willy," Emil said, pushing back his chair with a plate in his hand, "we live day to day. Our pleasures are books from the library, walking in the park, and sometimes a loaf of good rye bread from the delicatessen. Once or twice a week I go for a coffee to the local café where refugee men gather to discuss the war and their troubles. Now it's your turn. I want to hear about the *meshuganah* mutiny you got yourself entangled with."

"The problem began in France at the Czechoslovak army camp in Agde. Sophie and Pavel lived close by, in a village called Sillat."

"We know. We received two or three letters from there."

Sophie frowned. "Only two or three? In six months? We wrote you so many times." She took a breath. "Well, I'll tell you about our life in that village. The gypsy woman, Madame Escobar, whose cottage we shared was a bit of a witch, but underneath it all, good hearted. Everything there was so primitive. But the food … oh, yes … such wonderful fruit and cheeses … and beautiful fish." She smiled at the reminiscence. "Pavel loved being with that old woman because she let him do anything he wanted, even sent him off to play with the village children when my back was turned.

Sophie grinned at Judit. "Madame Escobar behaved like Pavel's grandmother, even giving *me* orders!"

Willy, chuckling, glanced at his mother.

"Every day," Sophie went on, "I had to carry slops down the hill to the cesspit. Blazing sun with stifling heat and insects everywhere… and…" Her mind went back to the shame she felt walking those disgusting buckets through Sillat every day, often with Czech soldiers calling out and whistling at her from the café terrace in the square. "

"In the mornings, we often found scorpions in our shoes when we got up," said Willy.

"Ooh, yes," chimed Pavel, his face alive with excitement. He nodded fiercely. "Madame Esco showed me. I killed them every day."

Willy laughed. He turned to face Emil. "Quite a story, eh? So … on my side of things, I was one of many soldier volunteers: civilians, Jews, Czechoslovaks, and communist fighters from Spain. We were supposed to be training to fight under the French but the Czechoslovak career officers despised and insulted us, especially the Jews. They handed out unfair punishments, and ordered pointless marches. When we were finally put on a British troop ship headed for Gibraltar, the communists from the Spanish Civil War and some of us Jews formally protested."

Emil was breathing heavily. His face had gone dark red.

Willy continued. "Our bad treatment didn't change in England. When the British accepted Beneš as president of our exiled government, the communists turned the protests into a full-scale mutiny. The communist volunteers under a man called Povídka who I knew pretty well from France were good organizers. About three hundred of us refused to follow orders. We were disarmed and confined under guard."

Emil shook his head. "We read it in the newspaper when we

took the boy to the hospital. Unbelievable. In Kaiser Wilhelm's army you would have been instantly court-martialed or shot on the spot."

Willy leaned forward, his glasses perched on the end of his nose. "Listen, Father. A soldier expects punishment for poor work, laziness, cowardice, or mistakes. But not for his race or beliefs." He gave his father a gentle punch on the shoulder. "In the end, the British High Command instructed General Ingr to offer us a choice; civilian life as a refugee or transfer to the British Army."

Judit put a cup of hot tea in front of Willy. Her hands were trembling. "Well then, my dear, why don't you leave the army now," she said. "We have missed you terribly—even your grumpy father has admitted it." She looked at Emil who nodded.

Willy looked around at his family. "Too late, Mother. I already agreed to a transfer into the British Army. I'm a private now."

Sophie caught her breath and looked away. She wanted to shake him. "How could you, Willy? Your mother is right. You care more about being a soldier than living with us. What have you turned into … a mercenary?"

Emil spluttered. "You are prepared to be a soldier in the trenches? Like I was in the Austro-Hungarian army? Cannon fodder. You are too intelligent."

Willy's laugh rang out. "I won't be in the trenches, Father. Here, like most foreigners I'll be in the Pioneer Corps. We don't get rifles, just shovels and hammers. We're supposed to maintain equipment and build huts and latrines."

Sophie put her face in her hands. "Why did you accept to do something as lowly as that? In France, you were in the artillery. You repaired weapons and got promoted. You even traveled all around the countryside negotiating food supplies for the camp."

Willy took a deep breath. "You all seem upset with me. I'm sorry for that, but how else can I thank the British for rescuing us from

France and taking us in?"

Sophie shook her head choking back the tears. She had been so happy to see him and now he was going to leave her again. She tried to keep her voice from revealing her anger. "There must be other ways to thank the British. What happened to your obligation to me and Pavel?"

"I have an additional, very personal reason for serving in the British Army," he said very quietly, after taking a sip of tea. "That way I will get my hands on a Nazi or two ... face to face ...." He gritted his teeth. And ... do as they did to me."

"I cannot believe you say this," Judit said, leaning forward earnestly. "You were always so gentle. Just stay with us. We love you." She looked at him hopefully. "Who loves you in your camp? Nobody. Stay at home."

Willy slammed his good hand on the table. Pavel and Judit gasped. "Enough, all of you. Love is secondary. Britain stands alone. The least I can do is serve in her army."

Willy looked around the table regretting the pain he was causing. He felt the tenseness of Sophie's arm pressed against his. "That's all I have to say. I don't want to discuss it anymore."

With eyes as big and shiny as half crowns, Pavel looked at his father. "Papa...I...it...one night... Maman and me, we were outside on the street. We watched the bombers fly."

Willy nodded. "Tell me." He lifted Pavel onto his lap.

Sophie exhaled, pleased that the boy had changed the subject.

"It was night, Papa. An airplane fell from the sky. We saw smoke. Then ... and then ... a big 'splosion. An ambulance came ... and a fire engine. We ran up the stairs to Granny and Grandpa's and I fell all the way down."

"That's an exciting story, *Pavlik*. You and Maman were lucky to escape."

Pavel nodded earnestly. "When bombers come, we go down in the shelter."

Willy laughed. "In that case, I will join you if it happens tonight. It will be my baptism of fire. It's strange, but it is you civilians who are really on the front line."

Sophie rested her hand on Pavel's head. "The poor darling gets nightmares. He wakes up frightened and has to cuddle up with me."

"And he wets the sheets," Judit said, taking Pavel from Willy and squeezing the boy against her bosom. "Almost every night. What do you expect after all he's been through?"

Pavel wriggled off her lap. "Granny is squishy," he said petulantly, "and she smells bad."

Judit gave him a reproachful look. "Don't be rude to *Babička*."

Sophie laughed apologetically. "I think he means the mothball smell from your clothes."

Willy yawned. "There you are. One of the penalties of living on top of each other. Obviously, Mother hasn't changed her Lučenec habits. I remember those mothballs from when I was growing up. Listen, I'm tired and we've heard enough today to fill a novel. We can catch up more tomorrow, after our meeting with George."

"We should all go to bed early," Emil said as he stood and stretched. "It's difficult to get to sleep with that burned wood smell in the air."

Sophie took Pavel's hand. "Bedtime, darling."

"Will we have an air raid in the night, Maman?"

"I hope not." Sophie glanced at Willy. "Your soldier Papa needs his sleep."

"The forecast is for bad weather," Emil grunted. "I think *Feld Marschal* Goering's bombers will prefer to stay at home."

CHAPTER TEN
The Meeting at Finetex
November 1940

For Emil and Judit, punctuality was a moral given and lateness a moral sin. Consequently, they arrived outside the Finetex headquarters in Golden Square half an hour early for the two o'clock appointment with George. Emil carried a shopping bag containing Judit's button box, a small blanket, a sandwich, and Pavel's furry lion. At Willy's insistence, Sophie had gone with him and Pavel on a shopping expedition to buy new clothes for the meeting.

Golden Square was pockmarked with holes and fissures that had turned into murky puddles after that night's rain. The central flower beds were choked with weeds and churned-up mud. In one corner, Air Raid Protection had built an enormous mound of shattered bricks, splintered wood, and plaster. DANGER signs hung on a rickety white fence surrounding a jagged bomb crater.

"It has stopped raining," Emil said as they stood in their overcoats and galoshes silently looking around the square. "We will wait here for fifteen minutes. Maybe the young ones will get here soon and we go in together.

"Such a mess the bombs made of this fine place," Emil grunted taking Judit's arm. "I am not surprised they have blocked off the traffic. It must be ten years since I was first here." He pointed to a bronze statue in the center of the square. "That's George the Second, King of England." He gave Judit a twisted smile. "He was born a German you know."

Judit kept her hands inside her fur muff and shivered. "I hate this English weather." She shook her head, despairingly. "*Apushkam,* why did we come? I am afraid we are wasting our time with this George. What can he do?"

"Nonsense. The weather is the least of our worries. We gain nothing by whining. But if you are too cold, we go inside. Come."

Finetex, one of England's premier textile companies, had occupied the second floor of 9 Golden Square, Soho, since 1883. The entrance to the limestone and brick building was an imposing portico, and there were bow windows on every floor. Each window was covered with anti-shatter tape. The building's elegance was further marred by a high berm of sandbags stacked against the outer walls.

After they entered, Emil noticed with satisfaction that little had changed since his visit in 1931. Such tradition was commendable. He liked the idea that the British way of doing business went back centuries.

As he and Judit walked along the wide, paneled corridors, Emil pointed out high-backed antique chairs, Persian carpets, and portraits of bewhiskered men in stiff collars and long jackets. "What a fine business this is, Judit. When Willy opened our store in Prague, I hoped we were well on the way to creating something like this." He shrugged as they passed a series of fire buckets filled with sand— silent sentries on polished wood floors. "I see that Finetex is prepared for the fire-bombs."

In front of carved double doors, an elderly receptionist, her smooth face framed by a sweep of grey curls, rose from her desk to greet them.

"Mr. and Mrs. Kohut?" she said, looking down at her appointment ledger. "You are expected. I believe the rest of your party will be here shortly. Overcoats over there. Then I will show you in to Mr. Kindell."

They hung their overcoats and hats on a bentwood rack set against the wall.

Emil wore his one bespoke suit and Judit was in a white blouse, a mothball-scented brown velvet jacket, and a grey woolen skirt. Willy had insisted they dress as well as possible for this meeting. "Like us, George is in the luxury fabric trade," he said. "He knows we have fallen on hard times, but if we look well-turned out, he'll understand we still have our pride. He'll make a special effort for us."

The receptionist took them into a richly carpeted room with a carved stone fireplace where a fire crackled and blazed. She indicated two armchairs. "Mr. and Mrs. Kohut," she announced to the man seated at the large desk, and left the room.

George Kindell rose, bowed slightly and shook hands. "Very nice to see you both ... and welcome to Finetex. Please excuse me while I finish my work." He sat down and continued writing. He placed a sheaf of papers in a tray muttering, "This stuff never ends."

"What a handsome man," Judit said quietly in Czech.

Emil nodded. George had his father's strong jawline and hollow cheeks. He nudged Judit's arm, pointing to the portrait over the fireplace. "That is old Mr. Kindell, my business partner. This son has the same beaky nose."

Emil guessed George was in his late twenties or early thirties. He remembered him from years earlier when they had met at the Finetex head office, before he and Willy went north to visit the textile mills in Huddersfield and Glasgow. Over those three weeks, Willy and young George became friendly.

As might be expected for an executive in the "rag trade," George wore a finely tailored tan herringbone suit and waistcoat. A spotted yellow bow tie graced his blue-striped shirt and a matching silk handkerchief drooped in extravagant folds from his breast pocket.

Gott zol ophiten, God Forbid, Emil thought, looking the young man up and down. *Such peacock colors ... but the suit ... it is beautifully made.*

"Forgive my surprise. You are both so elegantly dressed."

Emil bowed slightly in his chair. "We try, Mr. Kindell. My son Willy once had the same elegance as you. Now he is in uniform—badly made, coarse material—but tough." He pointed. "Please excuse, but where was your suit made? It is very well cut. Savile Row?"

"Ah, yes, my suit," George Kindell said with a smile of understanding. "You like it? Superb, eh? My father always insisted that my clothes and shoes were made in Savile Row. I had ten suits. He made me wear a different one each day." He paused, brushing back a forelock of fair hair. "So here I am—a walking, talking advertisement for Finetex. I believe Willy used the same strategy in Prague."

At that moment, the half-glassed office door opened and the receptionist re-entered. She acknowledged her young employer with a barely perceptible curtsey.

"It's the young Mr. and Mrs. Kohut, sir. They've arrived. They have their little boy with them. Shall I show them in?"

"Thanks, Marjorie."

A minute later, Willy and Sophie walked in—he in khaki battledress and she in shiny court shoes, a white crepe-de-chine blouse and a gray, pleated skirt with white pinstripes, bought that morning on Finchley Road. A dark blue beret perched on one side of her head. Pavel, in serge shorts with a gray pullover hiding his shoulder brace, stood silently behind his mother, taking occasional peeks.

Willy took off his cap, waving a greeting to his parents. Grinning broadly, he walked round the desk and took George's proffered hand with both of his. "It's wonderful to see you, George—after so many years. This is my wife, Sophie." He hesitated for a moment. "Please speak to her slowly, she is learning English."

Emil was pleased to see Sophie's charming, happy smile as she shook hands. It had been missing for a long time. As she sat down, putting Pavel on her lap, he watched George's eyes travel from Sophie's high-cheek-boned face down to the curve of her hips. The shimmering blouse accentuated her bosom. No doubt about it—her transformation and happy mood was Willy's doing.

George half rose from his chair. "It's so nice to meet you, Mrs. Kohut. Willy is a fortunate man indeed. If you remember—I hope I may call you Sophie—you and he graciously invited my family to your wedding. That must have been over five years ago. Sadly, I was in Paraguay at the time." He cracked open a slim silver case and lit a cigarette. He held it out. "Can I offer anyone a smoke?"'

Almost in unison, the Kohuts shook their heads. While Willy translated George studied Sophie with what Emil interpreted as appreciative eyes.

"And you, Willy old chap. Quite changed from the old days, I'd say. You've lost a fair bit of weight since we last met. I suppose the Czechoslovak Army thinned you down in France."

"Affirmative. We were in southern France—it was hot and the basic training was tough."

He sat down next to Sophie. "I must say, George, I kind of expected you to be in uniform, a fit-looking chap like you."

George leaned back in his leather chair and waved a debonair hand. "Dear boy, I *am* fighting—just not with a rifle. You see, instead of fine fabrics, Finetex makes military uniforms, greatcoats, vests, and underpants ... and we design canvas knapsacks as well. And His Majesty's government expects us to keep selling abroad—keeping the coffers of Finetex and our Empire jingling so that Britain can afford to churn out tanks and Spitfires. You just heard me mention Paraguay."

Willy nodded.

"When Hitler's antics eliminated our Central European market, we switched to South America. We've done jolly well there, actually. Now, how about some tea?"

George levered himself gracefully out of his chair and stepped over to the fireplace. He poked the fire into a blaze and pulled on a tasseled cord suspended from the ceiling. He smiled at Judit's' questioning look.

"A bell pull in each room … used for summoning servants. This building once housed the Portuguese Embassy. Marjorie will bring the tea shortly. I hope you and your boy like digestive biscuits."

Judit smiled. "He likes biscuits very much. Soon it is time for his sleep."

"He can take a nap here, dear lady. There's a couch in the room near Marjorie's desk. My father often took a snooze there after lunch. While we talk, she will entertain him if he doesn't nod off. "

A few minutes later, after Marjorie cleared away the china, she and Sophie led Pavel out of the office, carrying some of his toys.

Emil rose, and with a clunk placed the twisted metal fin on George's desk. "This is part of what destroyed our flat," he said abruptly. "We must move out of London, away from the bombing. Where to go and how it is to be done, we do not know."

George's eyebrows shot up. He turned the metal over in his hands, nodding. "An incendiary, eh?"

He looked at Emil and Judit. "It's clear you've been through a hellish time. So now …" He leaned forward, opening his arms wide—an invitation for someone to say something. "How can I help you?"

Willy shifted forward. "Listen, George. This is urgent. My parents, Sophie and Pavel—he's only four—are terrified by the nightly bombing. The damage to their flat was the last straw. My father went for advice to the British Committee for Czechoslovak Refugees—but all they offered was a move to a transit camp or out of the country. I don't want my family in a camp or on a ship to South America. Not while I'm in the British Army."

Sophie slipped back into the room, nodded to Judit, and

returned to her chair. "He'll be asleep soon," she murmured in Czech.

George leaned his elbows on the desk, his hands joined in a contemplative arc. He smiled at her. "The problem, my friends, is that they are bombing cities and towns all over Britain. Don't you think it might be easier if you just stayed put? Anyway, moving out of London is damned difficult for refugees. Loads of paperwork and regulations."

"You're a man-about-town, you know people," said Willy with some force. He shifted forward in his chair. "Finetex must have fingers in many pies, all over the country, even up north. My family has nowhere to stay. I'm afraid they will be ill, injured or even killed and I won't be there to help."

George nodded his head sympathetically.

Willy adjusted his spectacles. "Sophie, Pavel, and I slept on a bare mattress on the floor last night. It was icy-cold and damp—ash everywhere."

"The landlord cannot help us," Emil interjected, shifting forward in his chair." He told us to leave so they can repair the place. We can go back when it is ready but that will take months. We must find somewhere quickly."

George tapped the end of a fresh cigarette on the desk top. He lit it and blew a smoke ring. "You were damned lucky the awful weather kept the Jerries away last night. Why not look on the bright side, Willy. You're all alive and Finetex helped your father accumulate funds in the Westminster Bank—not like some of our luckless Londoners."

Willy shrugged. "I admit we are more fortunate than most refugees. But wherever my family ends up, I can't stay and help them. I have to be back in camp by late tomorrow, and I'm not in my commanding officer's good books anyway. I want to be sure my family will soon be safe and warm."

George blew another smoke ring, his face animated as if by

some memory. "Gosh, yes. That camp of yours. I heard about you chaps having a sort of riot—up north wasn't it? Is that where you are still stationed?"

Willy frowned. "That's over. I'm not there now."

Like a schoolteacher disciplining his class, Emil raised a finger. "Please—stop. This is no time to discuss Willy's army problems. Tell us where should we go, Mr. Kindell ... and how should we go? Do you know of a town with no bombing?"

George rubbed his forehead. "Mmm ... difficult question. You need a place where there's no industry and isn't in the path of returning Jerry bombers. They often drop their unused explosives on the way home to save fuel."

"We need your creativity, George," Willy urged. "Remember, in the old days, how we used to brainstorm business ideas over lunch and dinner. How we talked about setting up a distribution network in Eastern Europe—British suits and coats all the way to Russia and beyond."

George laughed. "As I remember those days, you had the ideas and I had the resources. It was fun to dream. I do have a suggestion though." He swung round and pointed a silver letter opener at the varnished sculling oar on the wall above him. Around it hung photographs of young men in blazers and straw hats holding oars in front of rowing shells. "How about living in Cambridge? Got my degree there. Lovely university with parks and a river; almost no industry. It's about fifty miles northeast of London, almost no bombing, I believe."

"What is this Cambridge?" said Sophie anxiously.

"The *famous* university, of course." Emil shifted excitedly. "This is good. We must act immediately."

George spread his hands, as if trying to calm Emil's enthusiasm. "Not so fast, Mr. Kohut. You probably know this, but refugees can't move about this country as they please. You'll need permits, the greasing of a palm or two, and a little time." He winked.

Emil's shoulders slumped. He looked at Judit and shook his head. "Not for us then."

Willy felt disappointment welling up. He could only guess at the bureaucratic and financial hurdles his parents would face. That could take weeks.

George fiddled thoughtfully with his letter opener, but then his face lit up. "Wait a mo'. There's someone I know of in Cambridge who might help out. A chap called Carnegie-Holston. He's an engineer, works at Duxford airfield where the Spitfire squadrons are stationed. His wife is a local doctor and a stalwart of the church: community-minded souls. I can ask them."

"Explain please," Judit said to Willy. "He speaks difficult words."

Sophie sat silently with her hands folded on her lap, eyes alert.

Willy put a hand on hers. He spoke in Czech. "George has friends in Cambridge. They may help us find a place."

"*Aah, gut,*" said Judit, her face wrinkling into a satisfied smile.

George flipped through his desk-top card index and scribbled something down on a card. "This is their address and phone number. In any case, I'll telephone them early this evening and explain your predicament as persuasively as I can. Call me at eight tonight. I will let you know if it's yea or nay."

Emil rose and, with a slight bow, picked up the note and slipped it into a waistcoat pocket. "We are most grateful, thank you," he said, shaking George's hand.

Judit also stood. She put a hand on Willy's arm. "Please, you will visit this Cambridge with us and help arrange everything."

Willy groaned. "Please, Mother, that's impossible. Tomorrow, I go back to the camp. I have no idea when I can visit you again."

Emil patted Judit's shoulder. "We will go together to Cambridge, my dear."

George rubbed his hands, looking pleased. "Good, I gather Cambridge is a go." He pulled a pen from his inside pocket and looked at Emil. "To save time, sir, I'll write an official Finetex letter approving your travel to Cambridge. Show it to the clerk when you buy your train ticket. If the Carnegie-Holstons can't help, then you can use this letter for some other journey."

After a few moments of scribbling, George buzzed his secretary and when she came in, handed her his draft. "Type this up straightaway, Marjorie. It's for the Kohuts when they leave. Use the special rubber stamp from the Foreign Office. "

George stubbed out his cigarette and came round from his desk. "Now you must excuse me; I have an important telephone call to make. Please wait in the hallway until Marjorie has done the letter. Then I'll see you all out to the street. We'll talk more tonight."

Emil shook his hand." Thank you very much. We hope for the best."

The Kohut family accompanied by George Kindell stood outside the Finetex office building, umbrellas spread, waiting for a cruising taxi to appear. George drew Willy away from them, close to the stack of sandbags. "Listen, old boy," he said quietly, "it seems a bloody shame that a capable fellow like you should serve as a simple foot soldier. I've got an acquaintance in the Foreign Office, Bill Strang. A few words from me and he could likely get you something better."

Willy froze. "This Strang—isn't he the official who advised Chamberlain to give a third of my country away to the Nazis? If so, I want nothing from that bastard. He betrayed us."

George put up a hand. "For God's sake, Willy, shut up. That's water under the bridge. Concentrate on your future. The British Army needs people with your brains and language skills. For a start, I could ask Strang to talk to the Czechoslovak military and have them review your background and languages. An eventual commission in the British Army might not be out of the question. What d'you say?"

Willy raised his eyebrows. "You could fix that, George? It's hard to believe an ordinary businessman like you can pull such big strings."

George patted Willy's shoulder amicably. "I'm all over the place these day, old chap—parties, briefings, meetings, sometimes at pretty high levels. I get to hear things from old school chums, friends, and acquaintances. I'm often asked to keep my ears pinned back. But if I'm going to smooth your way, I would need some help from you."

Willy laughed. "What? Me, help *you*?"

"I need information. Not too onerous, really. Reading that newspaper article about the mutiny at your camp, it was clear that ex-combatants from the International Communist Brigade were heavily involved in setting up the whole thing. I checked and discovered that one of the leaders was a commissar chappie with strong Russian connections. The *quid pro quo* is this; I want you to keep an eye on him, if he's still in your unit. Let me know if anything odd or interesting turns up: snippets about plans, conversations overheard— that kind of thing."

Willy frowned and shook his head. "I did something like this in Prague. I ended up in jail."

"Bad luck, old boy." A sympathetic look flickered across George's face. "Come on, Willy. Britain has given your family a safe haven. This is something you can do to help. The Russkies have a pile of operatives in Britain, many more than the Nazis. Supposedly they're on our side, but they're fomenting unrest in our factories, trying to disrupt war production. Your eyes and ears will be working for me—right?"

Willy's eyes widened. "You want me to *spy* on my comrades?"

George dismissed Willy's protest with a wave. "In a way, yes. I'm supposed to help people like Strang."

Willy's stomach twisted. Risky business. He would be informing on Povídka, Boho Serbin, and the other communists at the camp; people he disliked and who made him physically afraid. In Prague, not long after Colonel Moravec of Czechoslovak Intelligence had asked him to "keep an eye" on a pro-German acquaintance, Willy was arrested by the Gestapo. On the other hand, here was George Kindell, a friend, offering to help his family get away from the Blitz and find a place to live.

"Look, Sophie sailed from France with the kind of people you are interested in. They're at my camp … unreliable, touchy and dangerous types … and mutineers like me. I might easily lose contact with them."

George frowned. "Come on, Willy. It's just keeping an eye open. These days there's a risk to everything."

Willy paused for a moment, and sighed. "Okay, I'll do it. At least I'll be returning the favors you've shown me. I've had a number of dealings with commissar Povídka. He trusts me about as much as he trusts anyone. I'll keep an eye on him—even though he and his henchmen scare my pants off."

"Splendid fellow."

Willy nodded. "As to the rest of your *quid pro quo,* I'm very skeptical that you can guarantee me a commission in the British army. That would be a miracle."

"Miracles can happen. Telephone me tonight, old chap." George turned on his heel and went back into the building.

CHAPTER ELEVEN
Dinner at the Carvery
November 1940

Outside the Finetex offices in Golden Square, Willy stood in the road waving his umbrella. After some frustrating minutes, a taxi swerved and stopped with a squeal of brakes.

"Watch it, soldier," the driver said in an aggrieved tone as he clicked down the for-hire sign. "You'll get yourself killed before the fucking Jerries get a chance."

Willy guided his parents inside the cab and Sophie passed Pavel and his bag of toys in to them.

Emil sat forward "Come on, Willy. Get in."

Willy shook his head. He already had a plan. "I want to show Sophie the West End and Piccadilly. Mother, be an angel and look after Pavel for us."

Sophie leaned into the cab. "You go home with Grandpa and Granny," she said, smiling at Pavel as he scrambled up onto the fold-up taxi seat. "We'll see you later … and be a good boy."

Judit's plaintive voice came out of the cab's dark interior. "I made a special dish for supper. Emil fought for the meat at the butchers. Noodles and *pörkölt*."

"We will be back after supper. Leave the front door unlocked." Willy did not give his parents another chance to speak. He stepped back, shut the cab door, and waved goodbye as the taxi sped off.

Willy took Sophie's arm. "They will be very disappointed … but I want us to be alone."

The drizzle had turned into genuine rain and, as they walked, Sophie clung to him under the umbrella.

"Let's forget them for a while," he said. "What did you think of the meeting with George?" They spoke in Czech.

"I didn't understand much. It turned out well, didn't it?" Sophie said as they turned into Lower James Street. "George is nice … and very handsome."

Willy laughed. "He is *charmant* as the French say. And I hope he will charm his Cambridge acquaintances into helping us." He stopped, turned her head with a finger on her chin and kissed her lips. "Now, my sweet, you and I are owed some fun and then a good talk. What could be better in this horrible weather than a film and a proper dinner? At least you're already dressed up for it even though I'm not!" He looked down at his tunic and the wet bottoms of his khaki pants and laughed.

She smiled. "Sounds wonderful, *miláčku*. You've planned everything out, just like our old times in Prague. You are spending money on me, but you didn't bring a present for Pavel. "

Willy looked up at the scudding gray clouds. "I'm sorry. Had no time." He took her hand. "Now … you've been in London nearly three months. Have you visited the West End yet?"

She shook her head. "I was afraid to go out until I had my identification papers, then your parents did not like the idea that I wanted to go out and explore on my own. I didn't want to upset them and ask them to look after Pavel."

"Well, we're going to change that. On the train yesterday, I borrowed an *Evening Standard* and got some ideas." He looked at his watch. How about the cinema?

Sophie's eyebrows arched in surprise "My God, a film? I haven't seen one since Prague."

"There is a film called *The Four Feathers*." he said, tilting his umbrella against gusts of wind as they turned the corner. "A British colonial adventure full of action. Good for your English."

"I have been studying very hard," she laughed, again threading her arm through his. "And I was so happy that George's secretary understood me when I explained to her how to watch over Pavel. I think you will have to whisper translations in my ear in the cinema."

Willy grinned at her. "It will be a pleasure to nibble on your ear, and maybe get a kiss in return." He stopped as if undecided. "We have an hour before the film starts. On the way to Leicester Square, I'll show you the department store called Dickens and Jones. The newspaper said it was the only one undamaged after last week's air raids. And on Regent Street we can look inside one or two of the famous shops." Willy hoped the fashion displays would raise Sophie's spirits. What woman could resist the glamor of expensive clothes, even though she had an empty purse and was looking through taped-up windows?

Sophie gave him a quizzical look. "What do you mean, famous?"

"They have a very English character. Liberty's sells wonderful fabrics and Aquascutum specializes in women's outdoor clothes."

"And where will we eat after the cinema?"

"At the Regent Palace Hotel, next to Piccadilly Circus. George persuaded his secretary to reserve us a table. He goes there all the time. It's time you tasted good English food: roast beef, lamb, pheasant, pies and desserts."

"There's a food shortage, *milačku*. Your father will be shocked if he finds out."

Willy tapped the side of his nose and winked. "The rich and the privileged always find a way. Anyway, at the hotel restaurant they carve meat at your table, as much and as often as you like. It's splendiferous."

Sophie raised an eyebrow. "You make me hungry just talking about it. But … this circus next to the hotel. Why is it in the middle of London? Does it have acrobats on prancing horses, tigers and clowns?"

"If only!!" Willy had almost forgotten the light-hearted lilt of her voice. "Picadilly is just a traffic roundabout surrounded by fine buildings in the center of London."

"How can you afford to pay for the film and dinner?" she said as they stopped to look at a tiered display of ladies shoes and handbags. "I hope this isn't one of your famous impulse splurges. Spend like a pasha, starve later, that's what you used to say in Prague."

Willy made a face. "Don't worry; I managed to make some extra money at the camp—playing piano at officer's parties." This was only partly true. He had performed just once. He had borrowed two pounds from Emil that morning, promising to repay it from his wages. He wanted her to have a good time and eat well, hoping that doing so would help repair the distance between them.

"Did you play the same pieces you mentioned to Emil?"

"More American tunes than anything else—you know, Glenn Miller and Tommy Dorsey: but also a Chopin sonata and a couple of Czech folk songs."

On their way toward Piccadilly Circus, Willy couldn't stop noticing the graceful swing of her hips and legs: something he dreamed about often since leaving France. He thought back to the previous night, squeezed into her bed with Pavel close by them on the floor; the awkwardness of holding her—no longer pliant against him as she used to be.

The rain stopped and Willy closed his umbrella.

Sophie pointed up at the sky. "Those clouds are floating away like ice floes in a blue sea. Looks like a clear night coming. Maybe the Luftwaffe is planning to join us for dinner!"

"I damn well hope not!"

"Please, *milačku*, can we talk about the future while we eat? You leave tomorrow. We don't have much time together, you and me."

Willy slipped his arm round her shoulders and kissed her cheek. "Of course we will talk. It's time we attended to our marriage. I want you to feel happier than I know you've been." He took her shoulders. "I have to admit, I'm hoping for more than just a hug in bed tonight." He scanned her face, trying to judge the effect of his words. She blew him a kiss—neither a yes nor a no, as far as he could tell.

After the film, they walked from Leicester Square to Piccadilly Circus. Cars and buses with dimmed headlights cautiously rounded the boarded-up Eros statue. The Regent Palace Hotel was just off the Circus. Willy pointed out the celebrated art deco glass dome as they walked through the Rotunda Court where guests were chatting on leather couches and chairs. The large wood-paneled dining room was hung with chandeliers and full-length velvet curtains. Guests, many in evening dress, sat at most of the formally set tables. Sophie inhaled the enticing smell of roasted meat.

A waiter pulled out a chair for Sophie. She sat down opposite Willy, scanning the half-opened silk curtains at the tall windows and oil paintings on the wall—hunting scenes, racehorses, and seascapes. "This is very quiet place, Willy. I expected a livelier crowd."

Willy nodded, unfolding his napkin. "You are right. The English are not noisy, unless, of course, they've had a few drinks or they're watching cricket or football. I suppose you might say they were a bit dull. By the way, there is no menu. It's a kind of buffet on wheels. The waiters roll their trolleys from table to table, and you can eat as much as you like. Our dinner is *prix fixe* and everything is included, except wine." He shrugged regretfully "And I can't afford wine. I'm using up all my savings as it is."

Sophie, smiling, shook her head. "The last time I drank wine was in Sillat. Remember Monsieur Robineau, the village mayor? He tried to seduce me with his wine. When you were on night patrol at the camp, he would magically appear with a couple of bottles from his vineyard."

"I hope you resisted."

"Didn't have to. I just sat there while he showered me with compliments and drank himself to sleep in one of the garden chairs."

"For heaven's sake," Willy laughed. "You never told me!"

A waiter wheeled a heated meat trolley to their table, opening the domed silver cover to reveal a fragrant roast pork joint, a shoulder of lamb and rare roast beef. He carved generous slices of the meat and crispy skin according to their choice. Another waiter served roast potatoes, Brussels sprouts, baked pumpkin, and thick gravy, with side dishes of chutney, red-currant and horseradish sauce, and Yorkshire pudding.

As they ate, Willy reminisced about their happy times in Košice and Prague. Sophie was glad. It was better than revisiting their current problems. Half way through the lemon syllabub dessert, Sophie covered Willy's hand, leaned over, and kissed his cheek. "I'm content, *milačku*. The food is tasty, and I love having a brave Czech soldier show me around London."

The muffled sound of the air raid siren stilled conversation in the room.

Willy slammed his utensils down and jumped to his feet. "Damn it. Those fucking Nazis won't even let us eat in peace."

Sophie tossed her napkin onto the table and waggled a finger at him. "Don't get upset, Private Kohut. You are finally seeing action. But it's completely one–sided … German bombs against a Czechoslovak soldier eating in a luxury restaurant. Not what you would call a fair fight, is it? "

Willy gave her a grim smile. "*Touché, Madame.*"

Guests were leaving their tables, food half-eaten. They meandered, still chatting, toward the dining room entrance.

Willy looked around, surprised. "I don't get it. They are not in any hurry." He had expected Sophie to be frightened, but she was calm. Impressed, he gave her a quick smile.

Their waiter came up to the table, a gloomy expression on his thin face. "Dinner service suspended until the raid is over, sir."

"What do we do? Is there an air raid shelter nearby? Where is everybody going?"

"Basement, sir. It's a bit cramped, but if the raid goes on long enough, refreshments will be served. A bell rings when the All Clear sounds."

Feeling reassured, Willy pushed his chair back. The dinner wasn't over. There was just the small matter of sitting through a few explosions, after which he and Sophie would resume their tête-à-tête. "Okay, we'll follow the others."

Willy and Sophie were among the last to arrive in the dimly-lit basement. Willy led the way as guests squeezed themselves onto benches and chairs between stacks of boxes and laundry carts. Waiters circulated offering water and oatmeal biscuits. Two ARP guards tested stirrup water pumps and repositioned sand-filled fire buckets along the passageways. By the time Willy and Sophie had found an end spot on a distant bench, explosions, thuds and occasional clatterings shook the walls.

"These people look nice," Sophie whispered to Willy, nodding to the elderly couple sitting next to them. "Should we introduce ourselves?"

After a particularly loud explosion, the silver-haired man in evening dress put an arm reassuringly around his companion and looked sideways at Sophie. "Goddamit! That was a big one, eh? Third time down here in the last month. How about you?"

Willy leaned forward. "It's our first time here. We came for a special dinner. My wife is used to the Blitz but it's my first time. Unsettling, to put it mildly."

The gentleman gave him a circumspect look. "You're unsettled?"

"I'm still in training, sir."

"We usually see only officers at the Regent Palace." What he said next was drowned by a quick series of explosions. Then, " ... being a soldier, I expect you'd be interested to know that most of this god-awful noise comes from the anti-aircraft battery in Hyde Park—three point seven inch QF guns, twenty rounds a minute. Damned accurate."

There was a distant boom; the basement walls shook. Willy grabbed Sophie's hand. He wasn't a coward but this was more than unsettling. "Now I understand what my parents and you and Pavel have been going through."

She pulled his hand to her lips, giving it a kiss. "Those explosions are far away. I'm used to nights like this. Actually, I was thinking less about the bombing and more about what Cambridge will be like. I don't know what to expect."

Willy slid an arm around her shoulders and spoke into her ear trying to block out the noise. "They say it's a lovely city. You will be happy and safe with my parents."

"Yes, well, perhaps. But—I want to say something important, *milačku*," she said. "I do not like living with your parents."

He stiffened. "*Gott behüte*. Why ever not?"

"There is a bad atmosphere, especially between Judit and me. Your parents have changed." She sighed and laced her fingers into his. "*I've* changed. Haven't you noticed? If we go to Cambridge, I would prefer to find my own place with Pavel."

"I don't understand. When I arrived at the flat, we all talked and ate and laughed. My parents love you, Sophie. Ever since we were betrothed they treated you like their own daughter. What has gone wrong?"

"Emil is a grump and a dictator, although he has a good heart, and he adores Pavel. But, everything I do seems to be wrong. They lecture me all the time. They treat me as if I'm still a young bride with no sense or experience."

Willy pulled her close. "I'm really sorry, I know they are demanding. I'll try talking to them. I can't do more than that, since I'm leaving tomorrow."

Sophie squared her shoulders in defiance. "I don't need you to defend me or fight with your parents. I'm just explaining how I feel and why. But having dinner with you tonight has made me understand what I really want; for us to be together, as much as your soldiering will allow. If that means bringing me and Pavel to live close to your camp, then that is fine."

In his mind, Willy pictured the drab village cottages not far from his camp. Would they be willing to rent a room to a foreign woman and her son? There were no shops nearby. How would she manage? "You don't know what you are asking."

"Find us somewhere to stay—anything."

Willy stared, surprised by her determination. "Of course, I want us to be together. But I don't know if it's even possible to do what you ask."

"Do you understand what I've been through, Willy?"

"I can imagine some of what has happened between you and my parents," he said. "Circumstances have changed them, and us."

She reached up and put a hand on his arm. "My idea to live with Pavel close to your camp will solve our problems. I know it. We'll be far away from the bombing. That's what you told me. They only bomb cities and factories."

Willy sighed, his frustration leaching away at the sight of her tears. "Let's be clear about what this means. My unit has already changed location twice. And now, we're to move again under British command to Ilfracombe in the southwest. It will be hard to find you a place to rent each time I move and you'll end up not knowing anyone except me. Why not keep things simple and stable? Stay with my parents. Try harder to get along."

Sophie grabbed Willy's hands and pulled them against her chest. The softness of her breasts made him shiver.

Her lips quivered. "I'm ready to take that risk. I managed with Pavel in Paris and then at Sillat near your French camp. Why should it be any different?"

Willy wanted to tell her the obvious; that in Paris, to help her recover on her own, Pavel was placed in a residential kindergarten. And Paris was nothing like a hardscrabble, wintry English village where she would not understand the dialect. But, impractical as it was, he liked the idea of having her close by. She was right about one thing. It might be the best way to rekindle their marriage and for him to spend time with his son.

The look in Sophie's eyes melted his heart. "Okay, let's try it. If it fails you can go back to wherever my parents are living."

She drew in a deep breath. "I don't care what happens as long as we can see you. Whatever the living conditions, we'll manage."

When the raid ended just over an hour later, they returned with the other guests to the dining room. The waiter brought fresh portions of sour-sweet syllabub. They ate in silence.

Willy moved his chair close to Sophie and took her hands. "Listen—darling. You told me how you felt about my parents, and now I want be honest with you. That's how it should be between man and wife, eh?"

Sophie nodded.

He pulled her head gently forward and kissed her, then sat back and gazed at her in admiration. "Last night, holding you in bed, I had the feeling that we were more like friendly strangers than a man and his wife. It made me think about our marriage."

She looked at him with glistening eyes, hands trembling on the table. "We should not be doing this in such an elegant place." She glanced around. "People are watching."

Willy, admiring the soft curve of her cheek and full lips, felt desire again. He rested his hand on her thigh and stroked it. "I don't care what people think. A man should be able to kiss his wife after an air raid."

She let his fingers stay there.

It was just past nine when they left the Regent Palace. The air was thick with the smell of cordite and burned wood. Patches of fog, or maybe smoke, Willy thought, from some house fire, drifted down the street. He put his arm around Sophie's shoulders and felt her shivering. "We'll catch the number 13 bus in Regent Street but I want to try to get George and see if he has any news about Cambridge. There … there's a telephone box." He opened the door. "Step inside with me and stay warm. I'm going to try to get hold of George."

"I thought he told you to call at eight."

"I'll take a chance. He won't mind."

Two minutes later, it was over. Willy smiled "Good news, my love. I have the address in Cambridge where Father is to meet a friend of George's tomorrow. A lady doctor. Apparently, she offered a couple of possibilities. With my military travel permit and the letter of support George gave us yesterday, I'm sure I can get tickets for Father and myself at King's Cross Station. Father will take the Cambridge train and I'll leave for Birmingham."

Sophie turned him to face her. "What if they stop Emil getting a ticket? He doesn't have a travel permit."

"I'll work something out."

At the bus stop, they stood at the end of a line of glum-looking people. He kissed her again, whispering in her ear as he held her. "Tonight, if Father is still up, I'll tell him about the Cambridge arrangement. Then, at breakfast, I'll break the news about arranging for you and Pavel to live near my camp."

A bulky man in a peaked cap and uniform cycled up to the bus stop and slowly dismounted. "Sorry about this, everyone," he said, breathing heavily. He straightened his jacket. "No more buses tonight. There's a bloody great hole in Baker Street and another one along Finchley Road. They think one of 'em might be a UXB."

Sophie looked askance at Willy. "What is a UXB?"

"Unexploded bomb, missus. Everything inside a six 'undred foot area is blocked from the public. You'll 'ave to walk home."

People at the stop started arguing and grumbling about how far they would have to walk, and that everything in London was falling apart.

Willy took her hand. He looked at his watch. "Nine fifteen. I hope to God there isn't another damned raid tonight. I don't have enough money for a taxi, so we'll have to walk." He turned to the bus transport man. "How far is it to Swiss Cottage?"

"Three miles, mate. Take you an hour."

"I'll have to wake Father up when we get in," said Willy. "Come on, fast pace now."

As they set out, Willy gave her a kiss. "I have to hand it to you. You were so calm and sensible during the raid. All those explosions shaking the building ... I nearly wet myself."

She gave a ringing laugh. "Like Pavel."

CHAPTER TWELVE
6 Park Parade, Cambridge
November 1940

The next morning, at the ticket counter of Liverpool Street railway station, Willy and his father showed the clerk George's letter and both of their identity cards. "We're traveling together," said Willy as he tucked the return tickets to Cambridge in his breast pocket. He bought two newspapers at a stall, gave one to Emil, and then hugged him. "Good luck, Father, with your first trip on the GER. Just be sure to keep to yourself on the train. A foreign accent means "German spy" to most people."

"I am not sure what to expect from this lady doctor," said Emil, tucking his folded newspaper into the side pocket of his raincoat. "Dr.Carnegie-Holston; I hope she is not as complicated as her name."

Willy slapped him on the back. "Dig down deep, Father. Kiss her hand. That's always a good start."

A bleak smile crossed Emil's face. "And I have to find a place to live … on top of digesting what you announced at breakfast; Sophie and Pavel coming to live near you. Is that a final decision?"

"It will be an adjustment for all of us," Willy said, sliding an arm around Emil's shoulders. "They want to be close to me, Father. Even though I am skeptical about how it will turn out, what they want is what I want."

In Cambridge, Emil took a taxi. He had not talked to anyone on the train, and, after reading every word of the *News Chronicle*, he'd had time to develop doubts and anxieties about how the day would unfold. It was raining, and the taxi ride through the town's narrow, twisty streets only made him more pessimistic.

He paid the driver, looking around at the same time, unsure whether they had stopped in the right place. There were row houses on one side of the road, and railings demarcating a lush green park on the other. He had missed the street sign. "Is here Park Parade?"

"S'right, mate," said the taxi driver pocketing the money. "Number six, you said. Over there, see." He grinned. "Or mebbe not. That could be a bent-over nine."

Emil's hat blew off as he walked toward the front door. He retrieved it.

A woman got out of a Wolseley saloon car parked nearby, and approached him. She wore a beige raincoat and yellow sou'wester hat. "Are you Mr. Kohut?" She was a head taller than him.

Emil nodded, removing his hat.

"I thought there'd be two of you. George Kindell said your wife was coming."

"My apologies, madam. It was too difficult to get a travel permission for both of us." He extended his hand. "I am honored to meet you. You are the lady doctor?"

She accepted his greeting with a gloved hand. "How do you do. Yes, I'm Doctor Carnegie-Holston. George told me all about you— said this was an emergency." She pointed to the shabby door with its tilted "6" "I did my best to find something for you. This one is church property. Needs some cleaning up."

Emil bowed slightly, forcing himself to stay calm. He could hardly contain his joy at this miracle. His heart went out to George Kindell. The thought of he and Judit making things workable, clean, and correct in this house, was surprisingly pleasurable. *Alles in Ordnung.*

"It's got a lovely view over the park," she said in a friendly tone.

Emil took stock of the proposed rental property. Number six was part of a terrace of two story red-brick houses that extended down the street to a dead end. The houses had slate roofs and high chimneys, their windows criss-crossed with tape. He saw that the windows on the top floor of the house had been boarded up. The glass in one window adjacent to the front door had a giant crack and was held together with strips of sticky tape. On the sill inside, a white Angora cat licked its paws and looked directly at Emil as if waiting for him.

The doctor sneezed, covering her nose with an oversized handkerchief. "Sorry about this." Her muffled voice turned into a fit of coughing. "I'm … at the end of a *horrible* cold, so don't come too close. Please call me Dr. Emily. *Everyone* does, even some of my patients. Welcome to windy and waterlogged Cambridge."

"You are so kind to arrange this, madam." Emil bowed again.

"This park," the doctor gestured at what lay beyond the head-high rusty railings across the road, "is called Jesus Green. That's because it's close to Jesus College, part of the university. You can easily walk to the river from here. Ten minutes. It's the river Cam, the reason for Cambridge's name."

Emil noticed the doctor's mud-smeared Wellington boots and suddenly wondered if she wasn't a medical doctor at all, but some kind of a veterinarian. But she had mentioned patients. Still, in Czechoslovakia, medical doctors never dressed like this.

"You didn't bring any luggage? I expect you just wanted to have a look-see first."

As soon as the doctor unlocked the door, the cat appeared in the hall.

It meowed, arched its back and stretched its front claws in welcome. Emil liked cats, Judit did not ... because they were automatically dirty. He decided on the spot that if they moved here, this cat could stay ... and be *his cat.* Judit would just have to put up with it.

"I paid a retaining fee for you" said Dr. Emily with a sniff that turned into an encouraging smile. "The house belongs to the Diocese of Ely. I managed to twist the dean's arm. Do you understand me?" She took a quick breath, strangling a sneeze with her handkerchief. "Oh, dear I am sorry about this."

"It's cathedral property," she said, after wiping her nose. "At first, the diocese didn't think it was in good enough condition to rent out. They're asking one pound, twelve shillings a week—rather expensive for what you're getting. Can you afford that?"

Emil half-smiled assent. Better, at this stage, not to show his cards; he had hoped rental rates would be much lower in a town so far from London. This number six rent wasn't cheap.

"The diocese agent, Hargreaves, will be here soon. He's the person who'll help you get a refugee permit from the council housing office. The diocese also requires a British guarantor." The doctor smiled, pointing at her bosom. "That's me." She sneezed and blew her nose again. "You also have to apply to the Alien Registration Board for permission to live in Cambridge.

"What does this mean, madam, British guarantor?"

She laughed, more of a bark that ended in a paroxysm of coughing. "If you do not pay the rent on time or disappear, I'm financially responsible." She arched a sardonic eyebrow. "Please don't do that. That will ruin my reputation."

As they entered the hallway, Emil tried to sort out his feelings: exultation that he had found a place to live, and shame that he had to rely on kindness from a stranger. "You are a very generous person, madam," he said. "I am very grateful, but we do not need a big house like this. Before the fire, we had a small flat in London. I cannot afford to pay what you say it costs."

"Well, this place does need a lot of work," she said looking around again. A smile spread across her face. "The asking rent *is* rather high. Are you good at negotiating?"

She switched on the hallway light.

Emil gasped at the silence and dilapidation. The ceiling lampshade was festooned with cobwebs, the linoleum floor covered in dust and mouse droppings. The air smelled musty. Shreds of green and yellow patterned wallpaper hung down from the stained walls. His heart sank; he had just said he was grateful—for this?

"Oh, heavens," spluttered Dr. Emily through a coughing spell after they entered the front room that had a bay window overlooking the park. "It does look awful, doesn't it? But then George said anything with a decent roof would do. He told me that four of you will be living here: you, your wife, daughter-in law and a little boy—apart from any visits your son can wheedle out of the army."

From behind her, Emil glimpsed the fireplace: cracked bricks, and two feathered bodies, possibly pigeons, lying on a pile of ashes. He imagined Judit's horrified—more likely hysterical—reaction to this place.

The doctor gave him a sympathetic look. "What do you think?"

"With repairs, I could make it livable," Emil said, an idea fermenting in his head. "It will cost money and much time." He thought about the possibility of negotiating to buy this house instead of renting, using his account at the Westminster Bank. The war had depressed property values all over Britain. He might get a real bargain. He tapped the doctor's arm. "What if I do improvements? My rent could be reduced. Is this possible?"

He felt a growing excitement. It was not so bad. Remove all the *dreck*, then repair and paint it. This was what they needed: safety from bombs and enough space if Willy, Sophie, and Pavel ever needed to come back and live with them. Perhaps for the first time in his life, Emil was ready to discard his slow, measured reasoning and rely entirely on intuition and emotion.

"Oh, my, that's a grand idea," said the doctor quickly. "I'll do my best to persuade Hargreaves, the diocese agent, to rent it to you. He'll be here soon, I expect."

While they were inspecting the upstairs rooms, Hargreaves came up the stairs. As they shook hands, Emil, with some distaste noted the man's heavily pomaded hair and a double chin. At Dr. Emily's insistence, he delved into his briefcase, produced a draft rental application, and quickly agreed to a rate of two pounds a month as long as Mr. Kohut would clean up the house and perform minor repairs—with the diocese paying for the materials as long as he provided all the receipts.

On the grimy kitchen countertop, Hargreaves recorded the details of the Kohuts' alien registration cards and London residence permits. Emil signed the rental agreement, they shook hands, and Mr. Hargreaves handed him carbon copies.

"You've got yourself a bargain," said Mr. Hargreaves, cocking his head in admiration. "This place has got good bones: three fireplaces, two coal stoves, running water, and a working toilet. There's a gas cooker in the kitchen and room for a vegetable garden in the back. I saw a nice clump of rhubarb when I was here last. All the doors lock tight and the neighborhood is safe and respectable. When do you plan to move in? "

"As soon as we can—a few days."

Dr. Emily looked at her watch and began to button up her raincoat. "I must rush. I have patients starting at two. Now, about the big job of cleaning up this place, Mr. Kohut—as soon as you move in, I've recruited some helpers from my church to get you started. Our congregation at Holy Trinity has a committee for refugees like you."

Emil blinked, astonished at this offer. Whatever her religious beliefs, this doctor was a fine woman with kind compatriots. These ordinary English were kind-hearted and active people, unlike their politicians who had helped bring about the downfall of Czechoslovakia. "Thank you so much," was all he could manage.

Emil took a deep breath. "For the moment, only I and my wife will live here. My daughter-in-law and grandson were to join us, but now they will live close to our son's camp." He squared his shoulders with pride at the thought of all the Czechoslovak men training with the British army and air force.

Dr. Emily nodded, and then sneezed. "Oh, dear, this awful cold. Well, Mr. Kohut … I think that's it. I'll leave you to work everything out with Hargreaves. And when you're settled in, you must come and have tea. Toodle-oo!"

Rubbing his hands together, Emil turned to the agent. "Please, mister, you show me everything in detail now. We check the locks, water taps, the toilets and light the gas stove—you have matches, yes?—then if everything is good, I sign the papers."

A week later, Emil and Judit moved to 6 Park Parade, occupying one bedroom and the usable ground-floor room with the bow window.

Two days later, at eight in the morning, Pickfords Moving Company delivered their few possessions: second-hand furniture, beds and linens that Emil and Judit had bought at a local auction in Swiss Cottage. It took no more than an hour because Judit insisted that everything be stacked in corners until she came up with a detailed cleaning plan.

At ten o'clock there was a knock on the door.

Emil opened the door and the cat scooted in—a flash of silky white.

"Good morning, Mister—er—Cahoot." A plump red-faced woman stood on the threshold. Behind her were five other women dressed in aprons and headscarves holding long-handled mops and brushes. Buckets, bulging shopping bags, and dustpans stood at their feet. One of the team hefted a vacuum cleaner. "My name's Molly Biggs, from the Ladies Refugee Committee of Holy Trinity Church."

Emil noticed a white van parked at the curb. Hanley the Florist was written on its side in curly blue letters. What was going on? He felt Judit's presence behind him. "Good morning. Can I help you?"

The team leader unleashed a ringing laugh. She wore bright red lipstick and her cheeks were heavily powdered. "Other way round really. It's *we* that's come to help *you*."

All through the day, the house was full of noise and the whistle of tea kettles boiling. By five o'clock the Holy Trinity ladies left to prepare high tea for their families. They promised to return the next day to "finish the job" and bring "some bits and pieces we know you could do with."

"What a day," sighed Judit as she and Emil crawled into bed that night. "I tried to show them what had to be done, but they took no notice. To think that I grew up in my father's hotel and spent years in Lučenec supervising our domestics. Today, I felt useless."

Emil leaned over her and kissed her forehead. "They were a great help, and you restrained your remarks very well. I'm satisfied. Much was accomplished." He was amazed that these church women had done such a fine thing for foreigners who do not even belong to their religion. Would this ever have happened in Lučenec?

The Kohuts registered as aliens at the local police station, explored the Jesus Green Park, walked along the river to the barge locks, and bought food at the shops on Bridge and Magdalene streets. At the Cambridge council offices they were issued replacement ration books and received the government's refugee allowance of one pound a week.

Two weeks later, nearly every room in the house smelled of polish and bleach. There were still substantial repairs to be made, so Emil, with only simple tools and little experience, turned his attention to the outside.

Emil and Judit's first agreed priority was to build frames and sew blackout curtains for the windows on the ground floor. The Luftwaffe was attacking the RAF airfield at Duxton a few miles away and the Cambridge police had implemented stiffer fines for contravening blackout regulations.

After that, Emil turned to a few simple tasks to get some handyman practice. In Lučenec, he had employed a gardener and paid workmen to make repairs. He hardly knew how to use a screwdriver.

His first project was to turn the deviant house number back to a 6 and screw it tight. At the back, he weeded the small rectangular garden, surrounded by a dilapidated wood fence which he would have to straighten and repair. An exploratory dig revealed rich black humus, once the legacy, he guessed, of a dedicated gardener. One corner of the garden, close to the kitchen, held dustbins and a half-full coal bunker, and a tiny wooden shed slumped on its foundation. He oiled the rusty-hinged gate into the back lane and listened with satisfaction when the screeching stopped.

The interior and window tasks were more daunting and within a month, Emil regretted offering to rehabilitate the house in exchange for a lower rent. It seemed beyond his skills and knowledge. At the hardware shop, he found it difficult to understand the answers to what seemed to be his simple, even stupid questions. The tools the manager recommended were either unavailable or costly. Emil was disappointed. He would have to admit defeat, and probably pay more rent. In which case, they could not afford 6 Park Parade for more than a few months. Then what?

The Kohuts were saved by Alf Tidmarsh, a small wiry neighbor from three doors down who was registered as unfit for service in the military. He had been in the building trade until he caught polio but he still did odd jobs in the neighborhood. He wore a brace on his right leg and always called Emil, Mr. K. They met through the connivances of the white Angora cat who spent part of her life at each house. The wily cat begged and received food from both households, which led to neighborly conversations. Her name, Emil learned, was Susanna.

Emil persuaded Judit that a cat was the only proper and natural way to control rodents in an old house that was next to a park and had been empty for a long time. His supporting evidence was that each morning, Susanna left at least one partly chewed mouse on the front doormat. She became an essential member of the Kohut's household.

Alf Tidmarsh loved to talk, and as Emil was the only other man on Park Parade who did not go out to work, Alf became a mentor, lending tools and demonstrating how to re-glaze cracked windows. He repaired the coal stove in the front room where the Kohuts spent most of their evenings and he taught Emil how to hang wallpaper.

"When we did the wallpaper in the hall, I noticed your bannisters was rickety," Alf said one day. "You've got a couple of splintered stair rails—a bit dangerous I'd say; especially if you've got people comin' to stay. Come round tomorrer an' I'll show you how to use my lathe. I've got plenty of wood."

With no Mr. Marconi to weave its soporific spell, Emil became an enthusiastic learner, an apprentice of sorts. Alf instructed him in tradesman skills, in British working-class culture (food, greyhound racing, soccer, and pubs), and in the British workman's way of seeing the world (trade unions, bloody foreigners, and Britain's position as a world power and beacon of democracy). For Emil, his work in the continual rehabilitation of 6 Park Parade was like a doctor's prescription. He felt better and stronger—he lost some of his paunch and much of his bitterness.

In spite of Alf Tidmarsh's friendship, Emil and Judit felt more isolated than in London, for there were no delicatessens, cozy cafés, or places where foreigners could mingle and feel comfortable. Dr. Emily had mentioned that other foreigners lived in Cambridge, but she was unaware of any place that acted as a refugee social center.

"This is a fine place to live," Emil said to Judit as they took one of their daily walks along the Cam, "with beautiful university buildings and old streets. We are lucky."

Judit stopped to look at him. "*Apa*, I feel out of place and lonely. Mr. Alf explained to me once that in Cambridge everyone knows their place. The university professors and rich students are at the top, then people like Dr. Emily—and lower down workers like Mr. Alf. I'm not sure we can be happy here."

"We shall see. Making the house nice gives me a good feeling and I enjoy working in the garden.

Judit took his arm. as they ambled along the towpath. "Apart from gardens and boats on the river, I wonder what the English do for pleasure."

"Mr. Alf told me some interesting things," said Emil. "The upper class has their own special sports: golf, riding horses, and tennis parties. They love literature and theater—music much less. The working class prefers dance halls and pubs. Of course, now everyone goes to the cinema."

They stopped to admire the rhythmic precision of eight young rowers perched on a slim wooden shell surging along the river. "There you are," said Emil, pointing. "That kind of rowing is upper class. Working people play bowls and football, bet on horse-racing, and belong to darts clubs in the pubs. I suppose that is where they make friends … in the pubs."

Judit took Emil's arm as they started across the bridge to Logan's Meadow "Ah, yes, friends" She stopped for a moment and looked at him "What about all the people we left in Lučenec. I am afraid to think of what happened to them. Did you know that the women from Dr. Emily's church invited me to join one of their clubs?"

Emil's eyebrows shot upward as he smiled. In the past, Judit had been a sociable woman. "That is nice. You were in many clubs at home. Maybe this is a good sign."

"They called it the Women's Institute. They earn money to buy things for the troops by baking pastries and cakes, and they knit scarves, pullovers and socks. I suppose it is like the Women's Zionist organization I belonged to in Lučenec."

"Nice gesture. So will you join? "

Judit shook her head sadly. "My bad English! I would be ashamed."

Emil put a commiserating arm round her shoulders. "Perhaps later, my dear."

A few days later a letter arrived from Willy. Emil and Judit sat eating hot cabbage soup and bread at a table by the window overlooking the park. A steaming pot of tea, a plate of cookies and two empty cups stood on a tray in the middle. Emil read aloud between noisy mouthfuls.

Ilfracombe, Devon.
Dearest Parents, We have been here three weeks.
This is a seaside town with steep hills and a rocky coastline.
Sophie and Pavel are quite happy here though the weather
is often bad. Soon my unit is moving and once again, I will
have to find a room for Sophie and Pavel. She gets more and
more unsettled by these moves (four since London). I regret
that we made that decision. Gamlingay, where we are going,
for the next three months is very close to Cambridge; it will
be easy to visit you.

Judit looked at Emil, her eyes shining with happy tears. "Willy is coming to a camp near us, *Gott sei dank*. We shall see them soon."

Emil reading on, frowned, flattening the flimsy paper with his fingers. "Always it seems that wrapped inside good news there is bad. Listen."

We have a new problem for Sophie. She is in danger of
being sent to a camp. She has a Czech passport, but she was

*born in Hungary and grew up in Berlin. The new regulations
now put her in the "dangerous alien" category. The refugee board
might decide to change her security rating to "A". High risk!*

Emil slammed his spoon down and shook his head. "This is very
serious, Judit. At the Dorice Café, before we moved, I learned about
those internment camps. Bad conditions, and they keep children,
Jews, and Nazi sympathizers all together. In one place called the Isle
of Man, there are fifty thousand people in one camp. We can't let her
go there. And Willy says nothing about Pavel—what would happen to
him if Sophie is sent to a camp? "

"Read more of the letter, *Apa*.—and put that filthy cat down. I
saw her jump on your lap. You and Mr. Alf both look like tramps
because of her."

*I contacted George for help. Apparently, Dr. Carnegie-Holston
knows all about how to get an internment waiver. That's how
she saved her German cook from a camp. She said it would help
if Sophie found a job. If it is in or near Cambridge could you look
after Pavel while she works? Dr. Emily has offered to meet with us.*

"We will take Pavel, anytime," Judit said as she tore soft white
bread into fragments and dropped them into her soup. Emil saw the
joy in her eyes. "He can help you in the garden and there is the park
opposite and other children to play with. We will take him for walks
along the river." She laughed as she sucked the soup off her spoon.

Emil adjusted his glasses again.

Also we need to arrange a nursery school for him. He's coming

up to five and should be with other children—and learning
to speak proper English. I can send you money to help cover the
costs of food and school—ten shillings a week, that's all I can spare.

"He's right," muttered Emil. "Schooling is very important. The boy has been too much alone with his mother."

"Does Willy say anything else?"

"Let me finish reading. He says … "

After we are settled in Gamlingay, we will come to Cambridge to discuss all this with the doctor and say hello to you. It may be a month or two. Thank you from the bottom of our hearts. A thousand kisses. Willy

Judit smiled over her teacup at Emil. "This is wonderful, *Apa*. Pavel will be with us. He can even have his own room."

"Listen. I'm not quite clear what Willy means. He says he wants us to look after Pavel while Sophie works. Is that just during the day? Or does he mean she stays with us at night and at weekends?"

Judit pushed her chair back, frowning as she put the empty soup bowls and spoons on a tray. "If she comes to live with us, I am afraid things will soon go wrong again. Why did she want to drag the poor child around England, following Willy? Because *she* wanted to be with her husband. She didn't think of the effect on Pavel. She thinks more about herself than the boy. Me, me, me!"

Emil rose and placed his hands on Judit's shoulders as tears coursed down her cheeks. "Enough of this anger, Judit."

"*Apushkam*, here we have all that Pavel needs: no bombs, school and grandparents that love him. Soon he'll be settled and happy. Sophie can visit as often as she likes but she will never stay with us."

Emil released Judit's shoulders and sighed. Most of the time, he had a dutiful wife but, at times she could dig her heels in and was immoveable. "Pavel will be good for us. We can watch him grow and become a *mensch*."

CHAPTER THIRTEEN
Tallard House, Cambridge
May 1941

The village of Gamlingay where Sophie and Pavel had found lodging through one of Dr. Emily's church contacts, lay only eighteen miles from Cambridge. Compared to the other places she and Pavel had recently occupied, Sophie was overwhelmed by the size of the attic room at the vicarage of St. Mary the Virgin. There was no flat ceiling, just a network of solid beams soaring to the roof line. A low wall hid the vicar's stacks of old trunks, boxes and furniture from two single beds, a threadbare carpet, easy chair, table and a large wardrobe with a full length mirror on its door. The doll-house-sized bathroom was one floor down.

Sophie welcomed the view from the dormer window: on one side, a walled graveyard behind the church guarded by giant yews, and on the other, a small apple orchard.

She even had use of the kitchen when the vicar's cook wasn't there. The only real drawback—as the vicar's chatty wife pointed out—was that the roof leaked when it rained. "Trouble is," she said dolefully, "we haven't found the leak yet. Anyway, just use the buckets from the landing to catch the drips. Empty them in the bathroom."

Sophie had reported Pavel and herself as refugee aliens to Gamlingay's solitary policeman, a beefy sergeant who told her—after telephoning some higher authority—that their registration was only temporary. She should check with him twice a week until she was called to attend an official hearing in Cambridge. "We're like parcels being moved around the countryside," she complained to Willy. "We pack and repack, our alien cards get a new stamp and I have to get used to another landlord's rules and whims."

Eventually, Willy wangled a twenty-four hour leave to bring

Sophie and Pavel to Cambridge. Their first step was to visit Dr. Carnegie-Holston to discuss possible ways to deal with threat of Sophie's internment —and then on to his parents to chew over the outcome of the meeting.

The Carnegie-Holston family lived in Tallard House, in the western part of town: a substantial Victorian mansion with a velvet lawn, flowering shrubs and tall sculptural cedars. At the front door, framed by a climbing rose, Sophie bent to inhale the scent of one of the dark red flowers. "Smell this, Pavel darling," she said drawing him close. "Isn't it heavenly?"

On tiptoe, Pavel sniffed and Willy pushed the bell button.

A tall matron with an erect bearing, piercing blue eyes, a long face, and a mass of gray curls opened the door. She wore a blue cardigan and an ankle-length skirt. Half-moon spectacles and a silver cross dangled from her neck. Sophie sensed intelligence and a no-nonsense attitude in her look and demeanor.

"Ah! The young Kohut family," she said in a throaty voice, looking down at Pavel. "And this is your nice little boy." She bent down and gravely shook his hand. "How do you do, young man? I like your eyes, they're like blue searchlights. What's your name?"

Sophie smiled inwardly. This woman appreciated children … a good start.

"How do you do," Willy said. "This is my wife, Sophie, and I am Willy. Pavel is close to five years old."

Pavel's lips parted as if he wanted to say something. He snatched his hand back and glared as the doctor straightened up.

Willy stepped in front of him. "You are Doctor Carnegie-Holston, of course."

She smiled briefly. "Yes, I am she."

Sophie liked how she spoke: a pleasant, lilting accent … different from the Londoners.

"Just call me Dr. Emily. Everyone does. Come in, come in. Hang your coats over there. I'm afraid we're short a maid. I already met your father, Mr. Emil Kohut. A very nice man. I'm glad they're well settled at Park Parade. And young George Kindell filled me in about—Sophie isn't it?—about your camp problem. Come along. We're having tea in the conservatory. We have a guest. He's Czech too."

On the way to the back of the house, the doctor took them past a broad staircase. At the foot of the stairs a snarling black bear, erect on its feet, held a silver letter tray in its paws.

Sophie stopped and looked at its open jaws. A terrifying sight at first, but then she felt pity for the stuffed animal. It seemed so realistically alive.

Pavel, seemingly unperturbed, stroked the hairy coat. He raised himself on tiptoe and pushed Furry Lion onto the tray. "Furry Lion says hello to bear," he said, grinning at Willy and Sophie in turn.

The doctor laughed. "I see your bairn's not frighted. Brave little chap. That's Teddy. My father bagged him in Canada, thirty years ago."

Leaving Furry Lion on Teddy's silver plate, they followed Dr. Emily through rooms filled with sprawling, comfortable furniture. Flower-patterned chintz covered everything—curtains and furniture—and Sophie caught the pervasive scent of beeswax polish.

In the living room, the doctor paused in front of the unlit fireplace, guarded by two sleepy Labradors.

Pavel began stroking the two dogs, letting them lick his face. "Nice dogs," he said in Czech. "Can I play with them?'

Sophie smiled at him, happy that Pavel had lost his shyness so quickly. "Maybe later."

The doctor led them into a glassed-in conservatory filled with tropical plants in pots and hanging creepers where two men, smoking cigarettes and deep in conversation, sat at a bamboo table set close to large glass windows. Behind them, a multi-colored parrot sat on a perch, nibbling on something in its claw.

"Look outside, Pavel—those birds by the big tree," said Sophie, crouching down beside him. She pointed to the cloud of birds circling round a feeder, hanging from the low branch of a massive cedar.

She smiled as Pavel looked at her with bright eyes. "I want to go out and play with the birdies."

"After tea," said Willy soothingly.

"I love birds," said Dr. Emily indicating an assortment of binoculars in leather cases standing on a wickerwork table nearby. "Watching them is one of my greatest pleasures any time of the year. Now, let me introduce you."

They shook hands with Dr. Emily's husband, Dermot, a florid balding man, shorter than his wife. He, in turn, introduced the other guest, a handsome man, heavy-shouldered with piercing gray eyes and straight flaxen hair.

"This is Flight-Sergeant Spaček, from the Czech squadron at RAF Duxford. He's a pilot, one of your countryman. That's where I work, supervising all the aircraft maintenance."

The cloth-covered bamboo table had been set for afternoon tea; a translucent vase of small blue irises graced the center along with a lemon sponge cake. The doctor poured tea and offered finger sandwiches of fish paste, marmite, and sliced cucumber.

Sophie took one bite and then stopped. She looked at Willy with an odd expression. "Strange food," she muttered in French. "Tastes nasty, almost rotten. I can't eat anymore."

"Don't worry. Just leave it."

Astonished, she watched Pavel gobble his way through several sandwiches and two slices of cake.

"Go outside, Papa, please" he said after he polished off a glass of milk.

"He wants to play outside," Willy said. "Is that permissible?"

"Of course. Don't worry about your little chap," Dr. Emily's husband said in a gruff, not unfriendly voice. "Our gardener will keep an eye on him."

"I see from your uniform, Mr. Kohut, that you're in the Pioneer Corps," said Mr. Carnegie-Holston, cradling his cup in both hands. "The dogsbody regiment for foreigners who aren't allowed to carry rifles."

"I was a volunteer with the Free Czechoslovak Army in France. At the moment, I'm being considered for transfer into the Royal Engineers." Willy looked at his countryman. "What about you, Spaček?"

"We are twenty-four Czech pilots at Duxford—310 squadron. Most hardly speak English. We have a British commander."

Willy was impressed. The pilot's English was excellent.

"With the damned Nazis pounding us in Africa, and the Luftwaffe playing havoc here, the British need as many pilots as they can get, even foreign ones." Spaček puffed on a cigarette. "In '39, our army was the best in Europe—but then we gave the country away: a damned tragedy."

With a flushed face, Pavel re-joined them from the garden. "I had fun, maman," he said as Sophie brushed bits of grass off his shirt.

Willy leaned forward, smiling. "Our air force always had superb pilots. Forty of them were evacuated with the troops on my ship. Do you fly Spitfires?"

Spaček waved his cigarette nonchalantly. "Mostly Hawker Hurricanes. We hunt Stukas."

Frowning, Mr. Carnegie-Holston raised his hand. "That's enough gossip, Vitus. Airfield security, remember?" He gave Willy a confidential wink. "Duxford is a high-security zone." He bit off a piece of shortbread and spoke with his mouth full. "Even though all the German and Italian folk who've lived in Britain for years have been sent to camps, there are still plenty of spies tootling around."

Dr. Emily turned to Sophie. "So, tell me, dearie, where are you living now?"

"You will please excuse, my English is not so good," Sophie said as Willy nodded encouragingly. "Pavel and me. We live close to my husband—in rented room."

Dr. Emily patted Sophie's hand. "Ah, a tight family. I like that. You must be happy that your husband's parents live in Cambridge."

Willy smiled at the doctor over his teacup. "With your permission, I wish to come to the point of our visit. In ten days, my wife will attend a hearing at the Cambridge Alien Registration board at Hobson House, St. Andrews Street. They have changed her alien status and we are afraid she will be sent to one of those camps your husband mentioned." He paused. "We are not sure what to do about this."

"Doesn'a sound right to me," said Mr. Carnegie-Holston, frowning. "Tell us a wee bit more. Why are they doing this?"

"She was born Hungarian and grew up in Berlin. With the new regulations, her alien category becomes an "A". If she is interned, it will be devastating for us. Who knows if my boy will also have to stay in the camp?"

Sophie dabbed her nose with a handkerchief. "No camp please."

Doctor Emily stared at both of them, fingering her silver cross. "I would like to do something to help you."

Willy looked hopefully round the table.

Spaček lit a new cigarette from the glowing butt of his last smoke. "This is true. Refugees officially employed by British citizens can avoid internment," he said, blowing a smoke ring. "But at least two British citizens must vouch for them."

Dr. Emily coughed and waved the smoke away. "Listen, Dermot," she said as she picked up the teapot to refill the cups. "It's three weeks since Iris left us. I advertised but that was a waste of time. What if we hired Sophie to take Iris's place: help clean the house, greet my patients, and do some cooking when Helga has her day off?"

Willy remained silent. With the cards plainly on the table, he saw understanding and alarm dawn on Sophie's face. At the same time he was pleased that Dr. Emily had made the suggestion. She was on their side. The big hurdle now was Sophie's acceptance of a menial job. Fearing an outright refusal, he hadn't warned her about this possibility before the meeting. She needed to understand, it was for her own good. Better to earn money as a maid with family living nearby, than languish in a camp.

Mr. Carnegie-Holston wiped his mouth, sprinkling crumbs on the table. "We only hire servants with impeccable references." He shrugged. "One thing I insist on, if you take her on, my dear—nothing is to be touched in my office, not even scraps of paper."

Beaming, Dr. Emily sat back in her chair. "Well that's settled. She'll share a room with Helga."

Willy's heart sank when he saw Sophie's startled expression.

"I am to work here? Share a sleeping room," she said slowly. "I no understand. Who is this Helga?"

"Helga? My cook. She's German. Came to England in '34. Been with me three years. About a month ago, the immigration people wanted to put her in a camp but I got her a waiver, signed the necessary affidavits and guaranteed her wages. She lives here with us." Dr. Emily pointed at the window, smiling. "She feeds the birds for me. The sign of a good cook!"

"I…I will be a *maid*? With a cook?" Sophie exclaimed in French, hoping that no one else there would understand. She stared at Willy."This is so mean of you, *milácku*. You told me we were invited for tea and a discussion about how to avoid my going to a camp. Do you think I can accept being a maid for them, following orders, cleaning and scrubbing? And what happens with Pavel? No talk of that so far."

Willy took her hand, responding in the same language. He had expected such a reaction and was taken aback that she was so distressed. "Listen, *ma chère*, I did it this way to avoid you going to a camp and splitting up the family more than we have to. I was afraid you would refuse to come to the doctor's."

"Hunh! And Pavel? I'm not going anywhere without him." She looked across the conservatory where Pavel was hiding behind a rubber plant in a ceramic pot.

"Will you agree to work here if Pavel stays with you?"

Sophie looked down at her fingers and nodded glumly.

Willy turned to face Dr. Emily, returning to English. "My wife is willing to work for you. But only if Pavel stays here with her."

"Not possible." Mr. Carnegie-Holston snorted, putting his teacup down with a clatter. "I won't have another child in this house. We tried it before. Besides, with a child, she would need her own bedroom. That reduces how many guests we can invite to stay."

The doctor's eyebrows shot up in protest. "Dermot, be reasonable, I—"

Her husband braced his shoulders "No, Emily. Absolutely not. For one thing, I'm not particularly fond of children, and when we housed those church brats a year ago, they damaged our furniture, broke things, and ran all over the place shouting. I couldn't concentrate on my work. Never again. Fine if Mrs. Kohut works for us, lives here, and shares a bedroom with Helga. Eighteen shillings a week, food and bed. But, no child. That's final."

Apart from the clink of china, there was a long moment of silence.

Sophie grabbed Willy's arm. "Is this correct?" French again. "He refuses to have Pavel stay with me?"

Devastated by the man's blunt refusal, Willy's mind buzzed. He sipped his tea, playing for time, trying to think of some other solution. There was none. He looked at Sophie and felt sad for her, caught in the middle of this negotiation. But the most important thing was to save her, and Pavel, from being sent to a camp full of strangers; some even Nazi sympathizers. Thank God, he had asked his parents to house Pavel for a while.

Dr. Emily took Sophie's hand and patted it reassuringly. "If you agree, my dear, you can start here after this coming Monday—I expect Dermot might be willing for us to keep the bairn here for a few days until you have settled in and found a way for your boy to be looked after."

"Well, perhaps, but under strong protest," Mr. Carnegie-Holston grunted, pointedly looking out through the conservatory windows. "He'd better behave as quiet as a mouse."

Willy pushed his plate away, enthused by his host's turnabout. "In which case, if Sophie is able to work here, I can arrange for Pavel to stay with my parents in Cambridge. She'll want to see the boy regularly. She *is* his mother. Once a week, at least, perhaps?"

With a benign smile, Dr. Emily looked up at the ceiling, fingering her cross. "Of course. And he can even come and play in my garden and have fun with the dogs."

Sophie, cheeks burning, hissed at Willy. "What can I say now, *miláčku*. Why did you keep so much from me? "

Willy opened his mouth but Spaček pre-empted him. "I can see your wife is upset, *Pane* Kohut ... but whatever her reason, you should accept the doctor's offer. Avoid the camp."

Dr. Emily stood at the top of the marble doorsteps of Tallard House and shook hands with the Kohuts. She handed Pavel a small packet tied with cotton thread. He was clutching Furry Lion. "Here's some cake for when you get hungry on the train," She smiled at Sophie. "What time will you be here on Monday?"

"Probably, early afternoon," Willy butted in, putting his arm around Sophie's shoulders. He wanted to get her out of there and for this visit to be over. The pieces of his jigsaw plan had come together quite well but he expected recriminations on the way to the station.

"Good. My patients start at five-thirty. We can discuss Sophie's duties when you get here."

"I'm very pleased that our meeting ended this way," Willy said as they walked to the bus stop. "The best result in the circumstances. You'll be safe, you have a paying job, and…" he took her arm and turned her to face him, "you won't have to live with my parents."

She glared. "And I'll be a mother separated from my child?"

"Cheer up. I am also separated from him … by the army."

"You chose to fight. I didn't choose this. You chose it for me."

"Enough now. What is done is done. And there is something else we must do immediately. Call the boy, Paul instead of Pavel. He has to get used to England and the English have to get used to him. He will go to school as Paul. Do you agree?"

Sophie looked away and nodded.

"It's not so bad. You'll see him every week, maybe more often. It is obvious, isn't it, that Dr. Emily has a good heart? Don't you see how lucky we are?"

They were the only ones waiting at the bus stop.

"You are very persuasive," said Sophie with a slight smile. "My complaint is not *what* went on in that house just now, but *how* it all happened, with me knowing so little. This is what you used to do to me in Prague. I don't like it."

Willy sank dramatically to one knee, took her hand and kissed it. "I'm sorry. I'll do better next time."

Pavel watched both of them with curious eyes. "Autobus arriving," he shouted pointing down the street.

As they mounted the bus, Willy congratulated himself. Sophie had acquiesced. Everything would be fine. But he had a strange feeling that the emotional equilibrium between them had shifted slightly. It was like the clatter of tiny pebbles that sometimes foretold a landslide.

CHAPTER FOURTEEN
The Hand Off

July 1941

On the Monday morning that Sophie took Pavel to live with Emil and Judit, she told him as she dressed him that, from now on, he would be staying with Granny and Grandpa. "It's because I have to work at the doctor's house, and, as you won't be there, I have to share a room with Helga, the cook. I'll come to see you at Grandpa's once a week, on my day off. It's only a two mile walk."

Pavel listened silently, eyes wide. "But the doctor's house is big," he said with a hurt look." I can sleep there on the floor or in a cupboard. I want to be with you."

"This is the way it has to be, darling. It will be fun at Grandpa's house. Remember, it's next to the park and close to the river."

It took just over an hour to walk from the doctor's house to 6 Park Parade, carrying Pavel's small cardboard suitcase with Furry Lion tied to the handle. In bright sunshine, they meandered through the city's narrow streets with stops to look in shop windows. There were lines of customers waiting outside the bread and grocery shops and old Market Square was full of produce and second hand clothes stalls. Sophie had come to enjoy the extra bustle of Cambridge's Monday mornings. It reminded her a little of her Old Town neighborhood in Prague but without the smell of roasting sausages

On this occasion, she ignored the invitations of the stall-holders. Her mind was full. She would miss Pavel, but she felt relief as well. She would have some time to herself.

"We were expecting you to bring him two weeks ago," said Judit with a glum face as she led them from the front door into the hallway. "Your note about bringing him only just arrived. I don't like last minute arrangements."

"I'm sorry. I had so much work and you have no telephone." Sophie felt her pulse quicken. Keep calm, Willy had said. She watched Pavel drop his drawstring bag of toys on the floor so he could stroke Susanna who had come to greet him, her tail twitching like a feather duster.

"We were lucky," said Sophie, dumping Pavel's suitcase at the foot of the stairs. "The doctor's husband gave in and let Pavel stay longer than expected." She sniffed the aroma of braised paprika and onions. Judit only cooked in the mornings, but the smell lingered. Her mouth watered. Even if Judit could be irritating, she was a fine cook.

Half an hour later, Judit brought tea to the front room that served as living and dining room. Pavel took Grandpa's cloth bag of dominoes from a shelf and emptied it on to the floor. He started to build a wall around Susanna while she swished her tail and watched him.

"I can't stay long; I have errands for the doctor. I have explained everything to Pavel about staying with you." Sophie fiddled with her teaspoon. "He understands and seems fine with it."

"We shall see how it goes," said Emil gravely.

Sophie reached into her handbag and passed an envelope to Emil. "It's all in here." She looked away. "Instructions from Willy. Pavel's new kindergarten is called the Shrubbery. It is on Barton Road. You don't have to take him. The parents of another boy who goes there own a jam factory. Their van will be here at eight-thirty every weekday to collect Pavel. It has CHIVERS JAMS written on the side. They will bring him back at two."

Emil looked at her over his spectacles and smiled at Judit. "Excellent, daughter."

Sophie warmed to him. She needed someone saying good things to her. Dr. Emily was usually too busy to give compliments and her husband was a grump. "Thank you. Also, I put two pounds in the envelope to cover the first month's school fees. That's my own money," she said, glancing at Judit. "What I earned. It's not from Willy."

Emil put the envelope in his jacket pocket. "I will read this later. Thank you for the money."

Judit leaned forward. "Tell me, daughter, I am curious. Is your work the same as our maids did in Lučenec?"

Sophie nodded, stirring a quarter-spoon of sugar into her tea, wishing that she could add a squeeze of lemon. Tea with lemon was her favorite drink in Prague—there were no lemons now.

"My main job is *hausfrau arbeit*," she said as gaily as she could. "Also, I show the patients into the waiting room where the doctor holds a clinic—they call it a 'surgery' here. I like it because the patients talk with me and so, slowly, I understand English better. And when Helga, the cook, has a day off, I take her place and cook. We are a kind of team."

Emil and Judit exchanged glances.

What are they thinking, Sophie wondered? Good or bad thoughts about me doing maid's work?

Emil polished his glasses. "Does the doctor treat you well?"

Sophie laughed. "Well enough. It is a business arrangement. If I need something, I ask."

"You will learn to speak good English at this house," Judit said, with an approving look. "And this cook, Helga, she is from where?"

Sophie raised her eyebrows. "Would you believe, Berlin?—a good cook by English standards. Dr. Emily prevented her being sent to a camp, just like me. Still, we get on quite well," Sophie said earnestly. "I share a bedroom with her."

"This Helga will teach you to cook."

Sophie looked heavenward. "How many times have I told you, *babička*? I learned to cook in Paris, at the café there. A few days ago, the doctor's husband asked me to cook a French dish. He was very happy with what I did. So I have cooked some more for them."

Judit pinched her lips together as if she didn't approve. "And the doctor's husband. What is he?"

"An engineer. He works at an airfield outside the city."

Emil levered himself out of his chair and brought some brown paper and some colored pencils from the kitchen. He put them on the table. "Leave the dominoes, Pavel. You are getting Susanna annoyed. Draw something for me instead."

Pavel rose to his feet and fingered the pencils. "Draw what?"

"How about birds in a tree?" Sophie asked him with a fond smile.

Pavel grinned. "Not a tree. I draw … a Spitfire with guns." He flattened the paper on the table and bent to his task.

Judit watched her grandson intently. "So, daughter. When you take Pavel from us on your day off, what will you do with him?"

"Oh! I don't know. This and that. The lady doctor says Pavel can spend time with me at her house—as long as her husband isn't there. Her children are grown, but their playroom is still full of toys and a rocking horse. The garden is lovely and their gardener always asks Pavel to help him. I'll come to you every Thursday after school and bring him back after an early supper."

"That is well done." Emil looked at Pavel's drawing "Now is this plane on the ground or in the air?"

"In the sky, Grandpa."

"So, put in some clouds and draw another plane chasing it."

"He must take his lunch every day," said Sophie said. "He gets vitamins at the school. Rosehip syrup and cod liver oil."

"There is something I must tell you before we talk anymore," Emil interjected, hooking thumbs around his braces. "We agreed with you and Willy to take the boy for four months, perhaps longer. But we have had news from London. They will soon start repairing our

Northways flat. It will be ready sometime early next year. Then we will go back. Cambridge is a beautiful place, but not for us."

Sophie jerked upright. "Oh, no, Father. Not after all the work you put into this place." Her mind raced. If Emil and Judit left Cambridge, what on earth would she do with Pavel? The pit of her stomach hollowed out. Keeping Pavel with her would mean leaving Dr. Emily and looking for some other job. Another desperate thought struck her. "Has Willy suggested you take Pavel to London with you?"

Emil leaned back in his chair. "He knows nothing about our plans. But we would never keep the boy away from you. As for working on this house, we did just enough for the place to feel a little bit comfortable. No more."

Judit wiped her hands on her apron. "Cambridge is too English for us. Mr. Tidmarsh next door and Dr. Emily are nice, but others are not so friendly." She looked questioningly at Emil, as if for approval. "We prefer the place where we know the foods and where people understand us."

"I finished my drawing, Maman. I want to play in the park."

"I can see you made a very good drawing. And yes, we can go to the park. But first, I have to finish talking to your Grandpa and Granny about how long you are staying with them."

Pavel's face darkened. His mouth recast itself into an ugly twist and he swung his legs violently, kicking the table leg and shaking the cups and saucers. With each kick, Judit blinked or flinched, but she said nothing, compressing her lips.

"I don't want to stay here anymore," he said, his voice suddenly whiny. He kept on kicking. "I want to go to the river and catch a fish."

Sophie glared. "Not now, *Pavelko*." She had feared something like this would happen.

"Enough with those kicking feet," roared Emil slamming the table with his hand. "If you can't behave, there will be no park or anything else for you." He got up, pulling the boy and his chair away from the table.

Pavel dived for the floor and lay there spread-eagled on his back. He started to roll from side to side. "Park, park, park, park… park," he shouted, eyes flickering. His heels drummed the floor. "Park, park, park." Judit rushed into the hallway with her hands over her ears and then peered back as if unable to resist watching how the drama would unfold.

Sophie sprang from her chair, grimacing at the wet patch visible at the front of Pavel's corduroy shorts. A voice in her head hissed—these old people will never manage him. "Stop this, Pavel, I beg you."

"Judit," Emil shouted, his gaze fixed on the raging boy. "Fetch me a blanket."

Within seconds, and with remarkable dexterity and strength, the old man had rolled Pavel inside the blanket and put him across his knee like a wriggling parcel. "You can shout and scream all you like, young man," he said gruffly. "I won't let you out until you stop showing off."

Sophie was at first alarmed that Pavel might suffocate, but seeing how well immobilized he was she felt admiration for Emil. He had done this before … perhaps with Willy when he was small and had tantrums.

Judit stood in the doorway, hands on her hips. Her face was calm, almost decisive. "Time for you to leave, daughter" she said, raising her voice above Pavel's whines and groans. "This display of temper happens because he is spoiled. When you have gone, he will calm down."

"How dare you say I've spoiled him?"

"I've seen you. You let him do what he likes."

"School will do him good," Emil grunted as the living parcel twisted on his knees.

Sophie looked out of the window again, swallowing her anger. She wanted to explain how hard it was to have Pavel demanding attention day-in, day-out, wetting himself—and how, ever since they'd left France, she had been worn down with loneliness. But she had neither the time nor the courage. And, looking after him, well … they would soon find out how hard it could be.

Helplessly, Sophie watched Paul squirm and complain inside the blanket. "You see—how difficult he can be," she muttered.

Judit shook her head. "Don't expect sympathy, daughter. You chose to follow your husband around England. Now you pay the price. It is better you leave. "

Sophie made for the front door, grabbed her coat and bags from the standing rack and opened the door. "Why should I expect sympathy from you? You know nothing about what I've been through," she shouted. "I followed my husband from camp to camp because I wanted to be a good wife and mother—and so Willy could see his son. All I can say now is that there are two things you will no longer get from me, obedience and respect."

As she slammed the front door behind her, she heard Pavel shouting. "I want to go to the park!"

Sophie marched, teeth clenched, from Park Parade to Bridge Street, carrying her empty shopping bags. Her head throbbed until gradually her anger subsided.

Using the Carnegie-Holston's ration books, she bought three pounds of cod at Mac Fisheries in Falcon Yard and five pounds of potatoes and two cabbages at the greengrocers. She went on to Heffers bookstore to buy the current issue of PUNCH, Mr. Carnegie-Holston's favorite magazine. He kept old copies stacked by the toilet seats of Tallard House and reread them while he sat there, laughing at the cartoons. Occasionally, Sophie would borrow a copy to learn new English words. But she never saw anything she could call amusing.

Waiting to pay at the counter, she felt a tap on her shoulder. A tall, stooped, gaunt-faced man in a well-cut suit smiled at her. Tired eyes and stained teeth. "Remember me. *Paní Kohutová*?" he said in Czech. "I remember you very clearly." He doffed his trilby.

She felt a frisson of familiarity. She knew him, but from where exactly? It had to be before England. Yes, got it ... on the SS Northern Fen, the refugee ship she sailed on from Sète to Gibraltar. She decided to play it dumb even though she knew who he was. "Do I know you?"

He took her elbow—rather too firmly, she thought. "Let me jog your memory, *Paní*. Do you recall the SS *Northern Fen*? I was one of the soldiers responsible for dealing with the Spanish Guardia Civil. You must remember? That was when your husband's buddy, Sergeant Kukulka, caught a bullet. You were right next to him." He gave her a wolfish grin. "I am Leopold Povídka, Ex-Commissar, International Brigade." He saluted and bowed from the waist. "Most interesting that we happened to meet here. I must say you are just as appetizing as I remember."

Like turning on a light switch, Sophie recalled the episode. She remembered him boasting of how he fought bravely in Spain. But then, after Franco prevailed, he and other communist comrades escaped across the Pyrenees and joined the remnants of the Czechoslovak army. He and a thug called Serbin had been billeted in the same French village as the Kohuts. Povídka was a dangerous man—Willy's exact words.

What the hell is he doing here?

She engineered a half-smile. "This *is* a strange coincidence, Mr. Povídka. But, please excuse me, I'm in a hurry. I can only talk for a minute. What are *you* doing here?"

Povídka kept hold of her elbow. "Political business. I'm a

civilian now. I work for a newspaper. Where is your husband?"

Sophie pulled her arm away. "Why do you want to know?"

"He owes me a favor. Actually, several."

"He is in the British Army." Povídka's face was close enough for her to see that his irises were yellowy-green.

"I need to get in touch." He held out tobacco-stained fingers. "His address—please?"

Sophie's antennae were on full alert. She would reveal as little as possible to this man until she talked to Willy. "I'm sorry, he just moved camp. I'm not sure where it is."

Povídka grabbed her shoulders and brought his face close. His breath smelled of onions. She jerked back. He held her fast.

Sophie caught a glimpse of other shoppers looking at them curiously. She had to get away. Speaking a foreign language in public could lead to an arrest by the police. "Let me go. People are looking at us," she hissed. "Willy is in the Royal Engineers. That's all I know."

Povídka released her and stepped back. "And what about you? Where do you live? I remember, you have a little boy. We should meet for a long chat."

Was this a veiled threat? Hands shaking, Sophie gathered her bags. "I have no wish to chat with you, *Pane* Povídka. Goodbye and please do not follow me."

He laughed. "Off you go then, pretty woman. But trust me. I will keep looking for Willy. He owes me a big favor."

CHAPTER FIFTEEN
Unsettled Times
March 1942

All through the winter, Emil and Judit had faced more challenges than they expected; having to call their grandson Paul instead of Pavel, and then cope with the cascade of illnesses he acquired from his classmates at The Shrubbery School: chicken pox, scarlet fever, ear infections, and bronchitis. He spent many weeks in and out of bed, lovingly nursed by Judit. Now, in March, he had the measles and coughed ceaselessly, spitting up yellow mucus.

At the height of Paul's fever, Emil left a message at Tallard House asking Dr. Emily to make a house call.

When she arrived, Paul was in bed, the grandparents hovering around him.

"The poor bairn has a wee touch of pneumonia, but he should recover fine" said the doctor after listening to the boy's chest and folding up her stethoscope. She pointed to the scar below his jaw. "With his story of surgery for a TB gland in France, I wanted be sure his lungs were clear."

Emil nodded. "You say he has pneumonia. What if it is TB? Why not take an X-ray?"

"That's verra expensive, he's not ill enough. If he gets worse, let me know. Otherwise bring him to see me when the rash fades. I'll check that all is well."

Two weeks later, Emil brought Paul to Dr. Emily's clinic. Sophie, in her dual role as maid and mother, showed them into the waiting area where three other patients were coughing and sniffling. "It is first come, first serve. Paul will be the last one she'll see before the surgery closes," she whispered to Emil. "I'm busy in the dining room. I'll come later, when Dr. Emily has finished."

"The bairn's doing fine," Dr. Emily said to Emil with a satisfied smile when she finished examining Paul's ears and listening to his chest. "But before Sophie joins us, I'd like him to stay outside with her for a few minutes. I want a word with you alone."

The doctor led Paul out through the door, and Emil heard her talking to Sophie in the hallway. He polished his glasses wondering what the doctor wanted.

He looked around the cluttered office—so this was how an English doctor worked: an open roll-top desk bulging with medical folders, an old leather examination couch pushed against the wall, a glass cabinet full of old-looking instruments, and a tall bookcase of gold-lettered textbooks. A Swiss cuckoo clock, looking out of place Emil thought, showed the same time as his wristwatch. All very similar to Dr. Horváth's office in Lučenec except for the embroidered silk panel hanging on one wall, the words picked out in gold thread: **Our Father Which Art In Heaven, Hallowed Be Thy Name.** Watercolors and photographic enlargements of birds were positioned on either side. Incomprehensible … how could Dr. Emily, a medical scientist, believe that it was God who created nature and man?

"The bairn's helping his mother in the dining room," said the doctor bustling back into the room holding a mug of tea. She gave him a broad, reassuring smile.

A female express train, Emil concluded, watching the doctor press her long frame into the creased leather armchair in front of her desk. She swept aside a pile of folders and prescription pads and put down the tea. "They'll be a while—Sophie and Helga that is—setting the table in the dining room. We have guests for dinner." She took a sip.

"So—about Pavel. We do not need to worry?"

"Pavel? You mean Paul, don't you?" The doctor fiddled with her silver bracelet and stared at him. "It's better for him that we're consistent with his name, don't you think? Anyway though he's better, he's lost a fair bit of weight. The rash will fade soon." She glanced at the front of a cardboard pocket folder. "I see from his record Paul will be six years old in June."

Emil nodded.

"How has he been getting on with both of you in Park Parade?"

Emil loosened his shoulders. Good ... there was nothing serious. "He is happy except his shame with the bed-wetting. Almost every night and still sometimes in the day. It is tiring work for my wife, all that washing, and trying not to punish him. Also, he has missed much schooling. But we are pleased to have him with us. He is our pleasure."

Dr. Emily put down the folder. "Sophie tells me that he's very shy at school," she said after a moment. "The other boys make fun of his accent."

Emil shrugged. "To be expected. He will adapt. He is already used to his new name. But for my wife and me, it is not so easy. We often forget to say Paul."

She peered over her spectacles. "I'm sorry to ask such personal questions but Sophie tells me you will soon return to London—permanently. Have you given notice to your landlord, the Ely Diocese, about leaving the house?"

"Yes, I warned them. Our flat in London is almost ready. But first, I have to check that it is in good condition. Luckily, the night-time bombing in London is much less now. They say there is still a risk here in Cambridge."

The doctor heaved a sigh. "The Germans think they can destroy our morale by bombing our beautiful towns and cathedrals." She looked up at the wall hanging, moving her lips silently and leaned forward, her chair creaking. "So what happens to Paul when you return to London? He can't stay here with his mother. My husband won't allow it. Has she talked to you?"

He shook his head. "My son Willy is still not sure what to do with him. I … I suppose we could take him to London with us."

The doctor nodded sagely. "Yes, well, Sophie will be joining us in a jiffy. She wanted me involved in discussing the bairn's future."

With a fierce stare, Emil jerked upright. "You—you—wish to discuss Pavel's *future* with us?" His thoughts skittered. *This woman is using her position to interfere in my family.* "With respect, doctor, I brought Pavel here for a medical reason, not a family interrogation."

Dr. Emily swung round in her chair to face him. "I agreed to help Sophie and her husband make a decision about Paul. At the moment, neither of his parents is in a position to care for him properly."

The desk telephone rang. She swung back and shouldered the handset, pencil in hand. She glanced at Emil. "A moment please. It's the hospital laboratory."

While the doctor talked on the telephone, Emil reflected on the rewarding months that Pavel had lived with them. Judit adored him. The boy was sensible and well-behaved except for his bed-wetting and an occasional explosion of temper. He had adapted to school, was fluent in English, and had accepted seeing his mother just once a week. A reserved child on the surface. I was the same at his age, Emil thought.

Dr. Emily put down the receiver and continued writing notes— while at the same time she skimmed the pages of what looked like a medical textbook, as if she was searching for something. She looked up and gave Emil a wintry smile. "Sorry, just a bit longer."

Emil shrugged and pulled the *News Chronicle* out of his pocket. He glanced at the headlines. U-boats were sinking British and American cargo ships all over the Atlantic. The rumor that trainloads of Jews and gypsies were being gassed at a place called Auschwitz was no longer a rumor. It was a fact.

There was a knock. "Come," Dr. Emily called out, still writing.

Sophie wore a cotton floral dress covered by a starched pinafore, a white nurse's cap over her short black hair, and pull-on slippers. "I sent Paul to play in the garden. I don't know how long he'll stay out there."

She sat down, hands folded.

Emil straightened his shoulders, jaw set in reproach. He frowned. "I was not expecting the doctor to interfere in our family affairs," he said to her in Czech. "Why did you ask her to do this?"

Sophie responded in English. "Father, the doctor and I have something to tell you. Now that you will soon move back to London, Willy and I talked seriously. We have decided to send Paul to the countryside."

"*Gott behüte*," Emil exclaimed, half-rising from his chair. His cheeks were red, chin quivering. "What do you mean *countryside*?" he said, waving an angry hand in the air. "And why is this doctor in the *gemisch*?"

Sophie again replied in English, glancing at the doctor. "Countryside means he will live far from Cambridge, far from London, far from the bombs—Paul will live with other children on a farm." She smiled. "It is a good solution."

Emil collapsed back into his chair and looked from one woman to the other. A sudden sense of loss welled up. He felt close to tears. He and Judit would miss Pavel's chirpy presence and disruptions. "Aie, why do you do this now? Why did you not discuss this first with me and Judit? "

Sophie cleared her throat. "Willy and I went round in circles. This is why we asked Dr Emily for her opinion. She cares for many families. She knows what children need. "

Dr. Emily's face was somber. "I must take some responsibility for this turn of events, Mr. Kohut. I admit I encouraged them to consider moving Paul to the countryside."

Emil's face darkened. "I think you do too much with my family. Sophie should have come to us first. My son mentioned nothing about this in his letters. We may have our differences but this kind of decision is what a family is for."

"Well, Sophie and Willy asked for my help," the doctor said frowning. Her cheeks flushed. She cleared her throat, dabbing a handkerchief to her lips. "Perhaps, it's best, Mr. Kohut, if I discuss Paul's situation from the perspective of a qualified English person who knows him well and has his welfare at heart."

Emil felt a hammering in his ears. He stared at Sophie. It felt like a betrayal of trust, and he feared Judit's reaction when she found out. "So, please, I am waiting. Tell me what is best," he stuttered, trying to control his anger. "Because from what has just happened here, it seems we grandparents do not know what is best."

"Very well." Dr. Emily smoothed her skirt over her knees. "I can see you are angry but that can't be helped," she said with a sharp nod. "What is best is to keep Paul completely away from the bombing. Being on a farm is an ideal solution."

Emil raised a hand.

Sophie frowned at him. "Please wait, Father."

Dr. Emily took a deep breath. "Sophie is required by alien regulation law to stay in my employ. If she leaves and breaks the board ruling, she will again be a refugee with an 'A' category rating. You know what that means. A camp."

Emil stared. "So?" In that angry moment, he did not care if Sophie and Paul went to a camp or not.

"On top of everything else," the doctor continued, "Sophie tells me that your son Willy is to be transferred to a military depot in

Scotland, seven or eight hours away on the train. That means he will hardly ever see Paul."

Emil frowned. "Scotland? I did not know this. But why must the boy go to complete strangers in the countryside? He can come back to London with us."

"London is still being bombed and Willy and I agreed that this is a chance for Paul to live with an English family." Sophie's voice quavered. "He will learn their way of speaking and doing things. If he lives with you and Judit, he will grow up different from English children."

Emil closed his eyes, massaging his lips with the tip of a forefinger. He had seen the misery in Sophie's eyes. A long minute passed.

Dr. Emily lit a cigarette and inhaled, picking flecks of tobacco off her tongue.

"Knowing my son," Emil said trying to shift the bitterness out of his voice. "I suspect you already have a specific plan for Pavel. Let me hear what it is."

Sophie pulled an envelope from her apron pocket, but kept it on her lap. "Willy talked with someone at the SSAFA office in London. They place children in the countryside. We were given the name of a farming family. Good-hearted people. Already they house evacuee children; a woman looks after them. We want Paul to go there. It is in Shrop ... shire."

"Shropshire," Emil grunted. "Where is that? And you wish to put my grandson in a place where he knows NOBODY? And what about his wetting? They will be cruel to him." He could already hear Judit's plaintive words.

"I agree this is a hard situation for your family," said the doctor. "But the same thing is happening to thousands of children all over Britain. Some are even being sent to Canada and Australia on their own."

Emil leaned forward abruptly. "How can you do this without any idea of what it is like on this farm?"

"We do know something, Father," Sophie continued. "Remember when Willy and I took Paul away for three days, after his bronchitis? In February. We visited the farm, a lovely place far from any town. We saw the other children there. They live with a kind of governess in a cottage. They have good, fresh food. It's a country paradise owned by an aristocratic family, Sir Edward and Lady Hilliard. Lady Hilliard said she would take Paul as soon as there was an opening." She looked anxiously at Emil. "You see, we made sure the place was good."

"Hunh." Emil frowned. For at least a month they had been hiding this plan from him and Judit. "So Paul was with you when you visited. How did he react?"

"Excited. He says he would like it there. He would be with the other children and play with the farm animals. Dr. Carnegie-Holston says that the farm will help him become English. Why should we keep feeding him Czechoslovak culture? The Nazis have destroyed it."

Emil went to the window, hands clasped behind his back, and looked at the gravel driveway and the trim lawns, trying not to think of his losses and his narrow escape from the Hungarian fascists. On the lawn, the doctor's gardener was pushing a wheelbarrow full of grass towards a mound of cuttings—on top of which sat Paul waving his arms, his face split by a wide grin. His grandson was resilient, an enjoyer.

He looked hard at Sophie and raised both arms in the air as if witnessing a tragic *fait-accompli*. "So ... what can we do? We are only the grandparents." He paced the room, shooting glances at the women. "Perhaps you are correct. It is just that we love him, and it is painful to send him away."

"This is very difficult for everyone, Mr. Kohut," Dr. Emily said, patting him on the shoulder. "But the war is not going well, and we have to do what we think is best for our children."

Emil nodded. "But this must not be a short arrangement, not less than six months. More than anything, he needs a strong, steady framework to his life, away from fear and crisis." He raised a patriarch's finger. "But you must understand the implications of your decision, daughter."

"What, for example?"

Putting his hands in his pockets, Emil thought for a moment about the Judaic rituals laid out in the Torah, the Shabbat greeting and wearing the Kippah, traditions and beliefs that he had rejected all his life. He thought about the loss of his home and country—and his fear that Britain would soon be overwhelmed. But, if the course of the war changed, and the Allies defeated Hitler, Pavel would grow up in Britain. He sighed. "On that farm, Pavel—I mean Paul— he will start to forget us. At least he should know where he came from and why."

*   *   *

After saying goodbye to Paul and Emil, Sophie hurried back to the kitchen to help Helga with preparations for the Carnegie-Holston's dinner party. She felt shaky and her pulse raced. Standing up to her father-in-law had been hard, but she was relieved that Emil had finally accepted the decision to send Paul away.

The Tallard House kitchen was old-fashioned. A coke-fed iron cooking range took up most of one wall. Floor-to-ceiling cupboards were full of mixing bowls and china, copper pans hung on the walls, and a large pine table stood in the middle surrounded by ladder-back chairs. Sophie loved this warm room with its green tiles veneered by the smoke of roasts and pies. Helga told lots of stories from Berlin where they had both grown up; working in tandem with her was stimulating and relaxing.

"What happened when you told your father-in-law about sending Paul away?" Helga asked as she scrubbed dirt off the potatoes.

"He was very upset, but eventually he agreed," Sophie said as she laid out plump naked pigeons on a cutting board. She was always surprised at how Helga never seemed to mind being relegated to food preparation.

"So what was decided?" The potatoes Helga was preparing were covered with shoots and black eyes. She threw a pile of peelings into a pail.

"Paul goes to the farm. Willy has been transferred to a camp somewhere in Scotland."

"So, your family will be split three ways," Helga persisted. "Why did your husband have to go up there? He should be with his family, don't you think?"

Sophie tried to hide her irritation. She might not feel as close to Willy these days, but she was proud of his promotion. Willy was about to become a British Army non-commissioned officer, a lieutenant corporal, earning twenty shillings a week plus two extra shillings for being married. As an army wife with a child she received thirty-two shillings a week. With no expenses for food and lodging, she was saving money.

"He'll be training up there as a Royal Engineer. He says the engineers do everything except fire guns, drive tanks and fight in hand-to-hand combat."

"What do you mean?" Helga laughed. "What is everything?"

"Well, um." For a moment, Sophie stopped stuffing the inside of a pigeon with breadcrumbs and herbs and tried to remember what Willy had written. "They build roads and bridges, repair trucks, and railway lines—and move heavy equipment. They even make maps, I think."

Helga laughed as she finished slicing the potatoes. "Your husband does all that? What a talent."

Sophie shook her head. "Don't be silly. Helga. He's only learning one thing in that camp; it's what he calls transportation logistics."

Helga wiped her hands on her apron and tipped the potatoes into a large pan of water. "So, dear colleague," she said. "When will Paul go to the farm?"

Standing at the kitchen table, chopping up cauliflower Sophie still wasn't sure how she felt about Paul going away. Was it callous to send your own boy away? The doctor had encouraged it. Paul was going to safety and would be with other children, but would there be anyone at the farm to hug him when he needed it? And how much she would miss his liveliness and affection.

"When there is an opening. At least another two months. We hope it will be in May when my in-laws leave for London. If they don't agree to take him, I'm not sure what we'll do with him." Sophie wiped tears off her face with the back of her hand. "Perhaps, he'll live with my in-laws in London where I can't travel to visit him … or we end up in an internment camp, after all."

Sophie was too wary and private to share her marital concerns with the German spinster, but often, when they talked, Sophie's thoughts ran helter-skelter behind the conversation. Since arriving in England, she had pretended to enjoy sex with Willy, tried to show that she still loved him—more than anything for Paul's sake. She had blamed her reluctance on the horrible tensions of their escape and the frequent separations, but if truth be told, she now found his mannerisms and, sometimes, even the scent of his body distasteful.

The past couldn't be undone. The world had changed and the Kohut family with it. Her marriage was now more like a tacit arrangement in which each partner was on a divergent path. She was trapped at Tallard House while Willy forged ahead in the British Army. He was leaving his role as husband and father behind. She didn't know what to do about it.

CHAPTER SIXTEEN
Queen's Gate, London
June 1942

In the early afternoon of June 16, Paul's sixth birthday, Dr. Emily's gardener drove Sophie, Paul, and two friends from his school to Scudamore's Boats on the River Cam.

It was the perfect outing: a warm sun with cottony clouds in a sapphire sky. No one fell into the river in spite of the boys scrambling to change places in the punt, and arguing over the use of a small fishing net Sophie had scavenged from Mr. Carnegie-Holston's garage. As she watched Scudamore's young man use his pole to slide the punt past the peaceful college back lawns, she had second thoughts about their countryside plan for Paul. Would it really be good for him to live on a farm? Or had she and Willy decided on this because asking Emil and Judit to take Paul to London was the only other option?

After the outing, she took Paul to his grandparents for a tea that included a layered hazelnut cake; a concoction that had necessitated Judit's visit to Cambridge's best provisioner and used up many ration coupons.

Halfway through the meal, with Sophie watching, Emil went to the couch eased a brown paper parcel from behind one of the cushions, and returned to the table. "A birthday present from your papa," he said a gold filling glinting inside his warm smile. "He sent it all the way from Scotland."

"Gosh, how super," said Paul, his mouth still full of cake as he reached for it. Emil hung onto the parcel for a few more seconds and waved a stern finger "Finish eating first ... now undo the string properly and don't rip the paper. No waste in this house, remember?"

Sophie nodded agreement. Dr. Emily hewed to the same parsimonious principle.

After some careful unwrapping, Paul opened a cardboard box and pulled out a toy deer, covered in hide. It had wooden antlers and brown glass eyes. His face crumpled. "Why did Papa send *this*, Mama?" he said, dejectedly turning the toy over in his hands. "It doesn't *do* anything."

"Hmm." Emil polished his glasses, tilting his head as if he was considering the situation carefully. "You could take it to the park and make up a game that you are saving it from the hunters."

Paul's eyebrows twitched and his lips clamped tight. "It just stands there."

Sophie had a feeling that the birthday party was beginning to unravel. "Papa sent you a card with the parcel," she said encouragingly, picking an envelope off the floor.

Paul tore it open. His face brightened. He showed her the photograph of a castle with writing inside. "Does Papa live in that castle with other soldiers?"

"Quite possible," Emil grunted, looking over the boy's shoulder.

"Come on, *Pavličku*, read what Papa says," Judit pleaded.

Emil nodded. "The teacher said your reading is almost as good as the English boys."

Nervously, Sophie watched Paul's face as he stumbled through the words.

> *My Dearest Paul, Happy Birthday. I'm very sad I can't be with you now that you are six and doing so well at school. This toy is made from a real deer that was shot by hunters. My camp is very close to the fine castle in the photo.*

Paul pushed the deer away. "A toy castle with soldiers would be better." He put the card down. "I don't want to read this anymore."

Judit frowned. "No more cake if you don't obey Grandpa."

Sophie gave her mother-in-law a leave-him-alone look. "I'd better read the rest."

I wanted to get you something better to play with but there
are no good toy shops here. In fact there's not much to do
here for us soldiers except work. Our camp is close to
Glasgow, a big port where they build navy ships with lots
of guns. Next time I come, I'll bring you a model boat.
A thousand kisses. Papa
P.S. No need to send a thank you. We are not allowed
to receive mail during training.

Paul stared, angry eyebrows knitted together. "When will Papa come back?"

Willy had done his best. She tried to keep her voice calm, not wanting to show her disappointment. "I don't know when Papa will be here. He sent the little deer because he loves you."

"Alright, I'll keep it." Paul looked expectantly at his grandparents sitting at the table. "Do you know Mummy and me are going to London? A nice lady there is taking me on the train to the farm where I'll live."

With a muffled groan Judit turned away, covering her face with her apron. Emil stood behind Paul's chair, resting his hands gently on the boy's shoulders. "We know that already. But are you still very sure you want to go and live far from us on that farm?"

Paul blinked as he picked up the toy deer and prodded his piece of cake with its antlers. "This is a him isn't it? I think I'll take him, after all—and Furry Lion."

"We've talked enough about the farm," Sophie said, tight-lipped.

"Willy is in full agreement." She wanted to leave … now. She felt dizzy and couldn't think properly. Paul leaving was like ripping a bright flower from its stalk. And there was too much distress floating around the table. If she so much as looked Judit in the eye, she knew she would burst into tears.

"It's been decided," she said. "He's looking forward to it." Trembling, she pulled Paul close and kissed him. "We've had a nice day, *miláčku*. It's time for me to go back to the doctor's house." Sophie took Paul's hand. "Thank you, Emil and Judit for a delicious tea party. Paul will see me to the door."

Farewell kisses for the in-laws were no longer expected or given.

*   *   *

A week after Paul's birthday, Sophie received a letter.

Soldiers, Sailors and Airmen's Forces Association
23, Queen Anne's Gate   June 19 1942
Westminster, S.W.1.

Dear Mrs. Kohut,
    Reference: Request by Corporal Vilém Kohut, (Royal Engineers) for rural placement of his son, Pavel, now known as Paul.
    I am responding to an earlier request (April 17, 1942) by Cpl. W. Kohut and his wife to have their son, Paul, placed with a family in the countryside. The prospective host family we identified in Shropshire is now ready to accept Paul on their farm. Attached is the Deed of Responsibility which assigns care of the child to Mrs. Hilliard, to be signed by at least one of the parents. The deed drawn up by Mrs. Hilliard states that she will maintain and educate Paul but indemnifies her, her servants, or employees against any damages in the event of illness, injury, or disablement.
    Mrs. Hilliard will be in London on June 28 to collect another

little boy to join her group of evacuated children living on the farm. She wishes to take Paul back with her. This will save you the cost and effort of traveling to Shrewsbury. Bring Paul to this office at noon. (6.28.42)

Please bring in a suitcase the following:
Wellington boots if possible. 1 pr, boy's plimsolls, or sandals, trousers, Mackintosh, Pullover, 1 pr. Pajamas, 2 shirts, 2 vests, 2 underpants, 2 pr. socks, 3 handkerchiefs, 1 toothbrush, a towel and a favorite toy. Also, his ration book, national registration card and gas mask.

Be sure that he has no skin infection (impetigo) or louse infestation. Lady Hilliard insists that Paul be able to dress himself, use a toilet and sit properly at a table when eating meals.

Our office will also facilitate the payment to Mrs. Hilliard of the usual government weekly allowance of 8 shillings 6 pence for evacuated children.

Yours Truly
William Landrieu, Captain, Secretary.

The letter's instructions were clear and specific, and Sophie was confident she could get everything organized in ten days. She got permission from Dr. Emily to take the appropriate day off and accompany Paul to London, and she asked Emil and Judit to pack a suitcase, following the directions in the SSAFA letter. But in spite of being pleased that the plan she and Willy had concocted was working smoothly, Sophie couldn't concentrate on her tasks at Tallard House. She lost her appetite and had stomach spasms at night—indigestion, the doctor said, and prescribed milk of magnesia.

As soon as she could, Sophie visited the Borough Police Station in St. Andrew Street to complete their applications for travel permits. She had the official SSAFA letter, a supportive note from Dr. Emily and enough money for taxi rides and the train fare back from London.

The jowly, alien registration official at the police station skimmed her application, rubbing his chin and frowning at the same time. He had smiled at her when she first sat down: a kind face, Sophie thought. Now he avoided looking at her.

With an embarrassed cough, he turned her file around, and pointed to the large, smudged black B in the upper right corner. "See that B, madam. That's your new refugee rating. The C's been crossed out."

Sophie jerked forward. "But … I was given a C rating when we arrived. Why is it gone? No one told me this."

"Listen, missus. I just follow the regulations. A "B" rating indicates a moderate security risk. There's a new note in your file. Says you grew up in Berlin. That's the reason, I s'pose." He drew in a deep breath. "It means that on no account can you travel out of this jurisdiction."

Sophie gasped. "I have to take my son to London next week. He will live on a farm far from the bombing." Her heart thumped erratically. "What shall I do now?"

The official held up his hand, avoiding her eyes. "Listen, lady. I'm sorry. All you can do is submit an appeal to central office. That can take a while. Shall I give you an appeal form?"

With her heart still pounding, Sophie pulled out the note Dr. Emily had written, just in case there was a problem. "Please, officer. Read this. From my employer who is a doctor here. On June 28, my little boy goes from London to a farm. I have to hand him to…" She looked down at her letter. "Lady Hilliard."

The officer adjusted his spectacles and read the note. He gave Sophie a wry smile. "Doctor Carnegie-Holston is well-known in town, but I can't help you. Your application is denied. Find someone else to take your kid to London."

Sophie trembled. She could hardly get up from her seat. The officer's face was a blur. "Thank you," she said automatically as her mind went into confused overdrive. Trying to get hold of Willy for his guidance was out of the question: not enough time, too far away, and no telephone number. It was only as she was walking away from the police station, trying to clear her head that the solution came to her: Emil would take Paul to London! But she didn't have the courage to go to his home and beg for help … not with Judit there.

She arranged to meet Emil on neutral ground at the Lyons Café and Confectioners in the center of Cambridge: one of a chain of cafes whose décor included white tiled walls, self-service counters, an aroma of frying fat, and waitresses with frilly caps. The café was always busy with women gossiping over tea and men stocking up with buns or cake as they studied the greyhound racing and football results.

Sophie sat at a table by the window, shopping bags at her feet. She smiled hopefully at Emil as he sat down and ordered tea. "Extra hot, please," he said, after hooking his umbrella handle over the back of his chair.

"Ugh!" he mouthed taking a first sip. "Lukewarm, and as usual it tastes of dishwater. I don't understand why the English are so famous for their tea." He glared at Sophie as if she were to blame. "I prefer the tea at the Waffle Café. Why didn't you come to my house for this talk?"

Sophie, sensing his irritation, shrugged an "it-can't-be-helped" apology for choosing the meeting place. She answered in Czech. "It was easier for me here. Close to the shops. I have to buy groceries for the doctor … and, er … well; Judit always makes it hard for me."

"So, why am I here, daughter? We have already prepared Pavel's suitcase as you asked. Do you know which exact day he leaves? Your note said this was important. I can tell you are nervous." He pointed a gnarled finger at the cigarette Sophie had pulled from its pack. "And…put that *dreck* away."

Not wanting to irritate him, Sophie carefully put the unlit cigarette away. She had wanted to calm her nerves. "I heard from the SSAFA office. I'm to hand him over to Lady Hilliard in London. She will be there in six days' time. Before she takes him to the farm by train we have to sign legal documents."

Emil sat bolt upright, spilling his tea into the saucer. "*Um Gottes*—so soon?"

She tried to stay calm though her heart was racing. "But now I'm forbidden to travel. At the police station they said my refugee status was downgraded to a "B" category. I begged and begged. I showed them the doctor's letter. They said no." She took Emil's hand. "Please, Father, it is you who must take Paul to London. You have a travel permit … to inspect your repaired flat in London."

"Not so loud, daughter." Emil glanced around the room. "Here speaking another language means spy talk." He took a deep breath. "So, now—you want me to solve a problem that you and Willy set up for yourselves. You could have asked my advice about this earlier. You and Willy—always rush, rush, without a thought for the consequences."

"Father, for once, be kind to me. Of course, it was our decision to send Paul away and my responsibility to make it happen."

He sighed deeply "Does Willy know about this problem with your travel permit?"

Sophie shook her head. "I'll send him a telegram when I know you can take Paul to London. You will do it, won't you? We cannot upset this Lady Hilliard by canceling the appointment because of me. She might not be willing to take him anymore."

Emil, taking deep breaths, stared down at his teacup. Rain pounded the sidewalk, slashing against the window glass.

Sophie fidgeted with her teaspoon. Why couldn't he make his mind up?

He pushed his cup away. "Very well. I will take him to London."

Sophie put a hand on his arm. "Thank you, Father." She wanted to kiss him, and put her arms round his broad shoulders, but she knew he was discomfited by displays of affection between adults. Instead, she gave him her best smile. "He is to be at the SSAFA office at noon on the 28th. I'll give you the letter they sent me."

Emil nodded, his face impassive. "We will leave early. I want to buy paprika and sauerkraut in Soho, something impossible in Cambridge. Afterward, if there is time, maybe we will visit Piccadilly Circus and Trafalgar Square. After the meeting with the farm lady, I will go to our flat."

Sophie laid a pleading hand on his. "Father, please, for Paul's sake, be nice to the English lady. No political comments about the conservative government. I'm sure she is one of those."

"Enough, daughter. You begin to sound like Judit. The important thing for me is a signed and dated note from you saying that that I am your representative. You must also inform this SSAFA office with a telegram that I am coming with the boy, yes? "

She grabbed his hand and kissed it. "Thank you. As the days pass, I feel more and more miserable about Paul going away on his own. I will hate myself if he is unhappy there. You know, Father, it was Willy who thought up this plan with SSAFA."

Emil patted her arm. "Pavel is a resilient boy. Think of it as a farm holiday. It is what middle-class people from Vienna and Prague did before the war. Summers in the country."

Sophie refilled her cup. Afraid to lose control of herself, she could not bear to look directly at him. She sighed. "Being in the countryside is not a holiday for a lonely six- year-old. There will be no one to kiss him goodnight or dry his tears."

Emil studiously polished his glasses. "Ah, yes. And the question of his name. We still can't get used to calling him Paul. Living on the farm will reinforce the name change. Did you tell him, carefully, why he is to be Paul for everyone?"

Sophie wiped her lips with a napkin. Emil was so organized. He thought of everything. Her cheeks burned. With other people she talked about Paul, but could not help calling him Pavel when they were together. "I —I mentioned it two or three times but you could talk to him about it on the train to London."

*   *   *

Later, when Emil told Judit about the Lyons Café meeting and his agreeing to take Paul to London, she burst into tears and rushed from the kitchen. No point in trying to calm her down, he thought and marched into the back garden to work on his new project—putting shelves up on the walls of the small shed.

Eventually, Judit, wiping her eyes with her apron, came out to where he was hoeing around the lettuces. "When that boy gets back from school today, how do you expect me to hide what I feel?" she said with a sob. "Why did you agree to do this for Sophie?"

Emil kept hoeing. He wanted peace and quiet, not hysterics. "She is part of our family. It was Willy's idea. She had no alternative."

"She is using you."

He straightened up and glared at her. "Using me? She is not allowed to travel outside Cambridge. There was no other solution."

"No, she can't bear the shame of leaving him with strangers. She passed that job on to you."

Emil slammed the hoe against the fence. "Enough inventing, woman. You have enough imagination for three gossips. Strangers can be kind. The farm is not a prison. It won't be as bad as you think."

PART TWO: A PATH TO ASSIMILATION

CHAPTER SEVENTEEN
June 1942
SSAFA

On June 28, they took the bus to the train station. Emil was in his only suit and carried the boy's cardboard suitcase. Paul skipped along beside him in a short-sleeved shirt, khaki shorts, and sandals. The weather forecast was good and the 7:35 morning train to London was expected to take just over two hours, although delays were possible if there was bomb damage on the line. The train was teeming with people in uniform, most of them smoking and standing in the corridors. Emil found an almost empty non–smoking compartment and hoisted the boy's valise on to the overhead rack above the only other passenger, a sour-faced elderly woman with pinned-up white hair under a gray cloche hat. "It looks like a nice day, madam," he said with a bow.

The woman blinked through thick spectacles, muttered good morning, and returned to a thick book resting on an embroidered bag on her lap.

As the train rumbled through a landscape of hedged pastures and ripening wheat, the lady stopped reading at intervals to glare disapprovingly at Paul's restlessness. He alternated between bouncing up and down in his seat, and looking out the windows, all while posing a stream of questions about the posters of thick-walled castles, rolling landscapes, and families picnicking on beaches displayed above the upholstered head rests.

After half an hour, the woman gave up reading and shot nervous glances at them when they talked. This was to be expected, Emil reasoned. He had twice been marched off to the local police station in Cambridge because of his accent. She seemed relieved when an inspector clipped their tickets and Emil spoke to him in English.

After a while, Paul calmed down and immersed himself in the two Beano comic books Sophie had bought him for the journey. Emil reread the appointment letter and wondered what this Mrs. Hilliard would be like. Perhaps haughty, with an aquiline nose and immaculate hairdo, or more likely, a buxom apple-cheeked farmer's wife with braided hair, probably with several offspring. She had to be a generous and good-hearted woman to offer shelter to so many evacuated children.

As the train rattled toward London, Paul continued to ask endless questions in Czech about steam engines, how cows and sheep got babies, why horses let people jump on to their backs, and how farms worked.

Emil was surprised at how much the boy was looking forward to living on a farm. Paul talked eagerly about his recent visit there with Papa and Maman. The farmyard was very big, he said, with lots of cows in a shed and some huge pigs. There were rows of little wooden huts and cages, filled with chickens and ducks, and a big building stacked with hay bales. They all watched a tractor pulling a big metal thing with wheels and shiny sharp blades. And in the middle of the farmyard there was a mountain of pooh and straw—as big as a house.

Pavel talked about the farm hands in dirty clothes who patted his head or winked at him. A girl in a pinafore like Granny's gave him cream from the top of a churn to pour over a bowl of stewed fruit. Papa and Maman talked to a lady wearing a headscarf who drove a car with wooden pieces stuck to its sides. She took them to the cottage where he would live with other children. But they were out on a walk with the lady who looked after them.

"What about Papa and Maman?" Emil said. "What did they think of it when you visited the farm?"

"Jolly super."

"Won't you miss them if you live there?"

Paul stared. "I don't know. They've got six children living on that farm. It will be fun like it was in France." Paul put his hand on Emil's knee, giving him a winsome smile. "But I'll miss school, and you and Granny."

"Has Maman talked to you about Granny and me not calling you Pavel anymore?"

Pavel nodded and then shrugged. "Why do I have to have two names?"

Emil sighed. "Pavel is your Czechoslovak name. Now that you will be living on an English farm, it is better they know you as Paul. What do you think?

Paul looked earnestly at Emil. "I don't know, Grandpa."

Emil chuckled. "Well, when we get to London, you will magically and permanently turn into Paul. Only when you visit your Granny and Grandpa will you still be Pavel." He put out his hand. "But we keep it a secret from your Maman and Papa. Agreed?"

Grinning, Paul shook it vigorously. "Agreed."

"I will tell the lady from the farm you are called Paul."

Later, after the ticket collector came by to check on their tickets again, Emil clicked open the cover of his silver fob, a relic of his previous life. "What time is it now, Paul?" He smiled.

The boy peered at the watch face, crinkling his eyes in frustration. "I haven't learned the time. Is that bad?"

"You should hurry up and learn. See here ... the little hand always shows the hour. At the moment it is close to number nine which means it's almost nine o'clock in the morning—time for us to have the fine snack Granny made for us: sandwiches made with real scrambled egg and lettuce. We each get a ripe tomato and some crunchy cookies."

Emil politely offered the bag of cookies to the lady. "Please, madam, would you like one of these pastries?"

Her face turned a bright pink. "Oh, no—no, thank you. I couldn't possibly."

"Why doesn't she want to share our food, Grandpa?"

"Stop staring at her funny hat and tell me where I said we were going after we get off the train."

"To buy stuff in a shop near Piccadilly Circus—will I see tigers and elephants there?"

Emil laughed. "It is not that kind of circus. It is the center of London, where the traffic goes round and round like inside a circus tent. In the middle is a statue of a boy like you shooting an arrow, only now it's covered up because of the bombing."

*   *   *

At Queen's Gate, they found the SSAFA office on the ground floor of an imposing Edwardian town house. The air was heavy with cigarette smoke and smelled of cleaning fluid. Emil felt a wheeze in his chest and coughed.

Vividly painted regimental plaques and sepia photographs of be-medaled military men covered the walls. An attractive woman in a silvery dress and a fox fur collar, lounged next to a uniformed official at his desk, pen in hand. Emil was impressed by the confident way she appraised him and Pavel.

Beside her, a scruffy-looking boy, a few inches taller than Paul, scratched at his neck.

Captain Landrieu, florid-faced and portly, introduced himself and then presented the woman to Emil and Paul. "This is Lady Hilliard … your host, and one of her evacuees, Eric." He shot a serious look at Emil. "Unfortunate times. We have just been discussing the disastrous Allied defeat at Tobruk. Still, I expect you're too busy coping with a hard life here to follow the ins and outs of the Allied campaign in North Africa."

Emil's face darkened. They always made foolish presumptions about foreigners. "Excuse please. I have a nephew who is with the 8th Army there."

Emil switched his attention to Lady Hilliard who was now standing. She was tall and handsome; very much like the English ladies he had read about in novels or seen in films.

"How nice to meet you," she said, shaking Emil's hand firmly. She spoke in the soft, well-bred English he recognized from the BBC. He was taken by her friendly smile, white even teeth between full, rouged lips and delicate floral scent. "I hope you had a trouble-free journey getting here, Mr. Kohut."

"It is a pleasure to meet you," he said as her words triggered an embarrassed thought. "Excuse please. I regret, my son did not instruct me in the cost of railway travel from London to your farm." Emil pulled out his wallet. "I hope I have enough. How much do I owe?"

Captain Landrieu raised a pudgy hand. "No need for that. This is an assisted private child evacuation subsidized by the government. I have a travel voucher for the two boys and a billeting certificate,"

Lady Hilliard smiled. "That's also my understanding." She squeezed Paul's cheek and tousled his hair. "A nice-looking boy. Lovely curls and smartly turned out. He and I will get on famously."

Emil noticed how smoothly the fabric of her skirt followed the shape of her hips and thighs. Finest quality cashmere. Only the best for this woman. His immediate impression was of a warm-hearted woman who cared about children. Pavel ... Paul, would be in good hands.

"This is a big moment for my grandson to which he is looking forward." He rested a hand on Paul's head and cleared his throat. "One important fact I must tell you now. At the farm, he is to be called Paul: the English way of saying Pavel. He knows this already."

Lady Hilliard raised her eyebrows. "Mmm, Paul. Very well, though I do like Pavel. It's rather a romantic name. Tolstoyan, if you know what I mean. Anyway, thanks for bringing him all this way." She turned to the officer. "Captain, please alter the contract so that the boy's name is changed to Paul. "

Eric seemed unable to stay still and poked around the office looking distracted, pulling out drawers as he rubbed at the skin on different parts of his body. Emil was shocked by Eric's crusted and inflamed eyelids and how he often sneezed, wiping his nose with his fingers and then wiping them on his tattered shorts.

"Does this child have some infection?" he asked Captain Landrieu, after Lady Hilliard had excused herself and gone to the bathroom. "Does he by chance have lice?" He had read in the newspaper that evacuated children from the poorest areas of Britain's cities suffered from lice and skin sores, ate their meals sitting on the floor, and relieved themselves on carpets.

"I reckon not," the uniformed officer said with a derogatory sniff. "But he's a working class kid, from Bermondsey. With that skin problem, she shouldn't take him, but now that she's seen him, well... I suppose ..."

Emil worried that his grandson was still vulnerable to some infection after his string of winter illnesses. But how could he cancel the arrangement with no authority from Sophie or Willy? He would convey his concerns to them but keep the information from Judit. Emil sighed. The boy would just have to manage.

At the end of the meeting, Captain Landrieu orchestrated the signing formalities, and Emil was satisfied that everything had gone smoothly. Sophie had set it up well. He kissed Paul on the forehead and rubbed his back encouragingly.

"I am sure you will be very happy on this lady's farm," he said in Czech. "This Lady Hilliard is a nice person. Your maman will be pleased. We will write to you. And behave properly. Remember you represent our family. Look after your clothes and don't lose anything. Wash your hands often and try not to wet the bed." He tossed a silver half-crown in the air and then folded the boy's fingers over it. "Pocket money. I'll bring more when we visit you ..."

Paul looked at him, and glanced at Eric. "Are you going now, Grandpa?"

"Yes, to our flat. Will you be all right by yourself?" Emil bent down to kiss him again. "Do you have Furry Lion?"

Paul blinked, his eyes moistening. "Of course I have, Grandpa." He lowered his voice to a whisper. "Nobody came with that other boy?"

"Maybe his family brought him and left. "Emil kissed his forehead and handed him a small, worn leather wallet. "This is a present from your granny with photographs of all of us. Look at them when you feel sad or lonely. Remember, we all love you.""

Lady Hilliard smiled a thank-you at Emil. "Time for us to go, my dears." She clapped her hands imperiously. "From now on, you boys will be carrying your own things—and no dilly-dallying. Captain Landrieu, please order a taxi. We cannot miss that train."

Emil waited for five minutes before leaving the office. He was pleased that Paul had been so calm. The big question now was how he would adjust to the farm and all the people there. They might not take to a little foreign boy who could not speak English properly. And farms were dangerous places with sharp tools, heavy machinery and big animals.

CHAPTER EIGHTEEN
Knapp Farm Cottages
June 28, 1942

It was early evening and still light when they arrived at Shrewsbury Station. Paul, lugging his suitcase and clutching Furry Lion under his arm, followed Lady Mary Hilliard to the exit stairs. Eric dawdled behind with a canvas bag slung over his shoulder.

On the four hour train ride from London, Lady Hilliard twice took the boys to the refreshment carriage. Once for sixpence worth of fish and chips, and later for cake and tea. Paul liked this part of a journey that seemed to go on forever, most of all. She regaled them with details of Knapp Hill Farm, hardly pausing for breath. She talked and talked, the words vibrating pleasantly through her nose.

He had never come across a grown-up who jumped so easily from one thing to another, as if she didn't have to think about what was coming next. She was the opposite of Maman or Grandpa who shushed him and taught him to be obedient and watchful in public—saying the English expected children, to be quiet and well-behaved.

Lady Hilliard explained that she had been given the nickname Popsie from her days as a young, much-photographed young lady in London—debutante was a word she used. That was where she met her husband, Sir Edward.

"At the farm, the children all call me Aunt Popsie," she said, her lively eyes twinkling. "It's so much easier to say than Your Ladyship. So you two can call me Aunt Popsie, too." She laughed, her wide mouth and chin forming a perfect triangle and talked to them as though she was a friend, not a grown-up.

With nothing better to do than look at the countryside sliding by, Paul spent a long time comparing her to Maman. Aunt Popsie was taller and slimmer, with long chestnut curls that bounced on her shoulders. Maman's hair bounced like that as well, but it was shiny and black. It was only when Aunt Popsie said she had four teenage children at school—one of them an adopted Polish girl—did he understand why she looked so much older than Maman. She had wrinkles around the eyes and lots of makeup.

She told them that Sir Edward Hilliard was an ex-army officer. Welsh Guards, she said. He had a mustache and a stern face and didn't usually say much to children. But they shouldn't be afraid of him. He was really very kind. The farms came from his great grandfather, a coal mine owner who made a lot of money during the Industrial Revolution.

Leaning close to Paul, Eric whispered, "Wot's an industible revolushon?" He smelled bad. Like socks that had been worn too long.

Paul had no idea what this was about and turned away to look out the window. He soon tired of looking at the endless fields, hedges, and grimy stations they stopped at to take on more passengers. His mind wandered. From Aunt Popsie's descriptions, Knapp Hill Farm sounded like a terrifically exciting place. Maybe Eric and the other children would become his friends.

Paul pulled out the wallet and looked at the grainy family photographs. He didn't think he would miss them much if he was living on a busy farm. He was not even sad about leaving Maman and his grandparents behind. He had never been one for much hugging and kissing, and this was a new adventure. But he did hope the food would be as good as Granny's.

In the station forecourt, Paul and Eric waited, looking at each other, unsure of what would happen next. The sky was overcast, the light beginning to fade from gray to purple. Aunt Popsie patted her neck and face with a flowery handkerchief and with an irritated expression pointed up at a large clock above the station portico. "Look at that, boys! Past eight and still damned hot. What a summer! Storms, one after the other. Ruining my wheat."

She puffed on a hastily-lit cigarette, looked around again and stamped her foot. "Where the *hell* is that man?" Her face cleared when a dusty, wood-framed car with a long square back drew up at the curb beside them. "Aha, at last … the Light Brigade."

Paul noticed a dark face at the driver's window looking out at them. The man's cheek jerked sideways in a twisted smile "Evenin' your ladyship. On time am I?"

"At last, Bert," she frowned, throwing away her cigarette. "Why the hell are you always so damned late. Now, load up our stuff, and be careful with that big red box, there's china in it. Show the boys where to put their things, and keep Jason down on the floor."

"Yes, your ladyship." The old man slowly maneuvered his way out of the driver's seat and limped to the back of the car.

Paul guessed Bert was nearly as old as Grandpa. He was thin and bent, wearing shapeless trousers, an open-neck shirt, and a jacket full of stains and rips. He wore heavy polished boots and under his faded green beret, the old man's black hair shone like boot polish. Why was an old tramp driving Aunt Popsie's big car?

Eric put his hands on his hips and whistled. "Smashin' motor, this. Bet she goes fast."

"Wolseley shooting brake," Bert said with a wink at the two boys, "Do sixty-five if she's pushed. Now, get your skates on and shove your stuff inside. Not my job!"

Paul plucked up courage. "What's shooting brake, Mr. Bert?"

"A big car with a square back wot opens up so's we can put a load of stuff in: guns, dogs, equipment, and shoppin'. Sir Edward bought it for grouse 'untin' in Northumberland. That's a long time past."

Lady Hilliard directed the boys into the back seat where they squeezed between cardboard boxes, rolls of netting and twine, a crate of beer, cans of food, bags of rice and sugar, and tools that Paul had never seen before. A light-colored, short-haired dog with a gray muzzle sprawled on the floor between the boy's legs. It started to lick Paul's hand.

Eric shifted his knees out of the way. "Look at those teeth, will yer. Keep 'im away from me, mate. I don't much like dogs."

Paul, used to Dr. Emily's Labradors, put his arms around Jason's neck, and rubbed his face into the fur. "I *love* dogs."

Lady Hilliard sat in the front passenger seat, filling the interior with her floral scent that out-competed the smell from the dog's dirt-stained coat. She smiled at them. "Come on, boys, say my name."

"Aunt Popsie," chorused the boys.

"Good." She lit another cigarette and threw the dead match out her window.

Paul, feeling a shiver of expectation, pressed his nose to the window, watching Bert get in the driver's seat. He couldn't wait to see the farm.

Eric nudged Paul. "Our bloke's only got one eye—'e looks like a pirate," he whispered. "Only 'e don't 'ave no patch. "Ow can he drive this banger with jus' one eye. Bet he's got a dagger 'idden somewhere."

Paul silently agreed and his knees began to quiver. Bert, with his dry eye socket, looked like a criminal from an adventure comic. What if they crashed? What if they weren't going to a farm at all? What if Bert was taking them somewhere to be locked up like prisoners of war? What if Lady Hilliard was just pretending to be nice? He closed his fingers around the money Grandpa had given him.

"A pleasure to meet you two young 'uns," Bert said, touching his forehead with a stubby forefinger. The frightening face suddenly revealed a yellow-toothed smile, glinting with silver. "Yus, lads, I may look a mess but I kin still work an' drive." He turned the ignition key, the engine coughed and then burbled. "Off we go, then."

Paul liked the way Bert talked; words rumbled softly from his mouth just like the car's engine.

Aunt Popsie twisted in her seat. "Don't let Bert's looks bother you," she said with a smile. "He was badly wounded in the last war. He's worked for my family since he was a boy. You'll love his stories."

She shifted in her seat and tapped the veneered dashboard with painted fingernails. "For God's sake, Bert, don't dawdle. I've done enough traveling today. Take the Longden road and give me a rundown on all the local gossip. "

"Yes, m'lady."

Bert motored through the hilly town's winding streets, lined with bow-window shop fronts set below timbered houses. Paul hardly understood what Aunt Popsie and Bert were talking about. He concentrated on what he could see through the window, all the time caressing Jason's head which had found its way onto his lap. Soon, the car swayed and lurched between trimmed hedgerows on a narrow country road, with Bert grinding the gears and brakes as they swerved around bends.

Aunt Popsie began a commentary on what they were seeing, using words that Paul often didn't recognize. He surprised himself by asking her to explain what she meant by meadows, barley, pasture, Herefords, Guernseys, and black-nosed sheep that she called Kerry Hills. He wondered why Eric stared at him when he asked questions.

"Wot's that tall yeller grass called, missus?" Eric suddenly asked, as if he had just found his tongue.

"You mean out there? That's wheat, dearie," said Aunt Popsie pointing a slender hand through the open window. "W-H-E-A-T," she spelled. "Two more weeks, if the weather holds, we'll bring in the harvest, even though it's been flattened by summer storms. We use a big machine, called a combine harvester. All the children come and pick up the rabbits that get shot when they run out of the last patch of wheat in the center of the field. That night everyone bakes rabbit pie for dinner. It's fun, and we have a picnic and a big celebration when the harvest is over. Pray God, we have good weather."

"What's wheat for, missis?"

"To make bread, dear. And we grow other things: beets, peas, and mangel-wurzels for the animals. Our milk goes to United Dairies. You've probably seen their carts and horses where you live in London. And we raise pigs and chickens on one of our other farms."

"Gawd! Can we watch 'em killin' the pigs??" Eric dug his elbow into Paul's ribs and winked, as if he was proud of his daring question. "My uncle's a butcher, but 'e only chops up the bits. Y'know, the legs an' that."

Paul wanted to ask what a mangel-wurzel was but couldn't bring himself to say anything.

Bert swung the shooting-brake into a small lane and stopped to have a coughing fit.

"It's his lungs," said Aunt Popsie calmly. "Gassed in the war. He'll be better soon."

"Sorry about that, m'lady." Bert wiped his nose with a dark rag, crashed a gear and drove up a low hill along the twisting high-hedged lane. "Me lungs doan like this time of year."

Paul rolled down the window and looked out at the passing brambles, tall grasses, and wildflowers. He felt warm and comfortable. This was turning into an adventure in which he imagined he was an important person like Winston Churchill, traveling in a big car to somewhere secret and special. The only problem was that he desperately wanted to pee, but was afraid to say anything. Often, if he waited a little, the urge would go away, but then, sometimes, he would realize he'd wet himself.

A few minutes later, at Aunt Popsie's behest, Bert stopped the car where two other lanes met at a junction. They got out. "This is Henry the Eighth," she said, pointing to a massive oak tree on a grassy knoll, its roots curled round a mound of stones.

Paul had never seen a tree so huge. Its boughs reached out like giant twisted arms and he was astonished at the thickness of the rough fissured bark and the fairy doors. Grandpa would like this tree, he thought. He nudged Eric's thin ribs and they both looked up. "Do you think we could climb it?" he said.

"Gawd no," said Eric, shaking his head in wonder. "It's a bloody giant. You'd likely fall on to those stones and break your bloody neck."

If Papa had been there, Paul thought, he would have laughed and clapped him on the shoulder. "Go ahead, young man. You won't know till you try." He always said things like that.

"I knew you would be impressed by old Henry," Aunt Popsie smiled. "Do you know who Henry the Eighth was?"

"A boxer," said Eric with a knowing grin. "Knocked 'em cold in the eighth round.

"A ... a king?" Paul ventured.

"Good. He was a big fat, famous king who had six wives. And this tree is big and fat and has six main branches thicker than your two bodies glued together. We think he's four hundred years old which is about the same time Henry the Eighth lived."

Paul returned the smile. He liked her story and the way her red lips twisted a little when she talked, and how the skin on her face moved so easily over her rouged cheeks. She might be older than Mummy but she was just as nice. Then he saw Aunt Popsie looking down toward his knees and his heart leaped in shock. What would she say about the wet patch? Or think?

With a brief nod of what he took to be kindness and

understanding, she switched her gaze back to the tree. "This tree was planted by one of my husband's ancestors, a man called Cucleth Paraford who owned lead mines around here."

Paul's relief was a tidal wave of joy and gratitude. She wasn't going to say anything. "Whenever anyone in my family returns from a journey, we stop to give Henry a glad-to-be-home kiss. That's what I want you to do now."

Moments later, the two boys were hugging and kissing the tree, and examining the deep fissures and colored lichens on the trunk.

Lady Hilliard spread a tartan rug out on the ground. She slipped off her shoes and wriggled her stockinged toes. Paul sprawled on the grass with Eric, watching the ants, bees, and other unrecognizable insects scramble and buzz around dandelion seed heads.

Eric cleared his throat as if embarrassed. "Er…my mum told me you was a farmer. I've bin wunderin'. You don' look like a farmer—more like a toff."

Aunt Popsie's eyelashes fluttered. "Well, my dear, I suppose I'm a bit of both. How about you? The SSAFA application said you come from Bermondsey. Where is that?"

Eric nodded. "London, missus. Southwark, London Bridge way. Six of us live in two rooms on the third floor. It's near Guys 'ospital."

"It will be very different for you here," she said with a smile. "As of today, there will be seven of you children living at Middle Knapp Cottage, next to the farmyard. So it'll be a tight squeeze. Mrs. McAlistair will be looking after all of you: keeping you clean and teaching you spelling, sums, and reading. A farm girl helps her."

The two boys looked at her, wide-eyed. Paul wanted to ask who Mrs. Mucklister was. He imagined an old lady like Granny, always cleaning, and fussing and giving him soppy kisses.

"Mrs. McAlistair is from Scotland: she's a nanny and governess rolled into one. I want you to be nice and polite to her just like you would be with your own family. All right?"

"Please," said Paul timidly. His stomach lurched. He wasn't sure this was the right question or a good time for it. "Will missis Mucklister let my family come to see me?"

Aunt Popsie patted him on the back. "Oh, yes, of course. Whoever in your family comes to visit, they can stay with me at the big house. There's no room for them in your little cottage. And the lady looking after you—her name is Mrs. Mc-alis-tair, not Mucklister!"

She laughed and bent down to kiss his forehead. Paul inhaled the spicy scent from her hair. She was beautiful, and he loved her already.

Eric observed the kiss, and drew back, horror splashed all over his face.

"Come on then boys. Let's walk along the road and say hello to Mrs. McAlistair. Bert will drop your things off at the cottages."

Lady Hilliard took Eric and Paul's hands and they walked a hundred yards along a lane to a cluster of single-story brick-and-beam buildings. She opened a creaking iron gate and led them across an expanse of roughly cast, sloping concrete, surrounded on three sides by farm structures and a stone wall facing the lane.

"So, boys, this is the farmyard. Just over there is the barn where we keep the hay for winter feed. On the right, that long brick thing with opaque windows: that's the cattle shed—for forty cows. We bring them in every night from the meadows and milk them in the early morning. Sally Manders, our cow woman, will show you how we get the milk and prepare it in the dairy. I bet you'd like to try milking a cow, wouldn't you?"

There was silence. Paul remembered the short rosy-cheeked lady who had given him cream when he visited this farm with Maman and Papa.

"Don't wanna touch no cow tits," Eric whispered.

Paul had no idea what he meant.

Eric pointed at a mound of brown sludge and straw that occupied the center of the concrete farmyard. "Wot's all that stinky brown stuff piled up in the middle?" A bevy of clucking hens pecked delicately around its edge, watched by a multicolored cockerel with jerky black eyes.

Paul knew what it was. From when he came to visit with Mummy and Daddy. But he kept silent wanting to hear what Aunt Popsie would say.

She smiled indulgently. "I'm afraid, Eric, living here at the cottage, you'll just have to get used to the smell. That's manure; hay mixed with the poo the cows and pigs make. Very valuable. We put it on the fields and in the vegetable garden because it's wonderful for making things grow."

She guided them past the manure heap to a row of three white cottages, joined together under a single thatched roof. "Here we are— Knapp Farm Cottages. They've been here for at least two hundred years. Our farm workers and the land girls live in the Upper and Lower Cottages. You're in Middle Cottage. Come along."

Aunt Popsie lifted a brass knocker on the plank door and gave two sharp raps. A moment later the door opened and Paul inspected his new "mother". This woman looked much older than Maman. He had expected a welcoming look but her face was stern. He could usually guess what a person was like by their look. But he had no idea what *this* lady was thinking.

"There y' are then. Aboot time." The woman laced bony fingers across her apron and looked questioningly at the two boys and then at her employer. She had dark eyes, steel spectacles, and her brown hair, twisted into braids, formed a spiral on the top of her head.

The radio was playing in the background and Paul recognized the song everyone was whistling or singing in Cambridge—all about bluebirds and the white cliffs of Dover.

"Good evening, Mrs. McAlistair." Aunt Popsie rested a hand on each boy's head. "Here are two more lads to add to your herd—Eric from London, and Paul is a six-year-old from Czechoslovakia."

Paul noticed another face, framed by stringy, uncombed brown hair, peering at the newcomers from behind the new lady's skirt. "This is my Alice," said the governess. "She's just five." The girl stuck her tongue out and waggled it.

There was a moment of silence while Paul and Alice stared at each other.

Mrs. McAlistair looked down at her daughter. "Say hello, Alice. Eric's from London." Alice hid herself again. The governess looked at Paul as if she'd cracked her tooth on a walnut shell. "And this is … Paul," she said in a tight voice, taking in a deep breath. There was disapproval in her eyes. "Listen, m'lady, I didn'a take this post to look after *furriners*. You expressly told me when I applied that the bairns would only be comin' from British army families in trouble."

Aunt Popsie closed her eyes and sighed. She waved a dismissive hand. "Exactly right, my dear Mrs. M. We exclusively house children from military families sent to us by SSAFA. Let me explain one more time. Paul's father, in spite of being a foreigner, is a soldier in one of our Royal Engineer regiments. This is wartime, Mrs.M. We welcome soldiers from many countries to fight the Nazi tyrant."

Mrs. McAlistair's eyebrows shot skywards. "It's na reet to allow *furriners* to serve in our army. How are we not to know if they happen to be spies and sabotagers? What's more, I worry this bairn doesn'a understand or speak proper English. I have neither the time nor the inclination to teach him to speak proper."

Paul, aware that Eric was peering sideways at him, understood very well what this woman had said, in spite of her strange way of talking. She was arguing, being nasty. His stomach lurched. What if she was like this all the time? Maybe she was in a bad mood, like Maman was sometimes. It was then that he registered another surge of warm wetness in his underpants. He crossed his legs and turned sideways.

Lady Hilliard straightened her shoulders, a frown creasing her face. "Please, do not complain, Mrs. M. This youngster and his father have been thoroughly vetted by the SSAFA office. That's good enough for me." She rested a hand on Paul's shoulder. "Paul and I talked on the train. His English is quite good and I'm sure he will learn fast. I want you to treat him the same as everyone else. Just let me know if you have any concerns. He's a nice little fellow." She pointed at the stacked luggage in the hallway. "Ah, good, I see Bert dropped off their things."

"You'd best come in. Bring your cases." Mrs. McAlistair led Paul and Eric through the short passageway to a large, brick-floored room where two stout wooden pillars shored up the ceiling beams. Alice followed them, sucking a finger.

Paul gazed at the uneven off-white walls covered in cracks. Grandpa wouldn't like those. A strangely-shaped black stove with little glass windows stood inside a huge chimney breast, steaming black kettle on its flat top. Heat radiated from the stove. A table surrounded by several wooden chairs stood at the center of the room. A velvet settee and two stuffed armchairs faced the fireplace.

"That's Jingles," squeaked Alice, pointing a wet forefinger at a tabby cat curled up on one of the armchairs.

"We eat and do our lessons here," said Mrs. McAlistair. She pointed to a pair of plank doors. "That's my room where Alice and I sleep, and next to it is our bathroom. You are not allowed in there, except for once a week when you get a supervised bath. Otherwise you use the outhouse at the back of the cottage or the chamber pots upstairs. Now, follow me."

She took them up a dark, narrow, twisting staircase into an attic illuminated at either end by small dormer windows.

The floor's uneven planks creaked as they walked. The attic space was empty apart from two chests of drawers set against low walls and differently-shaped and colored chamber pots clustered around seven mattresses. "The floor is aboot two hundrid years old," she said, switching on the light—one bulb under a green shade—that dangled from a cross beam. "As ye can tell, the floor creaks terrible and there's nae ceiling. I sleep downstairs, so ye better be as quiet as mice at night."

Paul looked up at the slats and bundles of thatch that formed the cottage roof. The vegetal earthy smell suddenly reminded him of the stifling room Papa had rented in Paris. He remembered how the mice scratched at night. He studied the straw thatch above his head. What if spiders and biting creatures lived up there? He didn't dare ask.

The mattresses, made up as beds, were lined up in two rows, side by side. "The two beds at the far end are yours," Mrs. McAlistair said.

Paul was glad to see that some of the beds had stuffed toys on the pillows. Two teddy bears, a kangaroo, and a clown. His heart leaped with joy. Furry Lion would have friends.

Alice lurked behind her mother, sucking her forefinger again. "I have a proper bed," she gloated. "Not like you."

"There's rubber sheets under the bedding," Mrs. McAlistair said sternly, "so your pee doesna' ruin them. We boil the dirty sheets once a week. That's Sheila's job."

Paul winced, turning away to hide the wet patch on his shorts. How did she know that he was a bed-wetter?

Grinning, Eric nudged him, whispering "we'll soon take the piss out of the night-pissing kids,"

Paul, fear pounding deep inside, noted the severe line of Mrs. McAlistair's eyebrows. But he also felt a surge of relief. There were other bed-wetters here. And who was Sheila?

"Put your belongings in the box by your pillow. Empty bags and cases go over in the corner. Put a chamber pot by your bed afore ye go to sleep. Each one has a name label. "

Scratching his scalp, Eric looked around the attic. "Where's the other kids?"

"Sheila has taken the bairns on a walk before it gets too dark."

"Please missus Maclaster, wot will we be doin' all day? Can we go look around the farm?"

Paul stood silently behind his new comrade, hands in his pockets. Eric was brave asking such important questions.

She frowned, interlacing her hands over her pinafore. "Eric, isn't it? Well, first thing you do is say my name reet. It's Mrs. McAlistair, not miss or missus. Second thing, keep your hands *out* of your pockets when you talk to me. And I will nae tolerate vulgar words and runnin' or shoutin' in the cottage, especially up here in the dormitory. There's big gaps between the floor planks, so I can hear every word you say. Even your whisperin' and breathin'." She chuckled, a dry, scratchy sound. "I can even hear your dreams! As for the rest, every mornin' we have two hours of lessons, readin' and writin'. After lunch, ye take an hour's rest, up here. Am I understood?"

Paul nodded dutifully. Eric followed suit.

"Guid. Then, in the afternoon, Sheila takes you walkin' for exercise. After that—though I dinna approve of it—her ladyship insists you're free to do for yerselves unless she wants you helpin' with some task she takes into her mind would be good for you. Every mornin' there's porridge and tea for breakfast, a sandwich and an apple at noon. You get a glass of milk and a biscuit at four every afternoon, followed by story time and prayers. I cook the supper at five-thirty, bedtime at seven after a cup of Horlicks and a spoonful of rose-hip syrup."

Paul wanted to ask who Sheila was.

"You, Paul. Did you understand what I said? What did I just say aboot the timetable?"

Timetable? What was that? Paul's heart beat fast. Those threatening eyebrows again. He wanted to make her like him. What could he do? He had a feeling that what he said or did next might affect everything that followed.

"She wants you ter copy wot she jus' said", Eric muttered. "Jus' tell 'er wot 'appens all day,"

Paul looked down at his sandals. "You said... lessons after breakfast, a sandwich for lunch, and then we can play until four when we get milk. Then, I'm, I'm not—"

"Useless boy!" spluttered Mrs. McAlistair. "If you want to get along with me, just remember what I say. I've no time to waste explainin' stuff to silly *furriners* like you." Alice, hiding behind her, giggled again.

"She's a fuckin' mean ol' bag," Eric whispered out of the side of his mouth.

Paul, impressed at Eric's skill with bad words, stood very still, not daring to speak. She was a mean old bag all right and he could not figure her out. At home, he could tell a lot of what Mama, Grandpa and Granny were thinking from their faces and how they talked and moved. He even thought he could decipher what people were like from their eyes. But not this person—her pale cheeks were thin and covered in veins—and her eyes flickered, like butterfly wings. And there was something else he didn't like. When she spoke her fingers and wrists jerked, a bit like a puppet. Paul had an inkling that Mrs. M.

might not turn out to be nice; but he wasn't sure about that, not just yet.

"He's wet hisself," said Alice, pointing. "That new boy with the curly hair."

Paul felt the tears welling in his eyes.

CHAPTER NINETEEN
Spills
September 1942

"How's my blue-eyed scrap today?" Sheila said in her lilting brogue, squashing Paul's curly head against her blouse; it was something she did every morning when she came to work.

"Lovely," he would reply, his voice muffled by the soft bosom that smelled so nice.

Within three months of his arrival at the farm, Paul had fallen for Sheila, a red-haired Irish girl of twenty-three. She and two other girls replaced the Knapp Hall farmworkers who were had enlisted in the military. Usually, the Land Girls herded cows and drove tractors on the farm, but Lady Hilliard had assigned Sheila to help Mrs. McAlistair.

What Paul wanted most of all was for Sheila to help him fit in with life at the cottage. He was a foreigner with a funny accent and he wanted to make friends with the children, and be liked by the farm-workers, and Mrs. McAlistair, and Aunt Popsie and her fearsome-looking husband with the giant mustache.

As far as Paul could tell, Sheila was always working. She collected produce from Knapp Hall's substantial vegetable garden, prepared food, washed and ironed clothes, cleaned the attic, and took the children for a daily walk. Each day, according to Mrs. M.'s strict instructions, she bathed only one child. Paul could never remember which day was his.

"Seven bairns, seven days, and seven baths," Mrs. McAlistair would often say in her high-pitched voice. "And only lukewarm, mind ye; coal bunker's close to empty."

Paul couldn't keep his eyes off Sheila's hair which hung like a coppery curtain over her shoulders, and he loved the way she was always laughing. She said she enjoyed the way he mangled English and did her best to correct him. She never called him Paul, just "blue-eyed scrap", sometimes shortened to just BES. "We have to stick together, BES," she would say. "'Cause we're both of us foreigners and doan' talk high and mighty like they do on the BBC."

And when he undressed for his weekly bath, he liked the kind way she asked about the pink scar on the right side of his neck and the tender scald on his right shoulder. He only vaguely remembered the operation on his neck in Paris—the tall doctor and nurses, and Maman crying all the time—but the air raid and his broken shoulder seemed like they had happened only yesterday.

Paul loved Sheila most of all because she was the only one who kissed him—apart from an occasional peck and hug from Lady Hilliard when she turned up. On Sundays, Sheila always kissed him before she went off for holy services at St. Winefrede's Catholic Church in Shrewsbury. She smelled of flowers—"lilac fragrance" she called it. Besides being beautiful, she knew a lot about animals, trees, plants, and insects.

On the days Sheila wore her Land Girl uniform—a green pullover, corduroy breeches, beige socks, and brown shoes or Wellington boots—she looked like a soldier. The first time she bathed him, he asked her why she wore a uniform.

"We're soldiers of the land, y'see … standin' in for the farm lads that's gone to fight."

He shook his head. "You're a pretend soldier then. Wait till my Papa comes here; he's a real one."

"Are you warnin' meself? If he's as charmin' as you are, I could get into trouble," she said with a laugh that Paul thought tinkled just like the tea bell at Dr. Emily's house when Maman served the cakes and pastries.

Sheila's preference for Paul seemed to irritate Mrs. McAlistair.

"I'll not have any favoritism in this house," she said often enough. "Every bairn gets equal supervision, justice and punishment."

One day, on one of the children's walks past the Knapp Hall stables and around the beet fields, Paul asked Sheila, "Why doesn't Mrs. McAlistair like it when you're nice to me?"

She laughed, a throaty musical sound, and tossed her hair. "I could care less what people think," she said, giving him a playful punch. "I'm a free spirit. God gave me a strong mind and I'll do as I please."

She had told him that her real name, Siobhan O'Ranahan, had been rejected as an "Irish mouthful" by the workers at Knapp Farm. To them she was plain Sheila.

In some ways, Paul had never felt better or happier. Sheila was at the cottage every day, and Aunt Popsie made appearances from time to time, usually with some kind of treat made by the cook at Knapp Hall. On the farm, everything followed an unwavering routine and as the days passed, his memories of certain things faded, mostly about bad things that happened before they came to England.

The evacuee children nested in the attic. They were small enough to run around on the squeaky floor and not bang their heads on the low crossbeams.

Paul liked Hilda, a blonde, pink-faced four year old with long braids. Vince was seven years old. His parents lived in bombed-out Coventry and he wore a cross around his neck. Marigold had thick, black curls and a scabby skin. Chrissie was six, a thin as a stick with ratty brown hair and an ugly birthmark on her neck. Gerald was fat. His nose ran all the time and his wire-rimmed spectacles kept sliding off his nose. And there was Eric, of course.

Each morning at a quarter past six, Mrs. McAlistair rang a hand bell. The children had thirty minutes to brush their teeth, wash, and get dressed. Paul was often last and if Mrs. McAlistair noticed she would give him a slap. "Lazy bairn!"

They used a dipper to transfer water from the open tank in one corner of the attic to the single washstand basin. Eric took on the daily task of inspecting the tank and fishing out the occasional mouse or rat that fell in from the thatch. When this happened, the children held a burial ceremony in the cottage's untended flower beds, saying prayers that Paul couldn't understand. Choirboy Vince made them sing Run, Rabbit, Run over the tiny grave.

After morning prayers led by Mrs. M., they had a bowl of hot oats and milk, sweetened with a blob of sticky Golden Syrup that they stirred in as it melted. Paul was glad of the sweet taste that persisted long enough to disguise the slippery cod liver oil and diluted rosehip syrup that followed. The meal never varied, and Paul often yearned for Granny's paprika-flavored egg on toast.

On Sundays, Mrs. McAlister read the letters their parents sent each week. When it came to the letters Mama, Granny, and Grandpa Kohut wrote, Mrs. M. would often stop and laugh in a mean way that made the other children laugh along with her. Paul was ashamed, and he hated her for it. The first time she read one of Paul's letters, she scowled and thwacked the paper with her fingers.

"This isna reet, Paul. Your mother's signed herself as Maman— and she called your Dad, Papa. That's not how we call our parents in this country. From now on you are to say Mummy, Mum or Ma for your mother, and Daddy, Dad or Da for your father. I will send a note to your parents instructing them that in future letters they must sign their names properly. Understood?" She looked around at the other children sitting on the floor. "And you bairns, if you don't hear Paul saying mummy and daddy the right way, you tell me."

After breakfast, the children had to carry their chamber pots downstairs and empty them in the toilet. Only then would Mrs. McAlistair give them their daily portion of warm, creamy milk that Sheila collected from the dairy. Each day, a different cow provided the milk. Aunt Popsie wanted her "adopted" children to understand that milk was not created in a bottle. She liked to talk about milk when she visited the cottage. Paul never forgot what she said. "Milk from each cow has a different color, texture, and a subtle flavor to the tongue. It even changes with the weather and how contented the cow feels. Just like us."

Supper was the main meal of the day. Sheila called it "plain fare." Paul found it dull. Eric always asked for salt and pepper. "Be quiet, you, or, I will not allow the guid food I cook to be spoiled," was Mrs. McAlistair's usual response.

Mrs. McAlistair posted the weekly schedule on a cork pin board on the bathroom door. On Paul's third day at the cottage, he remembered how she stood him in front of the board while the others crowded round. "Let's see if our wee Paul can read proper English. Hurry up now."

His knees felt shaky and he suddenly felt a need to pee but he wanted to show he could do it, not give in or cry.

"Monday... Welsh rabbit; Tuesday... shepherd's pie; Wednesday... scrumbled eggs and, er, bacon; Furrsday... chicken soup and chicken sandvich; Friday... cornt beef and cabbige; Saturday... told-in-the-hole."

He looked around, happy to have got through it. "What is told-in-the-hole?"

Mrs. McAlistair nodded grudgingly. "That'll do."

Sheila laughed. "It's spelled T-O-A-D. That's a kind of frog. It's what the food looks like, see."

On Sundays there were no cooked meals. They ate spam, bread and butter, and salad. Whatever day or meal it was, the children were expected to eat everything on their plates.

Sometimes they had a treat. Mrs. Spencer, the cook up at Knapp Hall, would send down leftovers like a half-finished pheasant or remnants of beef or pork joints from one of the Hilliard's guest dinners.

Every day except Sunday, they ate thick, sweet pink or yellow custard for dessert. Paul hated it; the rubbery skin that formed on the top made him gag. On Sundays, Mrs. McAlistair steamed a pudding inside an old shirt sleeve. She called it Dead Man's Arm. Sheila had another name: Roly-Poly. It was slithery and chewy, like rubber, and stuck to Paul's teeth.

Bedtime was at seven. After a cup of Horlicks, they lay in the dark attic watching the downstairs light filtering up between the gaps in the floor boards. Whispering or talking was not allowed, but Eric taught them something else—to slide silently off their mattresses and peer down through the cracks to watch what Mrs. McAlistair was doing. For greater excitement—if they managed to stay awake—Eric and Vince crawled to another part of the attic directly above Mrs. M's bedroom and watched her undressing. Paul could never bring himself to join them. He thought it was mean to spy on someone naked who didn't know people were watching.

Paul's days were so full of activities that it was only at bedtime, as he began to doze off, that he had time to think about Mummy and Daddy, trying to imagine how they looked now. Sometimes he cried, remembering how he used to listen to them talking quietly when they all slept in the same room. He missed his soft bed at Granny and Grandpa's house and Mummy's laughter and kisses. He was proud of Daddy, the smiling soldier in one of the photos in Granny's wallet, but he did not feel that that he missed him the way he missed Mummy.

On Wednesdays, Mrs. McAlistair took a rest from her duties. Bert drove her and Alice to Shrewsbury to shop and go to the cinema. It was the best day of the week for the children because Sheila took them up to Knapp Hall.

She led the children through a high, brick-walled vegetable garden behind the cottages to where the lane from the junction ended in a stone gateway crowned by fierce lions. From there a long curved driveway, edged with lawns and giant rhododendrons, ended in a circular gravel forecourt in front of the beige-colored, green-windowed house—Knapp Hall.

They went through the cobbled back yard into the kitchen where Mrs. Spencer, always in a checkered apron and headscarf, served them lemonade and homemade fruitcake. After that they roamed the Hall grounds, racing along the flower borders, playing hide and seek. They pretended that Knapp Hall was a castle under attack. From the top of the wall, the defenders could see clumps of woodland among the valley's green and yellow fields, and smoke rising from cottage chimneys. Because he was foreign, Paul usually played the enemy. Sometimes a Red Indian, a pirate ... more often a Nazi Storm trooper. Paul thought it was unfair but he didn't want to be called a spoilsport. He wanted to be accepted by the group and be friends.

After the games, the children washed their hands and had lunch, served to them by one of the maids in the Hall's upstairs nursery. The food was always special: roasted chicken with rice or farm-made sausages and mashed potatoes, followed by stewed fruit and thick, yellow cream straight from one of the cowshed's stainless-steel milk buckets.

The part of each Wednesday that Paul loved most was when Sheila took them past the Hall stables, up a stony track that led to the top of Knapp Hill, a good half-hour walk when it wasn't raining. Smooth boulders studded the top of the whale-shaped hill. High grass, carpets of bracken, white heather, and a profusion of wildflowers covered its slopes.

Just below a stony outcrop near the crown of the hill, Sheila's expeditionary force usually stopped for breath next to a herdsman's shelter with a rusty tin roof. She would plop herself down on a mushroom-shaped stone outside the entrance.

Eric was very excited the first time Sheila showed them the shelter. "When the Jerries invade," he said with a swagger, "we'll hide here and fight them. Who built it?"

"I 'spect t'was a long-ago shepherd," she said. "Jesus, Mary! What a darlin' view. If only I had my Da's binoculars."

On each outing, she would teach the children something new: how to look for hawks, listen for skylarks, spot rabbits and hares—and, once or twice, she pointed out the bushy red tail of a fox slipping in and out of the fern cover. When the weather was good, she let the children spend the whole afternoon up there, making sure they did not get lost in the half-hidden paths that ended in deep mineshafts.

As the weeks passed, Paul felt less and less sad when he went to bed. It seemed like Daddy, Mummy, Granny and Grandpa lived in some dim and distant place. Sometimes in the middle of the night, awakened by a gust of wind howling in the eaves or by the clunk of a chamber pot, their faces appeared to him. Sometimes he heard them calling—Pavel, Pavlíčku, Pavliček, Paulinko—as if they were on the other side of the wall, in the next-door cottage. Only when he asked Sheila to reread the letters they sent did he feel sad. Sometimes, his tears flowed unchecked but he still wanted to know what his family was writing.

In the daytime, Paul forgot his unhappiness. He had Sheila, the farm, and playmates. He rough-housed with Eric and Vince and played hide-and-seek on the farm. The farmworkers were friendly, and he sensed the power of the Hilliard family. They were like kings and queens. They owned everything and kept him safe. The only person he could not fathom was Mrs. M., as Aunt Popsie sometimes called her. Most of the time Mrs. McAlistair ignored him unless it was to tell him off. When he asked her a question, if an answer came it was hard, sharp, and short. He did not know why.

*   *   *

Aunt Popsie donated two small bicycles—castoffs from her own children—to Middle Knapp Cottage. Paul and the others saw this as a miraculous gift, and on the first day, they bickered and shoved to get the chance to ride around the concrete farmyard. Venturing beyond the gate onto the public lane was expressly forbidden. No one knew how to ride properly, and Mrs. McAlistair tried to put a stop to it, raising the specter of head injuries and broken limbs. She was overruled by Sir Edward Hilliard, who persuaded one of the farm hands, sixty-year-old, bow-legged Jake, to teach the children how to ride. The old man leaned against an upturned barrel by the main gate, puffing on his pipe, watching them practice.

The cycling route was short and fast: an up-slope in front of Knapp Farm Cottages, a right in front the machinery shed, another right down the slope in front of the cowshed, and back past the farm gate to the cottages. In the center of farmyard loomed the mountainous, steaming manure pile into which the tractors dug their shovels every day to load up the spreader wagons. In spite of some scraped knees, Vince and Eric soon got the hang of how to ride fast round the bends. The girls were tentative and fearful. Paul managed to get round once without stopping. He wished Mummy or Daddy was there to watch him.

"Best ye be careful, lads," Jake called out. "There's patches o' tractor oil aroun'. Doan slam the brakes too 'ard or ye'll take a tumble."

After three days of practice, Sheila suggested a race. Her watch had a second hand. The fastest time of five circuits would win a slice of cherry chocolate cake made by Mrs. Spencer. The two women and several farm workers stayed for a while to watch the fun.

From the beginning Vince and, surprisingly, fat Gerald were the fastest riders. Paul did not think he could ever match them but he wanted to outshine Eric, who was third fastest. Except for school work, Eric was good at everything he tried, even getting away with being cheeky to Mrs. McAlistair.

When it was Paul's turn, he did his best to swallow his fear. After a fast first time round, he heard the cheers and glimpsed encouraging smiles as he sped past the spectators. He was no longer afraid. He was ready to beat Eric, or even *win*.

On the second circuit, Paul stood up on the pedals, zoomed up the first slope, turned and shot across the upper yard. At the cowshed, he angled the bicycle too tightly, braked, and skidded. Everything happened fast. His wheels went sideways. He felt his body separate and rise from the bike and for a split second, windmilling his arms, he was flying. Then SPLOSH, he was in a mass of warm squishiness and prickly straw. He didn't hurt anywhere. He could have laughed for joy if the breath hadn't been knocked out of him.

As he struggled to move, Paul felt a warm slime oozing over his bare legs and then the same stuff slid inside his shirt and up into his underpants. A nauseating smell swamped his nose. His chest felt tight, his eyes watered and began to sting. He heard the shrieks of laughter, looked around and saw the bicycle handlebars, a few feet away, sticking out of the manure heap.

The rescue was quick. Paul heard shouts and a sucking noise when someone got hold of his arms and legs. Then he was lying on a piece of canvas, spluttering manure from his mouth. Sobbing at the shame of his terrible failure, he tried to wipe the brown mess from his face. He wanted to leave the farm and hide forever. Someone said, "clothes off and hose him down."

"Right from the start I knew you would be trouble." Arms akimbo, Mrs. McAlistair and a giggling Alice watched Sheila bathe Paul for the third time in succession: each time using an unheard-of *twelve* inches of warm water. "You horrible child," Mrs.M. shrilled at him. "You've dirtied my bathtub. It's bad enough having to smell that manure every time I open the front door of this cottage. Now, it's *inside* my cottage … God knows how long it will last."

Sheila dried him, trying to reassure him with her warm eyes and gentle touches, while Mrs. McAlistair glared.

Paul kept looking down. He hated the way Mrs.M. talked. She was nasty.

"Pardon me, Mrs. McAlistair," Sheila said as she helped Paul dress. "It was an accident. He's only a little lad. Could have happened to anyone."

Mrs. M. grabbed him behind the neck and started pushing him up the stairs. "No supper for you tonight! And you won't get another bath for a month."

Paul pulled helplessly at the fingers that dug into his neck. "Please … stop. It hurts."

"Poor blue-eyed scrap," sighed Sheila, shaking her head as she followed up the stairs.

In the attic, Mrs. McAlistair let go and scowled at the both of them. "No afternoon walks for him 'til that smell is *completely gone* from *my* bathroom. He'll stay indoors studyin' his vocabulary."

A week passed, and Paul was still confined to the cottage. At night, he wet the bed and his nightmares came back. Sometimes he couldn't go to sleep or he would wake up at night and cry, wanting to go home and see everyone he loved. No one wanted to play with him anymore, and giggling Alice called him Poo-Poo Paul. Only Sheila and Furry Lion were good to him.

One night he woke from a bad dream and lay on his mattress thinking about Maman and how they used to play together in the lady doctor's garden. Even though rain rattled the roof thatch, he heard Mrs. McAlistair downstairs, swishing and creaking in the oak rocking chair where she liked to read. The other children were fast asleep.

Paul, restless and bored, decided to try Eric and Vince's trick; look between the cracks in the floor and "have a gander at the old fart," as Eric would say. Eric was brave and said rude words to Mrs. McAlistair that made her go red in the face and rap him on the knuckles with a ruler. He never cried and even stuck his tongue out at her. Paul wanted to be as brave as he was.

Next to Marigold's mattress, Paul found a wide gap between the planks and lay looking down into the room below. Mrs. McAlistair, in a red dressing gown, sat in a rocking chair with an open book on her lap. She twiddled her hair braids with one hand while she read.

She pulled up her nightdress, put a hand between her legs and wiggled her arm back and forth. With audible intakes of breath she began to groan softly. Her head tilted back, and Paul saw that her eyes were closed, and she was actually smiling. What she was doing was so strange that he could not stop watching. As he shifted to get a better look, his elbow caught the handle of a chamber pot. It half-tipped over, and cold liquid splashed on his skin. He moved the pot sideways so he could lean and look down again. She was still doing it. He felt wetness under his hand and in the faint light coming up from Mrs. M.'s room, he saw a puddle on the plank. His heart beat wildly, he could hardly breathe. Pee was dripping through the crack down into her room.

Mrs. M. jumped up with cry that turned into a scream.

The children sat up in their beds.

"What the fuck 'appened?" Eric growled. He turned on the light bulb.

Footsteps pounded the creaky stairs. In the next moment, Mrs. McAlistair, breathing heavily, was in the attic aiming her flashlight on the mattresses. Paul scuttled toward his bed but she saw him. The only child out of bed.

She shone the light in his face. "It was you knocked the potty over, wasn't it?" Her voice was shrill and angry. She looked around. "Which one of you saw him?"

"Please Missis," Marigold squeaked, pointing a finger. "It *was* Paul."

Mrs. M. bent down and grabbed his hair, lifting him off his mattress. He screamed and struggled, needles of pain tearing at his scalp. "You horrible children," she shouted, eyes flashing, her mouth working as if she was chewing meat. "All of you, stay up here 'til I've finished with this little divil. No coming down the stairs or you get the same as him."

Paul's feet slipped and his shins banged on the wooden steps as she dragged him downstairs. He shrank at the fury in her face as she shoved him into a corner, but his fear wasn't as agonizing as the pain in his right ankle. He held his breath.

She dragged him by his pajama top into the bathroom, slammed the door shut and forced him face down over the closed toilet seat. "This is where ye get what ye deserve. And naebody's watchin'."

He tried to resist but she was strong and kept his head and chest pressed painfully against the wooden toilet cover.

"I'll teach ye a lesson you won't fergit, disgustin' little tyke."

Paul struggled but the pain of her fingers digging into his neck was too great. He went limp and waited, terrified. He heard her grunt.

She pulled something out of a bucket.

He caught a glimpse. The long-handled wooden toilet brush. He heard a whistling sound and excruciating pain exploded across his buttocks. He screamed, clenching his fists, waiting for the agony to flow out of him. He hadn't felt bristles, just hard wood. Then the back of his thighs exploded. And seconds later, another smash … high up on his buttocks and onto his back.

Paul screamed "Stop!" He tried to pull her fingers off his neck, and cover his rear end with the other hand. Another blow cracked his fingers. He wriggled desperately, flailing and scratching at the hand around his neck. Every part of his body stung and throbbed. Every time she hit him Paul heard her shout "Wicked, wicked, wicked, wicked, wicked."

When the beating stopped, Paul was relieved, almost happy. All he could hear was his heart pounding and Mrs. M.'s heavy breathing. Moaning, half-crying and still face down, he sucked at the fingers of his left hand that now hurt worse than his backside. He tasted blood.

Fingers grabbed his hair, her lips right up against his ear. "Dinna tell anyone about this," she hissed. "If you do, your life here will be more than horrible—an' I'll beat you again if need be."

She released him. "Stop your caterwaulin' and get back to bed. Go."

As Paul hobbled to the stairs there was knocking at the front door.

A man's voice. Paul wondered who it was. He hoped it was old Jake come to save him. "What's that racket? Anythin' wrong?"

"Just dealin' with a frighted child, that's all. Nightmares, y'ken. Nothin' to worry about."

Sobbing, Paul stumbled up the steps, his buttocks and thighs on fire. The children, clustered at the head of the stairs, stood round his mattress as he crawled under his blanket and covered his head.

"Sounded like cats an' dogs fightin'," said Chrissie in her squeaky voice. "What did she do to 'im?"

"A bloody good wallopin', that's what." It was Eric, laughing. "Didn't you see what he done? He doused Mrs. M. with pee from your potty. He's got gumption 'as Paul. 'E had blood on 'im. Wish I could of seen 'er doin' 'im."

Paul felt as if his stomach was being punched. Why was Eric so mean?

"She never walloped none of us like that before," said Marigold in a trembling voice. "It was our potty. Maybe she'll do us next."

For what seemed a long time Paul stayed awake, holding Furry Lion tight. Through the throbbing pain, he seethed and struggled to understand why she beat him so badly. Spilling the chamber pot was his fault and he deserved punishment, but surely not the hard force she had used—all that for a little accident?

Next morning, instead of breakfast Mrs. M. sent Paul to the bathroom. By dint of twisting and standing on the toilet seat, he caught a glimpse in the mirror of violet indentations and horizontal lines of crusted blood on his buttocks and thighs. He touched the welts and winced in pain. They were as hard as the rungs of a ladder. He spoke to the mirror pretending Mrs. M. was there. *You hurt me. I'll get you, somehow.*

Paul was ashamed of what he had done and of being beaten like an animal. He wanted to tell Mrs. M. he was sorry for spilling the potty, but he knew from the way she looked at him and gave him his food last, and always the smallest helpings—that she would find a way to beat him again. Trying to be nice to her, as he did with Sheila and other grown-ups, wouldn't work with this nasty witch. Sheila, of course, saw it when she bathed him a week later. He could tell she was very upset, but all she said was, "You poor wee thing. I've a mind to tell Lady Hilliard."

"Please don't tell. Mrs. M. will find out."

Knapp Farm wasn't so super after all. He didn't know what to do about Mrs. M. He needed someone to defend him or rescue him and punish Mrs. M. Sheila would help him write the letter.

CHAPTER TWENTY
The Peacock Café, Cambridge
November 1942

Sunday breakfast, always the same menu, was a relaxed affair for the Carnegie-Holstons … though not for Sophie and Helga who were already up at six, snacking on scones and coffee before starting their chores.

Helga, aproned-up, baked the scones and cooked the eggs, smoked haddock, bacon rashers, and grilled mushrooms, which were all served in the dining room and kept warm in chafing dishes. Dr. Emily's extensive network of patients and church friends ensured that rationing did not affect the quality or quantity of the family's food.

Sophie, in a frilly beige cap and pinafore, set the dining table with napkins, silverware, condiments, marmalade and farm butter. She laid out the Sunday newspapers, sliced bread for the toaster and lit the burners for the chafing dishes. She replenished the food from time to time and made sure that hot coffee and tea were on hand.

On this occasion, Sophie had more on her mind than setting out the breakfast. The previous day, she had received an unsigned letter urging her to visit Paul at Knapp Hill Farm. It gave no details, no reasons. That night she slept badly, half-awake, wondering if Paul was in some kind of trouble. In the five months he'd been there, she hadn't been able to visit him because of the travel restrictions on refugees and her new "B" status. She had to find a way to see Paul. Now that they shared the "café project", Helga might have some useful advice about this worrying letter.

A month earlier, when Sophie revealed that she had worked at a Hungarian bakery in Paris, Helga told her about her dream to open a European-style café in Cambridge. She was fed up with being a servant. She had saved two hundred and forty pounds. Much better to make a business from her cooking. Doing this alone was almost impossible.

After much discussion around the kitchen table and stove, Helga had come up with an offer. In exchange for Sophie's savings from her wages and her full participation, they would be co-owners of a café. Sophie said she had forty-two pounds in the bank. One of the benefits of this arrangement, Helga explained, was that the government allowed refugees owning British businesses to travel without restriction. As a co-owner, for example, Sophie could visit Paul more or less at her own convenience.

Sophie loved the idea. She often dreamed about the café and, as she went about her chores, she imagined exactly what it would look like. It would have a friendly atmosphere where good food and conviviality were priorities. Cambridge was the perfect place, because there were so few restaurants and lots of hungry students. Many of the university professors had visited other countries. Surely, they appreciated continental food.

Meanwhile Helga spent most of her off-duty hours exploring the regulations regarding catering establishments, obtaining permits, and learning about area food suppliers and possible locations, all of which she collated in a box file snaffled from Dr. Emily's office.

Helga and Sophie's first step would be to quit their jobs, but Cambridge Alien Registration Board rules stated that they needed permission from their employer. Of course, there was a good chance Dr. Emily would refuse point-blank. What a terrible shock to lose two good servants at the same time. Sophie suggested they show iron-clad determination and tact to overcome the doctor's resistance, coupled with a well-thought-out plan backed up by evidence. Dr. Emily was a stickler for facts and justifications.

There was another obstacle—Willy. In one of her regular letters to him Sophie had mentioned that Helga wanted her to help run a café in Cambridge. "An interesting, idea," he wrote back. "Too ambitious. I'm snowed by work here so let's wait till the war is over when I'll have more time to advise you. For God's sake, don't waste good money on this. I'm more worried that the doctor will be angry at losing two good domestics. She has been so good to us. This is not how we repay kindness."

Willy was clearly too enmeshed in his training to understand that she wanted to do something constructive for herself. Enough scrimping and being a domestic.

Dr. Emily, of course, knew nothing of this, yet.

As Sophie finished her coffee, a headline in the day-old newspaper caught her eye. "Look at this, Helga. Good news. An Allied victory in North Africa. Tobruk has been retaken, Benghazi is about to fall and they have General Rommel on the run." She laughed. "If we win the war, the success of our café in Cambridge is guaranteed." The Allied victory was a sign to her that she was had made the right choice to join Helga.

Helga frowned. She was at the marble counter, unwrapping a slab of sliced bacon. "What are these places you speak about? Arab towns in the middle of a nowhere desert? Pfui. I've had enough of the war." She shook her braids, looking annoyed. "Anyway, fighting in Africa is not so important. Not like Europe."

"How can you say that?" said Sophie. "The newspaper says it's a turning point." She laid down the newspaper. "Listen, Helga. I have to visit Paul. I got a worrying letter from the farm. Today, I want to tell the doctor about our plans."

Helga spun round, knocking uncooked bacon rashers onto the floor. "*Du bist verrückt*, crazy!" With a curse she picked them up and wiped the grease stain off the floor with Sophie's newspaper. "What is wrong with you, girl? We are *absolut* not ready."

Sophie pulled a sheet of crumpled paper from her pocket and

flattened it. "Listen. This message is from Paul's farm. Not even signed. Paul is unhappy, and someone from his family should visit soon." She dabbed her eyes with her apron. "With the café approved, I will be able to visit Paul. We must tell Dr. Emily about our café, after breakfast."

With a sour look, Helga shook her braids. "*Überhaupt nicht!* We are not properly ready. We have the place but the lease is not signed. We don't have permits for a kitchen. We don't have a detailed estimate from the builder. We don't know how to get tables and chairs." She patted Sophie's shoulder with sympathetic fingers. "I understand your worry about Pavel. No panic. Just telephone the farm owners and ask them what's going on."

"I thought about that. Paul might be afraid to tell them that something is wrong. But me … he would tell. And what if this letter is from someone who only wants to cause trouble? Talking in English on the telephone is hard for me. I must go there myself."

Helga shrugged. "You are a foolish woman. Ask your husband to visit Paul."

Sophie gazed mournfully at Helga. "He already requested leave from his commander to visit Paul but I don't know when it will be."

"Well, there you are. Problem solved. Stop whining."

"But it could be weeks. He's a soldier and follows orders. The army controls him." Sophie poured herself some coffee, weighing the possibility of upsetting Helga so much that she would simply cancel their plan. "Like it or not, Helga, you and I will talk to Dr. Emily this morning. We'll explain why we want to leave. You *have* to help me."

Helga slammed her hand on the table. Her eyes blazed. "*Mein Gott*, Sophie, why should I do this for you and risk failure? I dislike very much being forced. This café is *my* dream, not yours. I have spent half of my savings. Every step must be carefully considered and taken."

Sophie washed her cup in the sink. "As they say here, keep your hair on, Helga. We have a good plan. I can't possibly trust Willy to turn up at the farm. I must visit Paul soon. Without official permission from the doctor to leave our jobs, our café is finished."

Helga grimaced, heaving her shoulders with a sigh. "So ... we will ask her ... and show how we are prepared. You are a good talker, so you start, and I join in." She pulled two large frying pans off their hooks, tightened the apron around her stout waist, and looked around at Sophie, who was slicing a long loaf for toast. "Does Willy know about this?"

Sophie felt a shock and tried to hide it. Revealing Willy's strong resistance would give Helga ammunition to delay everything. "All he knows is that I am trying to find a way to see Paul at least once a month. Owning the café with you will get me a travel permit."

Helga raised a suspicious eyebrow. "And your husband agrees?"

"He's happy that I'm planning to visit Paul. To tell the truth, Helga, he doesn't know how far we are in this venture."

Helga cracked six eggs, into a bowl, two at a time. "Your family was never my business, but what your husband thinks about our café *is* my business." She switched on the fan above the cooker. "Remember," she shouted above the whirring, "I'm the one with the big bank account. If your husband stops you, your money is gone."

Sophie stiffened at Helga's harsh words, caught by her determination to get to Pavel and her fear of what Willy would do when he found everything out. Emil, and certainly Judit, would be outraged. But what could Willy actually do? Write furious letters or stop sending money. He might belong to the Royal Engineers; but she did not belong to him.

"Let's see what happens when we talk to Dr. Emily," she said.

Breakfast in the dining room, apart from the click of silverware on plates and the twang of the toaster, was as quiet as a museum reading room. The Carnegie-Holstons were buried in newspapers. When Sophie was not refreshing the coffee pots and milk jug, carrying food in and dirty plates out, she sat at the kitchen table composing a letter to Willy. Helga was at the stove preparing for lunch.

"Time I got ready for church," Sophie heard Dr. Emily say to her husband through the partly open swing door that needed oiling. She knew that she and Helga had to act soon.

"Don't dawdle, dear. The domestics have to get the table ready for lunch. Remember, your cousin's family is coming at one."

Sophie recognized Mr. Carnegie-Holston's usual grunt. "Don't expect me in church today. The only God I look up to is General Montgomery."

"Not a nice thing to say, dear."

A bell jangled in the kitchen. Sophie pushed through the door into the dining room. "You called, madam?"

Dr. Emily smiled. "Yes, dear, come in. You may clear the table."

Mr. Carnegie-Holston looked up from his newspaper "Sophie, didn't you once tell me you lived in Vichy France?" He tapped the paper. "It says here that the Jerries have just occupied the south of France—kicked the Vichy blokes out for being too wimpy."

"We lived there just before the Vichy government was formed. My husband was in the Czechoslovak army. We were evacuated to England."

Helga appeared beside Sophie who was reassured by an encouraging look and the cook's solid presence.

"Ah, now this *is* a surprise," said Dr. Emily, pushing her egg-stained plate away. She drained the last of her coffee. "The two of you at once? Is this some sort of delegation?"

"Excuse me, please," Sophie said. "We wish to speak to you about our employment." She had a pencil and notepad in her pinafore pocket.

Helga was silent. Sophie noticed her frowning and twisting her apron strings.

Mr. Carnegie-Holston looked at the two servants and groaned. "I can tell from their faces that they're going to ask for a raise." He rose and dropped his folded newspaper on a chair. "This is your turf, Emily. I'm off—just don't let them play on your sympathetic nature. Times are hard, money's tight."

Dr. Emily leaned back, waiting for the dining room door to close behind her husband. She frowned. "What is it? You both look so serious. Anything wrong?"

Sophie attempted a curtsey, a maneuver she detested. In this case, she thought it might help to soften what was coming. "Doctor, I am sorry. It is not easy to say, but we wish to leave your employment. We need your permission."

"You … what?"

Helga nodded. "We wish to leave Tallard House, please."

Dr. Emily sprang to her feet, shaking her head. "I … Sophie—for heaven's sake."

"Yes," said Helga with a stubborn look. "We have decided."

A red flush suffused Dr. Emily's face. "Both of you, at the same time? This is ridiculous. What's going on?"

Sophie's heart beat faster. This was the moment. In a way, she felt sorry for the doctor, someone who worked hard and relied so much on her staff to run the household and her practice.

The doctor sat back down, her mouth an angry line. "Sit down. I can't talk with both of you standing there." She swiveled to face them. "You've decided, you say! Have you lost your minds?"

Sophie sat, her eyes lowered.

Helga pulled up a chair.

Sophie pressed her palms together. A gesture of hope, an appeal for consideration. "Please, for me it is difficult to explain. I'm very grateful for your kindness to my family. But I have to leave for Paul's sake."

The doctor fiddled with the silver cross hanging from her neck. "We depend on both of you. You can't just quit. So, talk, I'm listening."

"Leaving has been on my mind," said Helga. With an embarrassed look, she rubbed stubby fingers back and forth across her knees. "I always wanted to have a café or little restaurant. Since coming to you, I saved money." She shifted in her chair. "Sophie ran her husband's business while he was in prison and she learned to cook in Paris. You and your guests always say how good we cook."

Sophie waited for Helga's words to sink in.

"Another big reason for me to help Helga," Sophie said, "is that it is five months since I saw Paul. Five months! Because I am not allowed to leave Cambridge." She could not stop the tears coming and took out her handkerchief. "Helga explained that refugees are permitted to travel if they run a business." She dabbed her cheeks. "As part-owner of a café I could visit Paul."

Frowning, the doctor pulled off her glasses and tossed them on to the table. "Why give up a safe position with me? Don't you realize you might lose all your money and end up without a job?"

Sophie's words tumbled out. "Helga already found a place to rent close to the university, where a hairdresser shop just closed."

"Glory be," said the doctor. "All this has been going on behind my back."

Sophie's face flushed. The doctor was angry but she had to go on, paint a picture, and try to explain how a dream could become reality. "In the beginning, we will offer only lunch—for the university students and professors."

"We will use herbs like garlic and paprika," said Helga with the hint of a smile. "Such things are not found in Cambridge restaurants. We will have self-service salads in big bowls on the counter, and every day we'll bake fresh bread and serve a different soup. No table service."

"No other place will be like this." Sophie's eyes gleamed. "We have the knowledge and skill. Our café will be good for Cambridge. Please, you must help us succeed."

Helga smiled her agreement, twisting her fingers nervously.

"For refugees, you have unexpectedly large ambitions," said the doctor, raising an eyebrow.

Sophie waited, ankles crossed, hands folded on her lap. She saw the twitch at the corner of the doctor's mouth and had a feeling her employer wasn't quite so angry anymore.

A long minute passed.

"Well, Sophie," said the doctor with a deep breath. "I understand what you want. I was the only woman in my class at medical school. It was hard work and often demeaning. Since then, I have tried to help women overcome their subservient roles. But …" She exhaled. "I am annoyed you planned this behind my back." She paused, screwing the top back on to her fountain pen. "Still… your aims are admirable even though my family, especially my husband, will be much inconvenienced. I expect you know other refugees in town. If I agree to your request, you could help greatly if you found me replacements."

"I know some people," Helga said. "We will do our best."

"Hunh." The doctor poured another cup of coffee and added milk. "For this café—do you have a financial plan? You'll need a solicitor to work on the property lease and the taxes. "Do you know anything about food regulations? You will also need a National Food Office permit."

"We can manage all such things," Sophie said, her heart sinking at the doctor's acute observations.

"Now, listen to me, both of you—I understand your wanting to make something of yourselves. But have you really thought this through. Starting a café in wartime would be a huge step for two Englishwomen, let alone refugees. Also you'd have to get business permits from the Aliens Board. Who is going to support your credentials in front of those officials?"

The two domestics looked at each other and then at the doctor with hopeful smiles.

The doctor glanced at Sophie. "I presume your husband knows all about this."

Sophie smiled confidently. "Of course, doctor, my family supports me."

Helga frowned. "*Frau Doktor*, we know what to do. We are comp...etent. I was a supervisor at the Deutsche Bank in Berlin. I understand business and finance better than I cook, yes."

Listening to Helga, Sophie had some regrets. Tallard House had been good to her. She had learned about middle class English families. Her English was fluent. Dr. Emily had taught her and Helga the names of everything in the house and garden, even taking them on bird-watching excursions. She had acquired a fine cultural education. Now it was over. She was not afraid of leaving.

"Do not be worried, doctor." Helga continued. "We already spend many hours on this. Also, we talked to Mr. Matthews, the owner of the Dorothy Café where Sophie goes for tea dancing. He gives us advice on permits and where to buy cheap equipment and supplies."

Sophie's face glowed. "We found a place for the café next to St. John's College—the hair-cutting shop in All Saints Passage. It will soon close."

"Tell me this, "said the doctor. "What if your customers can't afford the food you prepare ... or only a few want to come? Have you thought about that?"

"Yes, yes—and yes" said Sophie with a smile. "We will make

advertisements. Our restaurant is close to where educated people like your husband and university students live and work. They will come."

Doctor Emily got up from her chair and looked out the window, hands locked behind her back. "Here's a speck in your eye. What will people say when foreigners like you open your cafe? What if they find out that Helga comes from Germany? If they know I've helped you, it could damage my practice."

"Aha!" Helga's smile split her plump face. "It will not be called a German restaurant, *Frau Doktor*, but a European one. Sophie is beautiful and lively. Her English is already better than mine. She will be the hostess, and our customers will see her through the windows. I am plain and heavy and stay in the kitchen. Once they taste our food, customers will come back."

"With your cooking, I expect they will," Doctor Emily murmured.

"The café will be full of light and painted with happy colors," added Sophie, her feet tapping with excitement. "Peacock colors. Maybe we show artist paintings. It will be like a bistro in Paris."

The doctor stood, towering over her two employees. She smiled. "Well, maybe I'll let you go ahead with your madcap scheme."

Sophie took a sharp excited breath. She was sure now that Willy would cooperate when he knew the doctor had agreed to help them. It was for Paul's sake, but the idea that she was opening a café on her own initiative was exhilarating. "

"Well, I'll pray in church today for your success," the doctor said, lighting a cigarette. "Just find me good replacements."

Sophie and Helga curtsied and turned to leave the room.

"Just a minute," Dr. Emily said. "Have you thought up a name for this European bistro of yours?"

Helga looked at Sophie, eyes flashing with pleasure. "She chose it."

"The Peacock Café," said Sophie. "A beautiful place where people will eat good food, feel happy, and make friendships—a place where they can forget the war."

CHAPTER TWENTY-ONE
A Visit to Knapp Hill Farm
November, 1942

It was Wednesday at Knapp Hall. Paul rolled his tongue round his lips as he practiced his writing with the others, before going out to play. A maid burst into the big playroom and grabbed Sheila's arm, nodding toward Paul. "Her Ladyship wants the little furrin lad. Down in the farm office."

Paul looked up in surprise. He was the only furrin lad. Had he done something wrong? He didn't dare ask.

"I wonder what her Ladyship wants," Sheila said as they descended the stairs. "Maybe Mrs. M.'s bin tellin' on us." Paul couldn't tell if Sheila was joking or playing a scary game. He slipped his hand into hers, grateful for the squeeze he got back.

They found Lady Hilliard perched on the edge of her paper-strewn desk, smiling and puffing on a black cigarette. Paul had never seen her in a riding jacket and breeches. He sniffed … something about her smelled like the manure pile he'd fallen into. There were mud splodges on her boots. *Was it mud or pooh?*

It was his first time in the farm office, and he decided to stay quiet, look around, and wait. What he guessed were family photographs cluttered the walls. Several pairs of old gumboots occupied a coconut mat in a corner. The top drawer of a green filing cabinet was half-open. Immobile in a basket, gray-muzzled Jason wrinkled his eyes at Paul and twitched a hello with his tail.

Aunt Popsie handed Paul an off-white envelope and winked. "Guess what, my dear. You'll soon have a visitor—an important soldier."

Paul pulled out a sheet of typed foolscap. After a few moments, he handed it to Sheila with a shy look. "I think it might be my … er, daddy. Can you read it?"

Sheila skimmed the sentences, eyes bright with excitement. "Bless me, Lord! Your da *is* comin'. In all the time I've bin here, he'll be only the fourth visitor we've had to Middle Cottage, and never a father."

Aunt Popsie stubbed out her cigarette. Her smile coincided with Paul's grin. "Go on, Sheila."

Dear Lady Hilliard,
Nov 18 1942. Bothwell Camp. Scotland

I have been given some leave. I plan to visit Paul at the farm between December 5-7 Apologies for the short notice. The long complicated train journey to you means I will actually only have one full day with Paul. My wife will not be with me. She is not allowed to travel outside Cambridge. Also my parents are back in London. I'm sorry that none of us have been able to visit Paul over the past five months.

Please confirm that my visit is possible. I will book a hotel room in Shrewsbury (any recommendations?) and, if there is no bus that comes by the farm, I'll take a taxi. I'll send you a telegram two days before I leave. Please let Paul know when I am coming.

Thank You. In appreciation,
Lt.Cpl. Willy Kohut. Royal Engineers.

Aunt Popsie ruffled Paul's curls. "You're a lucky little chap. But we can't have your father waste his precious time and money buzzing back and forth from Shrewsbury in taxis. We'll put him up here at the Hall. Bert will fetch him from the station. Sheila, please make sure Paul knows exactly when to expect his father. "

"Yes, your ladyship." Sheila exchanged a joyful look with Paul.

He wriggled his toes, too excited to even smile properly. "Super-duper," he whispered; one of Eric's expressions he greatly admired. He suddenly felt an urge to pee and squeezed his thighs together, hoping it would go away for a while. A thought suddenly surfaced. *When he gets here I'll tell him what Mrs. M. did to me. I know he'll punish her.*

*   *   *

A few days later, Sheila took Paul to the calendar pinned on the cottage kitchen door. "What's the day today, and what's written there?"

"Friday, and that's my name, Kohut. Is that today?"

Her smile was accompanied by a tinkly laugh.

"S'right. Your da's comin' this afternoon. So, don't go getting dirty. I'm not washin' any extra clothes. And bundle up warm. There's a cold wind blowin'. "

Paul was too excited to take in more than her first sentence. He ran up into the attic and sat on his mattress with Furry Lion beside him, looking at his photographs and trying hard to stop the quivering feeling that ran up and down his arms and legs.

Soon enough, Mrs. M. called him downstairs to join the others for the reading and writing class. He spent the rest of the morning with Eric and Marigold in the cottage's front garden, building traps for moles. In the afternoon, Sheila took the children for a walk. Just in case his father came early, Paul stayed behind, wandering around the farmyard outbuildings. Even in the cold, he felt hot and shaky.

By the time the children were back it was almost tea-time. Mrs. M. sat them on the floor to do simple sums while she and Sheila set out plates and silverware and began to make fish paste sandwiches. When Paul recognized the pop-pop sound of Aunt Popsie's car he dashed to the front door and ran outside.

A man in a military greatcoat and cap strode up the gravel path toward him, a large satchel over his shoulder. Paul wanted to give a triumphant whoop but nothing came out. He stood rooted, not knowing what to say or do.

Daddy lifted him high in the air and spun him around, covering him with kisses. "Sooo, my little *Pavliček*," he said in Czech. "How are you?' He spun him around again and put him down and continued in English. "I'm very happy to see you. Are you glad to see me? "

Paul eyes glistened with tears. "You're here, but … er, Mummy. Did you bring her too?"

Willy crouched down and grasped Paul's hands. "I'm very sorry, Paulikin. Mummy is still not allowed to travel." He brushed the boy's curly hair with his fingers and then stood, laughing. He threw his arms wide to include the cottage and its surroundings. "This place is like a fairy tale … wonderful. Old and pretty and so English. Like the nursery rhyme about an old woman who lived in a shoe—with so many children she didn't know what to do."

"Mrs. M.'s a bit like an old lady, Daddy," Paul said, admiring his father's uniform as he led him by hand through the front door. "But she always knows what to do."

Mrs. McAlistair, Sheila, and the other children sat round the table drinking milk and eating their tea.

Willy took off his greatcoat and plucked the peaked cap off his head in the bowing style of a medieval courtier. "Good afternoon everyone."

Paul threw his shoulders back, wanting to add importance to his announcement. "This is my Daddy. He's a soldier." From the open mouths and stares, he knew that his friends were impressed by the pressed khaki trousers, tailored tunic, gleaming brass buttons and buckles, and the leather belt and gloves.

Willy bowed. "Lieutenant-Corporal Kohut, Royal Engineers, at your service."

Mrs. McAlistair half-rose from her chair, an unaccustomed smile on her face. "Will ye not join us for some tea, Mister Kohut? Er, I mean, Leftenant."

"Thank you, madam. That would be nice. It's been a long, cold journey, but … first, Paul and I have to discuss something privately."

In the surprised silence that followed, Willy took Paul outside. By now, there was a cold drizzle and they huddled together on the bench under the thatched entry porch. He unclipped his satchel and pulled out two shiny, dark brown cardboard boxes. "I want to talk to you about the gifts I brought. Ever seen these before?"

Paul shook his head and ran his fingers over the gold lettering, spelling it out slowly. "All Gold."

"The name of very special chocolates," said Willy with a smile. "Look." He tore the fastening tab off one box and raised the lid.

Paul looked at the top layer of chocolates nestled inside pleated black paper cups. Each one had a different shape. It was beautiful, like a treasure chest.

"Look here, at the underside of the lid. The drawings tell you what filling goes with what shape and what it's called. It's a sort of puzzle. This square one. What's that word under it?"

"Car-am-el?"

"Right. Now find a chocolate with that same shape and eat it, very slowly."

Paul popped the caramel in his mouth. It was gone in an instant. "Can I have another one?" he asked eagerly.

Willy smiled. "Good eh? Well, not another one just yet. Let's share this box with everyone else in the cottage," he said gently. "These chocolates are very special."

Paul rolled his tongue around the inside of his mouth trying to extract the last taste of smoky caramel. *Why should Daddy give my chocolates away?* "What about the other box?"

"It's for Lady Hilliard who has been so good to you."

They went back inside. Willy accepted Mrs. M.'s offer of tea and a slice of her homemade fruitcake, and a stream of questions followed. Did he live in a tent, did he shoot guns, and did he ever drive a tank? Had he killed a Jerry? Had he thrown a hand grenade?

Paul proudly watched his father answer. "My main job," he said, finishing off his cake, "is making sure guns and tanks get put on trucks and trains and taken to where the fighting is." Everyone listened open-mouthed and wide-eyed.

"Try a piece of *this* cake, mister leftenant," Sheila said, tossing her long hair. She pushed a plate bearing an unevenly-formed cake with yellow icing toward him. "Made it meself. It's sponge with rhubarb jam filling. Paul loves it. I'm Sheila, the Land Girl."

Paul's eyes gleamed. "It's jolly good cake, Daddy."

Willy tried to focus on cutting himself a slice but found it difficult not to stare at the Land Girl's creamy skin, full breasts, and trim waist. The rest of her body, hidden under the table, was surely just as delectable. For too many weeks, he had been cooped up at Bothwell camp with only the local pub and barmaids for entertainment. "It looks delicious, but I'll take only one small piece. I'm invited for dinner at the Hall. Come hungry, Lady Hilliard said." Willy gave Sheila a slow glance. "However, Paul and I do have something special for all of you."

He drew the opened chocolate box from his satchel and flipped open the cover. "Terry's All Gold. Special chocolates." He looked down at Paul. "How many pieces do you think each person can take?"

Paul poised a forefinger above the rows of chocolates, ready to count. He looked up at the eager faces, and then pushed the box towards Sheila. "Two each. You first."

Willy could see the happiness in Paul's face. He guessed it was something to do with the pleasure of offering of a gift, or perhaps also, the possession of something rare and powerful that others might envy.

As Sheila put out her hand, Alice McAlistair reached across the table and grabbed the box. She helped herself and gave two to her mother who passed the box on for the children to help themselves. Soon, only a few chocolates were left.

Willy pushed the box back toward Mrs. McAlistair. "Keep the rest for later. I think there's enough left to give one more to each child."

Mrs. McAlistair closed the lid. "Dinna worry, I'll keep this locked away until there's a guid moment. Now children, say thank you to Paul's faither."

Half an hour later, Willy, exhausted from his journey, kissed and hugged Paul again outside the front door. "I'm very tired, Paul. I'm going up to the big house now, but I'll see you tomorrow," he said, taking a pipe from his breast pocket. He paused to stuff it with tobacco and light it. "How about after breakfast?"

Paul nodded. "Okay, Daddy."

Sheila came out from the cottage, easing on her raincoat and tying a headscarf over her red-gold river of hair. "I'll show you the way to Knapp Hall, mister soldier—if you'd like me to. I've an umbrella." She looked up at the sky and gave him a quizzical look. "Just in case. Come on, then." She walked ahead of Willy, the raincoat swaying around her hips.

He hurried to catch up, wondering when and how he would find a place to make love to her.

*　　　*　　　*

The next morning, Willy clad in a borrowed slicker and Wellingtons, explored the farm. He was delighted that his son, the farm expert, was so eager to show him everything in spite of the cold rain and set the pace with questions about the farm. Willy was unsure how to engage with his son—they had become almost strangers—so he kept asking for information and guidance, an approach he used in the army. He desperately wanted to rekindle a loving relationship. He tried to show interest in the milking shed and cow barn, the pigsties and Emperor, the retired Clydesdale that the Hilliards kept for old time's sake.

Paul with an enthusiastic look explained that Emperor's only job—in the summer—was to pull a hay wagon at the annual Shropshire County Show, all dressed up with leather straps, brasses, and ribbons.

Willy thoughts kept returning to Sheila's swaying hips and her inviting eyes.

He was pleased at how much his son had matured from the frail, whiny child who broke his shoulder in London. The curls round the boy's head had turned to a light brown thatch and his slender frame had filled out and he was a bundle of energy. Paul ran from the pigsties to the barns, raced up a ladder in the hayloft, scaring out roosting pigeons and chickens. He picked up ducks and chickens and tried to show Willy how to hold them.

"I can see you like it here." Willy smiled as they sat together on a hay bale in a barn big enough to house two tractors and some plowing equipment. He had decided to talk only in English; Paul still flip-flopped at times. Willy remembered Dr. Carnegie-Holston's advice. "If you want Paul to have a bright future here, just submerge him in our British ways."

Paul looked down at his intertwined fingers. "Yes, Papa—Daddy," he said hesitantly. "It's super here, most of the time—only that …"

"Most of the time? Is there anything I should know?"

Paul shrugged and looked away.

Willy wondered whether this was the clue to the unhappiness that Sophie's letter (now in his pocket) had mentioned. "Is it Mrs. M? I expect she must get angry at times. She has to be strict to put up with all you children bouncing around that little cottage."

"Did you come here to take me home to Mummy?" said Paul in a small voice.

Willy flinched. Paul had put his finger on the heart of the matter. His son was homesick. He put his arm round Paul's shoulders and with an unexpected sob, hugged him, ashamed that he had transferred his boy's care to strangers. And Sophie had dropped a bombshell in her letter; she was leaving her job with Dr. Emily to open a café in Cambridge. Her words circled mercilessly in his head:

That's why I made plans and decisions without asking you. I did not want to worry you needlessly if nothing came of it. In any case, these days, you have so little time for us. The army has swallowed you up. I have to run my own life.

As soon as I get the travel waiver and internment exemption card I will visit Paul and also come to see you in Scotland. We have to talk things over.

Resentment coursed through him like a hot current. How could Sophie make a decision to start a café without his say-so? And yet, she had engineered a solution that would allow her to see Paul. No doubt about it … she had *chutzpah*.

He started at the sight of a large bird swooping out of the barn's open doors, and turned to see if Paul was frightened.

"Don't be afraid, Daddy. It's an old barn owl. He lives here."

Willy breathed relief, half-ashamed that he had shown fear. "That owl has a home," he said, pulling an arm around Paul's shoulders, "but we don't, not yet. When the fighting is over we'll find a place and all be together again."

Paul gave his father a stricken look. "How do you know the war will finish? What about Mummy—and Granny and Grandpa. Are they safe?"

Willy gathered Paul into his arms. The boy's heart was beating fast against his own. "Don't worry," he whispered. "We're all safe. Did you know that Granny and Grandpa went back to London?"

"Sheila read me the letter. They liked the house in Cambridge. I liked it. I had friends at The Shrubbery School. There was a white cat that loved me. Why did they go away?"

Willy sighed inwardly. Life was difficult, especially for a little boy separated from his family. These days, everyone was trying to balance what they wanted to do, what they had to do and what other people wanted them to do. In his case, the army was in charge of his life's balancing act, and that drastically limited his options.

"Granny and Grandpa had no good friends in Cambridge and their flat in London was repaired—and the bombing almost stopped. Now tell me from your heart, are you happy here, at the farm? Anything not right?"

"I … I don't know. I like it a lot … but…" Paul took his father's hand and put it against his cheek. "Sometimes Mrs. M. is nasty."

Willy felt his anger stirring. "What do you mean nasty?"

"She calls me stupid 'cos I don't speak good. Marigold and Eric wet the bed too. And I'm always the last to get everything. She never smiles, not like Sheila."

Willy took a deep breath, trying to control his urge to get hold of Mrs. M. and give her a good shaking. But Lady Hilliard had hired Mrs. M. and he owed the Hilliards a great debt for housing Paul. "So … what does this Mrs. M. do to you?"

Paul blinked. "I dunno … different things. She says I'm stinky and wet the bed, a liar, wicked, stuff like that."

"That *is* mean." Willy put his arm around his son's shoulders. "I'll talk to Lady Hilliard."

Paul slid off the bale and peered up his father's face. "Why can't I be with you and Mummy, all of us together?"

Willy's heart sank. "If we can stop Mrs. M. being mean that will help, won't it?"

Paul nodded.

Through the open barn door, Willy saw a woman in a headscarf swing open the farmyard gate. A herd of cows crowded in from the lane. Beyond the heaving brown backs, he saw a curved stick swing in the air and heard a man's whistle … and a burst of laughter. He envied these people their simple lives.

"Can I ask you a farming riddle, Daddy? Sheila teaches us riddles."

Willy didn't know this English word, riddle, or why Paul was asking him. He felt ashamed that he knew less than his son. He nodded.

"What makes twice as much noise as a squealing pig?"

Willy took out his tobacco pouch and filled the bowl of his pipe. Pipe smoking offered not only pleasure but an opportunity for extra thought. He raised his eyebrows in mock perplexity as he struck the match. "Oh, I don't know—er—what about a trumpeting elephant?"

Paul shook with laughter. "No, Daddy, *two* squealing pigs—I got you, didn't I? That's one of Bert's jokes."

Willy puffed out smoke, grunting. "Hunh! Simple and logical."

Paul grabbed his elbow. "We better go outside, Daddy. You aren't supposed to smoke in a barn. It's dangerous."

The morning turned sunny. Willy and Paul walked a half mile from the farm to watch frogs jumping into a pond. When they got back,

Sheila greeted them. With a coquettish shake of her hair, she picked a cloth-covered basket off the doorstep.

"At last, finally! I've been waitin' a while for you two adventurin' rascals. We've a forty-minute walk ahead of us before lunch. Lady Hilliard asked me to arrange a wee picnic on Knapp Hill, and when we're there, I have to be sure you don't get lost or fall down an old mine-shaft." She fluttered her eyes at Willy.

He grinned back confident that she would be his. It was a question of when and where.

They set out on a lane that wound through a small wood behind Knapp Hall. Paul showed the way, running on ahead and then back, interrupting the grown-ups' conversation. Silhouetted against the blue sky, bare trees gave way to fields bordered by hedgerows, willow and elder. To reach the lean-to shelter at the top, they walked through patches of dirt-stained snow.

For a long time they gazed over the valley. Below them, carpets of dry bracken stretched down to meet the waist-high stone walls that separated the rough land from the valley's lower pastures.

"Bring me some of that bracken, if you can break it off," Sheila shouted to Paul. "I'll pick some dried coneflowers and we'll make a posy after we've eaten our sandwiches."

Paul started off along a well-worn track, waving his arms at birds that fluttered from the undergrowth. In a few minutes he returned, crestfallen, with a handful of dilapidated stalks. "These were all I could find."

She patted his cheek. "That's the winter for you, darlin'. Most every plant's asleep."

After a short rest on a log trimmed as a seat in front of the shelter, Sheila guided them to a badger warren and demonstrated how to use twigs and wild clematis vine to set a rabbit trap. "And that's called Red Beard," she said as they walked past a worn boulder covered by clumps of gray-green mosses, "though it's not red at the moment." She stopped and pulled at the stalk of a tall dried-out plant. "And this is a teasel." She showed them the prickly seed head. "In the old days, when they ran sheep here, the local women used these to card the wool before they spun and wove the cloth. Of course, the factories do that now."

Willy was impressed by Sheila's intensity and love for country things. She seemed completely at home on Knapp Hill, in a world utterly removed from the detailed, mechanical training and drab existence of his camp. This hill was a dream world.

On the ridge, sheltered from a stiff breeze, they rested below the massive rocks, eating sandwiches, contemplating the line of thunderclouds that Sheila explained were "peein'" on the other side of the Welsh border. "That big wanderin' dark hill you see far off, that's the Long Mynd," she said in her lilting voice.

Willy was enchanted by her Irish accent and the way the wind blew her coppery tresses and flattened her cotton dress against her breast and thighs. He felt a stirring heat between his thighs. He wanted to wrap her in his arms.

She shaded her eyes. "Can you see that pile o' black rocks on top of that Long Mynd?"

He nodded, shielding his eyes from the sun with cupped hands.

"That's the Stiperstones—the dreaded place where Wild Edric, a Saxon noble, battled the Normans. They say t' devil himself still sits up there in a great stone chair, drummin' up storms and eatin' whole sheep for his supper."

Willy laughed. "So, it hasn't taken long for an Irish girl to learn the local legends."

She took his arm and looked earnestly into his face. "Legends are beautiful things, to be sure, mister leftenant. Legends are truth, imagining and poetry all wrapped up to make your heart beat fast."

"See there, Daddy." Paul interrupted, pointing at several grassy tracks that meandered toward derelict fences and wooden signs half way down the hill.

Willy nodded.

"Old Bert told me about those places. They're tunnels, dug by men looking for metal and coal. He says they're old and dangerous. We mustn't go near them."

"Mines, they call 'em. We'll have to start back soon," said Sheila, tucking the food wrappings back into her basket "We'll take another twenty minutes up here and then home."

Paul ran off into the tall bracken trying to flush out a rabbit Sheila had seen. When he gave up and came back to the shelter, her head was bent over his father's open palm. She looked up, eyes sparkling. "I'm telling his fortune," she said. "I see great things a comin' for this lovely man."

Paul put out his hand. "Can you do mine?"

Sheila pulled back her tresses. "Your palm's not yet ready for the world, darlin'."

*   *   *

That evening, Willy enjoyed his dinner at Knapp Hall: smoked Welsh trout to start, bacon-wrapped roast pheasant in Cumberland whisky sauce, roast potatoes, and leeks—apple pie with farm cream for dessert. The Hilliards had weekend guests from London, a financial broker and his wife. A widow friend and a teacher and his wife from Shrewsbury School were also present. The men were in tuxedos, the women in long dresses. Willy wore his uniform and presented his box of chocolates to the hostess.

They were served by Brackett—a wispy-haired, elderly man in

an old-fashioned waistcoat and breeches; a real English butler who poured Sancerre with the trout and then an aromatic claret. The two maids supervised by Brackett offered the serving dishes to each guest as smoothly as any Parisian waiter, and with considerably more charm.

The only awkward moment came when the investment broker asked, "Just curious, old chap. What's a foreigner like you doing in the Royal Engineers? Were you in that line in Czechoslovakia?"

Willy was quiet for a moment, calibrating his answer into a generic description that would reveal only what everyone knew about military engineers. His orders were clear: no specifics to be discussed with anyone. "I'm still in training, sir. Our courses cover mechanics, electrical systems, designing and building structures and equipment, communications, and transportation, to name just a few things. We work ten-hour days."

Sir Edward laughed, a kind of knowing guffaw. "Quite a shopping list, eh? I 'spect they're scoping you out to see where you fit in. At least you're getting a break with us here at Knapp Hall." He leaned over to refill the wine glasses.

Trying to suppress an urge to boast, Willy nodded silently. In fact, he had already been assigned to a special project. Because of his background in textiles, he was involved in the design and construction of canvas decoy tanks, trucks, and guns. All he knew was that these decoys could be inflated in twenty minutes, and they would be used in an operation called Quicksilver. His next assignment would be in the county of Hampshire, southwest of London. As usual, no one had said why or what for.

Once that sticky moment had passed, Willy enjoyed the wide-ranging conversation that covered the Nazi advance on Stalingrad on the Eastern front, the struggling British economy, the bitterness of party politics, and General Montgomery's resurgence at El Alamein.

But he was bored by their county gossip about milk prices and the shortage of farmworkers—until he heard Lady Hilliard explain that she delivered free milk to local families in need. His admiration grew for her thoughtfulness and kind heart. This was the English at their best.

More than anything, he was surprised at her transformation from rumpled farm owner into a tall well-groomed, attractive woman in a form-fitting satin gown. Every time he glanced her way, she was smiling at him. First, a lovely Irish girl, and now the lady of the house was making eyes at him. Maybe he would have a chance—it had been such a long time that he had made love to a woman.

After dinner, Willy and the other men left the ladies drinking coffee and enjoying the chocolates he had brought. Carrying glasses, decanters and cigars into the games room, they settled into comfortable armchairs around the fireplace with their backs to the full-size billiard table. Brackett brought in logs and revived the glowing embers with leather bellows.

Willy was surprised by the presence of a billiard room in a private house. Its atmosphere was manly, rather like the officer's mess at his camp. Photographs of hunters in tropical gear, standing beside the buffalo and tigers they had shot, festooned every flat surface. A cluster of binoculars hung from the hooks of a clothes stand. A few animal trophy heads glared from the wall: gazelle, deer, and wildebeest. A fox, frozen in mid-stride with a pheasant in its mouth, stood on top of a battered Challen upright piano.

Willy couldn't wait to get his fingers on the keys. "Sir Edward, would you permit me to play something?" he said as cigar smoke filled the room. "It's so long since I've had the opportunity. I apologize if I make a few mistakes."

Sir Edward waved a languid hand from a deep chintzy armchair. "Gosh, yes, old chap. Bang away. Don't mind us. The thing hasn't been touched for years, though."

Willy pulled out the worn stool and ran his fingers over the stained ivories. The tuning was off, especially in the upper registers, but he pressed on with Debussy's Clair de Lune. Within a few minutes, the ladies, all smiles and chatter, burst in from the sitting room, carrying their coffee cups. The men rose and offered their seats.

Willy finished with a Chopin waltz and a flourish of his hands. "Good God, Mr. Kohut, I had no idea—you…" said Lady Hilliard. Her lustrous eyes were full of excitement. "We heard music and had to come. Your playing is gorgeous."

Willy knew instantly from her look that his hostess was one of those women who, when the melodies flow and fingers run gracefully over the keys, cannot help but fall in love with the musician.

"I haven't played for a long time," he said feigning embarrassment. He raised his right hand. "The little finger that the Gestapo tried to chop off doesn't behave itself too well on the keys."

"Christ Almighty," said the grizzled London broker. "Is this true? You were in the hands of the Gestapo?"

Willy nodded and his audience murmured astonishment. They were in the presence of a real live Gestapo prisoner who had survived. Now they were admiring him. His heart swelled. "It happened just before we escaped Prague. If it's alright with you, I'll play a little more."

He dazzled them with two liquid sonatas from Liszt and Chopin. After the applause died away, Willy took a long drink from his brandy glass, sighing contentedly as the warmth spread throughout his body. "Good cognac, this. It's a very long time since I've felt this comfortable. A wonderful meal and charming companions." He glanced at Lady Hilliard who now lounged back in her chair, her dress pulled tight against her thighs. She was more alluring than ever. She gave him a long, lingering look.

"Impressive playing," said Sir Edward, a cheroot stuck under his bushy, graying mustache. "Your fingers galloped along that keyboard like I don't know what. But I must say I prefer somethin' easy and singable like 'We'll Meet Again' or 'Underneath the Arches'. Where is it you lived before the war?"

Lady Hilliard twitched her bare shoulders. "I've told you more than once, Edward. Willy's people are from Czechoslovakia. You should remember these things."

He waved a dismissive hand. "Czechosl—ah, yes. Now, I've got it. It's the place that Chamberlain back-pedaled on to please Hitler. Middle of Europe, eh?"

"You are quite right, Sir Edward," said Willy with a forced smile, thinking that some of the English were too wrapped up in their own empire to understand what had been happening in Europe before '39.

After Willy's recital, the guests resumed drinking. It was nearly one o' clock when they staggered to bed. Willy, feeling a little dizzy, and Lady Hilliard, who he now addressed as Popsie were the last ones to leave the billiard room.

"Which way do I turn at the top, Popsie," he said thickly as she helped him up the stairs and along the landing

"This is your room, Willy," she said at the doorway, coming close and putting her hands on his shoulders. She switched off the hallway light and bent down to give him a lingering kiss on the lips. He had never experienced an uphill kiss before but he pulled her close and ran his hands over her bare shoulders, sliding fingers inside her gown. The kiss went on and on as their hips rubbed together.

"From the way you played piano, I expect you are a very passionate man," she murmured, kissing him again briefly and giggling as he held her tightly "We're both a touch tipsy, aren't we? Once upon a time, I used to be a very naughty girl, you know."

"You could be naughty again," said Willy on tiptoe, licking her ear, "Your husband must be fast asleep by now."

She eased away and waved a no-no finger. "I don't do naughty things anymore … though it would have been nice to find out if European men do more exciting things in bed than the British." She sighed. "Edward's a bit clumsy—but then…. Better to say good night." She walked off and then suddenly swiveled around round. "Ooh, I just remembered. We got a letter addressed to you from SSAFA a few days ago. Mislaid it. I'll give it to you tomorrow. G'night then." She blew him a kiss.

In his room, Willy took a deep breath and collapsed on the bed. "All's unfair in love and war," he slurred. It was then that he remembered he still hadn't talked to Popsie about Paul and Mrs. McAlistair. "Damn it, I'll do that tomorrow."

CHAPTER TWENTY-TWO
Father and Son
December 1942

Willy slept late for the first time in weeks thanks to the previous evening's sumptuous dinner and a soft bed. At Bothwell Camp, he had a hard bunk and an acetylene lamp flickered outside his window all night with reveille at six. The Hilliards had invited him to church, but he wasn't sure of his exact plan for the day, except he needed to spend time with Paul and find a way to get Sheila on her own.

He opened the curtains and admired the terraced garden with its trimmed hedges and flower beds surrounding an expansive lawn. This visit to Knapp Hall was a welcome escape from the dedicated embrace of His Majesty's Royal Engineers. Far beyond the garden's stone walls, an opal mist hung below the distant hills, hiding the lower valley. Not so different from the look of the low Tatras near Luçenec.

After feasting on eggs, bacon, grilled lamb kidneys and chops, toasted farm bread, coffee and homemade jams, Willy presented Sir Edward with a bottle of Laphroaig whisky he had spotted on an upper shelf behind the bar of The Castle Inn in Bothwell. Sir Edward's eyes twinkled, his thank-you muffled by his mustache. "Splendid gift, old chap. Difficult stuff to get hold of these days."

Not wanting to appear churlish by refusing, Willy accepted the Hilliards' invitation to attend Sunday morning service in the nearby village of Church Pulverbatch. He was curious about a Church of England Sunday service. If Paul was expected to ape Mrs. McAlistair's prayers, Willy wanted to get an insight into the mumbo-jumbo his son was being fed.

The organist played an accomplished Bach voluntary as the Hilliard party walked out to the graveyard towards the shooting brake. "Have you thought of what you'll do with Paul today?" said

Lady Hilliard

"I'm not sure." Willy said as he got into the back seat. "But I'm looking forward to some fun." The church music had raised his spirits. He hoped there would be some fun with Sheila. "And Paul and I have to talk. Father and son stuff, you know."

"He's settled in well, I think?" Lady Hilliard glanced at him from the passenger seat as Sir Edward switched on the engine and turned on to the main road. "It's so lovely that you were able to come and visit him."

I'm delighted how well he looks, Lady Hilliard." He couldn't call her Popsie anymore.

"The poor mite does get homesick. His bed-wetting vexes Mrs. M. no end. Paul's not one of her favorites. What do you think of her?"

Out of respect for Lady Hilliard, Willy kept a lid on his feelings. "Mrs. McAlistair? Well … she seems competent but standoffish. Someone wrote an anonymous note to my wife saying that Paul was unhappy. One of the reasons I came."

Lady Hilliard put a white gloved hand up to her mouth. "Oh, dear. I know nothing about this, I'm so sorry for him. But I'll get to the bottom of it and let you know."

Willy looked out the car window, pleased at her response. Lady Hilliard was a can-do person; she would keep her promise. "Thank you, I'm grateful. I'll tell my wife."

"Popsie will sort it out, all right," said Sir Edward curtly, caressing his steering wheel with long fingers. "Me, I don't concern myself with the evacuees. Light me a cigarette, will you, dear."

Willy shifted in his seat. "About the rest of the day; I want Paul to have some fun. We'd best take another long walk. Not much else to do, is there? Knapp Farm is quite isolated isn't it?"

"We're not in the back of beyond, y'know," Sir Edward grunted from under his mustache. "Only thirty miles from here, we've got three military camps teeming with American GIs. That's not isolated!"

"Who'd have guessed it," said Willy with a laugh. "Yanks taking over the British countryside. Still, we need them to beat Hitler, and they've got top-notch, up-to-date equipment."

Lady Hilliard suddenly slapped the dashboard. "Oh, golly. Your letter. I nearly forgot it again. She dug into her purse and pulled out a folded blue envelope. "Hope you don't mind but I opened it in case it was something important to do with Paul. There was a cover note from the SSAFA office, saying a man asked them to send this envelope to Knapp Hall and give it you whenever you came to visit Paul.

"Thank you." Willy tore it open, turning sideways to get more light. How did anyone know of his arrangement with SSAFA? How did anyone know that Paul was here? That he would be visiting Paul? He took a quick look—handwritten smudged writing, in Czech. Signature … *Povídka* …

She refused to give me your exact whereabouts/address…I Need your help. Telegram ASAP. 46 Frognal Lane. London NW3.

He sensed Lady Hilliard watching him.

…A friendly warning, Yid. Your wife is more than busy these days. Seems she's opening a café …
… she spends time drinking with all and sundry at the Eagle pub. I'd keep an eye on her.

Willy's belly cramped. *The bastard! How did he find me?*

He looked out the window, his mind tumbling. Povídka was like a tracker dog. Now that he'd discovered Paul's whereabouts, he might come up with some way to force Willy to do what he wanted. But what in the hell did he want?

The decoy project was nearly finished, and he was about to be transferred. But what if the bastard was right about Sophie? She'd opened that damned café even though he'd told her it would a financial disaster. That meant she'd rejected his advice, gone behind his back! If she went bankrupt, he would be responsible. Maybe even, prison? And what about this partying at a Cambridge pub? What the hell could he do? Damn all; he was working his ass off, day-in, day-out. He would think about the letter on his way back to camp.

"Anything wrong?" Lady Hilliard's hand was on his arm.

"Unfortunately, yes. But it's hush-hush. Military stuff."

She gave him a sympathetic smile. "Forget your work for today. Enjoy your son."

He nodded, swallowing hard. Suddenly his life had got more complicated.

"Here's an idea for this afternoon," said Sir Edward, turning off the main road into the narrow lane that ran past the giant oak up to Knapp Hall. "Take your boy into Shrewsbury. Lovely old town, old walls, the Severn River—you could rent a skiff if the weather holds. Bert will run you there—a thirty minute drive."

"I'll get cook to make you sandwiches," Lady Hilliard said, "and send a message to Mrs. M. that you're taking Paul into town. When you get back, we'll talk about next steps for Paul, if you like. We're not sure how much longer you want him to stay with us, and he really needs to go to a proper school."

Willy stared at her. Another of Paul's issues he hadn't thought about had just landed on his plate. He was ashamed. He was the boy's father. "Thanks. Rowing on the river would be a fine way for us to get re-acquainted. And I could certainly do with some advice about the British school system."

A few hours later, Bert drove Willy and Paul into the calm of

Shrewsbury on a Sunday afternoon. As they got out, Bert limped over to Paul and handed him a paper bag. "Bits of toast from breakfast," he said. "For the ducks an' swans when you get to the river. Poor things don't get fed much now the war's on."

"It's just like Sundays in Cambridge," said Paul, skipping along beside his father. "Eric says Sundays are when Jesus keeps people inside their houses until night-time."

"Which one is Eric?"

"The tall boy at our cottage. He swears about God and Jesus all the time. Mrs. M. gets angry. She smacks him."

Willy stopped and looked at his son. He regretted that, in France, he and Sophie had smacked Paul more often than was justified. But it was far worse when a stranger did it to your son. "I don't know much about God and Jesus, Paul. It's a complicated business. Better not to think about God and Jesus until you're bigger."

"Mrs. M. makes us say prayers every morning before breakfast, and I can't remember the words. What are prayers for?"

Willy was not ready for this one. "Mmm … prayers? It's … when people think they're talking to God and ask for help. Just learn the words and don't worry about what they mean. Come on, let's go down this alleyway and see where it goes."

Following Bert's hand-drawn map, they explored the narrow sun-filled streets and multi-paned shop-fronts that Sir Edward had said were known as the "shuts and passages." Everything was closed. Afterward, they walked to the grassy expanse of Quarry Park overlooking a broad curve of the River Severn and watched local boys tussling in a pick-up game of soccer, their goal posts made up of mounded raincoats. On the river bank, Paul fed the swans and ducks. Willy was pleased that Paul, as he fed the swans and ducks, handed out his crusts to some children who sidled up to watch.

On the down-river side of Porthill Bridge, Willy hired a rowboat for an hour from a wizened attendant as darkly varnished as his boat. Rowing in the sun proved to be hot work, so Willy took off his army jacket and unbuttoned his shirt. "Come on," he said, smiling as they headed upstream. His shirt tail flapped in the breeze. "Take off your shirt. The sun's good for your skin. Gives you vitamins. When you're ready, I'll show you how to work the rudder properly." As he rowed, he thought about Povídka's letter. *Maybe that swine invented all this stuff about Sophie. He's playing me for a fool.*

Paul gazed at his father's muscled chest and shyly, reluctantly, undid his own shirt. He glanced down at his own skinny ribs, unable to believe he could ever look as strong as his Dad. As his father rowed, Paul pulled on the steering ropes trying to keep the boat in a straight line. Out on the water, with the both of them together, looking at each other, he wanted to tell Daddy that Mrs. M. had beaten him. But then he held back; it would ruin their fun.

After half an hour's rowing, they steered into a cluster of reeds by the bank, and Daddy rested his forearms on the oars. Rivulets of sweat stained the back of his shirt. He grinned at Paul. "It would have been nice to have Mummy with us on this excursion. She would have made us a delicious picnic."

"I miss Mummy," said Paul, scratching at his ribs.

"Me too. I'm stuck in my camp in Scotland, and as you know, she works for the lady doctor. She's all right, though. Are you getting our letters?"

Paul nodded. "Mrs. M. and Sheila read all the letters out loud. Chrissie and Vince never get letters, so they listen to ours."

"That's sad for Chrissie and Vince." Daddy buttoned up his shirt. "It's good of Mrs. McAlistair to do that."

Paul didn't think there was anything good about Mrs. M. anymore. He would be glad to get away from her. Perhaps now was a good time to tell Daddy about Mrs.M.

"You know Paul, we miss you very much. And now that Granny and Grandpa are living in London again, maybe it's time you went to live with them instead of being here on the farm."

Paul shivered. What a super idea. If he left Knapp Farm soon he wouldn't even have to tell Daddy about the beating. "Are there children to play with in the street where they live?"

"Not sure. Probably. Anyway, we must get back to the dock. There's time to buy an ice-cream in the park and then—I've got another treat for you up my sleeve."

"What's that, Daddy?"

"Mickey Mouse cartoons at the Empire cinema, and then high tea at the Prince Rupert Hotel."

"A film. Yippee! Wait till I tell Eric." *I'll tell Daddy after the film.*

*　　　*　　　*

It was nearly six when Bert delivered them back to Middle Knapp Cottage. The children were sitting round the table eating cabbage and fried sausages. Mrs. M. glowered when they walked in.

"We had our tea at a hotel," said Paul proudly.

"No one informed me about this." Mrs. M. frowned, pointing to his empty chair. "Sit down. No food for you." She turned to face Willy. "You did not say you would be late. I must be told everything concerning these bairns. In future, please inform me of your plans."

Willy boiled inside but, for Paul's sake, he played the diplomat. "Our apologies, Mrs. McAlistair. Bert was late picking us up. We waited for him in the wrong place. I'll just say goodbye to Paul. It's time."

Willy took Paul outside. "I'm going back to Knapp Hall now, Paulikin. I have to leave at first light tomorrow so we won't see each other until I come next time. But I think Mummy is coming to see you soon."

Paul, with his face burrowed into the crook of Willy's neck, couldn't stop the tears. "Please come back soon," he whispered. "The only one who really loves me here is Sheila."

"Lady Hilliard loves you too," said Willy, wiping Paul's eyes with his handkerchief. "We all love you, Mummy, Granny, and Grandpa. What is important is that you are safe here, away from the bombing." He gently disengaged Paul's arms from around his neck, set him on the ground, and gave his shoulders a final squeeze.

"Daddy—" said Paul, biting his lip. He scratched his hair and looked away. "Can I tell you what Mrs. M. did to me?"

The cottage door creaked open and Mrs. McAlistair appeared, wiping her hands with a dishcloth. Two children peered out from behind her. Paul looked away, rubbing away tears from the tip of his nose.

She patted him on the head, a little too roughly. "It's verra hard to say goodbye. But Paul needs to come inside now—it'll be his bedtime soon. We don't want him catching cold, do we? So, Leftenant, you're off back to Bonnie Scotland?"

"As you say, time to go," said Willy furious with himself for missing the chance to find out what Paul was about to tell him. The boy was back in Mrs. M.'s clutches. "Anyway, I also have to go up to the hall to prepare for tonight. Lady Hilliard wants me to play for all the people who work for her, including the land girls. Will you be there, Mrs. McAlistair? Is there someone else to keep an eye on the children?"

The governess frowned. "No, no one," she said abruptly, pinching her thin lips. "I suppose I'll be stuck here while everyone else enjoys theirselves up at the big house. Not very nice for me, is it? Come inside now, Paul."

Paul backed away from her outstretched hand.

"I want you on best behavior," said Willy, kissing the boy's forehead. Paul's mouth was smudged with traces of chocolate ice cream. "Goodbye, my little fellow. I love you. Don't forget Mama will be here as soon as she can manage it."

He trudged to Knapp Hall, pipe clenched in his mouth, berating himself. He had failed his son. He felt like a coward. He took a deep breath. No time for that now. *Sophie can sort it out when she comes. I'll write to her.*

*   *   *

Two days later, Paul was expecting Sheila to appear to clear the breakfast and get the children ready for their lessons. She wasn't there to take them for their afternoon walk. Instead, Mrs. M. made them stay up in the attic and look at picture books and comics.

"Where is Sheila?" Marigold asked at tea-time. There was stony silence until Mrs. M. said, "We've a new girl coming tomorrow. She's called Iris."

Iris was plump and kind, but she had none of Sheila's prettiness or funny talk. Paul couldn't believe she had disappeared without a hug and a kiss. Over the next few days, he asked the cowman, Bert the handyman, and the farm tractor driver if they had seen Sheila recently.

"Gone," they said, not looking at him. Not one of them smiled, and silently turned to their work when he asked where she had gone. Something bad had happened. Was she ill or been run over? Or had she fallen down a mine shaft on the hill? He couldn't sleep, thinking about her vanishing like that.

He was afraid to ask Mrs. M. but one morning before breakfast he spoke up. "Why didn't Sheila say goodbye to us?" The other children chorused, "Yes, why, Mrs. M.?"

"She's gone away," said Mrs. M. with tight letterbox lips, "and good riddance to the slut. Now, don't you children ever talk about her again."

Paul didn't know what a slut was and he asked Eric, the wizard of all bad words.

"Don't know, Pee-Pee," said Eric. He frowned. "Ask Aunt Popsie. She likes you a lot."

A week later, during the children's usual Wednesday visit to Knapp Hall, Paul was playing hide and seek in the garden and crept inside an upturned wheelbarrow. A few moments later, he heard Adam, the gardener talking.

"Whatever 'appened to that lovely Irish girl what was 'elping you at the cottages? I've not seen 'er around. She was a lively one— liked 'er, I did."

"Thrown out on her ear, gone." A woman's faint voice. He wasn't sure who it was.

"Why is that? She seemed a decent sort."

"I saw her comin' out of the big barn with a soldier, all covered with straw bits." With a shock, Paul recognized the Scottish accent. So, Mrs. M. hadn't gone into town after all. "It was that furriner kid's smarmy dad. I'm sure of it."

The gardener laughed. "Sheila always 'ad her own mind about things, didn't she? But then 'e was a soldier. These things 'appen doan they—what with the war an' all."

"*Not* as far as I'm concerned, Adam. Not with Land Girls. I told her ladyship. Of course, Sheila was sent packing."

Paul held his breath, his mind struggling with the mysterious word "smarmy". He screwed his eyes tight. He understood one thing. Papa, Daddy, was the smarmy soldier. *Did Daddy and Sheila do something bad enough for her to be sent away?*

In the following days, Paul always got his food last of all and fat Gerald—who wet the bed every single night—had his mattress sheet washed while Paul's would just be hung out of the window to dry. It got more and more stained as the days went by and smelled horrible. And Paul's underpants kept disappearing.

After Daddy's visit and Sheila's disappearance, Paul stopped getting family letters. And he couldn't find Furry Lion. He cried himself to sleep almost every night.

Two Sundays went by.

"Why don't you get letters no more?" said Vince on the second Sunday without anything in the mail for Paul. "We likes your letters."

"Better ask Mrs. M. then," added Marigold. "Somethin's gone wrong, int'it? Probably, your people got bombed or summat, in Lonnon."

Mrs. McAlistair was stone-faced when Paul stammered out his question. "How should I know, child? Mebbe your folks have got their own troubles. Just put up with it."

A few days later, Iris came up to him in the orchard. She hauled some bits of paper out of her britches.

"Mrs. M. told me to clean her room and I found these in the bottom of the waste bin." She showed him a fragment. "Isn't that your family's name?"

He read the letters KOHU and nodded. He recognized his mother's writing. It was like finding treasure—but why was it all torn up?

Paul felt his face go hot and he took a sobbing breath. "It's my Mummy's writing ... and someone took Furry Lion from my bed."

Iris frowned as she tried to piece the scraps together. "Difficult ... it says something on this bit. I—can't quite decipher it—ah, yes, it says: *visit soon ... thousand kisses, your l...*"

With a sad smile and a shake of the head she handed the paper pieces to Paul. "They're too small, but you keep 'em, anyway."

Paul looked at Iris, took her hand and kissed it, the way he had seen his father do. He didn't know how else to thank her for finding the torn letter. Of course, if she had been Sheila instead of Iris he would have given her a hug, and gotten one back.

"Please, can you tell Aunt Popsie you found my Mummy's letter in Mrs. M's wastebasket?"

Iris looked at him in surprise. "Is it because you think Mrs. M. tore it up?"

Paul nodded. "And tell her my Furry Lion is missing.

She pursed her lips as if reluctant to go on. "Sorry. Can't do it. She'll be angry."

Paul looked down at his feet. His chest felt as if it would break open. A tight band squeezed his head. Everything was against him. He wanted to cry. He put his hands over his mouth to hold back the emerging sob.

"Cheer up, little chap, said Iris. "Your Ma might be coming soon. I think that's what she wrote on that paper."

Paul smiled at her through his tears. Mummy would sort everything out.

CHAPTER TWENTY-THREE
Mother and Child
December 1942

The Peacock Café opened two weeks before Christmas. "A peasant look," said Sophie when she thought up the décor—walls a soft gray, the old wooden shelves picked out in cornflower blue. They built a self-service counter close to the kitchen at the back. At a church sale, Helga bought six round tables, chairs and four benches which they lined with soft multicolored cushions. In exchange for a week of free lunches, a local artist painted and erected over the front door, a board showing a strutting peacock in glorious display. To attract the Christmas crowd, Sophie and Helga decorated the windows and walls with holly dried in Epsom salts to make the leaves glitter. They bought a small radio so that customers could listen to the war bulletins.

At first, business was slow, a combination of stricter rationing and the end of the university's Michaelmas term. Unable to afford adverts, they relied on word of mouth about the new "foreign" restaurant. Remembering how Willy had advertised his Prague store, Sophie distributed leaflets whenever she went shopping. She did the same at the Eagle pub bar, where she encouraged British and American air force officers to eat at the Peacock. They could afford it. She had no compunction about using her looks and charm to promote the café—besides, it was fun to flirt.

Helga and Sophie each rented a small bed-sitting room in the same neighborhood. They used their savings to pay rent and buy supplies for the café. A tight budget, no treats, no fun. They worked much harder than at Tallard House: lunch from 11-2.30 pm, four hours of food preparation and washing dishes, then open again from five to seven. Helga was in the kitchen, with Sophie at the front, seating guests, refilling serving bowls and dishes and taking the money. She hardly had time to think about Paul and thanked her lucky stars he no longer was her immediate responsibility. Emil was right. Having Pavel with her would have been a disaster.

Within a week, there were lines outside the door at lunchtime and they had to hire a dishwasher. Helga and Sophie's lives filled up with creating menus, ordering food supplies, shopping, serving customers, cleanup, ironing tablecloths, and keeping track of income and expenses. The Peacock Café soon became a meeting place for students and intellectuals and Sophie, with unexpected joy and enthusiasm, was drawn into the conversations and met well-known people. Bertrand Russell came every day for lunch with his secretary.

"I'm getting a university education and earning money at the same time as wearing myself out," Sophie joked with Helga. She could not admit to her partner that she often felt listless and exhausted or just misplaced things like keys or her purse. She perspired a lot and had a short temper—similar symptoms, she realized, to her breakdown in Paris. At the same time she was immensely proud of the Peacock Café. They had plenty of customers and were making a profit.

At the end of January, a few days after the wonderful news that the Nazi armies had surrendered at Stalingrad, Sophie received a notice from the Cambridge Aliens board. Her permit to travel outside Cambridge was ready. Joyfully, she telephoned Lady Hilliard.

"Excuse, please. I am Sophie Kohut, Paul's mother. May I come next Saturday? Is this possible?"

"How marvelous. He'll be so happy. And do stay with us; like your husband did—he enjoyed himself no end. Such a charming, wonderful man."

Sophie liked the warmth in Lady Hilliard's voice. Perhaps, Willy had worked his musical magic on her. "I have only Saturday with Paul. Next day, I visit my husband near Glasgow. I will arrive in Shrewsbury on the Friday evening. I stay at Salop Guest House."

"Oh, dear, a commercial traveler place. A bit dismal. Anyway, Saturday morning get a taxi—though that's a bit expensive. We're seven miles away. How about this? My husband will be in town getting supplies from Swifftons. He could pick you up at the railway station entrance."

Sophie exhaled. She had been worrying about the cost and coordination of this last part of the journey. "Very kind. Thank you."

"Eleven thirtyish? How will he recognize you?"

For a moment Sophie was nonplussed. "Oh … I will have … a blue-and-white turban, with stripes, like the one Carmen Miranda wears in her films."

"Splendid." Lady Hilliard's laugh was warm and comforting. "Can you dance the Samba as well?"

Sophie was afraid to stay at Knapp Hall. She was ashamed of her dry skin, untidy hair, and worn clothes—especially as Willy had written enthusiastically about his dinner there with guests in evening dress. It had been no trouble for him, she supposed. Because of his uniform, he could fit in and go just about anywhere. Her English would not be good enough to hold a conversation with these high-society people.

The train journey to Shrewsbury involved two station changes and untold stops and starts. The carriages and corridors were crammed with soldiers and littered with newspapers, cigarette butts, sandwich crusts, and empty beer bottles rolling on the floor. To distract herself from the clumping boots, the dense tobacco smoke and the clattering ride, she worked on her business notes. Now that the Peacock Café had been open for nearly three months, she could estimate long-term income and expenses, review their work permits, and complete the insurance and sanitary inspection forms that she had put aside for too long.

Just before nine in the evening, directed by an amiable porter at Shrewsbury station, she found the Salop Guest House two streets away. Sophie rang the bell a few times and banged on the front door. A sour-faced woman opened the door. "We don't accept people after blackout. And you can't stay if you didn't book."

"I did book, and if you don't let me stay, I'll go to the police station."

Sophie's two shilling room was airless—the window had been painted shut—and smelled of old socks and perfumed hair cream. The curtains were thin and torn, no protection from someone looking in from the street. At least the mattress on the iron bedstead was springy and didn't collapse in the middle. She regretted refusing Lady Hilliard's hospitality.

She propped herself up on the one pillow, eating the last of the curled-up sandwiches Helga had packed, hoping she would be able to sleep. Her body cried out for rest, but her mind churned on over the state of her marriage and the worry of what had gone wrong for Paul at the farm. Only the thought of wrapping her arms around Paul and covering him with kisses gave her some respite.

"I told Lady Hilliard about Paul," Willy had written. "How Mrs.M. picks on him. Perhaps we should get him out of there. I expect you can keep him with you in Cambridge if you are still renting a room. Or should I again ask my parents to look after him in London?"

Sophie knew that taking Paul under her wing would overwhelm her. She was too busy and didn't feel well enough. She needed to focus her energy on the café. In two or three months' time, she would be able to afford to rent a flat for herself and Paul. The best solution was for him to stay on at the farm, for a little longer.

The next morning was warm and cloudy. Feeling nervous, Sophie walked to Shrewsbury Station to wait outside for Sir Edward. What would he be like? Maybe he'd look down his nose at her dowdy two-piece suit. Her dazzling turban had been an impulse buy, using café profits.

Almost immediately, a two-seater with its canvas top down drew up beside her. The tall, hollow-cheeked driver in an Ascot cap looked up at her, his mustache too luxuriant for her to actually see his lips. Two pitchforks lay lengthwise between the seats, the tines pointing toward the back storage which was filled with a mass of boxes and bags.

"Mrs. Kohut?" he said touching the brim of his cap with a gloved finger.

She gave him a tentative smile. "Sir Edward Hilliard?"

He leaned across, releasing the passenger door with a flick of his hand. "Sorry about having the top down, but the pitchforks won't let me put up the cover. Spiffy hat you've got on, so better hold on to it. Let's hope it doesn't rain."

She got in. "Nice car," she said in an attempt to return his compliment.

"1935 Lagonda Rapide." His mustache tilted upward.

The open car was too windy to hear Sir Edward's growly voice clearly. She gazed at the passing countryside. The neat hedgerows, broad sloping fields, and bare sculptural trees soothed the turmoil in her mind.

*   *   *

Paul was helping milk a brown Hereford in the cowshed opposite the cottages when he heard a car toot. He saw his mother through the open half-door and ran to her, whooping with excitement. She picked him up and swung him round in a bout of frenzied kissing and hugging, knocking the milk pail sideway.

He clung to her as hard as he could, his heart pounding with happiness. It was a dream come true.

The dairy woman started to mop up the mess. "Doan you tell Lady Hilliard 'bout this," she said with a frown. "I'll get in trouble for lettin' you do a bit o' milkin.'"

"My, my, you've grown so much," Sophie said moments later as Paul led her toward Middle Knapp Cottage. At the door, she cupped his chin and kissed his nose, elated and happy. Her tiredness and lassitude had vanished. "You look so healthy. Soon you will be as big as Papa— oh, I mean Daddy."

"Yes, I know, Mummy," he said proudly "I can climb over a farm gate all by myself."

She knocked on the door and looked down at him. "Are you all right, my darling?"

A shadow passed across Paul's face. "I lost Furry Lion—and other stuff. Like all my underpants."

"Underpants!" With an astonished look, Sophie shook her head but couldn't help a chuckle. "I don't understand? How did this happen?"

"Sheila's gone too. Ask Iris."

Sophie had never seen such a ferocious look on her son's face. Something very bad had happened. "Iris? Who is that?"

"Ask her about Sheila—and my letters that didn't come anymore."

"Are you wearing underpants now?"

Paul shook his head and pulled down his shorts.

Sophie gasped … and at that very moment the door opened. A plump young woman in an apron stood there, flour smudges and a smile on her face. "You'd better pull up your pants, young feller, before Mrs. M. gives yer a piece of her mind."

Paul pressed his lips together. "This is Iris."

Time at the cottage passed quickly, with Sophie quietly observing how Mrs. McAlistair taught the morning lessons in her sitting room. She wasn't able to talk privately with Iris or Mrs. McAlistair but Paul behaved well and paid close attention. He seemed happy enough among the other children.

At the end of the class, Mrs. M. had to go see to see Lady Hilliard, and Sophie offered to help make lunch: two stacks of sandwiches: one of ham, the other of bloater paste. She stood at the kitchen counter with Iris who was washing lettuce leaves. Sophie fitted a lettuce leaf and paper-thin ham between slices of soft bread. "Where do you get lettuce this time of year?" she said, knowing how difficult it was to get any for her café.

"Head gardener brings 'em from the greenhouses."

They worked in silence for a moment. Sophie put down a half-completed sandwich. "Paul said to ask you about Mrs. McAlistair and him. What's going on?"

Iris looked up and, glanced round the kitchen as if on the alert. Sophie could tell from her blinking that the girl was nervous. "I'm not sure I should say. Still, I s'pose, with you comin' all this way, you ort to know summat 'bout your boy. It's only what I 'eard, that is."

"Go on, tell me."

Iris took a deep breath and rambled on about Paul's accidents and his punishments—and how Mrs. McAlistair had got rid of his dirty underpants and tore up his letters.

"She's got her claws into the poor mite, that's for sure. An' there's another thing." Iris was warming to her task. "Mrs. M. keeps callin' 'im a bloody furriner. 'Course, I'm not sure your lad knows what bloody furriner means."

"*Gotteniu*," Sophie whispered to herself, *this Schottische is a devil*. She grasped Iris's arm so she could look into the young woman's eyes. "My husband did not tell me this."

Iris's face went pink and she turned back to washing lettuce. "Never met 'im," she muttered. "That were before I come, when Sheila were 'ere—before she were kicked out."

"Sheila was beautiful and kind. Paul loved her. What happened?"

"Um—I—something to do with Paul's dad, I think." Iris flushed again, hesitating.

Sophie stacked the finished sandwiches on a serving plate. In the past months, in Cambridge, she'd observed plenty of easy sex and infidelity between the soldiers and unattached women. In fact, the Peacock Café was a prime rendezvous spot. So what? It was good for business. And she quite enjoyed the banter of the intelligence officers who were her regular customers. Emil and Judit had a phrase for it: *war immorality*. Well, Willy had not always stayed on the straight and narrow, even in Prague.

After a few moments she simmered down, thinking of her own minor transgressions in Cambridge—going out to dances and occasionally to the cinema with someone she had met at the Dorothy Café. That wasn't betraying a marriage, was it? Anyway, this Sheila story reinforced the reason for her trip to Scotland—she was almost sure now ... she no longer loved Willy. In fact, the thought of him making love to her, his grunting and body sweat, was nauseating. She was ready to tell him this face-to-face. Straightforward, no hiding behind the half-truths in letters. She wanted—needed—a different life.

*   *   *

That afternoon, even though the sky was gray and a sharp wind gusted across the valley, Sophie and Paul walked up on to Knapp Hill. He seemed very happy, skipping along, pointing out clumps of unopened bluebells poking up through new grass in the hedgerows.

Sophie tried as gently as she could to find out what was troubling him. She wanted to be sure of the facts before she complained to Lady Hilliard.

At the top of the hill, sitting on the stone bench at the shepherd's hut, she put her arm around him and kissed him. "We are all alone up here, darling. I want you to tell me why you are unhappy."

Paul entwined his fingers, inspecting them intently. He shook his head. Tears flowed down his cheeks. "Don't know. I … nothing. I'm all right."

Several times on their way back, Sophie asked the same question, in different ways. Paul would not answer. He just looked at her with serious eyes and shook his head.

It was nearly five when they got back to Middle Knapp Cottage. In the farmyard, Bert lounged against the driver's side of a black Wolseley, smoking. He was waiting to take Sophie back to the Salop Guest House. In the doorway, Mrs. McAlistair wiped her hands on her apron. With a solemn face and no tears, Paul kissed Sophie goodbye and went inside for supper.

Sophie had wanted to cover him with kisses but with sour-faced Mrs. M. watching she held back. She resolved to come back as soon as she could and stay longer. There was no time now to properly convey her complaint about Mrs. M. to the Hilliards. An expression she had learned from a café customer came into her head: she would "put a cat among the pigeons." She put out her hand. "Goodbye, Mrs. McAlistair. Thank you for letting me watch the lessons today. I saw how well you looked after the children. Paul and I had a very nice time on our walk."

Mrs. M. squeezed out a faint smile and took the proffered hand. "I'm verra glad you enjoyed it, Mrs. Kohut."

"By the way, Paul showed me he had no underpants. I find this very strange. He'll catch cold. He had enough when he first came here. Where are they?"

Mrs. M. flushed, twisting her fingers in the strings of her apron. "I canna really explain it. He does wet the bed a lot, ye know. I think Sheila, the girl that was sent away, she must have got rid of them. A bad lot she was."

"That's not the point. You get him some underpants, immediately.

Mrs. M. shrugged. "No one told me he didna have any."

"That is a lie. Paul said he asked you about his underpants. I believe him. We looked in the suitcase by his bed. No clean underpants."

Mrs. M. looked up at the darkening sky. "O Lord, give me strength," she muttered.

Sophie squared her shoulders. "I'll send some in a parcel as soon as I get back to Cambridge. This problem must not happen again, Mrs. McAlistair. Not under your eagle eye."

Mrs. M.'s face turned a darker red. Her mouth was a closed zipper. "With Sheila gone there'll be no more of that problem. But I have to say, she and your husband got verra close when he was here."

Sophie felt the heat rise in her cheeks. She forced a casual smile, thinking how best to strike back. "I see—well, my husband *is* a friendly man, especially where pretty women are concerned. Of course, that's nothing for middle-aged woman like you to worry about. But there is something else, much more serious. Paul told me that he didn't get any letters from us recently. We certainly sent them ... every week."

Mrs. McAlistair's eyes flashed. Her eyelids fluttered. "Dearie me, Mrs. Kohut, I'm not sure what you mean?" Tossing her braids, she looked away.

"Also you have been calling him bad names. That's cruel."

Mrs. McAlistair took a long deep breath. Her eyes blazed. "You're bein' verra rude. You'd better leave." There was spittle on her lips. "You turn up for just a day an' then throw vicious accusations at me. D'ye have any proof? I tell you, fair and square, her ladyship will nae be pleased when I tell her about this. She might even have to get rid o'your bairn."

Sophie clenched her fists, trying to control her desire to slap the woman and kick her in the shins. She pulled a wad of shredded paper from her purse. "And this … in your wastebasket. My handwriting. Paul gave it to me."

Mrs. M. gripped the door latch. "Goodbye, Mrs. Kohut," she said between her teeth.

Sophie adjusted her turban. "I expect you to remedy these problems," she hissed. "You *will* return his stuffed toy. And you *will not* hold back our letters. If I have to inform the SSAFA office in London about your cruel behavior, Lady Hilliard will be furious. It would be a pity if you lost your job here, wouldn't it? Sweet little Alice, seems so happy here. "

Sophie turned away, breathing heavily. Her pulse raced with rage and triumph. She could tell from Mrs. M's look that she had been understood.

In Shrewsbury, Bert stopped at a fish and chip shop and bought fried cod wrapped in newspaper. They ate the greasy, acrid-smelling food in the car outside the guest house. Almost immediately, Sophie handed him her portion. Her stomach surged at the surfeit of lard.

"Thank you for your kindness, Bert," she said as she prepared to get out with her small valise, "this is not my kind of food. You finish it, if you like."

"I surely will, ma'am."

"That girl Sheila who left so suddenly. Iris told me that my husband had something to do with it. Can you be honest with me? What actually happened?"

Bert sucked in a breath and then let it out slowly, massaging the steering wheel with gloved hands. "It was probably nuthin'. Mrs. McAlistair said she saw 'em both coming out of the barn. They was …" His voice trailed off and he looked away, out of the side window. "Sorry, missus."

Back at the Salop Guest House, before she went to bed, Bert's words whirled around her brain. Whether it was from the back-and-forth with Mrs. McAlistair or the greasy fish and chips, her stomach felt wretched. She wondered what she should do about her marriage, how could she keep Paul safe and happy, and what should she say to Willy next day about the café?

But all was negotiable. If he was willing to let her run the Peacock Café the way she wanted, well then … she would not mention the Sheila episode and maybe give the marriage another try. She and Willy would have to work out how Paul fitted into this puzzle. She had worked hard to fund and arrange this trip. In Scotland, she intended to make her time with Willy worth the effort.

CHAPTER TWENTY-FOUR
Blow Up
Bothwell, Scotland
February 1943

Willy commandeered a bicycle from one of the sheds behind his temporary billet, a converted classroom at a refurbished schoolhouse. It was evening and very cold. Wearing gloves, a pullover under his battledress and a scarf around his neck, he rode unsteadily through dark streets to the Douglas Arms. After the German raids on the Clydebank shipyards, blackout precautions were mandatory, and his only illumination was a sock-covered headlamp.

He had suggested to Sophie that they meet in the room she had booked at the Bothwell Station Hotel, but she wanted to talk in a public area. He guessed she feared a shouting match, or perhaps she thought he might persuade her to make love. The Douglas Arms was the only other place in Bothwell where he and Sophie could meet comfortably at this time of the evening. They hadn't talked face to face in three months and he hoped they would patch up their differences … and that she would come to her senses about this café of hers. Then they could solidify plans for Paul's future.

Willy sat at a corner table, nursing his second malt whisky—a peaty double from Islay— after first gulping down a hot meat pie. The pub smelled of wood smoke, beer and tobacco and a coal fire glowed in the brick fireplace. Three men were huddled on stools at the bar counter guarded by a long-faced publican. Two other others played darts.

While he waited, Willy skimmed the Daily Mail. "Rommel batters US forces at Kasserine Pass," said the headline. God, this was such depressing stuff! If the Americans failed in North Africa, an invasion of Italy was doomed. He drained his glass and glanced impatiently at the battered clock hanging above the GENTS. Half-past eight, dammit. Forty-five fucking minutes late!

Willy had been up since five. Even though he was exhausted, his right forefoot kept jiggling—a tic he couldn't stop when he got tense.

He would start the conversation with the news of his promotion, higher pay and his name change. Best of all, he'd tell her his grinding stint in Scotland was almost over. But what he really hoped for was a chance to snuggle up together on her hotel bed and make love.

The brass-studded door squeaked open and he saw Sophie framed in the doorway, muffled in a wool coat and scarf. Below a perky blue-and-white turban, waves of black hair flowed down over her shoulders. She had let it grow long. He liked that. Even bundled up, she looked attractive, though her face seemed thinner and there were dark circles under her eyes.

"Finally," said Willy, pulling her close and kissing her cold lips.

With a gentle smile, she hugged him back and hooked her purse over the back of the chair. "Here I am at last, *milačku.*"

He took her coat and scarf, admiring her stockings, the mid-calf pleated skirt and cable-knit maroon sweater that emphasized her bosom—an outfit he had not seen before. The nylons could only have come from some GI or the black market. Willy remembered Povídka's comment that she was having a good time in the Cambridge pubs. That's where she would have met some Yank, pockets full of cash.

But Willy was impressed that she had made the complicated journey alone; her first time outside Cambridge. "I'm glad you're here," he said, trying to stay calm. "Obviously, you've had an exhausting trip. A strong drink will warm you up."

"Yes please," she answered in English. "I'll have what you are drinking. My walk from the hotel was freezing." She rubbed her hands. "God help us, this weather is awful. It's cold in here, even with the fire."

Willy waved his glass in the air. The people sitting round the bar looked over. "Landlord, two whiskies please" he called out. The barman's assistant, a florid-faced man with a patch over his left eye, brought their drinks. "Pay at the bar," he said turning away with Willy's empty glass.

They clinked to good health and Sophie took a sip. She spluttered. "*Oy vay*, this is strong—like slivovic. Tastes of burned wood. What is it? "

"The best Scottish firewater." Willy grinned, studying her more carefully.

Still beautiful … where the hell did she get the money to buy nice clothes? Café profits? Or maybe the Yank who supplied her with stockings.

To settle himself down and start with some common ground, he pointed to the newspaper. "I read this while I waited. We're still battling it out with Rommel in Africa." He paused. "Did you know that my cousin Lači is there … with the 8th Army? Father wrote that he'd turned into a rabid communist."

"At least he's alive and fighting on the right side," she responded, leaning over to look at the newspaper.

"Do you remember those scummy Communist Brigade soldiers from France? The ones in my battalion, Povídka and Serbin?"

Sophie blew her nose. "Only too well. They sailed on our boat from Sète to Gibraltar. Serbin propositioned me. Your friend Kukulka's death was all their fault."

Willy grimaced. "Bastards. Those fellows taught me all about Communist treachery and viciousness. If Lači stays a communist, he'll come to regret it."

She looked around, as if taking stock of the pub. "It's easier for me if we speak in Czech. I don't think anyone can hear us. You mentioned that Povídka man. I bumped into him a couple of weeks ago in Cambridge … at a grocery shop. Quite a shock. He wanted to know where you were."

Willy jerked upright, eyes narrowing behind his glasses. "What a hellish coincidence. What did he want?"

"Wanted to know where you were. How you were getting on."

Willy grabbed the edge of the table, his foot jiggling again. Of course, it was no coincidence. Povídka was not the grocery type and the fact that he had found Sophie was worrying. Bloodhound Povídka was sniffing him out. "You didn't tell him?"

She gave him a reproachful look. "I had to say something. I said you were in the Royal Engineers, somewhere in Scotland. He said you and he were friends at that first English camp—comrade mutineers, he said."

Willy sank his forehead into his hands. "*Báječný*, you shouldn't have said anything."

"Why not? I'm not stupid. I was vague, doing my best to protect you and myself. He frightened me."

"You can't trust that bastard. He needed me when we sailed from Gibraltar to Plymouth—and then later, he helped me slip out of the Cholmondeley camp to call George. But he's a sly devil, and dangerous. He even sent a letter to Knapp Hall wanting to make contact. I ignored it."

Sophie frowned. "How did he get the farm's address? He must know Paul is there."

"From the SSAFA office, I suppose. He must have posed as a friend of ours. Don't worry. I don't think Paul's in danger."

Willy could see from Sophie's stricken face that he should not have mentioned the letter to Knapp Hall farm. She was tired and his tongue was loose from the whisky.

Yawning, he stretched. "How about we change the subject and I give you some good news?"

"I'll listen if you can get me something to eat. I've had nothing since noon. I'm tired and you look tired too. But after your good news, I want to talk about Paul and what happened when I was at the farm … and then one or two other important things." She gave him a wistful look. "Such as our life together as a family."

"Oy vay." Willy rolled his eyes and waved the barman over. He ordered egg sandwiches and another hot meat pie.

As Sophie munched, he talked. "First good thing. I've been promoted to second lieutenant."

Sophie smiled, her mouth partly full of sandwich. "Wonderful … but why were you promoted?"

Willy laughed. "Not allowed to say really. How about … no one else in the battalion speaks six languages?"

Sophie took out a pack of Sobranies and lit one "That's silly. Don't be afraid. I won't gossip. I'm your wife. What do you do?"

He watched the rising smoke, amazed. She had never smoked. Moreover, he didn't like the fancy way she held her cigarette, fingers curled like some movie star. He suspected she would smell of tobacco in bed. "Well, I'll explain a little more, if you keep it to yourself," He lowered his voice. "We design decoy tanks and guns. We've just about finished."

Sophie laughed behind her cigarette hand. "Decoys? Something to do with hunting?"

Willy shook his head. He emptied his glass and a dribble of whisky ran down his chin. "We design decoys to mislead German surveillance planes. That way the Nazis drop their bombs in the wrong places."

"Yes, I see." She paused. "But now I'm wondering how many drinks you've had. Your voice sounds squiffy. This is not like you."

Willy scowled. "Squiffy? That's—very British slang. I expect you picked it up from some upper class customer at your café—or maybe at the Eagle pub in Cambridge."

Sophie gave him a withering look. "You've definitely had too many drinks. How do you know about the Eagle?" She shifted in her chair and looked away. "Do you have anything else to tell me," she said faintly.

Willy saw that his mention of The Eagle had struck home. "There is something else. I have a new name: Second Lieutenant William Coulter."

Sophie almost knocked her whisky tumbler over. "*Kristus.* You're joking. Why?"

Willy's grin widened. He bit into one of her sandwiches. "I'm surprised too. Happened two weeks ago. My CO insisted. It's because we'll soon be back in France. With Kohut on my ID tag, the Jerries might identify me as not being British but a deserter from Bohemia. Probably execute me. So, no more Willy Kohut. I'm a British officer with a foreign accent."

Sophie squeezed her eyes shut and took a deep breath. "God in heaven! How can they do this to you—and to us? What about me and Paul? Don't we get a say on a new family name? Do your parents know?"

Willy waved a dismissive hand. "Not to worry, my dear. For the moment, you and Paul stay as Kohuts. But I've been promised British naturalization. When that happens, we'll all change to Coulter. You might as well get used to it and start calling me Bill instead of Willy. As for my parents, I haven't told them yet."

"This is shameful," Sophie said, dabbing her lips with a napkin as she finished off the last sandwich. "Where is your pride? Don't you think it's important to keep your family name?"

Willy drummed his fingers on the table. Sophie talked as if he was just someone to argue with—as if she had no respect for him. "Look, Sophie, over the last forty years, my family name changed three times: Cohen to Kohn and then to Kohut. Your family changed their name too. Grossberger to Gador."

He put what he thought was a friendly hand on her arm. "Look, let's not discuss my name anymore. What I wanna say is that you're terrific. It must have been exhausting to get here from the Hilliard farm. So, you visited Paul?"

"The farm has been a wonderful place for him. But that *Schottische* woman is a nasty one. Iris, the new land girl helping with the children, told me what that woman did to Paul. She's like an old crow pecking at helpless insects. I can see that you have no idea about this, even though you were there recently. I would expect someone like you, a father, to do a lot better. And Iris also said you had something to do with that other girl leaving. What was that about?"

Willy flinched inwardly. How did Iris know about him and Sheila? Better to say nothing and hope for the best. He knew he had missed an opportunity to hear Paul out, but he damned well wasn't going to admit that now and have Sophie pile on more criticism. "Paul and I had a good time at the farm. He did say Mrs. McAlistair was nasty, though he wouldn't tell me how or why. Anyway, I asked Lady Hilliard to tell the governess to stop being mean."

"I don't suppose her ladyship knows much of what goes on in that little cottage. When I was there yesterday, I told Mrs. McAlistair, face-to-face, that I would make sure she lost her job if she was cruel."

Willy raised his eyebrows and applauded. "Con … congratulations. Super. You did well." No doubt about it, Sophie had shown chutzpah. Maybe she shouldn't have had that scotch. One minute she was ebullient, next critical and now weepy.

Sophie dabbed at her eyes. "I was very upset—I even thought about taking Paul back to Cambridge, there and then. I may not have asked your permission to open my café but Paul is your son too, so I decided to talk to you first. Lady Hilliard did mention that we ought to get Paul into a school. That's a big reason I'm here."

Willy nodded thoughtfully. "As long as he goes to a good school."

Sophie heaved a sigh. "And where do you suggest this good school will be, *Herr Macher*?"

Willy tapped his glass with a cardboard beer mat. "Let's leave him on the farm until we've worked something out and hope Mrs. McAlistair mends her ways."

"That woman will never mend her ways. We can't leave Pavel there."

They sat in silence, not making eye contact.

Sophie's brain whirred. She had seen how well Paul fit in with the other children at Knapp Farm. He was accepted, talkative, a little wild and full of mischief. His assimilation was well underway. Why take him away from his friends? Maybe Lady Hilliard could be persuaded to get rid of Mrs. McAlistair.

It was time for her to take control of the conversation. She closed her eyes, preparing herself. She had hardly touched the second scotch Willy had ordered for her. She wanted a clear head.

In the previous two weeks and on the train to Bothell, she had rehearsed this meeting many times: Paul's immediate future, the café, and her lack of feeling for Willy. How to start? A burst of laughter from the group of men at the bar brought her out of her reverie. She saw Willy waving for another drink.

"I want to tell you a little about the Café," she said and described how hard she had been working and how people flocked to eat there. "Cambridge has nothing like it. I brought three months of accounts with me, to show you."

Willy glowered and slapped the table. "Beyond belief" he growled. "Where the hell did you get the money for this?" He shifted awkwardly in his chair. "I can't figure why Doctor Carnegie-Holston let you go. She needed you."

Sophie spread her hands in protest. "She understood what I wanted for myself. It gave me the opportunity to visit Paul regularly and create something successful that I enjoyed. Did I do such a terrible thing?"

"You didn't ask my permission for this café fantasy."

"*Your* permission?" She saw him look away, frowning. He was angry. She felt her own temper rising.

"I don't need your permission to do something for myself. The doctor approved of it and we've already made enough to cover a year's rent and four months' running costs. Doesn't that sound like the start of a successful business?"

Sophie watched Willy screw up his eyes and massage his temples, recognizing his familiar gesture of frustration. Abruptly, he stood, walked toward the dart players and then paced around the lounge, hands behind his back.

Sophie ignored him, rubbing her hands to warm them. She remembered how stubborn he was when he lost his temper or did not get his own way.

When Willy returned, he bent over her, swaying a little. "This is how I see it," he said in a thick voice, gripping the table with both hands, knuckles white. He coughed, clearing his throat. "The fact is … you planned the café behind my back. That is not how a good wife behaves."

Sophie was ready to get up and walk out.

He flopped into his chair. "Wasn't it enough for you just to be a mother and wife, and get paid to work for the doctor? *I'm* supposed to be the businessman of the family. For God's sake, woman, close the café down."

Sophie was shocked by his harshness. "Willy, how could you be so rigid? Frankly, I'm fed up with your domineering ways."

Willy swung round. "What if the damned café fails and goes bankrupt?" he said, thumping the table. "I would have to pay your debts and deal with the mess. I don't need another burden in my life."

Sophie spat out the words. "Don't talk to me about failure. Once you were going to be a great pianist. That never happened. You mismanaged our first store and your father lost his investment. Then you overspent extravagantly in Prague. We ended up with almost nothing. Don't treat me as if you own me."

Willy looked at her, open-mouthed.

"Remember, mister *macher*, how I got you out of prison. In Paris, I was the one who found the surgeon for Pavel. Here in England, with so little access to you, I've had to make decisions on my own."

Willy slammed his hand on the table. "Shut up, woman. I can't believe you're blaming me for everything that went wrong in Prague. You've changed, Sophie. You're not the loyal wife I married. I want her back—that's not too much to ask."

Sophie stared at him. *Why can't he see that I want an equal partnership? If he loved me, he would listen.* "I'm no longer your obedient wife. The truth is, it has all gone wrong between us. You haven't even done your part in looking after Paul. With all those separations we've been through we're almost strangers. Our marriage is—"

"Look, I admit that marriage and war don't go well together. But in wartime, wives should stick with their husbands and put up with hardships. I'm a soldier with a new name and a job that sucks me dry. Don't make my life even more complicated. Just get rid of your damned café."

Sophie looked up at the sound of a cough. The gaunt publican stood at their table. "Would ye be wantin' anythin' else?"

Willy shook his head. "No, thanks. I'll come over and pay in a few minutes."

"Verra well, but I must tell ye … your arguin's a wee bit loud. Best keep it to yoursels." He headed back to the bar.

Willy looked round. "Why should they care what we say," he said, his voice even huskier than before. We're speaking Czech. None of their business."

"I know the army dominates your life," said Sophie quietly after another silence. "But cleaning someone else's house, day in day out, isn't going to dominate mine. Our café will prosper. I'm earning my own money—even saving it." She pointed a finger. "In Prague, you gave me an allowance every month but most of the time you made me do the things *you* wanted. Now I'm going to do something I want."

"What are we talking about here? The café or our marriage—or both? "

Sophie couldn't help a harsh laugh. The bonds of her marriage were suddenly parting, strand by strand. Fear and optimism swirled in her head. "Unless you allow me to continue to run the café, our marriage is over. That means separation … or divorce. Of course, we will have to cooperate regarding Pavel's future."

Willy flung his spectacles on the table, rubbing his eyes. "Ridiculous. You need serious grounds for divorce. Besides, in our tradition, you can't ask for a divorce. Only the husband can."

Sophie sneered. "How can you, an atheist, bring up religion as an excuse? All your life you rejected Judaism. But I'm willing to negotiate. We can stay married, be polite to each other, and make decisions for Paul. Separate beds and probably separate lives."

Willy jerked forward and grabbed her hand.

Sophie winced at the pressure of his grip. She was suddenly afraid. Would too much whisky make him violent?

"Whaddya mean, no sex?" Willy said, his voice hoarse with anger and liquor. He leaned back in his chair, a tight, hard smile on his face. "Which reminds me. Povídka described some recent antics of yours in Cambridge: The Eagle pub, tea dances and outings with military officers. What happened?"

Sophie peeled his hand off hers. So, Povídka had been spying on her. "No sex, yet, husband."

Willy reared back, eyes wide.

"What do you expect from me? At the café I meet pleasant, well-educated men and women. Just because you're cooped up in a camp doesn't mean I can't enjoy a social life."

Willy jabbed a finger in her face. "What else have you been doing that I don't know about?"

Sophie looked down at her drink in silence. On top of the hard work and rewards of running the café, she had been having fun while he slogged away in Scotland. And then there was Captain Mottram, handsome and charming, a member of the RAF Intelligence Corps. One day, George Kindell had come to the Peacock Café to look it over and say hello. He found Kenneth, an old school chum, eating there and introduced them. Kenneth fell for her, and she was strongly attracted.

"You're no better. Yesterday, I found out about you and that Irish land girl. That must have been quite a farmyard scene. Poor Sheila was Paul's only real protection from that witch and by seducing her, you got her fired."

The two of them sat there, saying nothing. The fire crackled, darts thwacked into the target board and the men at the bar were laughing.

Willy's face, at first stony, faded into sadness. Tears trickled down his cheeks. He wiped his face.

Sophie was surprised. He could be harsh, clever and

entertaining, even rant and rave, but he rarely cried. Probably the whisky.

"I—I shouldn't have done it with that girl. It just happened. You know, one of those wartime moments. Please forgive me. I—we should try to make the marriage work." He reached for her hand. "Paul needs us and I still love you."

Sophie pulled hers back. But his appeal moved her. She had learned so much from him and enjoyed so much with him. He had protected and cared for her on their long journey from Prague. She had given him her loyalty, her body, her love and a dear child. But now, clear as crystal, she knew what she wanted to say.

"I don't love you anymore."

His mouth gaped, and he blinked as if blinded by a flash of light. "Do you have someone else?"

She shook her head and took a sip from her whisky, considering the lipstick marks on the glass's rim so that she didn't have to look at him. "How about this? Our marriage will be a practical arrangement: you in the army and me running the café. We live separately but can still pool our resources for Paul's education. But if you oppose the café, our marriage is over."

"Aie-aie. If your café fails, I won't pick you off the floor. You'll suffer for your woman's freedom."

Sophie pulled her coat tight around her shoulders to signal finality. "In that case, it's over. I want at least a separation."

Willy slapped the table. His face was grim. "Such an arrangement will not be easy, *Frau* Coulter," he shouted. "You will beg to come back."

Sophie pushed her chair back. She had come all this way because she wanted to negotiate a sensible agreement with Willy. "You are too stubborn and old-fashioned for me. And don't worry about my asking for money. I won't. I'm going back to the Station Hotel."

With a sense of accomplishment and relief, she put on her hat and coat, picked up her bag and gloves and walked briskly to the door.

Willy bellowed out. "What about Paul then? Will you desert him too?"

She stopped abruptly and noticed the men at the bar, heads turned, beer mugs frozen in their fists. "Goodnight, gentlemen," she said in English and closed the door firmly and quietly, as she had just done with her marriage.

*　　　*　　　*

"I'd like a word with you, laddie."

Startled, Willy looked up at the two men, feeling slightly dizzy. One was at least six feet, red-haired and heavy set with grizzled hair, one of the darts players. The other man was smaller, in a blue uniform. Under his arm he carried a peaked cap with a diced tartan band round the brim.

Willy rose, swaying slightly and then plopped down again, rocking his chair. "What is it?" *What are these idiots doing here? I don't need a chat, I need to be alone.* With an unsteady finger he pointed at the uniformed man. "Are you a soldier—oh, no, you must be a Scottish policeman. Anything the matter?"

The policeman indicated his companion with a nod. "Jock here telephoned the station about a suspicious disturbance. He said you and a woman were arguing and shouting in German. Where is she? "

"Okay, we were arguing. It was in Czech. Is that against the law? That woman is my wife. And me—well, I'm Bill Coulter, Royal Engineers, stationed at the camp." With some wriggling and a burp, he produced a card from an inside pocket.

Willy felt himself being lifted off the chair by his armpits. He was looking into the red-haired man's pock-marked face. Then at the policeman.

"Fockin' hell, Derek," said the red giant. "For sure, this feller might have somethin' to do with that ship that blew apart in the Clyde, the other day. They said it was sabotage."

The policeman slowly circled round Willy, inspecting him from head to toe.

"You're reet, Jock," he said finally. "Best to be on the safe side, eh? More than strange for a British officer to be speakin' German with a woman what's disappeared." The policeman looked down at Willy's identity card. "Well, this is a turn-up. The card says your name is "K-O-H-U-T. And Vilem? That's a bloddy foreign name if ever I saw one." He jabbed a finger into Willy's chest. "Just now you said your name was Bill Coulter. Your identity card says different."

"See what I mean," said the giant, placing a numbing grip on Willy's shoulder. "False identity, a fockin' liar. Guilty as hell."

"Look, chaps," croaked Willy, feeling trapped, outnumbered, and woozy. The men's faces were blurred outlines. "I'm a Czechoslovak citi-zen—we … er …escaped from the Nazis. We Czechs … we fight with the British. I'm … er, expecting a new identity … card."

Willy felt a hard shove and nearly toppled over.

"Fockin' bawface! You cain't fool us with your blather."

Willy bristled. "Morons like you should know who your allies are. I'm with the British Army—Royal Engineers. Billeted here in Bothwell." He cowered as Jock raised a massive fist.

The policeman took Willy's arm in a gentle but firm grip. "Come along, mister whoever you are. We're off to the police station and sort this thing out, peaceable-like, eh?"

*   *   *

The next afternoon, in the CO's drab office, dry-mouthed and head still buzzing, Willy faced Colonel Daffyd Swinton, Royal Engineers, a Welshman with graying hair. Willy could see from his expression and the prominent veins above his tunic collar, that the man was angry. He saluted and stood to attention, trying to brush away memory snapshots of the previous night's disaster.

"Blood-y dis-grace last night, Coulter," he growled, cracking his swagger stick on the metal desk top with each syllable. The humming from an electric coil heater fixed to the wall pounded Willy's head like a drill.

"Yessir."

"You were bloody stupid, speaking German to your wife in a local pub."

"Those blokes had no idea what we were speaking."

"Be that as it may, I had to crawl on my knees to get you out of this fix. Me, the commanding officer of this dump. So from now on, I'm expecting blood, sweat and tears from you. Savvy?"

Willy nodded, picturing with amusement his CO crawling under someone else's desk. "You're here for more than a dressing down, Coulter. We're shipping out." Swinton pushed his swagger stick out of the way and opened a buff-colored dossier. He jabbed at it with a forefinger. "I've something special in mind for you, in spite of last night's fiasco."

Willy kept quiet. Was Swinton's "something special" going to be good or bad?

"You're assigned to a new posting. If you do it right and on time, you'll be set for better things—that is, if you're looking for a military career. Maybe even make major, one day."

Willy felt a surge of excitement. All morning he had been feeling depressed. A hangover, the terrible shouting match with Sophie and a night in Bothwell jail. Suddenly, he was being given an alternative to begging George Kindell for a slot in his company. "Thank you, sir. What do you have in mind?"

"Your base is Drayton Camp, next to a village called Barton Stacey. That's sixty-five miles southwest of London."

"What kind of operation will this be, sir?"

"Two tasks. First one—security ops at an armaments staging post. You'll head a team: ten men and a couple of officers."

Willy nodded, smiling to himself. A staging post for tanks and guns? Maybe the rumored invasion of France was really on. "Any details, sir?"

Swinton ran a finger down his file. "Hmm. Hidden American and British field guns, carriers, trucks, tanks, jeeps and sundry ammo. Your team will cover security. No prying by the locals, y'got it?"

Willy grinned. "You mean this will be the real thing, sir. Invasion? No more building decoys or inflatables?"

"Not funny, Coulter," snorted Swinton. He broke a cigarette in half and stuffed it into his pipe. After lighting it, he puffed a stream of smoke into the air and leaned forward to check something on his desk. He pushed a card toward Willy. "That's the address."

Willy scanned it: No 2. TRAINING BATTALION. ROYAL ENGINEERS. 'C' CAMP. DRAYTON. WINCHESTER. HAMPSHIRE. He put it in his wallet hoping it wasn't in the middle of nowhere but close to the town of Winchester where there would be pubs, entertainment and women.

"Task two: Supervise upgrading a gasoline storage facility. It's in a chalk quarry near a hamlet called Micheldever Station. It's about four miles from Drayton HQ. Mostly involves prodding technicians, reporting progress, making sure everything's done on time. Can do?"

Willy's thoughts raced like an express train. He ran a quick calculation. Winchester was close to London and from there it would be only four hours or so to get to Knapp Farm and see Paul. Even visiting Cambridge to check on Sophie's activities was doable, two to three hours at most. He had been mulling over their contentious meeting and her mention of divorce. Maybe she did have a serious lover. He had to find out.

He took a slow, satisfying breath of anticipation. He, Second Lieutenant Coulter, would be in charge of an important mission, and for the first time, giving orders. "Sir, I believe I can."

"By the way, Coulter, this morning someone came to the camp gate asking for you. You know we don't allow entry for unpermitted civilians. He left a note."

Willy knitted his brow. "Anything special about him, sir?"

"A damned foreigner." Colonel Swinton looked at a slip of paper on his desk and pushed it over. "I expect it's one of your countrymen."

Willy's stomach turned over at what he saw.

I'll be in touch, Povidka

CHAPTER TWENTY-FIVE
60 Northways, Again
London
March 1943

Back in London, Emil and Judit resumed their lives: food shopping on Finchley Road, occasional excursions to Hampstead Heath and Regent's Park, and a visit to the Odeon cinema once a week. After shopping one Friday, Emil was delighted to find a letter from Willy in their mailbox at the Northways' entrance. He waved it triumphantly coming through the front door of the flat. Judit was in the kitchen, adding chopped carrots and sliced potatoes to the onions sizzling in a pan. "It's from Willy. He's turned into a dutiful son ... writes regular as clockwork."

He examined the postmark. "Winchester, Hampshire," he exclaimed, lifting a folded map of Britain down from behind the clock on the mantelpiece. It took a minute or two to find Winchester. "*Wunderbar*, Judit! This town is close to London."

Judit hurried from the kitchen, drying her hands on a dishcloth.

At the table, Emil pulled two sheets of flimsy paper from the envelope, careful not to tear them "Hmm ... he used a pen this time, and there's more than just the usual few lines." He began to read, then jerked upright in his chair. "Unbelievable. Willy has been ordered to change his name." This was way beyond the usual bureaucratic screw ups Emil remembered from his army days. The idea that his own son was about to abandon the family name that for fifty years had been a fixture in Lučenec society was intolerable.

Judit sat down beside him, her face creased with worry. "I don't understand, *Apushkam*."

Emil slapped the letter down and threw up his hands. "Army orders. In case he gets captured by the Nazis and they suspect he is not

British. He says Sophie is very unhappy. She does not want a new name."

Judit went back to cooking. "Always something new," she called out. "What is the matter with Willy as a name?"

"It is not just Willy, my dear—he will be William Coulter." Emil turned over one of the pages and smiled. "Aha. *Ganz gut!* He is promoted to second lieutenant, an officer. Excellent. More pay ... and respect."

Judit came to the table and slid some of the contents of the frying pan onto his plate. "Will we also have to change our name?"

Emil cut a thick slice of bread and started to eat. "It is just an army matter, only for Willy. Still, the name Coulter has a good English sound. It will help him fit in more." He rested his knife and fork and tapped the letter with a finger. "Maybe it's not such a bad thing to have an English name."

Judit filled her plate and eased on to her chair. She began to eat. "Mmm, what else?"

Emil tilted his spectacles. His hands shook the letter, something that he had been noticing and worrying about recently. "The new camp is sixty-five miles from London. His work has changed."

Judit sighed. "Poor boy." She finished eating, brushed stray bread crumbs off the tablecloth into her palm, and dropped them on her plate. "He should be living with his family."

"He does what he has to do," said Emil as he slid a piece of nut strudel onto his plate. "In wartime, family takes second place to soldiering." He turned over a page. "Here he writes about Sophie and Paul."

Most of the other children at the Knapp Farm will go home soon. Sophie and I agreed that Paul should also leave but not until we have made suitable arrangements. He's old enough to be at a proper school, but we cannot choose one until we have decided where he is going to live."

Judit stacked the dirty dishes on a tray. "The little one needs stability. He won't get that if he goes back to live with his mother. Not a word from her since Paul went to the farm. Such disrespect."

Emil agreed with her sentiment but said nothing, not wanting to trigger one of Judit's diatribes.

He brought the letter closer to his glasses, not sure if he had read the sentence correctly. "*Mein Gott,* he said shaking his head. "She left the doctor."

"What?"

"She opened a café with the doctor's cook."

Judit grabbed the letter and scanned it, her face crimson with anger. "You mean that insolent girl left her good job?" She stared at Emil, her lips quivering. "So that was why we heard nothing. She wanted to keep it a secret. Sophie is selfish and cannot be trusted."

Emil ripped it back from her, annoyed with Judit. She jumped to conclusions too easily and spoke without thinking. In fact, he was impressed by Sophie. She had shown chutzpah and competence. A refugee woman, his daughter-in-law. Willy had to be proud of her, though he didn't say so in the letter.

Judit, bosom heaving, carried the tray to the sink. "And from where did she get money to make a cafe? From Willy? He did not tell us anything. Are we strangers to both of them?"

Emil was reading again. "He does not give details. But he says Sophie is too busy with the café to look after the boy properly." He looked up at Judit and a smile broke on his lips. "He wants us to look after Paul and find a school for him here in London."

"Why does Willy wait till the last minute to ask us such things? Is this the behavior of a good son? No!"

That evening, as Emil listened to in BBC news, Judit switched off the radio and stood in front of him, hands on her hips. "Listen to me, *Apa*. I have been thinking."

He glowered at this unjustified intrusion of his precious moment of the day.

"I am very happy for Paul to live here," she said enthusiastically, "but we cannot be a hotel for him to stay at for a night or two. Too disturbing for the boy and for me. I want a proper arrangement without that *meshuganah* Sophie turning up and taking him away."

"Sophie *is* his mother. The boy should be with her," Emil said, even though he partly agreed with Judit's sentiments. It seemed obvious that with running the café, Sophie wouldn't have much time for Paul. How would she take him to school on time and bring him home? When would she supervise his homework? The boy might have to sit in her café for hours, breathing in cigarette smoke.

"You turn little problems into big ones, "Emil said dismissively as he switched the radio back on. "Where Paul lives and for how long can easily be worked out by Sophie and Willy."

*   *   *

One Sunday, when the café was closed, Sophie took the train to London. Now that Paul was set to leave the farm, Willy had written, asking her to visit Judit and Emil and reinforce his request for them to look after the boy.

She dreaded talking to her in-laws. She would have to tell them about the café and why in the short term, she couldn't look after Paul. Her task would feel doubly difficult because they knew nothing about her terrible argument with Willy in the Scottish pub—what it might mean for their son's marriage.

The two hour train journey from Cambridge and the tranquility of the fresh spring colors of the passing countryside outside gave her time to reflect on the good and the bad of the past few months.

The café had turned out just as she hoped. Customers adored the food and the convivial atmosphere. Kenneth visited the café nearly every day. On weekends, he took her on picnics and outings in his Morris Minor. He taught her new words and phrases in English. Their flirting was developing into a more passionate relationship.

Did her in-laws know what she was up to? Probably not—and just as well. Cambridge had a small refugee community that might still have links with her in-laws—and its gossip leaked like butter through hot toast. In her new life, she had entered a different milieu filled with talented people who came to eat her stews and salads, and Helga's German-style pastries.

On the bus to Emil and Judit's, Sophie reset her mind to the task at hand. It was a simple request: keep Paul with them in London until the question of his schooling was settled. But when she and Judit were in the same room, nothing was easy or pleasant.

In the apartment at Northways, sitting opposite Emil and Judit, Sophie sipped a weak coffee, and tried to keep her hand steady. She looked around the living room, admiring the new French doors to the balcony and the beige wallpaper patterned with modernist squares and triangles. "Not a sign of bomb damage, *Tante*. Aren't you pleased with how they repaired the flat?"

Judit just stared at her.

Emil curled a grudging lip. "They used cheap wood instead of metal, and did a terrible painting job. But then it's wartime, daughter. We put up with it."

"Please tell me, how was Paul when you saw him in March?"

"Pleased to see us," Judit replied with a half-smile. "He knows the English alphabet. He writes his name nicely and speaks many words. He read to us from a picture book and a children's magazine. He can count up to one hundred and do additions, subtractions and times tables."

Emil his face softening, edged forward. "I was pleased to see how much stronger he was.

His neck and shoulder are healed, scars almost invisible. He gets good food and exercise."

Judit nodded enthusiastically. "And he runs fast … faster than the other children."

"Did he say anything about that Mrs. McAlistair?"

Emil shook his head "He asked if he would be coming home soon."

"It broke my heart, how sad he looked," said Judit wiping her nose with a handkerchief. He said to me—when can I live with Mummy and Daddy?"

Sophie felt tightness in her throat. "And what did you say?"

"I said we weren't sure yet; because Willy was fighting the Germans, and you—you were very busy working for the doctor." Judit looked pointedly at Sophie. "Of course, we only just discovered about the café from Willy's letter!"

Sophie flinched.

Emil frowned at Judit, leaned over and patted Sophie's hand. "I understand the main reason you did this was to get a travel permit. That was clever, and I'm sure it is very hard work. But didn't you think he would have to leave the farm sometime and come to live with you?"

"Or go to wherever his home might be," Judit said in a bitter tone. "Which nobody knows yet. Why, in God's name, don't you tell us what you are doing?"

Sophie didn't have the energy to explain. "As far as Paul is concerned, Willy and I want him to grow up to be an Englishman.

Willy has been promoted and, so far, my café is successful, so I'm sure our future after the war will be here. Until Paul is older, we do not want to mention Prague or tell him we are Jews. Please, we want you to agree to this."

Nodding slowly, Emil cleaned his glasses. "After school, he should follow a medical career. War or peace, a doctor can always make a living. The human body works the same way whatever race or language. Dr. Paul will become an *English* doctor."

Judit twisted her hands in the folds of her apron. "*Apushkam*, you are a horse with blinders. How can Paul ever become an Englishman if he is connected to us? When we open our mouths, he knows that part of him is different from the other boys. One day, he will look at the documents and photographs left from the fire and ask, "Why didn't I know I was Jewish?"

Sophie felt a moment of respect for her adversary. They both loved Paul, and Judit was perceptive.

"What Paul needs now," Judit continued, "is good food, a good school with friends, and family affection. He has been on his own long enough. And for certain, he should not live with a mother who does not have time for him."

Sophie gasped. This was too much. "You are being unfair, Judit," she blurted out. "If we want a successful life for Paul I have to work. And I'm doing my best."

Judit glared back. She poured more coffee. "So you and Willy think it will be easy for Jews to hide in England?" she said in a bitter tone as she glanced at Emil. "Even if Willy has an English name—does that hide what he is? In Germany, Jews changed their names and gave up their traditions to become patriotic German citizens. What were their rewards? Where are they now? Dispossessed, in slave camps—or dead. The same thing could happen here."

Emil paced around the living room, hands clasped behind his

back. Then he straightened his shoulders and looked at his wife. "Paul is too young to know the truth. So, what can we do for him at this moment? Willy is away until the war ends, and Sophie wants a success with her café. She cannot look after the boy properly. They want him to live with us." He opened his arms. "So, simple answer. He lives with us."

Sophie shot a surreptitious glance at Judit. What was her nemesis going to say? She had the power to ruin what seemed like a reasonable plan. By insisting that Paul stay in Cambridge, she would hang him around Sophie's neck and that might put the future of the café at risk.

Judit nodded vigorously, eyes suddenly sparkling. "I want Paul to live with us, *Apushkum*. We have nothing much else to look forward to in this country. He will give our life a new purpose." Judit's lips trembled. She pulled a handkerchief from her smock and blew her nose.

Sophie had been expecting invective; now she felt closer to her in-laws than she had for years. They were offering a good temporary solution. And they loved Paul. A wave of relief washed over her. In spite of their faults, they were good people.

She looked at her watch. It was time to get the train. She had arranged to meet Kenneth for dinner in Cambridge, at The Bull Hotel where he had booked a room for the night. Though Emil and Judit knew something about the Peacock Café, she was sure they knew nothing about Kenneth.

She pushed her chair back. "I'm sorry, I must catch my train. I'm very happy you have agreed to look after Paul when the time comes—that's very generous of you."

At the door, Emil embraced her. Judit hesitated. Sophie stepped into the corridor without kissing her mother-in-law. Kissing was too big a step on the path to reconciliation. Take it slowly, Sophie. She took a deep breath and hurried off.

On the Northern Line tube to Kings' Cross Station, Sophie pondered the family's intent to hide Paul's background and grow up an Englishman. Achieving this goal would need knowledge neither she nor Willy possessed. The only person Sophie knew who understood refugees and was trustworthy was Dr. Carnegie-Holston. She would ask her for lunch on a Sunday, the one day the Peacock Café was closed.

*　　　*　　　*

When Dr. Emily knocked on the café door at noon the following Sunday, Sophie, nervous and hopeful, showed her to a table by the window. Doing her best to appear calm, she brought a carafe of water, two plates, silverware, rolls and prepared salads.

"It all looks so lovely," said Dr. Emily, unfolding her napkin as she glanced around. "I brought something for you." From a thin roll of tissue paper she drew a glowing peacock feather. "This was in my attic—pinned on one of my grandmother's hats."

Beaming, Sophie turned the feather over and over. "Such a wonderful gift. You are so thoughtful. I'll find a good place for it. Thank you for coming."

"My husband will be jealous of me eating your cooking." The doctor laughed. "And I see you've stacked *Picture Post* and *Woman's Weekly* into a big basket for people to read while they wait for a table. Just like my patients. Very nice idea."

"Thank you." Sophie felt great pleasure in getting compliments from her mentor. She pointed to the serving dishes. "Helga's German-style mayonnaise potatoes with chives, egg salad, a stew of canned beans, ham and onions with parsley. I'm sorry, there's no Spam today. Will these do?"

"Mmm, looks delicious. We do miss your and Helga's cooking, you know."

"Please—eat."

After a minute or two, Sophie laid down her knife and fork. "I need some very personal advice, doctor. But, please keep eating while I talk. I don't want to waste your time."

The doctor was spearing chunks of potato salad. "Very …um … well."

Sophie launched into the introduction she had practiced. "This is just between you and me, doctor. I must tell you that things are going well for me, but also very badly … all at the same time."

Dr. Emily sighed. "Oh, dearie me. Well, you'd better spill the beans."

Sophie took a deep breath. "What goes well is this place, our café. We make a profit and get many customers. I am happy and grateful to you for letting us do this, even giving us encouragement in spite of the awful inconvenience we caused you."

"I'm delighted it turned out well, my dear. I suppose now you want to talk about what's bad."

"My marriage. I think people here say "rocky". It started with our escape from Czechoslovakia in '39. Too many long separations. Now he is furious about the café. He says I was deceitful not telling him our early plans, and I should have asked his approval. I should be obedient and not do things on my own. He wants me to give it up."

"Are you asking me to talk to him?"

Sophie shrugged. "If I stay as Willy's wife, he won't allow me to run the café. I cannot bear to give it up, you understand. I don't know what to do. Should I leave him?"

Dr. Emily shook her head as she finished her mouthful. "You and your husband have to resolve this on your own."

"There is also another problem, doctor. As you know, Paul lives on a farm. He must leave soon. We have arranged for him to stay with his grandparents in London."

The doctor helped herself to more salad. "Why doesn't Paul come live with you?"

Sophie picked at her plate. Opening her heart was hard—especially talking to a religious woman from a different culture. She tried to make sense of her jumbled and contradictory feelings. "I know Paul should come to me, doctor but the café is awfully time-consuming. I don't think I can manage a lively boy even if he is at school for most of the day." Sophie could not stop the tremble in her voice. "He would have to wait at the café and then sleep on the floor in my rented room."

"So your husband's parents will take him. Good. They are fine people."

Sophie nodded. "They speak bad English and live in a Jewish neighborhood. If he lives with them he won't learn to be an English boy. Willy and I want him to learn a profession and be a doctor, like you. "

Dr. Emily glanced at her watch. "This café has confused your life quite a bit, hasn't it? Listen, my dear, if you want to get him on the right path for university or a medical career, don't rely on your in-laws to know what to do. To get into a good school and then medical school, Paul must speak perfect English and have a formal Catholic or Protestant religious affiliation that goes on his application forms. Otherwise, he hasn't a hope."

Sophie frowned, confused. What did religion have to do with school?

"Talk to George Kindell. He has fingers in a thousand pies. He went to all the right schools."

Sophie nodded, pensively. George might be able to help. "Maybe he … I don't know."

Dr. Emily snapped her fingers. "How about this? Take the first step as soon as you can. Turn Paul into a Christian boy. He could be baptized here, at Trinity, my church—I'd be his godmother. His affiliation on the school application form would be Church of England."

Sophie held her breath. How could Dr. Emily suggest such a thing? Was it possible to change religion just like that?

"A Christian? I don't know what Willy will say. "

Dr. Emily put down her knife and fork. "Oh, I think he'll agree. Your father-in-law told me he was an atheist. I expect your husband is too. If you are interested in a high-quality school, I can explain the steps."

She made to rise from the table. "Delicious lunch. Simple ingredients, beautifully flavored. Now, if there is nothing else, I must go. We're attending a lovely charity concert. Myra Hess is the pianist."

Sophie coughed. She had come to her last, most embarrassing revelation. "Please, wait another minute. I'm almost sure my husband had relations with a young woman when he visited Paul at the farm."

The doctor gasped, her face beetroot. "Why are you telling me this? This is adultery."

Red-faced and ashamed, Sophie couldn't look the doctor in the eye. "I don't know what to do."

Dr. Emily leaned forward. "And what about you?" she said very gently, resting her fingers on Sophie's wrist. "You're very pretty. I expect that's why some of the customers come to your café. Have you been tempted?"

Sophie hadn't expected this directness. She felt the heat rise into her cheeks and shook her head.

The doctor paused, as if wanting to clear her mind. "Look, I'm sorry you brought this up. I can't take sides. You'll have to work the marriage problem out yourselves."

Sophie blushed and shook her dark curls. "I—I know."

"To succeed as a professional, the boy will have to go to boarding school. That's all I can say. As for your fragile marriage and your husband's fling, that is something you must work out for yourself. "

"I apologize for asking you, doctor."

After the doctor had gone, Sophie gathered up the dishes, the doctor's words resonating in her head. Was it so wrong to be selfish? Who decided? She wanted to have it both ways—to find her own path and still stay close to Paul. Dr. Emily talked about a boarding school for him. What was so special about a boarding school?

CHAPTER TWENTY-SIX
The Officers Billet, Bransbury Hall, Hampshire
May 1943

Willy dropped his knapsack on the parquet floor and with a grateful sigh sank into one of the deep-cushioned armchairs of Lord Ainslie's well-appointed living room. He nodded amicably to the blond crew-cut American officer reading a magazine on the settee opposite, and glanced through the French windows at the trim lawns and colorful flowerbeds that surrounded the lord's grand mansion.

The sun-drenched view gave him little pleasure. He'd been hammered all day by new problems at the disused chalk quarry where for the past six weeks he and the other officers supervised the activities of a mix of civilians and soldiers—skilled metalworkers, mechanics, and engineers. They were doubling the size of War Department fuel tanks, part of the secret build-up of an Allied invasion force. At first, he had been excited by the mission, but now it seemed more like construction drudgery in dank, unpleasant conditions. His other, easier task was to coordinate the patrols protecting a camouflaged military zone hidden in a forest a few miles away at Wherwell Woods.

The American looked up and grinned sympathetically, "You look wore out, Bill."

"So I am, Eddie. And you're still here. No news of the posting yet?"

The big man's khaki shirt was open at the neck and he chewed on a half-smoked cigar, his untied boots resting on the low coffee table in front him. A tattered copy of *Life* magazine lay across one bulging thigh. "Nope. But this place is a great place to hang out. Tough day?"

Willy sighed as he unbuttoned his battledress blouse to cool off.

He was ready for a quick nap before supper.

"Before you flake out," said Eddie, taking the cigar from his lips. "Some guy was here not long ago, asking for you. A civilian. Wouldn't give his name."

Only Sophie and his parents had the address of this billet, so who else could...? Willy scowled. His weary muscles tensed. *Surely not fucking Povídka again? This would be the third damned time.* "What the hell did he want?"

Eddie shrugged. "Said he was a buddy of yours, 'cept he wasn't wearin' no uniform. How come this guy walked in here, easy as you please? Ain't your Home Guard fellers supposed to guard this place?"

Willy could not dredge up the energy to explain or defend. "What did this chap look like?"

"Skinny and tall. Twitchy face. Looked like he'd handled trouble before. Late thirties, mebbe. Foreign accent. Gave me this. For you." Eddie pulled a brown envelope from his pocket and tossed it. It bounced off Willy's lap onto the floor.

Willy picked it up and glanced at his name penciled in capitals on the envelope. "Thanks."

"Talking of foreigners," said Eddie, "how come a second lootenant like you is in charge of this big project that no one round here wants to talk about—you're not even a real Brit."

Willy shook his head as he tore open the envelope. "A complicated story. Let's say it's my language skills, plus I'm a good organizer", he said unfolding the letter. He stared at Povídka's signature, heart hammering against his ribs. *What the fuck is the bastard after?*

Eddie yawned, stretching his arms over the back of the settee. "Last night someone told me somethin' inter—"

"For God's sake, Eddie," Willy interrupted, waving the note. "Shut-up and let me read this."

Povídka's note was in Czech. "Meet me at White Swan, Barton Stacey village. Seven o'clock … got news for you. Be discreet. Leo."

What "news"? Willy looked at his watch. Five–thirty. *Okay, the village is only five minutes' drive away. No panic. Think this through.*

He jumped from his chair, weariness forgotten. "See you later, Eddie."

He hurried up to the stuffy bare-bones attic he shared with three other officers. Apparently, Lord Ainslie's domestics had shared this room before the war started. It housed four cots with red blankets, a table, chest of drawers, Windsor chairs, and hooks along one wall. The small windows were too high to look out of without standing on a chair.

Willy tore up the letter, flushed the pieces down the toilet and then lay down on his cot. Taking deep, relaxing breaths, he cast his mind back to what happened after the army mutiny at Cholmondeley camp. He and many other mutineers had been transferred to the Pioneer Corps, but, unbelievably, that damned Povídka, one of the chief trouble-makers, was shunted into Civvy Street. In the Spanish civil war, he had been a commissar in the Dimitrov battalion, the sort of rabid communist type George had asked Willy to keep a close eye on.

Why was Povídka stalking him? Was it personal or something else? Willy sat up and wiped sweat off his face with a towel. Danger and premonition. Damned sure, he wasn't going to let Povídka interfere with his work or get away with any other skullduggery. Just last week, at Drayton Camp, Colonel Bloomsworthy had floated an acid comment as Willy stood to attention. "Some of you foreign chaps can be a bit dodgy," the colonel had said, avoiding direct eye contact. "Not sure we can trust 'em. But so far, Kohut, you've done reasonably well."

Willy had no intention of ending up on the CO's "dodgy foreigners" list.

After an hour's nap, Willy drove to the White Swan pub in Barton Stacey village. His van was a dinged-up black Austin 8, requisitioned from Nutters Garage. The steering was loose, the tires bald and the battery lost its charge whenever he left it on a slope—but it worked, most of the time.

He parked under the fronds of a weeping willow next to the village church and walked a hundred yards along the road toward the White Swan.

Inside, the smoky public bar was crowded with soldiers and locals playing darts and bar billiards. They were talking and shouting above the sound of Vera Lynn belting out "We'll Meet Again" on the radio. Beer had clotted the floor's sawdust into brown sticky patches. Cigarette smoke hung in the air.

Willy spotted Povídka alone at a table by the bay window. He disliked everything about the bastard who was staring into space, a spiral of smoke curling from the black cigarillo held between two fingers. He looked much the same as when he and Willy last talked at the Cholmondeley Camp, except that instead of a worn-out French uniform, Povídka now wore a well-tailored slate-gray suit. A black trilby rested on a folded newspaper on his table.

Willy shouted above the din. "How the hell did you know where I was?"

Povídka gave him a slow knowing smile and raised an eyebrow. His neck twitched. "I'm very pleased to see you again, Comrade Kohut," he said in English.

Same cynical sarcasm, thought Willy. "Can't say that *I'm* pleased to see you, Leo. And call me Bill, not comrade. Nice suit. Looks like you've gone up in the world. By the way, my name's William Coulter."

"You think I don't know? You are a wartime miracle, Bill. A simple Czechoslovak-Jewish private transformed into a junior officer with a very English name—that surely is a great achievement."

In spite of Povídka's sarcasm, it *was* an achievement. Willy kept his face blank. "What the fuck do you want?"

Povídka sneered. "Come, come, Second Lieutenant Coulter. No need to be rude." He looked around the pub, furrowing his eyebrows. "We need to talk somewhere without being observed or overheard. What do you suggest?"

Willy had expected this. "The only place I can think of is my van. It's parked by the church."

Povídka nodded his approval. "Good. We go there separately. You first. I come five minutes later. How do I find this van?"

Willy stood. "You can see the square church tower from the pub's parking area. The van is under a tree with low hanging branches, next to the graveyard."

Inside the van, Povídka twisted to face Willy, his eyes needle-sharp. "I need information," he said in Czech.

"You what?" Willy's foot started to jiggle. The man's demand probably was probably hooked in to the British Communist Party's attempts to provoke strikes in Britain, mostly in the mines and factories. "You work for the Russians of course, but who specifically?"

Povídka gave Willy a piercing look. "Let's keep this simple," he said in tight low voice "Officially, I work as a news reporter for the communist *Daily Worker*. I also collect information for British people friendly to Moscow." He carefully lit another cigarillo.

Willy wound down the window to let the acrid smoke escape. He rested his hands on the steering wheel, waiting. There was more to come … specifics, no doubt.

Povídka tapped Willy's arm with tobacco-stained fingers.

"Look, Kohut. Now that Russia has committed to defeating Hitler arm-in-arm with the allies, the British and Americans are supposed to be sharing intelligence. Well, that's a damned joke. All we get are tidbits. What my people want is depth: plans, numbers and specifics, as well as proof that what they are getting is reliable."

Willy laughed, trying hard to hide his nervousness. "Why are you talking to me about intelligence, Leo? I'm just a low level administrator, helping to run a small military camp."

"That's not true, my friend." The man pulled a small notebook from an inside pocket and flipped it open. "You recently arrived from Scotland where your unit built ghost tanks and decoy guns to fool the Luftwaffe. Here, you're involved in the expansion of a fuel reserve facility and also active in a hidden staging post for heavy military equipment. Genuine *matériel* … British and American. Isn't that so?"

Willy rubbed at his chin, glancing out of his side-door window, trying to conceal his concern. Povídka knew some of the *what*—but did he know *where* the fuel tanks were located, or what exactly was hidden inside the barbed-wire fences and locked gates surrounded by forty acres of dense woods?

"You're on a fishing expedition," he said, fidgeting with his pipe. "Throw out bait and see what bites."

"Fishing, am I?" Povídka sneered. "Here's something you may not know. Your work is part of Operation Bodyguard—preparation for the invasion of Europe."

Playing for time to think, Willy pulled out his tobacco pouch and lit his pipe, and looked away to hide his dismay.

Povídka stubbed out his cheroot, picking tobacco remnants off his thin lips. His neck and shoulder twitched. "What I want is the location of your military staging post and detailed specifications of the war matériel stored inside. And I want a look-see."

Willy cleared his throat, but the words wouldn't come. The

bastard wanted him to betray the country that had welcomed the refugee Kohut family. "Impossible," he finally stammered, the heat of anger pushing his fear into the background.

"Don't be stupid. I know you can do it." Povídka pulled an envelope from his pocket and lifted the flap, showing British banknotes. "A hundred pounds for your penniless family?" He knocked ash off his cigarillo and sneered. "To help pay for your boy's holiday at that nice safe farm. Why not? "

Willy clenched his fists. "You're a piece of shit. Leo. Your Soviet masters are also full of shit. How can they do this to their allies? You really expect me to betray Britain, the country that's harboring my family? Fuck you."

"No betrayal, Kohut old friend, just some in-depth clarification of what we already know." Povídka ran a hand through his pomaded hair, and with a menacing frown leaned toward Willy. "Consider your lovely wife, Sophie. I ate at her café in Cambridge, twice. Good food. We had a pleasant chat. Remember, Boho Serbin … the indestructible knife-man who sailed with me from France? He greatly admires your wife." He smiled. "He would enjoy visiting her, don't you think?"

Willy seethed inside. He kept his gaze fixed on the willow fronds hanging in front of the windshield. "Bastard" he whispered under his breath. "You'd better leave my wife out of this."

"Come on, old pal." In the manner of a schoolboy asking a question, Povídka raised his arm in the air. "Don't you think we ought to protect your family from harm? For example, I could arrange for Boho to keep a friendly eye on Sophie … when you're not around."

Willy took a deep breath. A trap was closing around him. "Piss off. I'll inform my commanding officer. He'll have you arrested."

Povídka slid a hand into his jacket pocket and produced a small pistol. He rested it on his lap. "It would be your word against mine. I expect you would be suspended from your post as an unreliable foreign soldier fabricating stories about spies. And if you don't do as I ask, Sophie might no longer feel safe in Cambridge."

In a quandary, Willy fiddled with his pipe. Probably, his Russian handlers were squeezing the *schmuck* with same threats. He needed time to come up with a way of dealing with Povídka. That meant delay and a display of apparent cooperation.

"Okay, you win. Put the pop-gun away."

Povídka sniggered. "Excellent—so now we can get on with business." He pocketed the weapon and wrote in his notebook.

Willy leaned across, staying Povídka's hand. He had to have more information about Sophie, though it was a gamble whether he would actually get the truth. "Just a minute—can you be straight, really straight with me. How did you find my wife in Cambridge?"

"I used a private English investigator."

"Oh! God." Willy bent his head forward, fiercely massaging both cheeks with his fingers, trying to control his anger.

Povídka grinned as if pleased with what he saw. "Not so hard is it? All I need from you is a list of heavy equipment, ordnance and supplies stored at the staging post. But I also want to take photographs—so my superiors don't think I'm making things up. Okay?"

He pulled a buff-colored envelope from inside his jacket and handed it to Willy. "Use this for the number, types, and location of the war matériel at the staging post. And if you can get it, the location of any other staging areas you know of. You've got two days. I'll wait for you in a hotel in Winchester."

"How did you get here?" said Willy through his teeth, stifling an urge to reach out and throttle the man.

"Taxi."

"So that phrase about news in your note was just bait."

Povídka slowly unwrapped the band of a new cigarillo. "Not

so", he said putting the cheroot between his lips. "My news is about lovely, spirited Sophie who is having the time of her life."

"What about her?" Willy spat out.

Povídka smiled his wolfish smile. "The Peacock Café is always packed. And when it's closed, she often goes out to a film or a tea dance. They say the samba and jitterbug are all the rage."

Willy shook his head, afraid of what might be coming. He remembered the bitter argument at the Scottish pub. "Sophie just likes to have fun."

Povídka looked in his notebook. "More specifically with an RAF intelligence officer: Captain Mottram. Lots of *amour* apparently. A wartime romance."

Willy felt as if he had been punched in the gut. *Is this bastard telling the truth or twisting the knife?* "As usual, Leo, you're lying."

Povídka scribbled on the back of a visiting card and gave it to Willy. "The detective I hired. Check for yourself."

Willy snatched the card and shoved it into his pocket. Outside, light was fading and heavy raindrops peppered the road, forming small puddles.

Povídka peered out, screwing up his face at the wet willow leaves stuck to the van's windshield. "I'm not going to telephone for a taxi in this rain. God knows when it would arrive. You can drive me to Winchester. I'm staying at the Vine. We'll talk about next steps when we get there."

On the drive to the hotel, Povídka launched into a diatribe about the siege of Leningrad, praising the indestructible stoicism of the Russian people who were resisting the Nazis, even as they died of starvation. Willy only grunted his responses. Apart from the difficulty of navigating country lanes with dim headlights, he was trying to think of a way to outwit Povídka and save Sophie. His mind darted about as if in a maze. *I need help. I need time.*

At the Vine Inn, Povídka seemed in no hurry. "It is Russia's sacrifice that will destroy Hitler, not the Anglos," he said as he inched his door open and stuck a tentative foot onto the drenched pavement.

Willy glanced at his watch—just after eight. Still light outside. "Come on, Leo. I have to get back. My suppertime."

Povídka kept the van door open. "Pick me up day after tomorrow, latest? Telephone the hotel about a rendezvous time."

Willy tried to keep his voice under control. He shook his head. "It will take me a few days to get what you want and for me to arrange to show you the heavy equipment. I'll leave you a message at the Vine. I guess in three or four days. Latest, Thursday."

Povídka heaved a sigh. "No yiddisher tricks, mind you. I'll go back to London tomorrow—and return in three days—with Serbin." He slammed the door shut.

Damn. Willy lit his pipe. A Browning handgun from the camp armory would handle Povídka … if Serbin was with him, it would shift the odds … the wrong way.

CHAPTER TWENTY-SEVEN
Incident in the Woods
June 1943

When Willy got back to the officer's mess, dinner service was over and the kitchen attendants were clearing the sideboard. Gratefully, he wolfed down two lukewarm helpings of chicken curry, dal, and Biryani rice, and then rushed to his office. He picked up the telephone and dialed George Kindell's home number.

"This is Mrs. Kindell. Who is speaking?"

"This is Willy Kohut. I'm sorry if this is inconvenient, but I must speak urgently with George."

Willy heard the deep sigh. "It's always urgent, isn't it? Wait a minute."

When George came on the line, Willy described his encounter with Povídka in detail. "Those communists you wanted me to keep an eye on. I've done what you asked," he said. "Now I really need your help. I've agreed to take them to visit the staging post in the woods. They're armed and threatened to harm Sophie, possibly even Paul. They're coming in a week and I have to confirm the rendez-vous in three days. I have to come up with a way to deal with them that won't get me killed."

George spluttered. "Killed! Good Christ, Willy, what a hellish fix. I ... I don't see how I can do anything from here. You're talking military emergency. Best thing, old boy, to do is notify your CO, pronto."

Willy clenched the handset. George could be so exasperating. Of course, he could do something—if he was pushed hard enough. "Listen, George, my meeting with Povídka happened only a couple of hours ago, and my CO is unreachable on a Sunday."

"So, who's the next in command?"

"Today? It's me. The other option is to contact Bulford Camp thirty miles away. There's an Armored Infantry brigade there. Do you really think their CO will believe an ex-Czechoslovak soldier who has absolutely no evidence for a spy plot except for a note inviting him to a meeting in a pub? You know what the Brits think about us foreign soldiers: unreliable, untrustworthy and sometimes dangerous."

"You'll just have to chance it and tell your CO on Monday."

"Bloody hell! I can't risk that! Bloomsworthy takes an age to decide things … if he believes me. You were the one who asked me to keep an eye on the International Brigade communists at Cholmondeley. Well, I've hooked a couple of spies for you. You *have* to help me."

"Good Christ, Willy! What kind of help do you expect?"

Willy groaned. "Those two bastards have to be caught in the act—before they get what they want and do something unpleasant to me. If we can put them away, Sophie and my family will be safe."

"My God, Willy! How—"

"Listen, even if my CO believed me, he'd probably lock me up. Sophie would still be at risk."

"I get the picture."

Willy felt a surge of hope at the sudden firmness in George's voice.

"This … war equipment viewing. When's it to be?"

"In a week, on Sunday. That's my duty day at the staging post. Povídka and his thug Serbin arrive in Winchester a day or two ahead of the rendezvous. I expect they'll be armed."

"Has this communist chappie asked you for documents?"

"Of course. They want lists of tanks, artillery, personnel carriers, ammunition … the lot. They want to take photos too."

"What's your CO's name again? He definitely needs to be brought in on this … though not by you."

"Colonel Bloomsworthy, Drayton Camp, Barton Stacey. Royal Engineers and REME. He's a bit pompous but okay. Listen … if Povídka is caught red-handed, wouldn't that actually be a feather in your hat?"

George chuckled. "Actually, the correct expression is "feather-in-your-cap". Now listen, Willy—I should really call you Bill now, shouldn't I? I'll definitely contact MI5—but I'm really putting my neck out for you on this one." He chuckled. "But then it's not very *kosher* to let a friend get topped and dumped in an English wood."

"Not funny, George."

"Here's what. I expect MI5 will want to check on you and your so-called spies. If it's all genuine, they'll coordinate with your CO. I'll get 'em to spin him a story … something like they're running an intelligence "sting" op, with you as bait."

There was a long silence. "Who is this MI5 contact of yours? What level?"

George grunted. "You'll just have to trust me."

Willy let out a long breath. "Okay. But Povídka and Serbin have to be caught in the act. I want them put away for a long time."

"Got it. Of course, Willy, you'll be in the thick of it. Risky. Could get your head blown off—throat cut … whatever. Still, that's your problem. But, as you suggest, my reputation might get a boost if we collar your communist friends in the act. Yours too. Telephone me at home as soon you know details, after six in the evening is best."

*   *   *

Back at Bransbury Hall, slumped in an armchair with a double scotch, Willy lit his pipe and closed his eyes, trying to stop distressing scenarios from flashing through his mind: the possibility that no help would turn up at the woods, or that things would go wrong … and he would be shot, throttled or sliced up by Serbin.

That night Willy slept uneasily. Half awake, his mind vaulted back seven years, or was it eight—to the moment in Lučenec when he first watched Sophie dance the Czárdás. It had been at a weekend concert arranged by his parents. He remembered her graceful movement and the smooth sheen of her calves as they swished the embroidered skirt. He'd played the piano for her solo dance and later, they strolled hand-in-hand through the surrounding wooded hills, talking and kissing with delight. And on the soft grass under the trees, he had satisfied his desire for her graceful arms, bare breasts and welcoming thighs. The marriage came a year later, with a happy move to Prague after Pavel was born.

Still dozing, another flash of memory landed him in the interrogation room at the Pankrác Prison pinned down by guards, feeling the agony of his little finger being crushed in a vise, blood and flesh protruding above its metal jaws. "And this is just the beginning…," the Gestapo interrogator had said with that twisted smile Willy got to know so well.

He woke up sweating and breathless. It was five in the morning. Why the vivid dreams? Re-living the past? Something to do with his fear of what was coming? His joints and muscles ached, stiff from the unforgiving camp cot.

*   *   *

Two days later on the telephone, George confirmed that a MI5 unit would be hidden at Wherwell Woods by 9:30 am on the coming Sunday. Willy was to do everything Povídka wanted and not try anything stupid. "Just do as you're told." Next morning, Willy found a copy of the equipment inventory lying on his office desk—Bloomsworthy's doing, no doubt. He contacted Povídka and confirmed their rendezvous for the following Sunday.

*   *   *

Too worked up to read the Sunday newspaper, Willy sipped his tea, worrying what Povídka and Serbin might do to him in the woods. He and his four brother officers were breakfasting on the lavish spread prepared by Lord Ainslie's cook. The sun slanted through the French windows. Band music murmured from a radio on the sideboard and the smell of toast and bacon filled the dining room. Except for requests to pass the toast and marmalade, there was little conversation. This would have been a fine start to a day of rest and leisure, except that Willy could not eat anything. What was on his plate looked and smelled more like grilled entrails than sausage, bacon and fried egg. *Why bother? I could be dead by lunchtime!*

"Which of you guys is assigned to patrol that forest, today?" said Eddie, layering two rashers of bacon and an egg on his fried bread. "I'd like to tag along, see what's what. I know it's supposed to be a secret, but you guys haven't stopped talking about it. And as an American citizen, I do own some of the equipment stashed there." He grinned.

"You mean Wherwell Woods?" said the fair-haired lieutenant called Otley sitting next to Willy. He nudged him. "Isn't it you today, Coulter? My turn's tomorrow."

Willy's heart raced and he was suddenly alert. He shoved his plate away. *Take Eddie to the woods now? Povídka or Serbin would kill him and me. Fucking disaster.* With the American on board, the whole elaborate arrangement was *kaput*. "What? Oh, yes, it's me. What makes you want to tag along?" he said as innocently as he could, trying to think of a way to nix the idea

Eddie bit into his toast. "I'm pissed, waiting for battalion orders," he said. "I need some fun, that's what. Those roasted pheasants we had for dinner the other day were terrific." He turned to Willy, coffee cup in hand. "Someone said those birds came from the place where you're headed today. I'll team up with you and get me one." He grinned, patting the holster at his hip. "This baby wants action. When do we leave?"

Willy's right foot jiggled. He needed an excuse ... fast. He tried on a crestfallen expression. "Sorry Eddie, no can do. Got to have the alternator checked—my van keeps coughing and jerking. It might break down in the middle of nowhere. Sutton Scotney garage opens in a couple of hours. Don't know how long it might take to fix. Sorry."

Lieutenant Otley grinned. "I don't know why you drive that heap of junk." He laid a hand on Eddie's shoulder. "Not to worry, old chap. Come with me tomorrow. It'll be drier. There's *mucho* rain forecast for today."

Willy felt a flood of relief. Maybe he should eat. Put something more than fear into his belly.

At about nine, Willy parked his old van outside the Vine Inn. He checked his watch and peered out at the sky: dense dark clouds—the rain wouldn't be long in coming. He'd borrowed Wellingtons, slightly too big, and wore a hooded waterproof slicker over his battle dress.

Povídka, in a sports jacket and corduroy pants, a slicker over his arm, climbed into the passenger seat carrying a small cardboard briefcase and an umbrella. Serbin, in some kind of a rubberized zip-up suit, eased in through the rear doors. He took the briefcase from Povídka and shrugged off his sou'-wester. As usual, his bullet head was shaved. "Hello, shitface," he said to Willy. A sneer distorted the scars on his cheeks. "We meet again."

Willy forced an obsequious smile.

Povídka pulled the same squat pistol from his pocket, stuck it hard against Willy's ear. "Have you got the documentation?"

Willy, wincing, tried to nod, patting the black clip file on his knees.

"Better behave yourself," snarled Povídka, waving his pistol in the air. "No tricks, friend. I can blow your nose off at forty meters with this. Serbin has a pop-gun as well." He rested the gun between his thighs. "*Dobře*, let's go."

Willy chose the back roads, squeezing past high hedgerows and pastures, some dotted with sheep or cattle. Povídka and Serbin chatted about the vast defensive system the Russians were building at the Kursk salient, and how that would stop General Guderian's forces in their tracks. Forty minutes later, Willy swung onto a lane, passing through groves of oaks and beeches. As raindrops began to splatter the windshield, he stopped the van. "We're here."

Fifty yards ahead, a red-barred metal gate topped with barbed wire blocked the track. Next to it, a painted white board as big as a door was nailed to a post. A skull and crossbones at the top, below it a warning in red capitals:

DO NOT ENTER. PRIVATE PROPERTY. PATROLLED. TRESPASSING FINE: 50 POUNDS

Povídka sniggered. "A fifty pound fine for breaking into a forest? So stupid ... it's like an invitation."

Willy stepped out of the van, holding a ring of keys.

Povídka pointed at a bird, the size of a small turkey, scrambling into the undergrowth. He lowered his window. "What the hell is that thing?"

"A pheasant," Willy said, trying to stay calm. Povídka had raised his pistol. *Is he going to kill the bird ... or me?* He took a deep breath, trying to still his hands as he keyed open the two heavy padlocks. He swung the gate open. Getting back into the driver's seat, he forced a smile. "A-Okay," he said.

Willy drove under the dense green canopy, along an asphalt road, intersected by narrower hardtop junctions on either side. A sudden clap of thunder shook the van. Willy jumped in his seat. Raindrops streamed down the windshield and he turned off the jerky wiper. "Easier to see without it." He edged the van forward.

Povídka and Serbin said nothing.

In sight of what looked like a giant metal frog underneath camouflage netting, Willy parked the van under the boughs of a beech tree. The grass was knee high and sodden. He pointed. "That's an American Sherman—white stars on the sides and front. Beyond that, the road continues on through the woods. That's where most of the stuff is parked. Armored cars and jeeps are stored on the side roads."

"Let's take a look." Povídka, sitting next to Willy, struggled into his slicker. He jammed on a peaked rain cap and opened his door. He reared back and slammed the door shut. "*Christus,* something out there stinks like spilled guts. Let's wait for the rain to slack off. Maybe the smell will go away."

Willy gave him a grim smile. "The aroma of the wild, Leo. Probably a fox or a badger, or maybe a dead pheasant." He was relieved the woodland odor hid the smell of his own fear.

The wind rattled small branches and leaves against the windows and on the roof of the van. Rainwater dripped through chinks in the doors into the foot wells. Povídka pulled his rain coat more tightly around him. "If this van is the best fucking transport the British Army has to offer, the Nazis will walk all over you. So what happens next?"

Willy opened the ring-bound file he had brought. He couldn't stop his hands shaking. He felt Serbin's hot breath on his neck. "Here's the equipment list you wanted."

Povídka smirked, obviously pleased. "Give me a quick idea of what's in it."

"There's about thirty British and American tanks parked close by. On other sections of the road network under the trees, there are amphibious vehicles, Vickers Mark 2 cruiser tanks, and medium M3 and M4 lend-lease tanks. We've also got a few artillery tractors, self-propelled Priest howitzers, and 75 millimeter US mountain guns. There are army trucks on the side roads, stacked with boxes of Browning machine guns and ammunition."

Povídka grunted. "*Dobrý*, that's perfect." He smiled, patting the notebook's cover. Easing himself out of the van, he rested the notebook on his seat and opened his umbrella. "We're going to take a look in the woods. Boho will pat you down and make sure you stay put."

"Okay," said Willy, shakily as he got out.

Serbin ran his hands over Willy's legs, chest and belly and searched his pockets, then sat in the passenger seat and lit a cigarette. "Get back inside," he growled.

Watching Povídka walking away in the rear view mirror, Willy lit his pipe, his heart pulsing. *I have to get Serbin out of the van.*

"I'm back," said Povídka moments later, looking pleased. His silent return surprised Willy. "It's just as you said, Coulter." He handed Serbin a small camera and pulled another from his pocket. "Even though it's raining, Boho and me are going to take some pictures. Hand over the keys … to the van and the gate."

Serbin took the two bundles of keys out of Willy's hand, put them in his pocket and got out of the van. He came round to the driver's side. "Out," he grunted, pulling open the door.

As soon as Willy was on his feet, Serbin grabbed him. "Hands behind your back," he growled as he turned Willy around, slamming his face against the van's side panel. Pain shot from Willy's forehead down into his neck and shoulders. Serbin's hand gripped the back of neck so viciously that he felt dizzy. Something wetted his lips. Salty. Blood. He seethed with anger, and lashed out with his foot.

Serbin grabbed him by the ankle and dumped him face down on the wet ground. "Don't try games with me, you scummy little yid." Willy felt rope being wound tightly round his wrists. He was half pushed and half dragged to the rear of the van. What was coming next? An execution … gun or knife. Or, with luck, they still needed him. He realized he had pee'd in his pants.

Serbin pointed to the fender. "Down on your knees, shitface. Hands against the number plate." Out of the corner of his eye, Willy could see Serbin knotting the rope around one of the rusting metal brackets on the fender. "We like to keep our pets safe." He grinned, showing discolored teeth.

Willy was still able to move his torso and head. With his back to the van, he faced the asphalt road leading deeper into the wood but, with rain smearing his glasses, he couldn't see much.

"We'll deal with you when we get back."

Willy only just made out the blurry outlines of the two men walking away from him. *Keep our pets safe!* Once they got what they wanted, they would kill him. He imagined Serbin's knife would slash into his neck. How many seconds would it take for the blade to sever his windpipe and turn his world black? He had a rush of panic. *Where the hell are the MI5 boys? They have to be here, somewhere.* On the telephone with George two days earlier, he had asked for a signal that would tell him that the ambushers were in place—and was told there wouldn't be any signal. He cursed his own stupidity. He should have gone to Bloomsworthy. But, if Povídka got away, what would happen to Sophie?

He couldn't stop shivering. Was it terror, panic or just the cold rain? He strained and struggled. No amount of twisting and turning loosened the ropes. Where in God's name were George's fucking rescuers?

He wasn't sure how long Povídka and Serbin had been gone. At least half an hour. He couldn't see his watch. He struggled to free himself again. Useless. The skin on his wrists felt raw and his knees throbbed. Trying different positions made no difference. Rain soaked his head and legs. The insides of his boots were soggy. He shook his head trying to get the water off his face and clear his smeared glasses. He heard little except for the clatter of branches and the swish of rain. All he could see was the blurred image of an asphalt ribbon surrounded by shimmering undergrowth and trees. He felt dizzy, and pissed in his pants again. What could he do if no rescuers turned up? Nothing except plead for mercy. He closed his eyes, trying to calm himself, stop the panic from swallowing him up.

Rough lips pressed against his ear. A hoarse whisper. "Keep your mouth shut, mate." An arm bumped hard against his shoulder. Fingers worked around his wrists. The rope fell loose. He sucked in a deep breath. "Who are…?"

"Shut it, mate. I'm cuttin' you free. Jus' stay put. If they see you've moved off, they'll do a bunk or start somethin'. I'll be close by. Two of our blokes are inside the armored carrier up there, another one's on top."

Taking deep breaths, with his hands suddenly free, Willy rocked slowly backward, and then righted himself to a tight sitting position in the same spot where he had been tethered. His dizziness cleared, his knees no longer ached. Rain ran down his face. He risked a glance at his wrists: raw, bloody. Quickly and careful not to break them, he wiped his glasses between thumb and finger, put them back on and looked around. About one hundred yards away, two figures were coming toward him: the tall Povídka ahead of stocky Serbin.

As they passed the armored carrier, men swinging batons jumped from the undergrowth. A third appeared on the top of the carrier, pointing a rifle.

Willy leaped to his feet. To hell with the soldier's instructions. Good old George had come through for him. He made for the tall grass, rolled over and looked back, catching a glimpse of Serbin grappling with his attackers. Willy flattened himself on the ground as Povídka broke away and came sprinting toward the van, gun in hand, flashes coming from its muzzle. Bullets clunked into the van's bodywork.

Gotteniu, my number's on the next one. Crouching low, Willy dived into the undergrowth, rolling over and over, oblivious to the wet grass and dripping shrubs.

Povídka kept running and shooting, getting closer and closer. A masked soldier in a rubber poncho holding a Sten gun stepped from behind a tree close to the van. "Throw down your gun," he yelled.

Povídka still running, veered off into the brush

The Sten chattered. Povídka took a few steps and crumpled to the ground, groaning and twisting, bony hands clutching his face.

"Stupid bugger," the soldier shouted.

Willy scrambled to his feet, rescued his glasses and joined the soldier. In the pouring rain, they watched blood pump from under Povídka's jaw, and out of a gaping hole in his left chest. Raindrops diluted the thick red gobs, washing them into the grass. Willy sank to his knees beside Povídka. He looked up at the soldier. "Anything we can do for him?"

The soldier's face was like a stone. "Fuck all, mate. He's only got a couple more minutes."

Willy panted, his pulse racing. He stumbled to his feet. The communist had done many bad things, but he'd fought fascists in Spain and the Nazis in France, and he'd helped Willy get out of Cholmondeley Camp. He knew he ought to feel pity, but he had no space for it.

Povídka's hands dropped to his waist then slid sideways onto the grass. His body jerked. A drawn-out moan came from his chest. His jaw slackened. Lifeless eyes.

"The fucker's dead," said the soldier, looking grimly at Willy. "Did you know 'im?"

Willy nodded.

The soldier pointed to the armored car. "See, they got the big bastard. Took a bit of a tussle. Now whatever you do, mate, don't scarper. Cap'n Henderson wants a word."

Half an hour later, as Serbin, glowering in handcuffs was bundled into the carrier, an officer in a helmet with camouflage paint on his face came up to Willy. He smiled, showing white teeth. He handed over the van's keys. "I'm in charge here. Henderson. Are you okay?"

Willy took a deep breath and nodded. "I suppose."

"*Nothing* happened here. Not a damned word to anyone—ever. Wait half an hour for us to get out, then take your van back to your HQ. Act completely normal."

"What unit are you?"

"No business of yours."

"And what about the bullet holes in the van?"

"That heap! Your CO will sort that out. He's expecting a report from you tomorrow." He put out his hand. "Cheerio, old chap."

Willy watched them drive off. His head, knees and wrists ached and he was half-drowned in water and piss. But he was happy. Good old George. He and Sophie were out of danger. The rain slackened and, apart from the sound of water dripping from the trees, there was silence. A pheasant called, a harsh clacking sound. Willy climbed into the van and smoked his pipe, replaying what had happened. *Why didn't I spot that extra armored carrier? So ... it's Colonel Bloomsworthy and me tomorrow. Could be good, could be bad ... could be disastrous.*

Back at the billet, Willy took a bath and changed into dry

clothes. Heart thumping, he made for the music room, hoping that if he came across someone they wouldn't comment on the bruise on his temple and the stiff way he was moving. He hoped his shirt cuffs would hide the rope marks on his wrists. The piano was the only way he knew to calm his agitated body and stop him from falling apart.

Alone in the music room, Willy sat at the keys of the upright Steinway and ran some scales. With many stops and restarts, he played the Raindrop Prelude, Chopin's prelude 15 in D Major. His knees and wrists throbbed. He wasn't going to let that stop him.

Three officers, one of them Eddie, came in from the living room and sat in armchairs, drinks in hand, listening while he played the Dvorak intermezzo, but with fewer pauses and mistakes than with the Chopin. His fingers had gained elasticity. When it was over, there were the usual compliments. Eddie came up and put a hand around the back of his neck where Serbin had grabbed him. "Did you see any pheasants today, friend? I'm hopin' for some action tomorrow."

Willy winced and eased himself from Eddie's grasp. "I did see one, heard one call. That's it."

*   *   *

Much later, Willy went to bed but he could not sleep. The fear and relief of what had happened in the woods looped round and round, and he could not get it out of his head. He got up, went downstairs for an hour and paced Lord Ainslie's sitting room, drinking whisky after whisky. Sophie was safe, but Povídka had left him with an unanswered question. What was she really up to in Cambridge? From inside his army blouse, he extracted the card Povídka had passed on to him.

CAMBRIDGE ENQUIRY AGENCY
E. Blivens, Esq. ex-Metropolitan Police
Discretion guaranteed.
Telephone: Cambridge 4428

On the back Povídka had scribbled...

Užijte si, Žide.

Enjoy yourself, Jew.

CHAPTER TWENTY-EIGHT
Compassionate Leave
June 1943

Willy's interview in Colonel Bloomsworthy's office at Drayton Camp was short and sweet.

"No need for an extensive post-mortem on this incident," said the colonel, locking away the black file that Willy had just handed over. He looked up at Willy, thoughtfully massaging his gray mustache with thumb and forefinger. "It seems that you were a pawn in this operation and instructed not to communicate with anyone, myself included. Suffice it to say, my confidence in you has been mostly justified … in spite of your unorthodox behavior. This morning I received an informal commendation from the War Office."

Willy smiled, relieved. It appeared that Bloomsworthy wasn't going to give him a wigging. "That's very good, sir."

"In fact, your part in this mysterious incident may help you. I'll try to speed your naturalization process—and your eventual promotion."

Willy couldn't help a grin. "Yessir. Thank you, Sir."

"Now, bloody well get on with your work. Dismiss."

After two weeks, Willy could no longer contain his curiosity about Serbin's fate. He telephoned George to congratulate and thank him,

"Glad we could winkle you out, old chap. A British citizen spying for Germany would get either life or a hanging, but then those wicked friends of yours were Czechoslovaks. My guess is that they'll both be shipped to Moscow sometime. In which case, they'll end up dead or starving in a Siberian camp."

"Didn't they tell you?" Willy exclaimed. "One of them, Povídka, was shot dead in front of me."

"Oh, well," said George with half a chuckle. "That's the mysterious MI5 for you."

Willy drove himself and his team hard. They were under extreme pressure to complete expansion of the fuel facility. He slept badly and was breathless even on mild effort. He felt hungry all the time but eating didn't help. Sometimes his heart beat so fast he had to stop what he was doing. Worst of all, he suffered bouts of sweating. His fellow-officers started making remarks about the "stinky foreigner."

At the billet, the radio hammered out interminable war news: the Allies were poised to invade Sicily, US Marines and Japanese were slaughtering each other in the Pacific. His parents wrote him about relatives and acquaintances sent to labor camps in Poland.

At times, he was overwhelmed by the gloomy news—and he couldn't stop thinking about Sophie. His doubts about reviving their relationship had multiplied. Povídka's insinuations chafed like a splinter. Wartime flirtations were two-a-penny, but this was his wife, and it seemed possible that her attachment to this RAF officer was more than just a fling. At the pub in Scotland, in the heat of their angry confrontation, she had mentioned divorce. If it came to that, Willy would fight to keep Paul. It was time to contact Ernest Blivens, the Cambridge detective that Povídka had used to spy on her.

He called from a public telephone box in the sleepy village of Wonston, four miles from the billet. As usual it was next to a pub, the Wonston Arms.

"Who's speakin'?" The man's voice had a rough nasal quality.

"You are Mr. Blivens?" Willy asked.

"That's me. What's up?"

"My name is Kohut. Mr. Povídka, a friend of mine, used your services."

"So what. What d'yer want?"

Blivens had a blunt, aggressive tone. Willy considered hanging up. This fellow was rude and over- suspicious. "He hired you to keep an eye on my wife. She manages a café in Cambridge. The Peacock."

There was a moment of silence.

"You say yer Mr. Povídka's friend?"

"He hired you on my behalf while I was away. I'm a British army officer. He said I could contact you."

Another silence. "Right, I remember 'im now. He smoked a stinky cigar in my office. Smelled for days it did. Look, I might be able to 'elp you. I charge two shillings an hour. Where d'yer live? What d'yer want done?"

"I'm stationed near Oxford," said Willy, "but I can't get away for a while. All negotiations between you and me will have to be by phone or letter. Is that acceptable?"

"Well, it's a bit irregular. But, what isn't these days? Anyway, I gets lots of requests like yours—from blokes stuck in a nowhere camp while their missis does hanky-panky at home. What yer after this time?"

"What did Mr. Povídka tell you about me?"

"Wait a sec. I'm pullin' the file."

A long silence ensued, then the click-click of metal and noisy breathing. "Ah, yes, 'ere we are. Willy Kohut you said, right? He gave me a letter wot you wrote from North Africa askin' to keep an eye on your wife. I'll say this; your wife's got a sheaf of admirers, one especially, an officer chappie. If I remember right, she's a nice-looking lady."

Willy frowned, squeezing the receiver tight. Povídka had made up the story about a letter from North Africa but he'd told the truth about Sophie. "Listen, I want to find out what my wife is really up to. You see, if she's having an affair, I might have to consider divorce. I'll send you two pounds to show I'm serious."

Willy's mind raced. He would ask Emil to forward the money to Blivens (with no return address). The postmark would be from London.

"All right, mate. I can tell you're a foreigner. How come you're in the British Army? Got a proper identity card? Registered with the police?"

"Rest assured I have the necessary documents; I'll bring them when we meet and explain everything."

The detective cleared his throat. "If yer thinkin' divorce, we 'ave to catch her in bed with a bloke. Witnessed evidence is what you need in a divorce case. Give me your address. I'll send a weekly report of her doin's and my fees."

Willy stared at the receiver, annoyed that he hadn't thought this through properly—he could not reveal his whereabouts. "I move around a lot. I'll telephone you Tuesday every week, about nine in the morning."

In two subsequent conversations with Detective Blivens, Willy discovered that Sophie enjoyed an active social life, frequenting the Eagle Pub and attending tea dances on Saturdays often with a group of friends which included British and American officers. She had rented a small flat and accompanied Helga in her Morris car when they bought supplies and food for the café. Once, on a Sunday, they were driven out of Cambridge by a local GP, Dr. Carnegie-Holston, all three equipped with binoculars. Blivens had no idea where they went. He confined his work to within Cambridge city limits. Petrol was expensive and in short supply.

In his third Tuesday call, Blivens' voice had a note of triumph and Willy feared the worst.

"Big news, Mr. Kohut. A certain Captain Kenneth Mottram, RAF Intelligence, spent the whole of Saturday night at your wife's flat.

He left at ten Sunday morning."

Willy was speechless. She had lied to him in the Scottish pub. Deceived and insulted him. He wiped reconciliation or separation from his mind. He looked at the wedding ring on his finger and twisted it until it hurt. It was time to act.

"You still there?"

"I want you to concentrate on Mottram. How much time he spends with my wife and how often he stays at her place. Don't they call it a stake-out? Don't bother with anything else. We'll talk next Tuesday, Okay?"

"If yer wants to go ahead with a divorce," said Blivens after a long silence. "I can set up a cast-iron case, for a fee."

"How would you do that?"

"We get into her flat late at night, when she and that Mottram bloke are in bed—and take photos. But it's a lot better if you're there to identify your wife. Stronger case in court. I'll need a couple of weeks' notice. Probably a Friday or a Saturday evening when she's tucked up with 'im. You want ter go ahead with this?"

Willy was shocked by the ugliness of what the detective was suggesting. "I … I have to think about it. I'll decide after we talk next week."

Two days later, Willy received a brief note from Lady Hilliard saying that Mrs. McAlister had left the farm. She could not find a replacement. The evacuee children had to return to their homes. From June 18 onward, she and Sir Edward would be staying for several weeks in London to attend Wimbledon, the Henley Regatta, and Ascot. They would bring Paul to London on the 17th and he would stay the night at their flat. Her last sentence brought him up short. *Please have someone collect Paul from our flat on 18th. 55B Cadogan Place. Chelsea. Tel: KEN 3846.*

Willy would now have to persuade Colonel Bloomsworthy to grant him a couple of days' compassionate leave to collect Paul in London. What if he used those same two or three days to get to Cambridge as well, and coordinate with Blivens to surprise Sophie with her lover? But after checking the train timetables, it was clear that his plan had too many moving parts. Bombing raids, and train delays might add to the uncertainty. The only practical solution was to get his *father* to collect Paul—while *he* was in Cambridge with Blivens.

*   *   *

"Second Lieutenant Coulter reporting." Praying silently, Willy stood at attention in front of the CO's desk and saluted. He put on the eager-to-please look that Bloomsworthy expected from his men.

Colonel Bloomsworthy glared. "God's sake man. I know who you are. You asked to see me. What's it about?"

"A personal matter, sir."

Bloomsworthy, scratching his nose with a forefinger, heaved a sigh. "Personal is it? Well, before you go on about this personal matter, bring me up-to-date on the projects. Then I'll make my judgment."

Willy took a notepad from his breast pocket. "At Wherwell Woods, daily monitoring and security are in place and tight. At Micheldever, the expanded fuel tanks are fully bomb-proofed and the rail gantries strengthened. We're still upgrading pumping-station capacity and need to test the generator and air filtration systems. Estimated completion, about two weeks from now."

The colonel flipped file pages back and forth on his desk. "Good, good."

"May I make my request now, sir?"

The colonel gave Willy a sharp glance. "What is it, then?"

Willy straightened his shoulders. Asking permission like this took him back to his schooldays, and the Czechoslovak army. Groveling to someone who had the power to deny, humiliate or punish. It had to be done. "During the Blitz, my son Paul was evacuated to a farm in Shropshire. His sponsor asked me to pick him up when he arrives back in London. I'm asking for leave to do that."

Bloomsworthy's eyebrows shot up. "God kiss my arse … you want to leave at this pissing time? Just get your family to pick the little feller up."

"I have to do it in person. SSAFA regulations." Willy was gambling on an outright lie. Hopefully Bloomsworthy would not bother to check with the SSAFA office.

"Damn it. What about your wife?"

"A refugee—in Cambridge. Not allowed to travel." Willy compressed his lips at the successive lies. Pretty convincing, he thought.

Bloomsworthy's face turned purple. "You foreigners are more trouble than …" He got up and looked out the office window, hands thrust in pockets. He wheeled around. "Gawd-kiss-a-pisser, Coulter. There's still a load of work to be done at the fuel tanks, and now you're begging for time off. There's a fucking war on."

"Sir, you have a reputation as a generous and perceptive senior officer. I haven't seen my boy for many months. And really, we're on schedule with our objectives. There'll be no holdups while I'm away. Captains Otley and Warrenton will cover for me. They're responsible chaps."

Bloomsworthy nodded, rubbing at his circlet of sandy hair "I dunno about this. Maybe yes, maybe no." He paused for a long minute, looking down at his file. "All right. Take your leave Coulter, and bloody well get back here and finish the job we came to do. Dismiss."

Willy saluted. The wheels had been set in motion.

*   *   *

Next morning, with a signed travel permit in his pocket, Willy dialed Blivens from his Drayton Camp office. He glanced at the *News Chronicle* on his desk, noting that the Allied invasion of Sicily was going well. Another column caught his eye. The French Vichy Regime was rounding up Jews and sending them to camps in the east. He had old friends in France, and Sophie's doctor cousin from Paris was still there somewhere. He felt sick.

"Blivens Detective Agency."

Willy recognized the detective's hoarse voice. "Kohut here. I've got a weekend leave in two weeks. Anything new from your end?"

Blivens grunted. "Lover-boy Mottram works at an RAF linguistics unit at Cambridge University, close to Caius College. He spent Saturday night with her again. He and your missis 'ave been tootling around the countryside with the woman what helps run the Peacock Café—Helga Hilderman. She's got an old Morris saloon and they goes on picnics where this Helga woman does bird watchin'. Shall I keep checkin' or are you ready. A Saturday night is when we should do it."

"I'm ready."

"When can you be here?"

" I'll come on the Saturday, two weeks from tomorrow."

"Telephone my office when you get to the station."

Willy put down the telephone. That afternoon he sent his father a telegram.

CHAPTER TWENTY-NINE
Collecting Paul
55 B Cadogan Place, London.
June 18 1943

Emil was intrigued. He had never ventured into the elegant neighborhoods of Knightsbridge and Chelsea where Sir Edward and Lady Hilliard had their town flat. He would experience how aristocrats lived and welcome Paul home at the same time. The last time he and Judit had seen the boy was at the farm, in March. Even though Willy had asked for yet another last minute favor, Emil was not too angry with his son, just irritated. In the past, an accomplished *macher* like Willy would balance asking for favors and offering quid pro quo's. But now, he only asked for favors. There was a reasonable excuse, of course ... he was in the British army.

From the underground station, Emil crossed Sloane Square and bought a posy of pink petunias from a grey-haired flower lady sitting under one of the plane trees. This part of London was clean and spacious and smelled of summer. Pigeons fluttered around a bowler-hatted gentleman dispensing breadcrumbs from a bench. Emil raised his trilby as he passed by. "Luvly day," the man said.

Checking his map, Emil turned up Sloane Street, admiring a row of imposing Victorian redbrick buildings with mullioned windows and parapets trimmed in Portland stone. Opulent and discreet ... very English.

At 55B Cadogan Place, a rosy-cheeked maid opened the door, curtsied and led him into a sunlit room. Lady Hilliard, with a smile and a tinkle of silver bracelets, rose from her desk to meet him. Admiring the cut of her gray pencil skirt and the peach-colored blouse with puffed shoulders, he presented the posy before kissing her hand. Despite the hardship of refugee life, he had kept his eye for good clothes.

"So kind. Lovely to see you. And what a rush—your stepping in for Willy."

"Lady Hilliard, I'm honored. I'm sorry my son could not be here."

Emil was impressed. Quite the contrast between this charming flat and the casual furnishings of Knapp Hall, where he and Judit had been invited for a sherry when visiting Paul. He was amazed at the number of flower-filled vases on the mantelpiece and side tables. What he liked about the English was their enthusiasm for flowers and gardens, and growing things. "Beautiful flowers," he said, beaming at her and taking the proffered seat. "So please, where is Paul?"

"Oh, let's not disturb him for the moment. He's having a lovely time playing model soldiers with Edward in the next room."

Emil was puzzled. "I did not know your husband played such games with children."

Lady Hilliard settled into her armchair and smiled. "Let me explain. My husband has a miniature soldier collection and he recreates famous battles—so you see there are, in fact, *two boys* playing in the next room. They will be finished soon."

She jumped up, and, from the mantelpiece, lifted down a statuette of a helmeted Hussar riding a white horse, saber drawn. She put it in Emil's hands. "One of his specials. Every time we come up to town, Teddy barricades himself in there."

Emil turned it over in his hands. "Very fine." The British aristocracy drove Rolls Royces, sailed yachts, raced horses, built model railways, collected butterflies and shot wild animals in India and Africa but he had never heard of toy soldier battles. A rich man's hobby but practical. All you needed was a room, a big table and hundreds of toy men with guns. Carefully, he returned the model to its place.

He watched her press her foot into the thick carpet, and when she moved it away he saw the brass button by her chair. "I'll ask Helen to bring us coffee. It's Jamaican, from Fortnum and Mason. And some cress sandwiches."

"Thank you." Her offer was a chance to learn more about Pavel's life and perhaps understand the thinking of British aristocrats. He looked at his watch. "We cannot stay long. Do you have Pav—Paul's suitcase?"

She nodded. "I have to explain a couple of things that I don't suppose he'll tell you. First, his bed-wetting has improved, but he's apt to overdo the sulking. On the good side, he's been attending day school in Shrewsbury and he can write and read quite well; mind you, he needs spectacles. Your son sent us money for the optician's fees."

Feeling indebted and embarrassed by her generosity, Emil did his best to absorb the flood of information. He touched his own metal-framed glasses. "Thank you for arranging the spectacles." He guessed Paul was near-sighted, like all the men in the family.

The door opened and the maid brought in a tray with two large china cups, a silvery thermos, sugar, a pitcher of cream, and perfectly stacked, triangular sandwiches.

Lady Hilliard poured. "I suppose Paul will live with his mother and go to school in Cambridge. I must say, we'll miss him and, of course, your son's marvelous piano-playing. But there you are. How is she getting on? Your son's wife, I mean."

Emil smiled politely. The smooth tang of this coffee brought him a memory of the Café Slavia in Prague. He guessed she was waiting for him to say something about Sophie—but he couldn't bring himself to expose the terrible rift within his family. This kind and generous woman spoke in a very personal way, almost as if she was part of his family. But she was not, so why reveal family secrets? Besides, if *he* could not understand what was going on with his son's marriage, how could he rationally explain it to anyone else?

Lady Hilliard put her cup down. "Let's go and look in on the boys, shall we?"

Entering the "Battle Room," Emil was surprised by the vision of Sir Edward's beanpole figure bent over a landscape of baize-covered hills and valleys, his face almost hidden by a mass of miniature trees, fields, roads, and scattered buildings. Between them, agglomerations of cannon, horses, and lead soldiers were stationed around tiny flagpoles flying British or French flags.

Paul crouched on a chair on the other side of the battlefield a crown of curly brown hair framing his face. His fingers hovered above advancing lines of uniformed figures with rifles and fixed bayonets.

"Aha." Sir Edward looked up with a grimace from his contorted position.

Emil thought he was either in pain or annoyed at the interruption.

"Greetings Mr. Kohut. You caught us at a crucial moment. The Battle of Waterloo is in its final stages."

Paul, knocking over a few soldiers, scrambled off his chair and ran to his grandfather. Emil picked him up, kissed his cheeks and set him down, pleased at his sturdiness and disheveled hair. With freckles on a snub nose, blue eyes with long lashes and a fair skin, Paul looked English. That was excellent.

"Do you see what is happening here, Mr. Kohut? Paul has Napoleon's army positioned in front of the town of Planchemont. His Imperial Guard is drawn up at the back, waiting to deal the usual crushing blow to the enemy. Me!" Sir Edward delivered his military commentary as if he were discussing the placement of fielders on a cricket pitch. "The British, with the Forest of Soignes behind them, are clustered around two farms, here on the right. Bony, is about to attack—"

Emil felt a hand on his arm. "Are you taking me home, Grandpa?"

He laughed, a deep and joyful sound that he hadn't experienced for a long time. "We're leaving soon, even though I see that the Battle of Waterloo is not yet lost or won."

Crestfallen, Paul looked at Sir Edward. "It's not fair. I was going to win." Sir Edward got to his feet and with a smile raised his hands in mock surrender.

Lady Hilliard patted Paul's cheek. "Can't be helped, dear. Fun and timetables rarely go together. Now be a good chap and find Helen. She has to pack your suitcase. We'll be in the living room."

Emil, on the settee beside Lady Hilliard, drained his coffee cup. Even though it had gone cold, it was too good to abandon. Sir Edward closed the War Room door and flopped into a leather club chair. He extracted his cigarette case from a pocket and waved it at Emil. "Would you like one?"

Emil shook his head. This was a good moment to take advantage of the Hilliards' knowledge and wisdom. "Excuse me, Lady Hilliard for asking. My son wants me to find a school for Paul in London. Do you have advice for me?"

Lady Hilliard frowned. "Why can't Paul stay with his mother and go to school in Cambridge?"

Sir Edward sat up. "Don't pry, dear. We'll be glad to help," he said gruffly, turning to Emil.

Emil nodded his thanks. "We want to hide Paul's past. Have him grow up a normal English boy. Go to school in London. Do you understand my meaning?"

Lady Hilliard's plucked eyebrows knitted together. "I suppose that means you want him to know nothing of your escape. He is to forget his past. And who is the *we*? Is it Willy and his wife, or you and your wife, or just all of you?"

Emil was taken aback by her bluntness. Embarrassed, he picked up his empty cup and pretended to drain it.

"Paul's a fine lad. He'll do well," said Sir Edward. "Your son's already in the British Army. That's as good a start as any to settling your family in Britain."

"I asked you before," said Lady Hilliard, "why can't Paul go to school in Cambridge where his mother lives?"

Emil winced. This woman was like a bulldog. "I'm not sure you know this, but my daughter-in-law opened a café in Cambridge. She rents a one-bedroom flat and works long hours. She cannot look after Paul properly. So, for now, he will live with us in London. Willy wants to find him a school that will get him to university."

"*Now* I understand," said Lady Hilliard with a heave of her puffed shoulders. "What you want for him is very commendable, but it's jolly difficult in Britain for young people in the middle and lower class to get into university. It will be even harder for a foreign boy."

Sir Edward cleared his throat and spread his hands over bony knees "There's really only two pathways, you see. A local grammar school leads to a factory job, a skilled apprenticeship, working in an office, or some sort of trade. If you want Paul to be a professional of some sort, a preparatory boarding school is essential. You have to pay fees for that."

Emil raised an eyebrow. "I am not sure…"

"He means that Paul will have to live *at the school* during term-time," said Lady Hilliard."

"At which age does this schooling begin?" Emil said. The system sounded more like living in an army barracks.

"He'd start at eight years old," said Sir Edward. "Home for holidays. At twelve, there's the Common Entrance exam to get into either a Grammar School run by the government or an independent private school. That's where he gets ready for the university entrance exams. If Paul went to a Grammar School, he would attend one close to where his family lived.

Lady Hilliard smiled. "There's a famous school in Shrewsbury that prepares boys for university. We have connections there. We could help Paul get in there when he's twelve. There are fees to pay on top of certain entrance requirements and recommendations."

Emil rose and circled the room, hands behind his back. What was the quality difference between the private schools and the government ones? Could they even afford a private school? He and Willy needed to discuss this in depth. Soon.

"This is difficult for me to understand, Sir Edward. In my country, schooling was free. Paul would be on his own. We would miss him very much." Emil stopped in front of the mantelpiece. "The school you recommend sounds more like it comes from Charles Dickens, perhaps?"

Sir Edward chuckled. "Not at all, old chap. Boarding school teaches independence, competition, responsibility, and discipline. You know, the boys don't really miss their parents that much. Our two lads are at Radley at the moment, where I went to school. They are perfectly happy, aren't they dear?"

Lady Hilliard leaned forward. "Please remind me, Mr. Kohut. How old is Paul, exactly?"

"He'll be eight next year. In June."

"Usually, there's a waiting list as long as your arm."

"And there *is* the cost," said Lady Hilliard, knitting her eyebrows together. "These schools give preference to boys whose fathers went there, and who have been on the waiting list since birth."

Sir Edward coughed, and glanced hesitantly at his wife. "I must be frank, Mr. Kohut, they don't like Jews."

Lady Hilliard gave Emil a sympathetic look.

Emil took a deep breath. His shoulders drooped. No need for further discussion. "Thank you for your explanations. Now I know that it is not possible for my grandson to enter university from a private school."

Lady Hilliard put her hand on Emil's shoulder. "Don't give up. We like Paul and very much want him to succeed." She smiled encouragingly at her husband. "Teddy is on the governing board of a wonderful Preparatory School near Brighton. A good friend has her son there at the moment. We could try to get Paul enrolled."

Lady Hilliard opened a silver case, lit a cigarette, and snapped the case shut. "If an opening came up soon, I think Mr. Moon, the headmaster, could be persuaded to take Paul early. How much are the fees, Teddy?"

Sir Edward stroked his mustache. "About thirty pounds a term, I think: four terms a year. Can you afford that?"

Emil felt a surge of hope. Just over 150 pounds a year. He and Willy could work something out. Regret instantly followed enthusiasm. Helping to pay for Paul's schooling would eliminate his cherished plan to buy a house. Owning a home and hopefully a little garden would have given him some self-respect—a small kingdom that was his.

"Believe me, we will find the necessary money."

With a laugh, Lady Hilliard clapped her hands. "How splendid. I'll make enquiries and let you know about the school. I'll have to be quiet about Paul being Jewish. There's nothing official, but it's a bit like our golf and tennis clubs. Jews are not encouraged to apply. I'm sorry. Now where is that boy? PAUL!"

Paul ran in, his furry lion in one hand, and a brown leather suitcase in the other. His eyes sparkled. "Here I am, Grandpa. Will we be in first class? On the train we had bacon and egg served by a funny-looking waiter. He had hair growing out of his nose."

Lady Hilliard smiled. "He's a bright, cheeky little chap, isn't he?"

Emil felt a surge of pride at how easily and smoothly Paul talked. Even the idioms he used were like those of the BBC announcers and English film stars. His year at Knapp Hall Farm had been a blessing.

"Are we going to Cambridge, Grandpa?"

"We stay in London, at Northways." He rested fingers on the back of Paul's neck, finding pleasure in the feel of it. "Give Lady Hilliard a kiss and shake Sir Edward's hand—and thank them for looking after you so well."

Sir Edward stood. He was a nearly a foot taller than Emil. He leaned over and shook Paul's hand. "Been a pleasure having you on the farm, young man," he said, his eyes twinkling.

From the side pocket of his Norfolk jacket, he extracted a small cigar box secured by a rubber band. "This is a souvenir from all of us at Knapp Hall. Mint condition. Look after them."

The boy dropped Furry Lion and put down the valise. He opened the box. "Gosh, how super," he said, looking wide-eyed at Emil. Six model soldiers nestled on white cotton wool, each one marching with a shouldered rifle.

"Thanks awfully, sir." He looked up at Sir Edward. "They're terrific. Look, Grandpa. The way they're painted. I bet everything is just right."

"Absolutely right. They're *chasseurs* from Napoleon's Imperial Guard," said Sir Edward with a proud smile. "My soldiers are handmade by Britains."

"Magnificent gift," said Emil. He picked up the soldier, holding it delicately between thumb and forefinger. The right arm holding the rifle was hinged at the shoulder "Look, Paul, his arm swings as he marches. Just like in your daddy's army."

Paul's face lit up. Then it clouded. "Where's Daddy? Why didn't *he* fetch me? And Mummy? Why couldn't *she* come?"

Emil's heart sank. He didn't know what to say. The boy had every right to see his mother and father after such a long time away. Willy and Sophie were trapped by circumstances, some of their own making. The Hilliard's flat was not the place to explain and untangle his son and daughter-in-law's complicated life. Emil guessed there was plenty Paul did not know.

"I'll tell you when we get home. We'll take the Number Two bus and sit at the top. That way you get to see Marble Arch and Oxford Street, full of sandbags. We might even see the anti-aircraft battery in Hyde Park."

"Golly, how super."

CHAPTER THIRTY
Incident at Farley Villas
Cambridge, June 1943

Dismayed by rumbling thunder and lightning flashes from a pall of rain clouds over Cambridge, Willy slumped in an armchair in Blivens's office. The storm reminded him of Rigoletto, Act Three ... a premonition of disaster or shame at what he was about to do. He had arrived at nine. Daylight was fading fast.

This is going to be very unpleasant, he thought, but I haven't come all this way to weasel out at the last minute. Soon, I'll be fighting in Europe—I might be wounded, captured or worse. Paul has to belong to *me*, stay in *my* family's custody. He sipped the tea Blivens had brewed for him, adding a shot of rum to calm his nerves.

Ernie Blivens, tall and heavy-jowled, looked at the clock on the wall. For the past hour and a half he had been hunched over his desk, a cigarette stuck between his lips, working on various files, "Just gone eleven. Time I told you what's goin' to happen. 'Ave you been to her place before?"

Willy emptied his pipe into an ashtray, his hand shaking a little. Sophie had probably found a comfy little flat. Much different from his lumpy attic bed at Bransbury Hall. "Never been there. Snowed with work. Anyway, I'm listening."

Blivens passed him a sheet of paper. "Made this sketch of your missus's flat at Farley Villas. Ground floor. I've a copy of the keys, don't ask me how. Me and Nancy go in first. You stay outside in the hallway and keep quiet 'til after we surprise 'em and do the photos. I get the guilty parties to say who they are. Nance takes more pictures. You enter and identify your missus. And for Chrissakes, keep your mouth shut." He paused. "Nance'll be here in a jiff."

"Okay, okay—simple enough," Willy's right foot jiggled with

tension. His mouth had gone dry.

A slim young woman in an ankle-length shiny raincoat emerged from a door at the back of the office. She was about Willy's height, with flat black hair cut in pageboy style that emphasized a curiously triangular face with high cheekbones and doe-shaped eyes.

"Hullo, Mister," she said unslinging a box with an attached reflector from her shoulder. "First outing for my new Brownie Reflex TLR." Beaming at Blivens, she patted a pocket. "127 film. I keep the flash bulbs in me coat."

Willy was surprised. She was fifteen or sixteen … seventeen tops. Attractive too. He worried that she might mess-up if any things went wrong. Better to say nothing and rely on Blivens judgment.

A few minutes later, they left the office and climbed into a Riley saloon parked at the curb. Rain drops the size of cherries bounced off the windshield.

"This 1938 motor is my only luxury," said Blivens, settling his bulk into the driver's seat. He ran a loving finger across the veneered dashboard. "Got a luvly feel. Purrs like a tiger."

Nancy curled up in the back.

Willy half-hoped the car wouldn't start. That way he would have an excuse to cancel everything. "Mr. Blivens … how many times have you done this … this thing we're doing?"

"Lots, mate. Usually, we do hotels and bed and breakfasts. Easy access." He rolled his neck. "Private dwellings is harder. Paid the landlord a tenner to copy a set of keys and oil the door hinges while your missus was workin' at her café." A deep chuckle shook his frame. "Illegal, o'course, but the guilty party's always too embarrassed to call a copper or register a complaint."

Willy twisted sideways to face the detective. He really had second thoughts now. If Colonel Bloomsworthy got to hear about this, he had no idea what would happen, except that all hell would break loose. "We've got to stop this. I don't need the police on my neck."

Blivens grunted. "Don't fucking piss me about, Mister Kohut."

Willy took a deep breath, screwing his eyes tight. He'd lost control of the situation.

"Cheer up, mate. Never 'ad no problem with the law, have we Nance? But … if you don't have the knackers to carry ahead, you still pay me in full—plus twenty quid on top for having me and Nance come out for nothing on a piss-awful night."

*   *   *

During the fast ride to Farley Villas, Willy clung to his seat, still wondering whether he was doing the right thing. How would he justify his actions to his parents? And if Paul ever found out what his father had plotted, there was no telling what his reaction would be. Hate? Rejection? Understanding? Acceptance? It was only now that Willy fully understood the reality of what was about to happen in Sophie's flat. She had said she didn't love him, but after this she would hate him.

Blivens shut off the engine and turned to face Willy.

"Here we are then. Nice neighborhood, eh?"

The street lamps were off and the sky had cleared. A quarter moon cast enough light to make out details of the houses—a row of identical Edwardian stone and brick villas, low walled gardens and front gates. Light glowed through blackout cracks in a couple of upstairs windows. The house they were about to invade was silent.

They shuffled quietly from the car, and Blevins shone his covered flashlight on to the arched porch revealing *Farley Villas* etched in the keystone.

Blivens slid a key into the half-glassed front door and eased it open. After a pause, he switched off the flashlight. "Shoes off," he whispered. They crept past the stairway, and after a few steps stood in front of a door ... Sophie's flat. With an unhurried movement, the detective unlocked the door. An imperceptible click. They moved forward, Willy bringing up the rear.

Willy steadied himself against the wall, peering at what lay beyond the outlines of Blivens and Nancy in front of him. As they stepped forward, everything exploded in a silvery flash. There was another flash, then another. A ceiling light glowed in the room. Silence at first, then a shriek.

Willy stepped into the room and caught his breath. Two naked figures struggled to untangle themselves from twisted sheets. Another flash.

Sophie, wild-eyed, her black hair disheveled, sat up in the bed.

Shame and regret sliced into Willy's gut and he had to look away. A heart-rending wail drew his gaze back.

Sophie threw herself face down, covering her head with a pillow. The man—handsome, stark naked, and silent—stood beside the bed, a dazed, angry look on his face.

Blivens stepped forward. "I'm Ernest Blivens, licensed investigator and ex-London Police. Are you Captain Kenneth Mottram, Army Intelligence Corps?"

Mottram grabbed at his clothes from a chair and started to dress. "What the hell is this? I'm going to telephone the police."

Willy swayed, his heart skipping and pounding. This was worse than he had imagined. He had to get out of there, blot the nakedness from his mind.

Nancy steadied him. "Stay put," she said fiercely. "An' keep your trap shut."

Blivens pulled him forward. "Is the woman on that bed your spouse, Mrs. Sophie Kohut?"

Willy nodded, spluttering out a harsh "that's her." To avoid looking anymore, he gazed up at the ceiling light, his mind whirling in anger and humiliation. The bones of his marriage had just fractured and would never heal.

"We are witnesses to adultery," Blivens announced his words clear and measured. "We are independent witnesses retained by Mr. Kohut. Before you call the police, Captain Mottram, think very, very carefully ... what with the photos an' all. Come on Nance, Mr. Kohut. We're finished here."

Sophie clutched a sheet over her breasts. She looked at Willy, tears streaming down her face. She was shaking.

"Why did you do this terrible thing to me?" she sobbed in Czech. "Do you hate me so much? You said you would be in London. You lied—to make *this* happen? You are a pitiful man. Get out."

"I'm sorry it had to be like this", Willy said hoarsely. "I was willing to consider a separation but now you have shamed me. You said you wanted a divorce. Well, now you'll get one, but it will be on my terms. Paul is with my parents in London. They don't know anything." Willy turned to face Mottram who was sitting on a chair tying his shoes. "No need to leave, scum," he said bitterly. "The performance is over. "

Blivens dragged him into the corridor and out to the car. Nancy followed, camera in hand.

They sat in the car for a minute or two. Willy groaned and mopped his face. "That was terrible." He was almost in tears. He had seen the shock and pain on Sophie's face. He hadn't wanted to hurt.

"You'll get over it," said Blivens lighting a cigarette. "People do. All in all, it went off nice and smooth. I'll send you my account if you give me your address. Of course, I *would* prefer cash."

"I'm not sure I have enough," Willy replied, still shaking. He couldn't wait to get back to the hotel "I'll give you a check." He had been saving up his wages but the bill might be higher than expected. "You quoted me two shillings an hour for surveillance?" Talking like this about money to pay for what he had just done made him feel sick.

"Fifteen quid for surveillance and ten for tonight's set-up. Nancy'll 'ave the prints ready on Monday. That's five quid. Your solicitor will need them for the judge. An additional ten quid for our affidavits that we witnessed the event. Forty quid. Is that agreeable, Mr. Kohut?"

"Yes, that's okay," said Willy shocked at the amount but relieved that he could cover the fee. "Please have Nancy make me an extra copy of the photos. I'll write you a check."

"Two quid for an extra photograph. We'll settle up when I get you back to your digs."

Outside the Earl of Derby hotel, Willy wrote Blivens a check for forty-two pounds. As he made to get out of the car, Blivens restrained him. "I never heard back from that feller—that friend of yours, Pivodka or whatever his name was. He still owes me ten smackers. I called his number a few times. No one ever answered. Anything happen to 'im?"

Willy bit his lip. Damn. It was Povídka who hired Blivens, and detectives were always suspicious of loose ends "I … I'm not sure. I've been trying to contact him as well." He pulled out his wallet and handed over two five pound notes. "He'll repay me when I see him." It was time to get Blivens and this whole mess out of his life.

Blivens thrust the money into a pocket. "Righty-ho, sport. It's obvious you and he are good mates. Well, goodnight then. Say goodnight to the nice man, Nancy."

The hotel desk clerk at the Earl of Derby had given Willy a late night key to let himself in. He was exhausted. He tossed and turned in bed, reliving the vision of Sophie's horrified face. He had no idea what to do next. Of course, he would tell his parents, and sooner rather than later. And that would create a firestorm! He imagined Judit's face crumpling into a flood of tears and his father's stern fury. They all needed to talk through the implications for Paul. Who else could he turn to? George, of course, his only close confidante. George was bound to have a suggestion or two.

CHAPTER THIRTY-ONE
Divorce Proceedings
Cambridge
November 1943

Sophie was tired and miserable. Nothing seemed worthwhile. Listless and careless, she had run that day's lunch session on her own; the new dishwashing woman never turned up. Only a handful of customers had trickled in since four, and the afternoon light was fading. She was ready to close early.

Ever since Helga disappeared in mid-July, about the same time as Kenneth, Sophie had prepped and cooked with only part-time help. The café was losing money, its reputation damaged by reports of her affair with an RAF officer and an upcoming divorce. She had been profiled in the local paper as a glamorous refugee intent on wheedling secrets out of a fine British officer. Silence from Willy and no word of Helga's whereabouts.

Sophie sought out Dr. Carnegie-Holston, talked to Kenneth's unit commander and checked with the police. No one could or would, she suspected—offer any information. The disappearances were a mystery. Sophie had been abandoned.

Only Jonathan's support and affection held Sophie's despair at bay—Jonathan Finch, a law student at the university and a devout admirer, had taken on the role of her confidante; for months he had been a fixture at the café. Not long after she opened The Peacock, he had offered advice on permits, food regulations and taxes. And from time to time, he took her out to dinner and for drives to the Norfolk beaches of Palling and Cromer.

As she buttoned her winter overcoat, she heard a rap on the door. Glancing through the window, a tall, trilby-hatted man stood outside, impatiently swinging a walking stick. He had an official look about him. Someone from the city council? She unlocked the door hoping that he was not bringing another problem into her life.

He took off his hat and bowed slightly. He pulled a card from his wallet. "Mrs. Sophie Kohut? Colonel Stephens. Military Intelligence. I would like a word … regarding Captain Mottram. Hope you don't mind."

His mention of Kenneth set her heart pounding.

Once inside, doing her best to stay calm, Sophie motioned for him to sit at a table, in two minds about making an effort to challenge his identity. She sat down opposite and blurted. "In God's name, where is Kenneth? What happened to him?" She wiped tears and felt anger burning her cheeks. "What have you come to tell me? Is he dead? Or … what?"

Colonel Stephens looked away. "An urgent posting, Mrs. Kohut. You were probably aware he was RAF Intelligence. We're not allowed to reveal his whereabouts."

Sophie gave a bitter laugh at the easy excuse. "You are hiding something else." Kenneth would have left her some word … even written a slip of paper with a 'goodbye' on it. "So, colonel, why are you here?"

He stared at her, thoughtfully massaging his chin. "I understand you have a divorce hearing coming up in London on November 16."

Defiantly, she braced her shoulders. "That is my affair."

"You intend to be present at the hearing?"

Sophie jerked backward. "Of course … fighting for custody of my son."

The colonel leaned forward, tapping a finger on the table. "We know you have been receiving advice from a man—a friend I believe—registered to attend court with you, Mr. Jonathan Finch."

"I don't know what you are getting at." Sophie had a feeling that she was falling into some kind of trap. This man was so confident, and he knew too much.

"You have also retained a solicitor." He leaned back, took a cigarette from his case and lit it, blowing rings in the air. "I expect they told you that the evidence is stacked against you: affidavits, photographs, public exposure—the whole package. Are you prepared to have your infidelity flaunted in public?"

"I don't care. I want my son to live with me." How did he know about Jonathan and all the evidence? And he was right about the adverse publicity. It would take all her courage to stand up for herself and keep Pavel.

Colonel Stephens folded his hands round the trilby resting on his knees. "Let me make myself clear, Mrs. Kohut. RAF Intelligence insists on minimal publicity at this hearing."

Sophie read hope in his expression that till now had been without emotion.

"Just stay away from court. You've nothing to gain, much to lose."

Sophie jumped to her feet. "Stay away? Because you want to protect your own. It's my right to be there."

The colonel, seemingly unperturbed, blew more smoke rings. "Of course, we can't stop you, but if you insist on being at the hearing, the license for your café will be revoked and your travel waiver canceled."

Sophie caught her breath. "To avoid publicity, you will destroy my life and prevent me from visiting my son? You are a callous, horrible man. What gives you the right to do this to me?"

Colonel Stephens tapped his pipe into an ashtray. "Your collusion with the spy Helga Hilderman, who is currently being interrogated. You accompanied her on several so-called ornithological excursions to the countryside, in the close proximity of allied airfields. Unless you cooperate, you will end up in a camp."

Sophie slumped, her resistance crushed. Protest and anger died in her throat. "So that's what happened to Helga." she murmured. Kenneth and now Helga—two close friends, had betrayed her. And maybe it wasn't over yet. What if Helga implicated her, lied?

"I believe I've covered everything. "Colonel Stephens picked up his cane and fitted the trilby at an angle on his head. "I'll see myself out."

Sophie slowly made her way to the back counter and picked up the telephone. Her thoughts ran helter-skelter, weaving in and out, not making sense. She had to talk to someone. Jonathan.

*   *   *

On November 16, Willy hurried through breakfast. He hadn't slept well and cut himself badly while shaving … high on the cheek where the divorce judge might see it and draw erroneous conclusions. He caught the eight-thirty London train from Winchester. George would be waiting at Waterloo Station. Their destination: the formidable Royal Courts of Justice, just off the Strand.

Two months before the divorce hearing, George surfaced from a business trip to Latin America and learned about Willy's marital rupture. George offered to escort Willy to the hearing in London and recommended a barrister, Mr. Noel Button, to coordinate the case with Willy's solicitor in Cambridge.

Lucky enough to grab a seat on the packed train, Willy leafed through the Manchester Guardian, his mood low at the prospect of having his life exposed to all and sundry in court. His gloom deepened on reading the news. Britain's economy was in a mess, the Germans were putting up stiff resistance against the Eighth Army in the Italian Abruzzo region, and sixty out of two hundred and ninety American bombers had been shot down in an attack on the

Schweinfurt ball-bearing factory. The popular argument that the way to defeat Germany was by bombing it to smithereens was losing favor with the public.

He imagined how it would go in the courtroom, especially with his parents there. Judit would burst into tears and his father would probably make derogatory comments under his breath, in German. And Sophie? He had no idea what she would say, how she would behave. It was going to be a circus. On the other hand, Mr. Button had reassured him it was an open and shut case. *Hope to God it will be over quickly, without fuss.*

*　　　*　　　*

George and Willy met under the suspended clock in Waterloo Station.

"Been a long time," said George. "Pity this get-together is for such a rotten reason. Anyway, when the hearing's over, I'll buy you and your parents' lunch. They'll be on hand, won't they?"

Willy, in crisp formal uniform, was embarrassed by George's get-up: brown bowler, suede boots and a fawn trench overcoat with a velvet collar. "Aren't you a bit overdressed, old chap? I've a feeling Sophie will wear plain clothes to gain the judge's sympathy for a nice plain mother."

"Quite the opposite. I hear the old judge is near-sighted. Besides, British justice tends to favor the well-endowed against the lower classes. How about your parents?"

Willy grimaced. "My mother wants to see Sophie punished, and my father wants to show that they are capable of caring for Paul. I'm nervous about them being here, especially if my mother breaks down. But I couldn't say no. They're the ones looking after Paul at the moment."

George raised his brolly to hail a taxi. "Your father usually comes across as a strong reliable person."

George's assessment surprised Willy. He often thought of his father as a man broken by the loss of his home, business and country. Maybe he was wrong.

As the taxi weaved its way through traffic, George lit a cigarette. "As it happens, Dr. Carnegie-Holston is here on some medical jaunt. I asked her to join us for lunch. I trust you're agreeable? I thought, as a GP, she could help smooth the family waters if the hearing doesn't turn out well. "

Willy frowned. As usual, George presumed too much. A lunch immediately after the court decision was sure to involve high emotions and probable misunderstandings. In any case, he doubted his ability to appear cheerful or charming during the meal, even if he won custody.

He patted George's knee. "Okay, an expensive lunch is a small price for you to pay. You were the one who introduced her to Mottram in Cambridge."

George grinned. "How was I to know they would fall for each other? And I expect you haven't been a monk yourself. We do our best to help each other. Sometimes things go wrong."

They were early, and alighting at Somerset House, they walked along the Strand to the Victorian-Gothic pile of the Royal Courts of Justice. George paused for a moment under the portico to point out the statues of Solomon and King Alfred.

"Don't bother with the guided tour," said Willy irritably. He guessed George was trying to distract him. "Can't think straight. I just want to get this over with." He had been wondering about seeing Sophie in court—what stories might she or her representatives invent to label him as an uncaring, disreputable, even promiscuous father?

Inside the building, George vaguely waved his hand at the elaborately carved oak ceilings. "I'll give you the fascinating history some other time. Let's take a peek at today's case list."

At the posting cabinet, Willy noted that Coulter versus Kohut was scheduled for Court 5 of the Probate Divorce and Admiralty Division. As their footsteps echoed down long corridors, he felt out of his depth. He had never in his life been before a judge wearing a horsehair wig and a black silk gown. How was he supposed to behave?

It was almost noon as they entered the unheated courtroom Willy signaled hello to his parents, who were three rows back from the Cambridge solicitor. As he expected, Emil looked solemn and gloomy in his best suit, a stiff collar, and a striped tie: a fashion plate from the 1920s. Judit, in her Lučenec winter coat with its black lambswool collar, gave Willy a weak, tremulous smile. They had left Paul at Northways with a kindly neighbor.

"I do not agree," had been Emil's emphatic response when Willy had telephoned a few days earlier to ask them to stay home and look after Paul. "We want the judge to see that we exist and are reliable grandparents. We will be at the hearing. The judge must be satisfied that we can care for Paul properly while you are in the army. A neighbor, who has a dog, will take Paul to the park and look after him until we return."

Willy accepted the inevitable. "Alright, Father, but no outbursts from either of you. An English court is a very formal place."

With the hearing set to begin in a few minutes, Willy's solicitor Mr. Royston and the bewigged barrister Mr. Noel Button were studying their briefs in the front row of upholstered benches, below the judge's dais.

Willy nudged George. "Why isn't Sophie here? It's not like her to be late."

George patted Willy's knee and looked at him with sympathetic eyes. "She's not coming." he said in a whisper. "I'll explain later."

Willy stared at him. What the hell was going on? "What—"

"The court will stand," intoned the clerk.

Everyone stood. "You've got a huge advantage," George whispered."

"You know something I don't! How the hell …'"

"Shut up, for God's sake."

Justice Maurice Ormerod, wizened and gaunt-faced, half-moon glasses perched over a thin, blue-veined nose, lowered himself into a high-backed leather armchair on the dais.

"He looks too old and ill," said Willy quietly. "Is he competent? In my country he would be retired and reading newspapers all day in a café."

"Actually, his mind's quite sharp, but the poor devil's overworked. Your solicitor said that the number of petitions for divorce has quadrupled in the last three years. I don't think these old judges were ready for this staggering amount of work. Still, an undefended petition like yours, should only take about twenty minutes."

Willy grabbed George's arm. "What do you mean undefended?"

At that moment, the Clerk of the Court, a middle-aged, burly man with a shiny bald head and a toothbrush mustache, stood up and banged a wooden staff on the floor.

"Next case, m'lud."

Noel Button rose. "Your lordship, this is a straightforward divorce case. The petitioner is Mr. Viliam Kohut, now known as William Coulter, Second Lieutenant, Royal Engineers. The offence is adultery by the respondent, Sophie Kohut, part-proprietor of the Peacock Café in All Saint's Passage, Cambridge, with co-respondent, Captain Kenneth Mottram, Army Intelligence Corps. We have submitted the affidavits of detective Ernest Blevins, who is present here in Chambers.

Willy craned his neck. The big detective was soberly-dressed, but his feisty niece, Nancy, wore a fluffy pink sweater and a mauve skirt, a black beret stuck on the back of her head.

"Thank you, Counsel," said the judge. "I have read the sworn affidavits entered by Mr. Blevins of October 20 and November 7, 1943, the affidavit of Mildred Atkinson, owner of 10 Farley Villas, and of the respondent on October 12. Are the petitioner, respondent, and co-respondent in court?

"Yes and no, your Lordship," the barrister replied smoothly. "The co-respondent, Captain Mottram, was posted to Salerno, Italy two months ago. The respondent is absent. Her representative, Mr. Jonathan Finch is here. The petitioner, Viliam Kohut ... er— I mean William Coulter, is present."

"Mmm," the judge mumbled. He seemed to be constantly chewing something. "Pray tell me, why does your petitioner have two surnames, Kohut and Coulter? Which are we dealing with here?"

"A simple matter, my Lord," said the barrister, stepping toward the Bench. "For his protection in the event of capture by the Germans, Lieutenant Kohut, was assigned the British name Coulter. He is shortly to go through a naturalization process."

The judge peered at Willy and seemed satisfied. "Aha, I understand. You're in the process of being Anglicized. Very sensible too." He paused for a moment. "Now, Lieutenant Coulter, step into the witness box and describe the circumstances of this case. In just a few words, please."

Earlier, on the telephone, Mr. Button had advised Willy to emphasize his daring escape from Prague and determined commitment to military service. In court, Willy explained how he joined the Czech army in Paris, describing the family's journey to

England, their traumas during the Blitz and his current service in the British Army. In the course of all these events he and Sophie had grown apart. He learned of her affair with a British officer and hired a detective to follow her.

"And you were present when the respondent and co-respondent were confronted in her flat?"

"Yes," said Willy quietly, his face red with embarrassment. He tried to stop the hurtful and shaming vision in his mind of Sophie holding a sheet over her breasts.

"Thank you, Counsel," said Judge Ormerod, still chewing. "The photographs in question are here with the affidavits of the enquiry agents and the solicitor." He nodded to Willy. "You may step down now, Lieutenant. Tell me, Counsel; is it correct that Mrs. Kohut is *not* defending the facts or the petition for divorce?"

"Kristus!" Willy halted, and looked questioningly at Noel Button. *She's not defending? What the hell is this? She has to defend … if she wants any chance to get Paul into her custody.*

"Quite so, your Lordship," the barrister said with a nod. "She is not here. Her affidavit admits the facts as described."

"What about you, Mr. Finch?" The judge switched his gaze to Jonathan Finch. He was tall with a long face, an aquiline nose and a head of dark wavy hair.

"Can you shed any light on why Mrs. Sophie Kohut offers no defense or mitigating circumstances in this case? And please explain your role in this case."

"I'm a close friend of the respondent, and in my second year at Cambridge Law School. For the past few months, subsequent to the distressing intrusion at her flat and the abrupt overseas posting of Captain Mottram, Mrs. Kohut has been distraught. She is in no condition to face the pain and hardship of this hearing. You have her affidavit, which states that she has a seven year-old son, Paul, and another from a local doctor recommending that she be spared further emotional turmoil. She does plead for custody of her son."

Judge Ormerod peered at a sheet of paper in his hand. "I see that she is the part-owner of a restaurant in Cambridge."

Finch nodded. "A business that will easily ensure adequate funds for the boy's long-term education. I have copies of accounts that show that the respondent's income is, in fact, greater than Second Lieutenant Coulter's pay. Also, one cannot dismiss the possibility that Second Lieutenant Coulter will soon be fighting in Europe. Mrs. Kohut's care would therefore be the more reliable choice for long term custody. A mother is essential to a child's happiness."

Willy felt relief as he sat down again. A well-reasoned but weak justification for custody. No match for Detective Blivens's evidence and photographs. Why hadn't Sophie made counter claims of infidelity or inadequate parenting? *Maybe she just gave up.* He could hear Judit sobbing.

The judge nodded to Noel Button. "Are there any other comments from the plaintiff?"

"No, your Lordship, said Willy's barrister." That is the case. We ask for a decree nisi."

"First step," whispered George to Willy. "A decree nisi means that the legal justification for divorce is fully established. Absolute decree in six weeks' time."

The judge looked around the courtroom. "Where is the boy now?" His voice penetrated every corner of the room.

"Seven year-old Paul Coulter currently resides with his grandparents in London. They are in court. We can provide details confirming their good health. and financial resources, over and above the income of the said William Coulter."

Judge Ormerod peered at Emil and Judit. He gathered up his papers, pulling the gown's padded shoulders around his thin frame. "With the solid evidence of adultery, the respondent Sophie Kohut's absence today, her admission of fault together with the lack of a counter-petition, custody is awarded to Lieutenant William Coulter. The child will live with his grandparents. It is regrettable that Sophie Kohut is not here to argue for her son's disposition."

The judge surveyed the court while he dabbed his lips with a handkerchief. "Access to the said child by the respondent Sophie Kohut, to be agreed, with liberty to apply to the court. May I remind you that a decree absolute cannot be obtained until satisfactory arrangements have been made in writing for the care of the child."

Willy whispered in George's ear. "What does this mean?"

"You have custody of Paul, but before the divorce is final, Sophie has to apply to the court if she wants to have Paul with her at certain times. It might be one day a week or, if he's away at school, she would have him for a portion of the holidays."

"The Court will rise," the clerk intoned.

"It's over. Time for lunch," George muttered.

Willy gripped his arm. "Wait a minute. You were going to tell me why Sophie wasn't here."

"All very unfortunate." George paused.

Willy jabbed George in the ribs. "Spit it out."

George looked away in embarrassment. "Kenny Mottram is an RAF Intelligence officer. He was ordered to keep an eye on the German woman, Hilderman. When Hilderman worked as a cook for the Carnegie-Holstons, our dear Dr. Emily encouraged her to become a bird-watcher."

Willy clutched his head. "What in God's name has bird-watching to do with my divorce?"

"After the café started, Hilderman got a car and did her own bird-watching, usually outside Cambridge, and damned close to our allied airfields."

Willy gripped George's elbow, making him wince. "What of it?"

George dropped his voice. "Hilderman was spotted using

binoculars in places where there were hardly any birds—the boundaries of Duxford, Bassingham, and Teversham airfields where American bomber squadrons and the Eighth Army Fighter group hang out. She also took photos. Kenny used his friendship with Sophie to keep an eye open."

Willy buried his face in his hands, speaking through spread fingers. "Are you saying that Mottram was *assigned* to befriend Sophie?"

George patted Willy's shoulder. "S'right, old boy."

"And that has something to do with Sophie not being here?"

"Those photos your detective took. Kenny naked. Super sensational. Did you see the reporter in the back? Scribbling away at a juicy story. RAF Intelligence shipped Kenny to the Italian war zone. The German cook is under arrest."

For a few moments, Willy couldn't speak. He clenched his fists and took several deep breaths. "Sophie was an *intelligence* assignment?"

George grabbed Willy's shoulder, holding him steady. "I don't think Kenny meant to go all the way with her, but I expect he couldn't resist. Your wife is a charmer. And I have a feeling she was ready for his spiel. I'm told it's one of his talents."

Willy ground his teeth. This revelation turned everything upside down. He thought he'd been the main victim of Sophie's affair. But she had been betrayed and shamed twice over. The newspaper reports about her were unjust and cruel. Mottram was no hero. Her reputation was in tatters and her beloved café might go under.

"Could we ask for a new hearing based on what you told me? She's been punished enough."

George shook his head. "Not poss, old chap. Secure information. I shouldn't really have told you. "What's done is done."

"What else haven't you told me, you bastard?" Willy wanted to pound George's nose so hard that his own family wouldn't recognize him.

George raised his hands in protest. "Come on, Willy. I checked with military intelligence. Kenny was following orders. They spirited him out of the country and pressured Sophie to stay away."

"She had a right to be here. Do you know how they persuaded her?"

George dropped his gaze. "I expect they suggested her café business might suffer … maybe something worse. Do you want me to find out?"

Willy considered what it might take to unravel all the strands that led to the divorce. He had no time. He was tired of it all and a new posting was imminent. "Let it go," He looked up and took a deep breath. His parents, wreathed in smiles. Emil held up two fingers in a victory sign.

"Let's go to lunch," said George as he clapped Emil on the back.

"We won," said Judit with a triumphant smile.

Willy bent to kiss his mother, dreading George's lunch. She didn't know the half of it, and Dr Emily would be there.

CHAPTER THIRTY-TWO
Lunch at the Savoy
November 1943

Willy and his parents accompanied George Kindell along the Strand to the Savoy Grill. The rain had stopped and the granite facades of the street's buildings glistened and glittered in the weak sun.

George slowed his long stride to let Emil and Judit catch up. "Let's forget the world's woes for a couple of hours," he said. "Lunch is my treat. There will be an extra guest, someone you know. Dr. Carnegie-Holston."

In the Grill Room, the Maître' d showed them to a round table covered by a damask tablecloth, set with Wedgewood china and a vase of yellow roses. A deep Aubusson carpet and silk curtains muffled conversation in the busy room. A waiter circled their table, flicking open white linen napkins for the guest's knees as they studied gold-printed menus. George ordered two bottles of Chablis. Another waiter took the order.

While they were eating, Dr. Carnegie-Holston arrived, removing a flower-strewn trilby and slipping her raincoat off into a young attendant's hands. "So sorry, to be late. My meeting went on and on."

Willy, surprised at the doctor's heavy makeup and hairstyle, nodded a dutiful welcome, still unsure whose side she was on. She was the one who had hired Helga Hilderman and probably encouraged Sophie to open her café—possibly even lent her money. He felt uncomfortable. This celebratory lunch might turn sour. Recriminations were possible. "The waiter will be back to take your order in a minute, doctor," he said. He wasn't ready to call her Dr. Emily until he knew whose side she was on.

George poured some Chablis into the doctor's glass. "Did you accomplish anything?"

Dr. Emily took a sip. "Mmm, that's lovely. My meeting? Well, the government has asked the British Medical Association to fast-forward training in all our medical schools. The army's desperately short of doctors, so they want to use medical students. I expect our troops are in for some rather patchy treatment."

"Are you aware, doctor," Willy said, "that I was just awarded custody of Paul at the divorce court?"

The doctor gave him a quick, sympathetic smile. "I expected it. I'm here because George thought I might be helpful in discussing Paul's future." She put on square, black-framed spectacles that hung from a chain around her neck and picked up the menu. "In my thirty-years of general practice, I've had a good deal of experience with all sorts of family problems. And Grandpa Emil here seems determined that the boy should have a career in medicine. I think I can help you figure something out."

Emil, taut-faced, fiddled with his silverware. "A doctor is always respected, and the science of medicine is the same everywhere. Look at me. I was a successful merchant. Now I am nothing—a *nishkeit,* a spoon without a handle."

"I don't think we should listen to Dr. Emily," Judit said forcefully, her eyes flashing. "Because of her, Sophie started the café and this terrible divorce happened."

Willy looked at her, in shock. "*Být zticha.* Be quiet!" As he feared, tension was mounting.

Dr. Carnegie-Holston untied her chiffon scarf and hooked it over the back of her chair. "Come now, my friends, be fair. I was just her sounding board. From what Sophie has been through these past three years, I know she is a brave and enterprising young woman."

"Enterprising?" Willy said in a sarcastic tone.

"Sophie ran your business while you were in prison in Prague, didn't she? And if I'm not mistaken, she cared for Paul in France when he got TB, and you were far away in the Czech army."

"Pardon, me madam." A waiter slid a plate full of food in front of her.

The doctor picked up her knife and fork. "I absolutely applaud that Sophie planned and set up her café— with determination and against all expectations. Of course, she was impulsive and probably did not consider the consequences of her actions." Dr. Emily looked earnestly around the table. "Be assured I have *all* your interests at heart, especially Paul's."

"What do you think about our idea for Paul's education, doctor?" Willy said after they finished eating and were taking coffee. Whatever his misgivings, he wanted to get Dr. Emily's perspective. "Lady Hilliard, the kind woman who took Paul on her farm, recommended a boarding school for him. She has offered to arrange it."

"Yes, Sophie told me. It's on the coast, somewhere near Brighton. Lady Hilliard must have a lot of pull at that place. From what I remember about Paul, he's resilient enough to handle it. He's a lucky lad to get the chance."

Tears welled in Judit's eyes as she scrabbled for a handkerchief. "In my country, children went to school where their family and friends lived, even when they went to university. How can a child learn when they have no love around them?"

Emil put a hand on her arm. "Please Judit, not now. There were enough tears in the courtroom."

Judit pushed him away. "The boy has been alone too much already. He is nervous. Why should he pretend to be an Englishman? When the war is finished, we should all go back to Czechoslovakia."

Willy was aghast. His mother had never said this before.

Emil waved an imperious finger. "*Nicht möglich,* Judit—impossible. Czechoslovakia, if she survives, will never be the same. Who knows if Jews can even go back there? I think we will live in England, unless we go to Canada."

Judit stared at him. "Let us see what happens. But I want Paul to live with us until the war is over."

George lit a cigarette. "You have a point about family ties, Mrs. Kohut. It will be hard for you to let him go. I was lonely when I went to boarding school. But, if you really want him to have a career, his pathway is pretty much set—if you can afford it."

"George is right," said Dr. Carnegie-Holston. "I will gladly help Paul with his applications. Private schools here have strong religious affiliations. They don't want to accept Jews. If Paul has C of E on his application for school, that would solve the religious barrier."

"C of E?" chorused Emil and Judit, looking around the table for help.

"Church of England—Protestant. I can arrange for him to be baptized in my diocese, at Trinity Church. I discussed it with Sophie and she is fine with it."

"That's quite an offer," said Willy. He looked around at the others hopefully. "I think it would work." He raised eyebrows at his parents. "I presume and hope that Paul still is unaware that we're Jewish. He laughed self-consciously. "I've been away too much."

"We have revealed nothing," Emil said with a firm shake of his head.

"That's settled then," the doctor said. "I'll contact the vicar."

Willy wiped his glasses on a clean napkin. "I agree with George and Dr. Emily. We should baptize the boy and get him into the school Lady Hilliard recommends." He took a sip of water. "Now that the Allies look like they might win, Paul will grow up an Englishman. I want to thank all of you for helping us so much."

He leaned back in his chair. "Soon enough, I will be in France playing my part in the invasion. He gave Emil and Judit a grim smile. "It's quite possible I'll never come back. In that case, I want to be sure Paul is on the right track."

George raised his wine glass high. "Here's to Paul's future ... and your safe return."

Judit drained her coffee and dabbed her eyes with her napkin. "Until Paul lives at this residential school, it is Emil and I who must look after him. So what do we do about Sophie? I don't want her on my doorstep whenever she wants to see Paul."

Willy was surprised at the strength of his mother's feelings. She tended to let Emil do the talking.

Dr. Carnegie-Holston shook her head in dismay. "That's not a very Christian thing to say, Mrs. Kohut."

"Thanks God, I am no Christian."

Willy waved a warning finger at Judit. "You are being rude and unpleasant, Mother."

The doctor shook her head. "It's alright. Mrs. Kohut has strong feelings about Paul. I expect she has been affected by the hearing this morning. She asks what's to be done about Sophie. My questions relate only to Paul. When and how are you going to tell him about the divorce? And are you *all* willing for the boy to be brought up Christian? And how are you going to explain sending him away to school?" Dr. Emily looked at Willy. "Someone must do it."

Judit compressed her lips. "Sophie. Punishment for the trouble she has caused."

Willy saw the anger on his mother's face. Her hands were trembling and he was not sure how to calm her down. She had a point. He couldn't tell Paul; he would be back at his camp by the evening. And, given his mother's outburst, he didn't trust his parents to do the job calmly.

"Look here," George interjected as the waiter presented the bill on a silver salver, "the boy's coming up to eight years old, right? Until he gets into boarding school, the divorce doesn't change his circumstances. He'll live with the grandparents, and most of the time Bill will be away, fighting or whatever he does with the Royal Engineers. Meanwhile, Sophie stays in Cambridge, running her café. What's the gain in telling the boy about the divorce right now? I think it'll upset him. Why not leave things as they are till he's older and well settled at school. "

Willy smiled gratefully. "Sensibly put, George. I agree, though there's a possibility I might not be alive when the time comes to explain. I'll let Sophie know about the plan."

Judit frowned. "I'm not so sure about waiting. Better Paul starts to learn what happened, bit by bit, starting now." She gave Emil and then George, a look of sadness and reproach. "It is high time for us to go home." She rose from the table. "Come Emil. Thank you, George, for a very nice lunch."

Willy put an arm around her shoulders and kissed her cheek. "You may be right, Mother. I need a few days to think this over,"

George signaled to the hovering waiter and laid a five pound note on top of the bill.

Dr. Emily looked at her watch. "Oh, my God, it's late. I'll need a taxi to get to the station. Thanks so much, George. Lovely meal. Must rush. Good luck telling Paul. Bye, everyone."

On the way out, Willy shook hands with George. "Thanks for offering us lunch. It didn't turn out to be a celebration, but we heard some opinions, and cleared the air a bit."

"And what are you going to say to Sophie?"

CHAPTER THIRTY-THREE
The Telling
December 1943

Four weeks after the divorce hearing, Sophie enthusiastically agreed to have Paul spend a long weekend with her in Cambridge. On the Friday, Emil would bring him by train from London and the next morning, under Dr. Carnegie-Holston's benevolent eye, Paul would be baptized at the Holy Trinity Church. Two days later, Monday, she would keep the café closed and take him back to the grandparents. She had something else very important to tell him. Perhaps on the train on the way back to London.

Paul's visit would be a welcome distraction. The Peacock Café had turned into a monster. She couldn't sleep properly, mixed up ordering supplies and even with part-time help was exhausted by the cooking and cleaning. She forgot to pay bills and was careless about ledger entries. She was ready to sell the place and salvage what was left of her savings.

Jonathan Finch had asked her to marry him and she had agreed. She was lonely and still terribly hurt by Kenneth and Helga's duplicity; she still had nightmares about them. Marriage to Jon sat before her like a golden pear, demanding to be picked. But until Paul knew about the divorce, how could she say anything about a wedding?

A week earlier, on the telephone, she told Willy about Jonathan.

"So he's more than just a handsome lawyer in training, eh?" Willy grumbled. "It didn't take you long to find someone else. What's so damned special about him? Money?"

Willy's remark made her feel angry and guilty. She was lonely, attracted to Jonathan and he clearly adored her. But he was rich and she was sliding into debt. "He's Jewish. His father came from

Lithuania twenty-five years ago and he insists I can't marry Jon until we go through a Jewish divorce. You have to be at the *Get* and sign the documents at the *Beth Din* rabbinical court in London."

Willy laughed. A bitter sound. "Sounds like a script for a Hollywood movie."

Sophie understood he was still angry. Surely he'd retained some understanding and affection for her. What if he found a Jewish woman to marry and was forced to comply with the traditions? "Will you or won't you help me with this divorce ceremony?"

"I don't want any part of that Judaic hocus-pocus. Besides, I'm up to my neck in army work."

"Don't be a *schmuck*, Willy. This is important. Do you want me to tell your parents about your romantic adventures? I bet I only know about half of them."

"What I agree to is this. Since you have just torpedoed our agreement not to tell Paul anything until he's older, you must take responsibility to break the news to Paul … and explain how he's gaining a stepfather. I'll write my parents that I've allowed Paul to spend to three full days with you."

Sophie slammed the telephone down. Was this to be her future where Paul was concerned … begging her husband for permission?

*   *   *

Paul thought it was funny to be staying with Mummy again, so soon after the Christmas holiday, but she said Dr. Emily had arranged a baptism at her church. Something to do with attending prayers at a new school he was going to. It seemed like a lot of trouble for not much. He'd already learned lots of holy stuff at Aunt Popsie's farm.

In the morning, Sophie took him shopping and bought him two comics, a Dandy and a Beano … and a second-hand copy of *The Wind in the Willows.* The man at bookshop said it was going to snow. They took a walk by the river and it was jolly cold. Paul didn't have any gloves. They walked to Holy Trinity church and met Dr. Emily for the baptism. On the way there, Mummy said she had closed her café for good.

The baptism lasted only a few minutes. It was fun having holy water splashed on his face. Paul wondered why Granny and Grandpa couldn't have done all this in London. The vicar filled out a little baptism card and gave it to him. They had sausage and chips for lunch at the Lyons café and went home on the bus, just as the snow started falling.

Paul sat with arms hugged around his knees on the broad cushioned window ledge of his mother's flat at Farley Villas. The gas fire's ceramic columns pulsed red heat. He loved the place. Full of knick-knacks and small paintings of mostly flowers and animals, and a big one, full odd shapes and super colors. She said it was like a picture that Picasso would paint, but an artist who often visited the café had given it to her.

He looked out onto a small garden. The snow was settling in big flakes, and the dead flower-heads looked as though someone had spooned cream on them. A bare, lonely tree stood in the middle of a patch of brown grass He watched a tabby cat stalk a robin hopping about in the snow. Mummy had said it was too cold and nasty to go out for another walk.

At tea-time, she read him the chapter about Toad and how he loved fast motor cars more than anything else. After that, Paul half-listened to music on the radio while she sat at the dining table and wrote what she said were "café accounts" in a special book.

"Damn." She slammed it shut and pulled out a handkerchief.

"Mummy, why are you upset?"

"Because I've closed my café … forever," she said, coming over to the small sofa. She settled down beside him and stroked his cheek. "I'm all right. I'll get over it. But I want to talk to you about something else: something important. Are you ready to listen?" She tucked the handkerchief into the sleeve of her blouse.

Paul smiled and leaned against her. "Okay, Mummy. Can we have some of that chocolate cake you bought, for tea?"

She took a deep breath. "Cake? Of course. But later. Do you … do you know what a divorce is?"

He looked up. Pity about the cake. He was feeling a bit hungry. "Golly, your face has gone all red, Mum."

She blew her nose. "The fire's a bit hot. Well, it's … I wanted to tell you … your Daddy and I are divorced."

Paul searched her face. "What's divorced, Mum?"

"When a mummy and daddy can't be together anymore."

"Oh, like you and Daddy. 'Cos he's in the army and you have the café."

"Not really like that. Divorce means a mummy and daddy stay away from each other. All the time. It's like when you and the children left the farm. You'll probably never see them again."

Paul suddenly felt like crying. "No one told us that would happen. I miss Eric. Where is he?"

Playfully, she pinched his nose. "I don't know, somewhere in London."

Paul wasn't sure why Mummy was talking like this. He picked up a paper bag and looked inside at the candies she had bought him. Scrumptious. Which one should he eat first: a lemon sherbet, barley twist, or a Cadbury's chocolate flake?

"Me and your daddy. We love you, of course, but we don't love each other anymore."

Paul's eyes widened as he sucked on the barley twist. What was she saying? "Would you like a candy, Mum?"

"No, um, this is very difficult for me, Paulikin. It's because you and I and Daddy were apart so much, even before we came to England. I'm not sure if you remember those bad times we went through—on that long journey from Prague."

Paul scratched his nose. "What's Prague? I remember France when we lived in a village with that old lady."

Looking surprised, she drew his face close. "You mean you don't know that German soldiers came to our flat in Prague and Daddy went to prison?"

Paul shrugged and looked out of the window. The flakes were still coming down.

"Your Daddy and me don't like each other anymore. Our love just slipped away. I think it's because of the war and all the trouble we've been through. Now, we argue a lot, and he hates that I had the café. I'm much happier away from him."

Paul chewed on the collar of his shirt. He picked up his Dandy comic. "Have we finished talking now? I want to read about Desperate Dan."

She sighed, kissing his cheek. "I'm not finished yet, darling." She took a deep breath and gently put his comic aside. "You see, divorce is much more complicated than just living apart. An official in London, called a judge, decided we should not be married. We won't live together anymore."

"Just like now?'

She put her arms around him and kissed his forehead. "That's right."

"So, what …?"

"And there's something else I have to tell you." Sophie caressed his forearm.

It looked to Paul that she was ready to cry again. He hadn't known she was so soppy. He hated it.

Sophie wiped her cheeks and bent down close. "After a divorce, the judge lets the mummy or daddy marry somebody else."

"That's sounds nice."

"You see, Paulikin, if I wanted to marry another man, then you would have two daddies. One would be your real daddy, and the other would be what people call a stepfather."

Paul sat bolt upright. This was interesting. "Two daddies? Gosh. Does that mean we would all live together? So, if one daddy was away somewhere, like in the army, the other one would stay at home."

"Well, no, it wouldn't be like that. Two daddies are not allowed to live together with the same mummy. What would you say if I told you, I'm thinking of marrying another man—a very, very nice man. He would be your stepfather."

Pavel's mouth opened, but he made no sound. He stared at her

"I mean it. I want to marry a man you haven't met yet. That's because you were living at the farm and then with Granny and Grandpa in London. He's called Jonathan. We met when he started coming to the café."

"So you love him, not Daddy?"

Sophie took a pack of cigarettes off the table and lit one. "I suppose so, dear, "she said stroking his arm again. She didn't look at him. She seemed to be somewhere else.

Paul picked up his comic.

Sophie absent-mindedly gazed out at the snow melting off the roof of the next door house, and thought about the time Kenneth and Helga suddenly disappeared. For days afterwards, she hadn't been able to sleep and suffered nightmares. It had been a terrible strain until Jon came to her rescue.

Even at the time of her affair with Kenneth, Jon, as he liked to be called, had been a regular at the Peacock. He dressed beautifully in silk shirts and clothes from Savile Row. He took her out to dinner, to pubs and for country drives in his car. She got used to his mustache kisses.

"Let the Peacock Café go," Jonathan often said. "With me you'll never have to worry about money or get up at five in the morning to get food ready. We'll live in one of my houses in London, a nice neighborhood called Chelsea." And for their honeymoon, he had promised her a fantastic voyage to visit her father and brother in Australia—a twelve day journey on a flying boat with hotel stops in Athens, Cairo, Aden, Rangoon and Singapore—and after a month's stay, back again. She hadn't seen her family since '38 when they fled Nazi Berlin.

Sophie felt a tug on her arm. She stubbed out the cigarette.

"Why don't you answer?" said Paul. "I asked you something."

"Oh, what? Sorry. What were we talking about?"

"You said you were going to marry another man. What's he like?"

Sophie was pleased that Paul had accepted the divorce without a murmur. She decided to go with Jon's appearance. "Taller than your daddy. Lots of wavy hair and a mustache. You'll like him."

Paul's eyes widened. "Will I see him soon?"

Sophie smiled at his enthusiasm. "He's coming to say hello tomorrow. In fact, he offered to drive us to the seaside in his Bentley."

"Golly whizz, Mummy. A Bentley? That's super. What model?"

Sophie laughed. "I didn't know that you were an expert on cars."

"He must be rich to have a Bentley."

"Well, yes, his family is very rich." Sophie could tell Paul had been well and truly hooked by the Bentley.

Paul nodded vigorously. "So if you marry him, you'll be rich too."

"He'll help pay your school fees until you go to university." She hugged him. "For eight years. Imagine that."

Paul was puzzled. "What do you mean, school fees?"

Sophie sighed. "Oh, dear, yes. I nearly forgot. Grandpa told me about your new school, St Justus. They've got an opening for you, sometime in the next month or two."

Paul jumped to his feet. "Ooh, yes, I remember now. That's the school Aunt Popsie said was so super."

Sophie hugged him again and kissed his cheek. "You'll make lots of friends there. And it's where the beaches are, near Brighton on the south coast. People from London go there for day trips and holidays."

Paul's eyes widened. "Do you know what it's like?"

She sighed at her loss of control over his life. "Not really, Paulikins. Listen, it's been a long day and we've talked enough. Time I prepared supper."

Sophie hoped with all her heart that Jon would like Paul and be good to him—and that Paul would love him back. Pleased that Paul had accepted the telling without the least protest Sophie gave Paul a long, loving embrace. All would soon be well for both of them.

CHAPTER THIRTY-FOUR
St. Justus School for Boys
March 1944

George Kindell guided the maroon Armstrong-Siddeley to the entry steps of Northways. He checked his watch and lit up a cigarette. Time enough for a smoke before Paul and his grandparents appeared. *Hope to God Mr. Kohut won't ramble on about his old days selling our fabrics in Slovakia. What if the lad's school trunk doesn't fit in the back?*

Two weeks earlier, Willy had telephoned, asking for a last-minute favor.

"Good heavens," George groaned. "Not *another* one. What's the crisis this time?"

"St Justus School sent a telegram. They've a mid-term opening for Paul, and they need him there within the week. There's no way I can get a release from my unit. Not now. Working all hours. Can you take him and my father?"

"Your father can take him."

"I can't ask him to lug a big trunk on to a train and then find the school in the middle of the English countryside."

"Why can't Sophie and her new husband do it? He has a Bentley for Christ's sake! She's still Paul's mother isn't she?"

"You're right, of course," Willy said apologetically. "But the thought of begging my ex-wife for help sticks in my throat."

"Sometimes you have to swallow your pride, old chap."

"Come on George … will you do it? And on the question of favors, don't forget that I was the instigator of the Povídka and Serbin caper. I have a feeling you were warmly praised for that incident."

George sighed. "So what's my reward?"

"My eternal gratitude and a free dinner at the Hungarian Csárdás in Soho."

"Oh, yes! And when will that be?"

"No idea."

George wound down the Armstrong Siddeley's side window, letting the cigarette smoke seep out. No smoking on this trip. Judit Kohut didn't like smokers. He glanced up at the blue sky, and then studied the open map on his knees. It would be a nice run to the coast; no hint of the dense fogs that had plagued London in the last couple of months. They'd stop for a bite at the Bear in Horsham and, when they reached Brighton, he'd take the coast road. St. Justus School was somewhere up there on the Downs, close to the little resort town of Seaford.

On the telephone, Willy had sounded tense—probably due to overwork and the aftermath of the divorce. In spite of his half-joking gripe, George was glad to help, even though it had meant canceling a trip to his fabric suppliers in Yorkshire. All along, he had admired the spunky but now splintered Kohuts. A promotion was "in the works" for Willy but Sophie, after a starburst of initiative, creativity and success had fallen to earth. George wondered how her second marriage would work out. Was it true love on the rebound or a calculated move on her part to achieve security and an easier life?

Paul, spruced up in a maroon-colored cap, grey shorts and blazer sporting an embroidered bishop's miter below the left lapel—emerged with his grandfather from the Northways' entrance, hanging on to a green and white steamer trunk. Together with George, they bumped it down the steps to the car, and went back for a wooden tuck box. Emil took off his Homburg and wiped perspiration from his face.

"Looks like there's not a country this fine piece of memorabilia hasn't visited," George said admiring the colorful travel stickers on the trunk as he helped manhandle the luggage into the boot. He wondered when Mrs. Kohut would appear. She wasn't a chatty one, so that was good. But based on her performance in the divorce court, she might fall apart when they said goodbye to Paul at St. Justus.

Paul scampered around the car, whooping with delight. "Gosh, how fast does she go? Can I sit the driver's seat? What if…."

George raised a hand to stop the questions. "She does eighty-five miles per hour, tops, but on this trip we'll stick to the speed limit." He opened the front passenger door. "It's high time we got going. Mr. Kohut, why don't you sit beside me in the front? Paul and Mrs. Kohut will be in the back. Isn't she ready yet?"

With a little bow, Emil took off his Homburg. "We are much in your debt for this journey, Mr. Kindell. You are a generous man. My wife has decided to stay behind. It will upset her too much to come with us. She already said goodbye to Paul."

George killed the cigarette with his heel. Sensible woman … make the trip simpler. "Do you want to sit next to me or in the back with your grandson? You can switch at lunchtime."

Emil looked at Paul. "You and me in the back before lunch, yes?" He patted the shopping bag he had brought. "Granny packed rugelach."

"Is Mummy coming too? She said she might." Paul's face was full of hope.

George exchanged a meaningful glance with Emil. "I expect she's ultra-busy with your new stepfather. I heard they were moving into a house in London." He watched the boy's eager expression crumble. "It's just us men on this trip."

Later, as they drove through Crawley, on the outskirts of London, Emil put his arm around the Paul's shoulder. "So, young man, you will be on your own again. I know you will study hard and obey all the rules at this school. Remember what Granny said. Look after your clothes properly. Remember how they disappeared at the farm."

Grandpa was neither a hugger nor a kisser, and Paul was surprised at his grandfather's intimate gesture. But he felt comforted with the old man's arm around him ... but he hated the lecturing.

"And don't get into fights. You do not know this, but when he was your age, your father often came home with bruises on his arms and legs."

Paul's eyes lit up. "He fought at school?"

Emil nodded. "He never started the fights. It was because our family was—" He checked himself—"different."

"I expect I'll have to fight at school." Paul wrinkled his nose at the thought. "I'm a foreigner. That's why Mrs. M. was nasty to me on the farm."

Emil tousled his grandson's hair. "That is in the past. Now you speak with a good English accent, and you are strong and clever. Study hard, and remember, we will always be thinking about you."

"Yes, Grandpa, I'll try hard." Paul saw, behind the thick spectacles, that his grandfather's eyes were wet. This was a shock. Grandpa never cried.

"What do you think it will be like at school?" said George from the front.

Paul wedged himself between the two front seats. He could see the road better that way and study Mr. Kindell's driving. "Classes every day, I 'spose. Sports, sleeping in a dormitory. Hope I can make friends."

George grunted. "Hunh … You may find it hard at the beginning, young feller. There are school rules and then there are the hidden rules made by the older boys. The main thing is to watch and learn how things are done. It'll help a lot if there's something special about you that other boys like or admire, like being good at cricket or telling good jokes."

Good advice, Paul thought. He might have to tangle with mean boys and submit to teachers like Mrs. McAlistair at the farm. He resolved to learn fast, and stay out of trouble.

Emil squeezed Paul's knee affectionately. "I have some good news. No more Northways flat. I just signed the lease on a house with a nice garden at the back with pear and apple trees. I want you to help me when you come for the holidays."

Paul half-smiled his agreement. He knew his grandparents had been looking for a place. A house would be a lot more fun than living in a flat. Perhaps, there would be friendly neighbors with children … not like Northways. But helping Grandpa in the garden sounded jolly boring. Grandpa would give orders and talk about seeds and plants and how they grew—though it might be fun to climb the trees and pick apples.

"Will I have my own room?"

Grandpa winked. "Wait and see." He lifted his shopping bag off the floor. "Granny and I have something for you." He pulled out a cardboard tube closed at both ends, as long as a six inch ruler, its surface decorated with colored circles and squares. "This is a kaleidoscope. At this end … here … you look through a lens. Hold it up to the light, like this, and you see … a beautiful pattern. Shake it and there is a different pattern. Try."

Paul took it. He held it up against the car window squinted through the lens. He had never seen such a dazzling and organized mix of colors. "That's super, Grandpa." Can I really take it to school?" He shook it again. "Super, now it's completely different. Where did you get it?"

"From the ruins of a bombed shop. You know I'm always on the look-out for treasures."

Paul grinned at him. Grandpa was a dustbin dipper and hoarder. He stacked and tied old newspaper into bundles, kept a cash box filled with padlocks and old keys, and stored twists of used string in a tin box.

"So, Paul, in the Greek language, *kaleidoscope* means seeing something beautiful. This is also how you should look at life."

Was this going to be one of Grandpa's boring lectures? "What do you mean?"

"Today, you start a new life—with a new pattern. Away from your family."

Paul eased the kaleidoscope into his satchel. He felt sad, and his eyes prickled with tears. He hadn't thought about it before, but now he was sorry to leave Granny and Grandpa.

"Whenever you look through this kaleidoscope remember that your grandparents love you."

Paul kissed his Grandpa's stubbly cheek. He looked away. He didn't want his tears to be seen.

After they stopped for a bathroom break and a sandwich at the Black Bear in Horsham, Grandpa sat beside Mr. Kindell. Paul lounged in the back reading a Dandy comic with Furry Lion snuggled against his chest. Keeping half an eye out for interesting things in the countryside like horses, tractors, different shaped church steeples, and sports cars, he fell to wondering about his new school.

Some time ago, Daddy had written that he had visited St. Justus on his own. He enclosed the school brochure with photographs of the school and its surroundings: buildings, playing fields surrounded by grassy meadows, and in the distance, the sea. The brochure described all the subjects the boys studied—a long, scary list. Paul had no clear idea of what the classes would be like. Most of all he was afraid no one would like him. He was a foreign boy. He'd learned that at the farm.

Early in the afternoon, they drove up a winding road to the top of what Mr. Kindell said were the South Downs, a great expanse of grassland with hardly a tree. Paul had never seen anything like it. A few minutes later he caught an exciting glimpse of a silvery gray sea, flecked with white, stretching all the way to the sky.

The car wheels crunched to a halt in the semicircular gravel driveway of a two-story brick building.

Mr. Kindell pointed out the blue flag flapping over the main entrance. "Same design as on your blazer, Paul. The outline of a bishop's hat." Paul remembered when they bought the blazer at Harrods. Granny had been frantic at the price but loudly refused Sophie's earlier offer to help pay. "I do not take bribes from the woman who deceived my son." That was when Paul realized how angry Granny was about the divorce.

The moment they climbed out of the car they heard a distant booming. Not sure of its source, Paul looked around and frowned. "What's that noise? Like guns or explosions."

Mr. Kindell pointed out to sea. "Waves pounding on the cliffs, my friend. They're slowly eating England up. I bet you can see France from here."

Paul was thrilled. The breeze had a sharp tangy smell—like when they went to the beach in France, only this was stronger. A fizzy, pleasurable feeling ran through his arms and legs. His worries vanished. Instead, all sorts of questions streamed through his head. Did they let the boys walk and play on the beach? Did they learn how to catch fish and crabs?

Above him a twisting squadron of seagulls wheeled low, as if inspecting the visitors. Paul's heart thumped. An adventure was beginning. Grandpa had said it would happen: Paul was about to shake his own kaleidoscope.

"Hello everyone." A beaming man in a black gown bounded

down the front step, waving a welcoming hand. His plump, veined cheeks wobbled as he spoke. "I'm John Moon, headmaster. Young Paul Coulter, isn't it? Welcome to St. Justus. You're right on time."

Paul looked up at him. The shape of the headmaster's face matched his name. His graying hair was combed sideways, and when he smiled he showed white teeth. His belly stuck out. His gown fluttered like a flag in the wind.

The headmaster gestured to a big man standing close by. He looked like a farmworker. "Sykes, be a good chap and take the boy's trunk up to the dormitory."

As Mr. Kindell opened the car's boot the headmaster ran his hand over one of the Armstrong-Siddeley's shiny mudguards. "Such a magnificent car, Mr. Coulter. We hardly ever see beauties like this hereabouts."

George stared at him. "I am not Mr. Coulter, headmaster. I'm George Kindell, a friend of the boy's father. Captain Coulter is away in the army. I'm helping out."

"I am Paul's grandfather," said Emil, bowing slightly "Emil Kohut. My son and I have different last names."

"Ah, I see," said Mr. Moon," looking bewildered." Well, welcome to all of you."

A fair-haired boy with a narrow face and muscular legs encased in dark blue shorts ran down the front steps to join them. He wore a gray blazer with the embroidered St. Justus crest. "You wanted me to help, sir?"

The headmaster drew him forward. "This is Pratt, one of the seniors. Over the next couple of days he'll take your boy around and show him the school's geography. There's high tea in the dining room at four-thirty. As we do for all the new boys, Pratt will keep an eye on Paul for a few days. It can be awkward arriving half-way through a term."

Mr. Moon bent down and rested a plump hand on Paul's head. "From now on you will be Coulter. We don't use first names here. It's too complicated. And address me and all the masters as Sir."

"Yes, sir," said Paul warily. This naming stuff sounded a bit like what Daddy said happened in the army. Soldiers were called by their last name and ordered about. They couldn't do what they wanted. Daddy said it was discipline. Paul didn't like the idea of being called Coulter.

Mr. Moon turned to Emil. "Mr. Kohut, I'm sure you would like me to give you and Paul a tour of the school. It will take less than an hour. Then we'll have tea in my study and he can come and say good bye to you."

"I wish to see the classrooms and then the place where he sleeps, and anything else of interest. You have a gymnasium? And, I hope, a library."

Mr. Moon's eyebrows rose. "I detect a strong foreign accent, Mr. Kohut. I'm guessing you're from somewhere in Europe."

Emil nodded. "Czechoslovakia. Refugees from the Nazis."

"Oh, yes. I remember now. It was on Paul's application."

"The sun's out," said George. "I'll take a stroll along the cliffs. Which way should I go?"

Mr. Moon pointed toward the sea flecked with whitecaps. "On the other side of the road, there's a sign-post and a path across the Downs. It takes you to Seaford Head. But take care; the cliffs are a bit crumbly with a hundred foot drop in places. You'll get a superb view of the Channel and the Seven Sisters cliffs. The footpath takes you on toward the coastguard cottages and Cuckmere, a lovely estuary with lots of sea birds. Used to be a smugglers hideout."

Paul could hardly contain his excitement. This was what he had dreamed it would be like. A place full of adventures. He wanted to go on the walk with Mr. Kindell.

An hour later, George returned from his walk and waited for Emil and Paul, leaning against the passenger door, hands in his pockets. He was impatient to leave but didn't want to show it.

Mr. Moon came down the steps from the school entrance. "I suppose you will be off soon, Mr. Kindell. Paul seems to be a nice, quiet boy. I expect being a refugee has toughened him. I hope so. You know how other boys can be when they deal with someone who is not quite like them."

George laughed. "You mean they'll give him hell. Par for the course, I'd say. Actually, I think he'll manage pretty well. You probably have no idea what he and his family have been through. He's a resilient little chap."

Emil and Paul appeared from the far side of the main building. They walked up to the car. "We were inspecting the outdoor swimming pool."

"It's empty and slimy," Paul interjected.

Mr. Moon waved an apologetic hand. "We clean it in April. All the boys must be able to swim two lengths by the summer."

"Excellent," said Emil.

George opened the passenger door and jangled his keys. "Time for us to leave, Mr. Kohut Sit next to me. We'll talk."

Emil bent down to straighten Paul's shirt. "I'm proud that you are so calm," he murmured as he hugged the boy. "Three months of school will pass quickly. In June you come home for holidays and spend your birthday with us. "

"Will I be staying with Mummy too?"

"Of course."

"Don't look so sad, Grandpa," said Paul when Emil kissed him on the forehead. "I'll be all right here. Pratt told me there's a model airplane club, an electric train layout, Ping-Pong, a film every Sunday, acting in plays and other stuff."

"Plenty to keep you busy." Emil handed Paul a paper bag with the last of the rugelach. Granny will send you a nice cake from time to time."

Paul offered a pastry to the headmaster. "Would you like one of my granny's pastries, sir? They're called rugelach; they're jolly good."

Mr. Moon selected one. "Mmm, delicious," he mumbled with his mouth full.

With some effort, Emil inserted himself into the low slung passenger seat. "We can leave now, Mr. Kindell," he said with a deep breath. He waved to Paul. "This is a healthy place. They even grow their own vegetables. The classrooms look well supplied, and there are only eighty-five boys. So far so good. I'm satisfied."

George pulled the starter; the engine hummed. He jabbed a finger at Paul outside. "Have a good time, young man," he shouted as he shifted into gear and the tires crunched the gravel. "Just make sure you stick up for yourself."

CHAPTER THIRTY-FIVE
St. Justus
April 1944

As Grandpa had predicted, Paul's life changed dramatically as he struggled to adapt to a completely different life. He tried to fit in, study hard, avoid punishments and, if possible, make some friends.

He soon resigned himself to the unchanging routines: wake-up bell at six, breakfast, mumbled prayers, and lessons with different teachers, each one with their own particular style. He found it hard to adjust to their individual demands and foibles. He hated the lunches that consisted of lukewarm vegetables, mashed potatoes and sometimes a sausage, boiled mutton or beef hearts. In the afternoon the pupils went on a supervised, rain or shine, one-and-a-half hour walk on the Downs. In the afternoon there were more lessons, a cooked high tea—beans or a soft-boiled egg on toast—45 minutes of homework, more prayers and bed.

Saturdays, soccer and rugby practice were compulsory. Paul was a fast runner and liked the competitiveness but he had a hard time absorbing the rules. He soon learned to keep his spectacles in his shorts pocket. On Sundays, there was an hour of prayer and hymns, a sermon by Reverend Fothergill, the vicar of St. Leonard's, followed by Sunday Bible Discourse. They had some kind of roast meat and potatoes for lunch, and a two hour walk—the highlight of the week for Paul—down to the shingle beach at Cuckmere. After tea, the boys wrote letters home.

From time to time, Paul remembered how he had expected boarding school to be fun, especially after Pratt had shown him round saying how terrific it was. Paul loved the sports, the model airplane and chess clubs, and the musical appreciation class when Mr. Lousada discussed classical recordings after playing them on a wind-up gramophone.

Paul was one of three new mid-term boys or "squirts" and almost every day, he absorbed more than his fair share of shoves and curses, and night-time short-sheeting. The bullies pulled off his glasses and hid them, or played catch. He tried to stop them, even lost his temper and fought back. That made the bullying worse. Because of his accent, some of the other boys called him Pedro, even the friendly ones. There was a song popular on the radio—Pedro the Fisherman. The man sang it with a Spanish accent, nothing like Paul's. He tried to shrug it off, but at night he chewed over all the insults and shoves he had accumulated that day.

The twelve iron bedsteads in Paul's dormitory housed boys of different ages. There was a pecking order and the most senior boy, Aitken, was supposed to supervise dormitory rules and good behavior. Bedtime for Paul could be shameful and risky. His bed was a prime target for taunts and tricks. A regular one was for one of the bigger boys to snatch Furry Lion and toss it around the dormitory like a rugby ball while Paul chased after it or was tripped up. He finally consigned his companion to the bottom of his trunk for safe-keeping. In his head, he kept a list of his main tormentors promising that the day would come when they would pay for being so cruel.

Before lights out, the boys were required to say their prayers out loud, kneeling by their beds, elbows propped on the red coverlets, palms together. Kneeling at his bedside Paul mumbled and stumbled through the Lord's Prayer. This placed him squarely in the category of a "blithering idiot" or "ignorant clot." Sometimes the boys were allowed read their own bible before "lights out". To celebrate his enrolment at St. Justus, Dr. Carnegie-Holston—now officially his godmother after the baptism—had sent Paul the gift of a leather-bound bible.

At the end of the second month at St. Justus, Paul's kaleidoscope went missing. He found it two days later lying on his blanket, twisted and torn, its colored glass fragments scattered. This was the final straw. Even though sneaking was thought to be an unmanly defect even worse than crying, he reported the damage after class to Mr. Arrowsmith, the crusty-faced history and divinity teacher.

A few days later, one of the smallest boys in the dormitory told Paul that the kaleidoscope vandal was a boy called Shackton, the gangling eleven-year-old, leader of the most feared gang of bullies. Paul added Shackton to his hit list, but there was nothing else he could do except mourn his Grandpa's precious gift … and, if he asked, tell him it had been stolen.

For a long time, Paul and the two other "squirts", Gurley and Evans, put up with hazing. At night, they sobbed into their pillows as silently as possible, so no one would hear them—"blubbing" was the scathing word used by their tormentors. They commiserated with each other and became friends. Paul discovered there were different ways to make friends.

Paul worked hard. He found Latin, Math and Current Affairs the hardest—and he hated the forty-five minutes of homework after supper … the words spun, he had to re-read sentences and his eyelids felt like logs.

Mr. Nauwelaars, the bespectacled schoolmaster who taught French, took an instant dislike to Paul and often punished him for fidgeting with his pen, banging the desk with his feet or gigling at the teacher's odd Belgian accent when he rolled his "r"s, as in *très traumatique*. Mr. Nauwelaars, Paul concluded, was jealous.

Paul unconsciously distanced himself from the other squirts. Something about him steadily diminished the bullying and generated interest, even respect. He was the only pupil in the school who came from somewhere in Europe and he answered questions about his travels to France, Budapest and Prague (words he had learned at Grandpa's knee while listening to Signor Marconi) by embroidering the origins of his "war wounds." The thin scar just under the right side of his jaw was where a life-threatening abscess had been emptied by a brilliant French surgeon. The scar on his right shoulder was caused by an incendiary bomb explosion that destroyed his grandparents' flat in London. He would prove that he was telling the truth by showing them the bomb casing the following term. Elated by his own inventiveness and the admiration his stories provoked, Paul guessed that any story he told would be believed.

The old steamer trunk turned into Paul's winning card. At first he had worried that he would be laughed at because of his battered old tin trunk. The other boy's had leather suitcases or wooden tuck boxes. Grandpa had bought it from a rag-and-bone man in London. The other boys pestered Paul about the multicolored travel labels plastered on its sides. "Gosh, did your family go all that way to Hawaii?" "What was Cairo like?" "Did your Mummy see the mummies in the pyramids? Ha! Ha!" "Did your Dad ever go to the top of the Empire State Building?"

And so, Paul learned that his stories brought admiration and kept him safe. His family were adventurers and world travelers. The story line was simple. "This is my daddy's old trunk. In Prague, he worked for the Czech Secret Service. Before the war, he traveled the world." At night, Paul would review, refine and embellish the story plots before going to sleep; much more fun than blubbing and thinking about how much he missed Granny and Grandpa, and Mummy.

The daily walks at St. Justus were the most fun. One of the teachers would stride ahead of a crocodile line of boys—usually twenty or thirty—on the footpaths of the rolling, grassy downland. No shouting or throwing stones, no running, and no breaking away or hiding. Certainly no fighting! They were allowed to talk and switch partners on the way back. Paul preferred to stay quiet, keep to himself, and watch the wooden fishing boats with their nets hanging and the gulls wheeling around them. France was just across that strip of water. He wondered how Daddy, on the other side of the Channel, was getting on, fighting the Jerries. When he came home he would be full of stories. If he came home.

*   *   *

Paul's first term ended in high drama. The Allied invasion of Normandy occurred on June 6, and on June 14, the last day of school, a rumor raced through the classrooms, dining room and the sports changing room. The Germans had fired a new kind of bomb that flew by itself all the way from France to London. Headmaster Moon tried to suppress the news, worried that the boys would panic, then gave up. In class, Mr. Claudet, the science teacher said the bomb had a rocket engine, was called a V-1 and didn't make a sound before it exploded. Looking stern and grim, he said it might change the course of the war. Paul told his friends that his grandparents lived in London. They might be killed if the Germans fired more rockets.

The day before the end of term, the school's top cricket team played a home match against its archrival Ladycross Preparatory. Cricket was slow and boring but watching and cheering the home team was compulsory. In the end, St. Justus eked out a narrow victory.

After the match, at supper, the headmaster gave a congratulatory speech. As he presented little silver trophies to each of the players, the whole school erupted into a hip, hip, hoorah! followed by the rhythmic clatter of spoons banged on trestle tables: the tradition of the "Spoon Racket."

As he pounded his spoon, heart swelling, Paul felt proud of something he couldn't quite understand. Even the bullies and other boys he hardly knew, celebrated the achievement. He was part of something fine and important.

*   *   *

On June 15, Mr. Lousada, who taught English, drove Paul and his trunk to Brighton Station and put him on the train with two other boys. Two hours later, when the train pulled into London's Victoria Station, Grandpa was waiting on the platform.

When they got to Wycombe Gardens in Golders Green, the taxi driver helped Emil and Paul manhandle the trunk through a gate and down a concrete path to the front door. A heavily-built tabby, swishing its tail, greeted them with an impressive meow. It arched its back against Paul's legs. He was surprised at the cat's strength.

"Here we are at number nine," said Grandpa with a wink as he slid the key in the door. "Your first visit to our new house."

His grandparent's home was a two-story, semi-attached house with a room at the back for Paul.

"And this animal is Chippy. Not affectionate, but a talkative hunter. I don't know how old he is but he came with the house. As a reward for keeping and feeding him, he usually leaves me a dead bird or mouse, even a rat, on the backdoor mat. While you are here, it's your job to bury them."

Paul stroked Chippy and tried to pick him up and hold him. The muscular cat escaped easily. What a cat! It would be fun to watch him pounce.

After a smothering welcome from Granny, and a peek at his room, Grandpa showed Paul all the newspapers he had kept since the allied invasion of France. "Here's some homework for you, Paul. I expect you to read all the front pages, so we can talk about what is happening in France. Your daddy is there right now. In the middle of it." He pulled a crumpled airmail letter from his pocket, and smoothed it on the table. "His unit is part of the Twenty-First Army Group under Lieutenant General Crocker of the British Second Army."

Paul grabbed the letter and scanned it. At the end, he read "Give Paul a big hug for me." He hoped Daddy was killing Nazis but not in danger. He wanted Daddy to come home and watch him play soccer at St. Justus. "Do you think he's fought with any Germans yet?" The out-of-date Pathé newsreels projected after the main film on Saturdays at school only showed British soldiers running behind tanks, hunkered down in trenches or frantically jamming shells into field guns. There were never any Germans, dead or alive.

Emil shook his head. "Your daddy is too important to be at the front. He manages supplies for all the soldiers who have landed in France. In the letter, he calls it Rear Lodgement. Most of the tanks and food come from America now."

Paul blinked. His jaw dropped. "Crikey." Daddy wasn't actually fighting in the trenches. He was someone who ran things, like a headmaster. Boasting about his father managing food and transport would fall flat as a pancake.

Grandpa put the letter in a large cigar box he used to store all Willy's letters, fastening it with a rubber band. "In a day or two, we will all go to the cinema to see the newsreels of the invasion, and then I will take you to the library so we can look up the places."

Granny took off her apron, and picked up her overcoat, ready to go out. "It's your birthday in three days. Perhaps the postman will bring something special from your father."

Emil gave her a sharp look. "Please, my dear, no false hopes. Willy is working all hours of the day and night. What time does he have for writing letters?

Paul felt a lump in his throat. He would have loved a letter from

Daddy. In the last few weeks, he had sent three letters to Daddy's camp, with no reply.

Paul hoped for a lazy time in the holidays, but Grandpa dragged him into the garden and started him on digging, weeding, moving earth in a wheelbarrow, raking flower and vegetable beds, and trimming overgrown fruit trees. Most of the pears and apples had set, some were beginning to ripen. "Climbing trees will be your job when the fruit's ripe," Grandpa chuckled. "You're young and agile, but for Granny's peace of mind, I'll tie a rope round your waist and tether it to a branch."

Two weeks later, Paul found what looked like a very old coin in the ashes of a recent bonfire they had made. In the kitchen, Grandpa washed and scrubbed it with a toothbrush. He dried it with a rag and handed a magnifying glass to Paul. "Lucky you spotted this. I think it's bronze, very, very old—a little like me." He winked. "Tilt it to the light. See, there's a head on it, and writing round the edge. Can you make it out? My eyes are too weak."

"Septim—Sev—something. How old is it?"

Grandpa picked up the magnifying glass. "I make out one word ... Septimus. That's old Latin." He passed the magnifier to Paul. "The coin is from the Roman Empire. One thousand years old ... when the Romans conquered England. Think of it. A centurion lost his coin right in this spot. I wonder what he was doing at the time? I believe an archeologist would love to own this coin."

Paul had no idea what an archeologist was or did. He was too excited to ask. "Golly, Grandpa. D'you think we can find more coins if we dig? What were they doing in England? The Romans were in Palestine. I learned that in bible class."

Emil nodded. "The Romans were everywhere. They were clever foreigners just like us. Most of them went back to Italy, but many stayed here and turned into English men and women. Just like you will be when this war is over."

Paul had never seen a coin like this. A thousand years old. It would be a sensation at school, another weapon against the bullies. "Should we take it to a museum?"

"Good idea but the British Museum was bombed. We can try the local library and look for an encyclopedia."

Grandpa laid the coin on Paul's palm. "You found it. But for the time being I'll keep it in my document box—until you are a little bigger. It would be a pity if it was lost."

Paul laughed. "Thanks, Grandpa, that's super." He wondered if the coin was worth a lot.

A week after Paul's birthday, the postman delivered a parcel. Grandpa handed it to Paul with a little bow. "A delayed birthday gift from a close relative … I think." He winked at Granny who was knitting a cardigan by the window.

Paul instantly recognized the stamp and his father's handwriting on the address label. His heart jumped. "Whoopee, it's from France." Daddy hadn't forgotten his birthday after all.

He turned it over. **Inspected—Military Security** was printed on a piece of red tape on the back of the parcel. He cut the string with a knife, opened the box and put the flimsy envelope lying at the top to one side. Rummaging through shredded newspaper he found the gift: a metal wristwatch wrapped in tissue paper. It had a white rectangular face and a black leather strap.

Granny put down her knitting and came over to look.

"Gosh, How super!" Paul could hardly believe his good fortune. Only a handful of boys at school had watches. Shackton the bully was one of them.

"Polished steel," said Grandpa. "*Sehr gut gemacht*. Very well made. And, Paul, there's a word on the watch face."

"Luft … Luftwaffe. That's German, Grandpa. German Air Force. Golly, how did Daddy find it?"

"Read the letter and you'll find out" smiled Granny, slitting the envelope with her scissors. She put it on the table in front of Paul. "Our first proper news from Willy since he went to France. At least he is alive. So Paul, read for us."

Paul took a deep breath.

Dear Paul. At last, I have found a good birthday present for you. A WATCH! It belonged to a Luftwaffe pilot now a prisoner. It's very special and glows in the dark. Grandpa will explain why! We are getting ready to move toward Belgium. I am sure now that together with the Americans we will win the war.
I often think about you, wondering how you manage at school. You have so much to do now. A new school, and helping with Grandpa and Granny's new house. And I expect you will get to know your stepfather better during the holidays.
Love you and miss you very much, Daddy.

Paul let Granny strap the watch on to his wrist. His hands shook with excitement. The leather strap was too big, but that didn't matter. He was now the proud owner of two treasures. A Roman coin and a Luftwaffe watch. He would ask Grandpa if he could take the watch to school. Who else at St. Justus could possibly own a captured German pilot's watch that lit up in the dark? Maybe it was waterproof as well. He would ask Grandpa if it would be all right to test his idea out in the sink.

*   *   *

For the last ten days of his summer holiday, Grandpa arranged for Paul to stay with Mummy and Uncle Jon on the east coast near the resort of Margate. They were spending the summer in a place that belonged to Uncle Jon's family: old coastguard cottages on a cliff near the village of Birchington. Toby Mullins, the sharp-eyed gardener with gray side-whiskers, mowed the lawn and Minnie, an older woman who limped with a built-up shoe, was dropped off by her husband to make breakfast and clean.

Paul was impatient to see Mummy and find out what his stepfather was like. He wanted to watch how they loved each other. Would it be different from how Daddy had been with her? Would he discover the reason she had married Uncle Jon.?

Within a day of arriving, Paul knew he was in paradise. A shiny bicycle, his first, waited in the back porch and Uncle Jon, always fiddling with his RAF style mustache, introduced him to an enthusiastic black and white spaniel. "You will have the good fortune to keep Colin fed and watered, he said. "And be sure to brush him every day. His hair is like a vacuum … fills up with twigs and grass. Ha, ha." Uncle Jon's laugh was a bit donkey-like.

Paul liked Uncle Jon, and Mummy seemed pleased all the time. But there was something about Uncle Jon that stopped Paul from telling the truth, or saying what he really wanted to say, or how he felt about something.

Epple Bay, a half mile away, was marvelous; hardly any sand, just tidal pools stretching right across the bay partially blocked on one side by a mountain of chalk boulders. The gardener said that the outcropping was all that was left of a well-known smuggler's cave. Paul spent hours in the bay, often cycling there on his own and bringing back tiddlers or crabs in a bucket dangling from the handlebars.

Mummy took him shopping on the bus every day, and once

Uncle Jon drove them to the pier and funfair at Margate. On the way home they stopped at the Odeon cinema in Ramsgate to see "Lassie Come Home". But Paul was often bored in the evenings. Every night, Uncle Jon and Mummy played cards with Ruth, a small red-haired woman who never stopped talking and was staying for the summer to write a book. Paul would go to his room and read while the grown-ups drank whisky and gin, played cards, and smoked cigarettes into the night. Most of the time, Uncle Jon was nice enough, but he and Paul never did anything together: no walks, flying kites, cycling, fishing at the beach, or playing checkers.

Mummy still kissed and hugged him, called him "my Paulikin" and cooked super food. But she hardly asked him stuff about St. Justus: if he'd made friends and if he was doing well in sports and in class. He tried to tell her about the bullying and how he had to put up with being a foreign boy, but she didn't seem to listen or understand what it was like. She was different … less lively, not like when she had the café.

*   *   *

The autumn term began on September 5. The class work was much harder and the weather changed. Almost every day, winds brought rain gusts off the sea.

The autumn term sport was soccer. Paul started out on one of the junior teams. Without exception, every boy was expected to attend practice and play on the sodden fields, even when rain streamed down their faces and mud covered their boots. Paul was proud that he was the fastest runner on his team, and a strong tackler. The sports master, an ex-Navy officer, promoted him to a mid-level soccer team and put him on the wing. Being good at sport meant you might get into a team playing other schools. It meant that you were special, one of the chosen. It was another way to beat the bullying and gain respect.

There was a routine to clean-up after a game or practice. The basement changing room consisted of a mud-room, storage for sports equipment, lockers and benches. White tiles covered the walls, red tiles on the floor. Mud-spattered boys threw their clothes into a giant wicker basket and either soaked in a communal bath with their team-mates or took a shower.

One afternoon, after vainly looking for a lost boot stud on the pitch, Paul arrived late. The changing room seemed almost empty. He stripped off and showered, eyes closed, hot water scouring his arms and legs while he savored a small triumph. That afternoon, the sports master had told him that he was good enough to play in the school's second-eleven team. A match against Newlands was coming up in two weeks.

As he rotated under the shower, one of the older boys—sallow-skinned with a shock of curly black hair—was scrubbing himself under the far shower. Paul didn't know him but Bender was supposed to be "brainy." He was useless at sports and therefore perfect bait for bullies.

Paul pulled a towel off its peg and started to dry himself. He stopped at the cry of "Don't—please!" Three older boys already dressed but still wet-haired, flicked Bender with wet towels, laughing, egging each other on. Paul flinched at the sound of the towel corners snapping.

"Cowardy, cowardy, custard, Jew boy's stuck in mustard," they chanted as they flicked again and again. Bender begged them to stop, vainly trying to cover his genitals and his backside with his hands.

Paul froze, towel in hand. He hated watching but what could he do. Anyway, what was a Jew boy? What if they turned on him? Why wasn't Mr. Claudet, the science and sports master, there? He felt sick.

The pleading and fear in Bender's face triggered vague, disturbing memories: Daddy beaten with a gun, blood on Mummy's legs, people splashing in the sea, a big soldier lying next to him, dead.

He recognized one of the tormentors. Floppy haired and beaky-nosed Shackton, the destroyer of his kaleidoscope. Paul decided that the unwritten rule of not snitching to teachers no longer applied. "Hey, Shackton," he shouted, resentment swelling into his chest, "you bloody well leave Bender alone. Three against one is not fair. I'll get Mr. Claudet on you."

Shackton strolled over while the others stopped to watch. Up close, he was a head taller than Paul. "All right, goody-goody Coulter," he said, flicking out his rolled-up wet towel. "How about some piggy squeals from you? No squirt tells me what to do and gets away with it."

With the towel's first lancing sting, Paul's mind shot back to Knapp Farm Cottages and how it felt when Mrs. McAlistair thwacked him with a brush handle. He grabbed a wooden mop from the wall and swung it like a cricket bat.

Caught sideways on the temple, Shackton slipped and crashed to the floor. Paul ran towards the other boys who were standing round Bender. "Stop it, you buggers!" When they turned on him, he swung again. The mop-head smacked an ear. He saw blood on the mop-head. "You've bloody gone an' dun it!" his friend Eric would have shouted gleefully at the farm.

Bender's shower hissed in the silence. Paul hesitated. Shackton had vanished. The others ran off yelling insults.

"Are you all right?" Paul asked, turning off the shower. If Shackton snitched he was in for a caning.

Bender, head down, dabbed at the red flick marks all over his lower body. "I suppose so." He spoke with a slight lisp—at least his s's and r's sounded odd. "Thanks for the rescue. Actually, I'm sort of used to this kind of thing."

Paul looked at him, astonished. Why hadn't he put up a fight? He was as big as Shackton.

"You're Coulter, aren't you?" he said. "One of the squirts."

Paul stared at him. "You're one of the boys that gets bullied all the time. Why did they call you Jew boy? Are you a foreigner?"

The boy looked away. "We're from Manchester. Been there forever. Anyway, thanks. Jolly decent of you." He paused, looking down at Paul's genitals. "You know, we're sort of alike. Is that why you rescued me? Anyway, I have to get dressed." He limped away to his locker.

As Paul was drying his hair, feeling like a heroic crusader defending the weak, he wondered why Bender thought they were alike. He felt a tap on his shoulder. It was Bender, a dry towel round his waist.

"I want you to know something, Coulter."

"Oh? What's that?"

"My family's real name is Birnbaum. We're Jewish."

Nonplussed, Paul hung the damp towel around his neck. "Why hide your real name?" What so different about being Jewish? There were thousands of them living in Grandpa and Granny's part of London. "Is being Jewish why you never play games on Saturdays? And you're never at prayers."

"My Papa won't let me. We have a different religion."

"Golly. I thought everyone had to go to prayers. Is that why other boys bully you? You're big enough to fight. I would."

"My family doesn't fight. My Papa says I have to put up with being picked on. You'll see. One day, I'll be better than them—cleverer and richer."

Paul shrugged. "I suppose you know what you're talking about." The idea of not fighting back seemed silly. You were bound to get hurt.

He'd often heard Grandpa talk about the Jews who lived near their house in Golders Green, and the poorer ones in the East End. They'd fled from Europe because neighbors and friends robbed and attacked them in their villages. "Tea's up soon. We'd better get ready."

Bender looked down. "You know, Coulter, your plonker's just like mine." He unwound his towel, and held up his penis. "No foreskin, see. You're the same as me, circumcised."

"What's that mean?" Right from the beginning at St. Justus, Paul had noticed that his own penis looked a bit different from the others. During the holidays he had wanted to ask Grandpa, but he felt too embarrassed.

Bender chuckled. "You must be blind and dumb. Jewish boys have the flaps at the end of their plonkers cut off just after they're born. Circumcision. It's a tradition, see. Golly, I thought I was the only Jew here."

Paul examined his penis in awe. "Are you telling me someone cut my flaps off?

Bender retied the towel around his hips. "A *mohel* did it, that's who." He shook his head pityingly. "Haven't your parents told you anything?"

"I haven't the foggiest idea what you're talking about."

"You're a *Jew*, Coulter. Why else would you rescue me? I bet your family had a different name once."

Paul ran a comb through his hair. What if Bender was right? Grandpa had shown him an advanced tailoring certificate of his from Vienna. His name was listed on it as Emil Kohn. "I'm jolly well *not* Jewish. I'm Church of England. I was baptized in Cambridge. Stop fibbing about my plonker."

"Doesn't your family celebrate Shabbat, Rosh Hashanah, and Hannukah?"

Paul frowned. What was this foreign jabber? Could it be true, and his family hadn't told him? Or was Bender making everything up? And yet, his plonker did look like Bender's. "Look, my stepfather is Jewish. But he doesn't pray or go to a Jewish church."

"Does he eat bacon and pork?"

"Heaps. For breakfast every morning. Roast pork on Sundays. What's that got to do with it?"

Bender shrugged. "He's a *hiloni*."

Paul didn't care a fig what that was. Anyway, what was so wrong with being Jewish that you had to cover it up? The Divinity class was all about Jews, Jesus, David and Goliath, Moses, miracles, and battles with people smiting each other. Jews were special people.

"I've no idea what you're talking about," Paul said. "Just shut-up, we'll be late for tea."

"But we'll be friends won't we? You could help stop me getting bullied. We'll be a team. I can't wait to see their faces."

Paul stared at his self-appointed friend and thought back to the flicking towels. Just going around with Bender was a dangerous idea. Besides, a friend was someone you knew, liked, and had fun with. Bender was no friend, and seemed a bit too clever to have fun with. Paul had a feeling that Bender and trouble chased each other's tails.

Paul wanted Bender to leave him alone. He also wanted to find out the truth about his plonker. Did it hurt when they cut off the flaps? Did it change the way you pee'd? Why have flaps cut off? Silly idea.

At high tea, Bender plunked himself down next to him. Paul edged away, tried to ignore him. He needed time to mull things over. He remembered the kaleidoscope. Grandpa said a single shake could change the pattern of your life. Well, he was right—even here at school, things changed suddenly, like learning about the end of his plonker.

Chewing half-cold beans on burned toast, Paul ignored the

dining room chatter around him and thought about what happened in the changing room. He was a foreigner. Mummy and Daddy said he was here to become like the other English boys. Why didn't they tell him about being Jewish … if he was Jewish? There was no one at St. Justus to turn to with such questions. No one to give him warmth or love. It was a place where he had to rely on himself.

He felt a sting on his cheek and balls of squashed bread bounced off his head. He dodged another and heard suppressed giggling. Boys sitting on nearby benches were watching and fashioning their own ammunition.

Bender gave him a nudge. "Shackton's lot started the bread fight" he muttered.

Paul glanced over to the high table. The schoolmaster who taught Latin and History was bent over a book, sipping tea, oblivious to the mayhem. Shackton and his sniggering cronies were three tables away. The battle was joined. Paul grabbed a slice of soggy bread from the platter and broke it into pieces and began to mold them.

"Don't do it," said Bender going red. "That swine Shackton never gets caught … but the rest of us do. It's inevitable, like one of the Ten Commandments."

Shackton pointed at Paul and then, with a sneer, twisted his hands together as though he was wringing out a wet cloth.

Paul stuck out his tongue.

"Now you're in for it," Bender whispered. "He's going to get you for helping me."

"Not if I can help it."

CHAPTER THIRTY-SIX
The Reckoning
September 1944

That fall, Paul's letters home from school were no longer filled with local weather patterns, his occasional high mark in class, minor infractions and gossip about other boys. He wanted answers. Was I circumcised? And where? Am I Jewish? Why didn't you tell me? Where can I read about it?

Mummy wrote that he had been circumcised, but the details were a serious matter only to be discussed face-to-face with Uncle Jon. Grandpa explained how the Kohut family name had once been Cohen, the priestly tribe of ancient Samaria, now called Palestine. Paul had been circumcised by a *mohel* in the town of Košice, Slovakia. Granny wrote that the whole family was Jewish. Paul was to keep all of this absolutely to himself. She copied Willy's one line telegram from Brussels.

"Liberation! We covered 120 km in a day. Delirious crowds. The Germans melted away. Love. Willy."

Paul waited for a reply from Daddy. Nothing came. Too busy probably? Daddy would have explained about being a Jew, and where they came from, and why the family wasn't really Jewish anymore.

*　　　*　　　*

On Sundays, the whole school attended morning prayer service and then after lunch, divided into groups of ten for Sunday Bible Discourse—always supervised by a teacher. It was the only class at St. Justus where boys were encouraged to ask questions and discuss their opinions.

Paul was in Reverend Arrowsmith's SBD group. He often had the feeling that the crusty, unkempt teacher, usually dull and boring, relished leading this particular class. The old man's eyes glowed and sparkled behind his half-moon glasses. Everyone enjoyed the exciting stories about miracles, good and bad people, pain, smiting, suffering, and revenge. But since Paul's discovery, his interest in the Bible was intense. If he was Jewish these tales were about the places his family really came from. His ancestors must have been swashbuckling adventurers.

One Sunday in October, Reverend Arrowsmith waxed eloquent on the wandering undertaken by Jewish tribes following years of slavery in Babylon and Egypt. "They are still being persecuted by the Germans," he said with a grim look on his face. "Anti-Semitism is everywhere. Sometimes hidden, sometimes flagrant."

Paul put up his hand. "Won't it all stop when the war is over, sir?"

Reverend Arrowsmith peered over his glasses. "I doubt it."

After he dismissed class and hobbled out, Paul stayed at his desk studying his palm-sized bible, the delicate gilt-edged pages bound in black leather. Flicking through Leviticus, he chanced upon the building of the tabernacle and was fascinated by the specifics of its construction, trying to picture how it looked. Why had Mr. Leviticus used up so much space in his chapter to describe every detail of the structure? What was the point? This part of the bible was an instruction manual: like the diagrams for building model airplanes.

"It's time to be crucified, Coulter."

Paul looked up and saw that Shackton and his grinning allies from the locker room, Stephenson and Meldron, had surrounded his desk. Daggers of fear and panic twisted in his gut. So, finally, they had come to retaliate. His knees and thighs twitched but he couldn't move. He glanced around. No one else there.

Paul held his bible up. The only way out was an appeal of some sort. "Come on, Shackton, be a sport. Today's Sunday. A holy day." He tried a winning smile. "Peace and kindness. All sins forgiven. No ragging on Sundays?"

"You're having me on, squirt." Shackton laughed, flicking back a lock of flaxen hair. He patted Paul's cheek. "No violence, I promise. Not like you did to me with that mop. But as it's Sunday, we're going to baptize you properly." He shoved his thin, sneering face up close. "It never pays to rag with the Shackton gang."

What did Shackton mean … baptize? He felt his arms being pinned round the back of his chair. He felt the wet in his pants. All he could do was kick out when the time came to fight back. Shackton sauntered over to the teacher's desk, opened the lid, and returned with the reservoir of ink used to replenish the inkwells. Paul struggled desperately, afraid of what Shackton was conjuring up. Meldron fastened a school scarf round Paul's ankles.

Taking great care, as if pouring tea from an antique porcelain jug, Shackton splashed ink onto Paul's hair.

"Now, doesn't that feel good?" he asked.

With the cold trickle on his scalp, Paul saw the pleasure on Shackton's face.

"With this ink I now baptize you. Ye will be known henceforth as Inky Stinky Farter Coulter." Shackton laughed raucously, obviously pleased with his own rhyming. He poured more ink over Paul's shoulders.

Paul could barely see through ink-stained glasses at his ruined blazer.

Paul strained against his captors ready to fight. "You horrible, awful buggers."

"There now," said Shackton with a satisfied smile, screwing the cap back onto the reservoir. "A job well done. Let him go, chaps. If he sneaks on us, we'll just deny everything and say he had a terrible accident—spilt the ink on himself."

"God, he looks a sight," said Meldron, grinning happily, hauling Paul to his feet.

Shackton nodded. "Okay, Coulter, you blabby piece of snot, scoot out of here. It'll be fun to see what happens next. You may depart, Inky Stinky." Releasing him, the three stood in a line, laughing and ceremoniously doffing invisible top hats as they showed him the doorway out of the classroom. "Depart, depart, Coulter the Fart," they sang faces alive with triumph.

With ink splashed on the desk and the floor in front of him, and his clothes ruined, Paul felt this was somehow his fault and he would end up being punished. He saw spatters of black all over his bible. On the gilded pages that told the story of his probable Jewish origins. Fury boiled over. Just like the Philistines, they would pay. What could he do? Blab to Reverend Arrowsmith or the headmaster? Snitch against three older boys? He sobbed at the enormity of his weakness. He pushed past scattered chairs and desks toward the door. Shackton's gang roared with laughter, pointing ink-stained fingers at him.

Voices screamed in Paul's head, his anger coiling into action. He hoisted a chair and blindly swung it.

With a stifled cry, Shackton crumpled, blood pouring from his temple and staining his hair.

Paul stared triumphant and terrified at the same time.

Shackton lay curled up, whimpering, on the floor, hands covering his face as blood seeped between his fingers. "Arrgh—oh, God, help me, help me," he moaned. "Please, Coulter. Don't—" The rest of the gang rushed out yelling for help.

Paul stood holding the chair, now missing one of its legs. It was like the stone from David's sling. Shackton was Goliath. In class only half an hour earlier, Reverend Arrowsmith had quoted from the bible. "How are the mighty fallen, and the weapons of war perished." Only Paul wasn't sure who that mighty person was, Shackton or him.

Four hours later, Paul steeled himself for punishment in Mr. Moon's office. Even though he had scrubbed and bathed, and wore fresh clothes, there were ink stains on his forehead, neck, cheeks and hands. Shackton, with matron hovering over him, had been rushed by taxi to the Royal Sussex Hospital.

The headmaster, in his dark blue Sunday suit paced about, hands clasped behind his back, apparently deep in thought.

Paul was in danger but he wasn't ashamed. He replayed every crystal-clear moment and was astonished by what he had done—amazed at the exhilarating feeling of power he felt just before he bashed Shackton. He couldn't help a smile.

"What are you smiling at boy?" The headmaster perched on the edge of his desk, glaring at Paul. "This is no joke. It's damned serious."

"Sorry, sir. I don't know why I smiled."

"Why, Coulter? Why did the hell did you do it?" Mr. Moon shook his head wearily.

Paul looked down at his ink-stained hands, not wanting to meet the headmaster's look. "Sorry, sir. I couldn't help myself. They ruined my blazer, my trousers and my bible. Ever since I got here, they've bullied us squirts. They break stuff or steal things from the other boys, and they get away with it. I—"

The headmaster towered over Paul looking sad and angry. "What you did was very bad. Serious, Do you understand? "

Paul had a shock of understanding. What if Shackton was badly injured? Oh God! What if he died? He couldn't stop twisting his fingers. His breathing felt tight. Tears trickled down his face.

"I've had no previous reports of you misbehaving. Your work has been good. You've the makings of a fine athlete. And now this—

this … madness."

Paul clung to his chair, even though he yearned to run away and hide. "Shackton and his gang were beastly to me because I stopped them bullying Bender."

Mr. Moon frowned. "What do you mean? Stopped them."

"In the changing room, they were smacking and flicking him with wet towels. They called him Jew boy. Three on one isn't fair. I hit them with a mop. Why doesn't Shackton get punished when he bullies other boys?"

Mr. Moon sighed, twisting the gold ring on his finger, back and forth. "Well, Paul, you may have been partly justified. Smashing his head with a chair was a terrible thing. Your parents can easily replace your clothes but the scar on Shackton's head will be there forever."

Paul pinched his lips tight. Easy for Moonie to say. He doesn't know we don't have much money.

"As you might expect, I telephoned Shackton's father. Of course, it's impossible to get hold of your father." Mr. Moon picked a file off the desk. "I'm obliged to telephone someone in your family about this, but I'm not sure who. Your grandfather? Your mother?"

Paul wriggled in his chair. The awful thing he had done was going to be shared with the whole world. He was frightened. What would they do to him?

"This is worse than you think, Coulter. Shackton's father is on our school board and works at the Ministry of Defense. I want him to be satisfied that you are sufficiently punished. Now, Paul - who in your family shall I contact?"

Paul sat up. Being called by his first name … nicer than just Coulter. Moonie wasn't a bad sort really. Grandpa and Granny would panic. Daddy was for sure unreachable, and Paul wasn't sure Uncle Jon or Mummy would understand what was going on. Moonie mentioned the school board. *Aunt Popsie*. Paul had a vague memory

… she had something to do with that. That was how she'd got him onto the waiting list.

"Please sir, telephone Lady Hilliard. She knows me really well. I lived on her farm for a long time. She knows all about this school."

The headmaster took a deep breath and stared at Paul, rubbing his chin. "I know who she is. You'd better wait here. I'll see if I can get in touch right away."

He returned some minutes later and sat on the edge of his desk, holding a slim bamboo cane. "Lady Hilliard was very disappointed to hear what you did and agreed you must be severely punished."

Paul looked at the cane. There was no one to take his side. He knew what was coming and his stomach turned over.

"As I see it, you have a choice." Mr. Moon raised a forefinger. "Option one: I can expel you from the school, immediately. You'll go home and never come back. Of course, your family would have to find you another school. He paused. "And if that school contacted me for a recommendation, I would have to tell them what you did to Shackton."

Paul's stomach turned over. Kicked out! He'd be letting his family down terribly, and Lady Hilliard, and Dr. Emily, and Daddy's friend George. But he could start a different school with a clean sheet. Staying at St. Justus meant facing Shackton and his gang, day after day … and maybe other boys would turn against him.

"Option two: Restricted privileges for a month. No walks, no films, and no sports. And you also get a caning on your backside—six strokes with that." He pointed to a bamboo cane on the desk. "Do you have anything to say?"

Paul was astonished that he had a choice. Being thrown out of school would be like an ink stain, a permanent record. His family would be ashamed. A caning would hurt like the dickens, but it would be quick, and he hoped soon forgotten. He could stay on at St. Justus.

And he did want to stay. Of course, none of this hullabaloo was fair; Shackton was the violent one. He and his gang had started everything.

"Cane and restrictions, please, sir. But—do you still have to tell my family?"

"In due course, boy, I'm bound to inform them. But I will explain how you were provoked, and that you stood up to three boys. You showed courage, I'll give you that."

Paul nodded.

Mr. Moon took off his jacket and picked up the cane. He flexed it in his hands. "Now let's get it over with. But before we start, I have news about Shackton. His injury wasn't as bad as we thought, and his father agreed not to bring any charges. He said he would be satisfied if you received a corrective flogging."

"Yes, sir." Relief flooded into Paul's heart. Maybe his own situation wasn't so bad after all. He felt like smiling but beat it back.

"Now bend over the back of your chair. Have you been beaten before?"

"Sort of, sir," said Paul.

"Well it'll hurt. Just keep your eyes closed and picture something you really enjoy, like eating chocolate or going to see an exciting film."

Paul bent over the back of the chair and gripped the edges of the rush seat. He was as taut as a bowstring. When the first stroke smashed into his buttocks, he thought how much he wanted to be hugged and kissed by someone he loved: though he wasn't sure who he wanted it to be. He gritted his teeth and blanked out his mind for the five subsequent excruciating strokes. The caning had been worse than he expected. The relief that followed was wonderful. It was over.

"Before I dismiss you," the headmaster said, returning to his chair, "I want you to listen very carefully." He dropped the cane onto his desk.

Paul nodded, gently rubbing his backside and feeling the painful ridges of beaten flesh underneath his pants. Agony radiated down the backs of his legs. "If you had been an English boy, I would have immediately expelled you. But Lady Hilliard talked about extenuating circumstances. Do you know what I mean by that?"

Paul nodded again even though he had no idea what "extenuating" meant and he wasn't quite sure how it was connected to circumstances. He smiled. Lady Hilliard was a jolly good sort. He would have liked a hug from her just now.

Mr. Moon mopped his face with a handkerchief. "She was very upset at what you did, but said that your family's Jewish and had a hard time escaping from the Germans. And that you lived on her farm. She thinks a lot of you. She wants to help you succeed here in England."

Most of the headmaster's words floated past Paul. Three stuck in his consciousness: *Your family's Jewish.*

So what Bender and Grandpa and Granny and Mummy said was really true. Even Aunt Popsie knew it.

"Because of your family's circumstances and Lady Hilliard's influential position on the school board, I will be lenient this time, but from now on I expect impeccable behavior—do you understand?"

Paul nodded and groaned. He kept shifting in his chair, trying to find a position where his buttocks didn't hurt so much. The pain stopped him from thinking straight. He couldn't even respond to what Mr. Moon had just asked.

Mr. Moon leaned back in his chair and lit a cigarette. "You will have to learn to control your emotions, Paul, and follow the rules. English boys are supposed to keep their anger in check and not get into fights. It's not a good idea to show what you really feel in tense situations, because that will likely land you in trouble. Do you understand? This must never happen again."

Paul discreetly rubbed his backside. This little lecture was rubbish. He'd seen lots of boys losing their tempers. Nothing happened to them. "Yes sir. Please sir, what will happen to me now?"

"Nothing else. Just go back to being one of the boys of St. Justus."

"But, sir, I'm a Jew? Bender doesn't fit in, does he? And I'm not even clever."

"Nonsense. I'm sure you'll fit in. You are good at sports and that engenders respect. Bender has an unusual face, but you don't look any different from the other boys. St. Justus will do its best for you, and of course, your family will help. But the person who directs your life must be *you*. It'll take effort and persistence. Are you ready to take some hard knocks down the road?"

"I suppose so, sir." His behind throbbed and throbbed. Everyone in his family was busy with their own life: Mummy with her new boring husband, Daddy fighting Jerries in Belgium, Grandpa and Granny, old and fussy. How could they help him? His mind, still foggy from pain began to clear. School, life, his future, it was … mostly up to him.

Mr. Moon gave a broad smile. "Righty-ho, Coulter. Get your sore tail out of here. The whole school knows what happened to Shackton and that I've given you the appropriate whacking. At suppertime, you'll have to face the dining room. Whatever reaction you get, show them you're brave."

"Yes, sir. Thank you, sir," said Paul as he limped out of the office door. He hadn't thought about the consequences of being caned. The prospect of facing the assembled school was terrifying. Better to hide somewhere, but then he would be called a coward as well.

Late in the day, as the boys filed in for supper, Paul could tell from the sidelong glances and half-smiles that everyone knew. There was silence while he walked stiff-legged and wincing, trying not to limp to his place at the long table by the bay window. They all remained standing while Mr. Moon recited the usual grace:

Benedictus Benedicat per Jesum Christum Dominum Nostrum. Amen.

The dining room filled with conversation and the clink of silverware and dishes. Paul gasped as he sat down, pain pulsing in waves through his buttocks. He tried to keep his body still. Everyone was watching to see if there was suffering on his face or tears on his cheeks.

As the kitchen staff set out plates of buttered bread, lettuce leaves and hard-boiled eggs, the boys at his table looked at him expectantly and then started in on him "What was it like, Coulter?" "Shackton got what he deserved, didn't he?" Someone else muttered. "I bet you blubbed." Grins and encouraging comments followed.

As the maids ladled out bowls of pea soup from the head of each table, Paul saw Bender look at him as the bowls were passed along his face, a picture of triumph—as if Shackton's downfall had been all his doing. Paul gave him a weak smile and began to eat his soup, not wanting to talk to anyone.

Somehow, Bender caught Paul's eye again, raised his soup spoon high in the air. He brought it crashing down—thwack—on the oak surface. Everyone turned at the noise. Conversation stopped. In total silence, he did it again, and then, again, and again—rhythmically. "Coulter," Bender shouted at the top of his voice as his spoon hit the table, "Coul-ter ... Coul-ter ... Coul-ter... Coul-ter ..." The repeated thwack of the spoon and yell of "Coul-ter" punched through the air like an insistent call to arms. Boys at the other tables turned to look at Bender and then at Paul. Some grinned, others raised their eyebrows in surprise. They took up the refrain, and picked up their spoons. A crescendo of pounding spoons and shouts of "Coul-ter" echoed in unison through the dining room.

Paul sneaked a look at the teachers, afraid that they might throw him and Bender out of the dining room. But they stood like statues, exchanging glances, shaking their heads. One or two were smiling. Paul grinned, his pain almost forgotten. Like a St. Justus sports victory, this was overwhelming approval of his defeat of Shackton and his followers. All those smiling, enthusiastic faces conveyed something wonderful. You are us. You belong.

EPILOGUE
Headmaster's Office, St. Justus School.
Five Years Later—May 1949

This was it! Moonie's farewell talk. The portly headmaster sat behind his kneehole desk, strewn with folders and papers. A coal fire glowed in one corner. Paul hoped it wouldn't take long. Calm on the exterior, inside he was exultant. This would be the last time he wore his grey blazer and striped school tie. The days of short trousers, knee socks and sandals were over—and Grandpa was here, sitting beside him, ready to take him back to London.

He looked around the headmaster's office fingering the packet of chocolate-covered Maltesers in his pocket, sent by Granny. He remembered the chair he'd bent over when Mr. Moon caned him but not the bookcase that occupied most of the wall behind the desk. Squeezed together on the top shelves, stood a phalanx of teddy bears, puppy dogs, tigers, and rabbits; a cornucopia of fuzzy colors, glass eyes and black noses, the bed-time companions of many St. Justus boys who were grown men, some fighting in the war. Over the years, the soft toys had been confiscated, left behind, or lost by departing pupils.

In preparation for the headmaster's goodbye "chat," Paul had brushed his hair flat and wore new wire-rimmed spectacles. He glanced at the sheet of paper his grandfather was holding. Was this term's school report good enough? What if Moonie brought up Paul's propensity for breaking rules and picking fights? And an important decision had to be made by his parents, Moonie had said, about the identity of the next school.

But Daddy was in Belgium because his stepmother Claire was expecting their first baby any minute, and Mummy was winging her way with Uncle Jon in a BOAC flying boat to Australia to see her father and brother. So, only Grandpa was here to talk about schools. Paul frowned. His parents could have come if they'd really wanted to.

Emil Kohut, spruced up in an old pinstripe double-breasted suit, placed Paul's grade report on Mr. Moon's desk. "Second in the school's top class," he smiled. "An excellent result, headmaster, I'm proud of him."

Paul felt a glow of satisfaction. Grandpa was patting his back. A rare display of praise.

"Your grandson also did well in the Common Entrance examination in January. That's the test that advances him into the next school. Even more important than his class performance will be the letter of recommendation I send to the headmaster of wherever Paul is going. Now we must decide which school he should apply to."

Paul straightened in his chair. He hadn't thought Moonie would have so much to do with all this choosing stuff.

Emil Kohut scratched his head. "I have trouble understanding your system here. What kind of school will this next one be?"

The headmaster hunched forward. "From where you come from, I think you would call it a high school. I understand your son discussed this issue with British friends and came up with St. Paul's in London."

"*Ach*, you mean *Hochschule*."

Mr. Moon nodded. "I have absolutely no doubt, Mr. Kohut, that St. Paul's School will accept your boy on my recommendation. He's an intelligent, self-reliant chap..." He shot a knowing look at Paul. "At times he has an unfortunate habit of solving problems with his fists."

Paul noticed his grandfather's scowl. *Blast!* He would get hard questions about fists on the train home, but... was it St Paul's, Moonie just said? Why on earth did Daddy choose that one?

"Forgive me for asking," said Mr. Moon with a brief smile. "I was wondering why Mr. Coulter had put Shrewsbury School on his list? It's a reputable boarding school, but way up in the Midlands. Much easier to apply to St. Paul's, Highgate, Merchant Taylors, or Westminster, all fine schools in London where the boys can live at home." He smiled briefly.

Paul's heart pulsed in alarm. Live at home? In Golders Green, he would have to put up with Granny and Grandpa's old-fashioned ways. In Chelsea, he'd have to live with Uncle Jon's chain-smoking, boozing and moodiness. "Walk on eggshells," Mummy had warned when Paul spent part of the last Christmas holiday with them.

"What if we cannot get Paul into one of the schools you mentioned?" said Grandpa.

Mr. Moon waved a dismissive hand. "This is the reason boys come to St. Justus—a smooth escalator into higher education and university."

Emil turned to Paul. "What do *you* think? I don't know enough about these places." He rubbed his forehead. "Such a pity your father isn't here."

Paul was taken aback by Grandpa's question and ashamed that he hadn't paid attention to the school talk in his parent's letters. He'd thought Daddy and Mummy would do the choosing after they had argued enough, and after Uncle Jon stuck his nose in because he was supposed to help pay the fees. All he could think about, at this moment, was to choose whether to live at home or live at boarding school.

He knew pretty much what he wanted next: a school with rules, where he could make friends, play lots of sports, and know who was in charge. He didn't want to live in two different worlds, school in the day and his broken family at night. He expected there would be more bullying at a boarding school, and he would have to defend himself. But he wanted a place where he would be Paul all the time, and not Paul and Pavel mixed up together. He could stay with the different bits of his family during the holidays, just as he had done before.

Paul looked at the headmaster. "Well, sir." he said in as confident a voice as he could muster. "What I've liked about St. Justus is why I want to be in the same kind of school again." He glanced at his grandfather for some gesture: approval or a signal to stop.

Receiving no clues, Paul took a deep breath. "And, I suppose, sir, you should know why I specially want to go to Shrewsbury? Well—'cause Lady Hilliard once took me around that school when I lived on her farm. I could tell straight off that it was a super place. Did you know that Darwin was a pupil there, and also one of the famous climbers who died at the top of Mount Everest? She said it was one of the best schools in the country, and, if I went there, I could visit her at the farm any weekend. Best of all, she said she could help me get in there."

Polishing his glasses, Emil said, "Lady Hilliard is a very fine person. She's fond of him."

Mr. Moon tapped ashes from his briar pipe into an ashtray. "Let's not rush this. Family ties are extremely important. Why doesn't your son in Belgium want Paul to grow up there, under his guidance and tutelage?

Emil squeezed Paul's shoulder and gave him a smile. "In his short life, Paul has lived in Czechoslovakia, France and England. Going to Belgium would add to the disruption. At the moment, Captain Coulter has a job in his wife's family business in Brussels. As a family, we have often talked this over and what my grandson needs now is stability—such as your school has provided. We always agreed that Paul must grow up to be an Englishman. Of course, that would be impossible if he went to a French-speaking school."

Paul silently agreed with Grandpa. He didn't want to grow up in Brussels. It was fun to visit, and eat mussels and *pommes frites* and go on trips in Daddy's car, but he had no friends there. Boys there didn't even play cricket or rugby.

Mr. Moon stuffed tobacco into his pipe and fired it up with his desk lighter. "Seems like your family's at sixes and sevens at the moment," he said between studied puffs. "However, I very much hope that what we decide will put Paul on the path to a fine career."

Emil took a deep breath, looking hard at Paul. "To be frank, Mr. Headmaster, I don't believe this young man knows *where* his home is. But he clearly wants to attend boarding school in England. Don't you?"

"Yes, and I want it to be Shrewsbury," said Paul firmly. As far as he knew, no other St. Justus boys were going there, but that was okay. He would make new friends.

Grandpa was right. He didn't know where he belonged. The divorce court had ordered that he belonged mainly to Daddy and a little bit to Mummy; though at sixteen Paul could legally decide where his home would be.

There was a sharp knock at the door. The school porter stood in the doorway "The taxi's here, headmaster. I brought down the lad's trunk. I'll be outside if you need me."

The headmaster nodded, and the door closed. "I'll write to your son about our meeting today. When and if he agrees on Shrewsbury, I will draft a strong letter of recommendation for Paul to the headmaster."

Bubbling over inside, Paul picked up his valise, smiling at his grandfather. "Let's go, Grandpa."

Emil Kohut pulled on his overcoat and picked up his trilby. "So we say goodbye, headmaster. It will not be so easy for us to visit the boy in Shrewsbury. It is twice as far as coming here, but it is the first big decision Paul makes by himself. Thank you for what you have done for him."

Mr. Moon walked over and pumped Paul's hand. "Dear boy, we

greatly enjoyed having you at St. Justus. You will make a fine doctor one day, if that's what you want. And come back and see us sometime."

Paul grinned as he put on his school cap. He liked what Moonie had said.

"Thank you, sir. I'll do my best."

He pulled Furry Lion, worn and one-eyed, from his satchel. Snapshots of their times together flashed into his head: hunting rabbits, finding the incendiary casing on Grandpa's balcony—and snuggled up on his pillow at Knapp Farm. Furry Lion was his past, just like Mummy and Daddy, whom he loved but who had their own families. It was better to wipe the slate clean.

He set Furry Lion on the headmaster's desk. "This is Furry Lion from Prague. He speaks Czechoslovak and just a little English. Could you add him to your collection, please?" He pointed to the top shelf of the bookcase. "He doesn't really need me anymore—and I want him to be up there, among friends."

Dear Reader,

Thank you for reading *Pavel's War*. I hope you enjoyed it enough to find a moment to write a brief honest review of it on Amazon. Authors like me depend on such reviews to publicize their work and get some recognition.

To submit a review –
Find *Pavel's War* on Amazon Books and click in Customer Reviews. Just a few lines on what you found particularly interesting/enjoyable/significant will suffice.

Pavel's War is the last volume of The KOHUT TRILOGY, three sequential novels based on my family's odyssey through Europe in WW11. If you have not read the other two, *The Dragontail Buttonhole* and *Café Budapest*. I urge you to do so. They have received good reviews. Each one in a different European country, with its own wartime story to tell—involving different engaging and unpleasant characters … at a crucial time in world history.

Visit www.petercurtisauthor.com to find the Gallery, an interesting photo background to The Kohut Trilogy

Many thanks,

Peter Curtis

ACKNOWLEDGEMENTS

I am most grateful to Jaroslav Bouček, former Historian and Archivist of the Military Institute, Prague for reviewing and correcting my manuscript. Thanks also to Tomáš Jakl of the same Institute for permission to use photographs on my website gallery of the Czechoslovak Army-in-Exile in France, courtesy of Státní Oblastní Archiv v Zámsrku- SOkA, Pardubice.

Immeasurable thanks to Marlin Greene of 3Hats for the design of my website (www.petercurtisauthor.com) and the covers of *PAVEL'S WAR* and its predecessors, *THE DRAGONTAIL BUTTONHOLE* and *CAFÉ BUDAPEST*—as well as his close collaboration with formatting and printing the text. My sincere appreciation to Lesley Dahl for prompt and efficient editing. I am indebted to the penetrating, constructive comments and steadfast support of two writer groups in Seattle, USA. Ravenna Writers: Lynn Knight, Lauren Basson, Eugene Marckx and Gary Bloxham. Third Place Writers: Teresa Hayden, Elizabeth Gage, Teri Howatt and Brian Schuessler. Special thanks to my wonderful writing colleague, Brita Butler-Wall, for her linguistic skills, incisiveness and incredible commitment to laboring over my manuscript.

Sincere thanks to Elizabeth Krijgsman, Helen Szablya, Howard Droker, Victoria Farr Brown, Danielle Carr, Mike Cory, Bill Taraday and Goldie Silverman for their valuable critical reading, support and reviews of the manuscript.

For information on Peter Curtis, my historical research and my other books, *The Dragontail Buttonhole* and *Café Budapest*, see www.petercurtisauthor.com or visit the author's page at Amazon Books, Facebook and Pinterest.

AUTHOR'S NOTE

Major sources for this book included family artifacts, maps, official documents, photographs, stories and a memoir dictated by my mother. The characters in this novel, except for Pavel, known as Paul later in the book, are either fictitious or deceased. Real people, places and events have been depicted as accurately as possible in the time frame of 1938 to 1949. Any resemblance to actual events, places or person, living or dead is coincidental.

Loose Ends: Some years after WWll, Bill Coulter became a travel writer and lived with his wife and two children in Brussels. Sophie moved with her property tycoon husband to Chelsea, London, and had two children. Paul entered Shrewsbury School and went on to train at Guy's Hospital Medical School. During his studies, he lived with Emil and Judit who spent their final years in London. St. Justus School closed down in 1982.

For many years, Paul stayed in touch with Lady and Sir Edward Hilliard. They remained true friends and sponsors of the Kohut family. Dr. Emily was Paul's godmother.

ADDITIONAL NOTES

For the Kohut Trilogy, I have relied heavily on certain published resources:

The Czechoslovak Army in France: 1939-1945. Roy E. Reader. Czechoslovak Philatelic Society of Great Britain Monograph #5.1987

Cˇeskoslovenská Divize Ve FRancia (1939-1940) Gustav Svoboda. Ministerestvo obrany Cˇeské republiky

Armada druheho odboje. General Oldrich Spaniel. Chicago 1941.Prague 1945

Master of Spies by General Frantisek Moravec, Sphere Books Ltd. 1975

Prague in Danger by Peter Demetz, Farrar, Strauss and Giroux 2008

Prague. My Long Journey Home by Charles Ota Heller. Abbott Press 2011

On All Fronts: Czechs and Slovaks in World War II. Editor, Lewis White.

East European Monographs, Boulder.Co. 1991 (Vols 1, 2)

Czechoslovakia in WW2, East European Monographs. Boulder Co. 2000. Ed, Lewis M White.

Prague in the Shadow of the Swastika, Collum MacDonald and Jan Kaplan. Facultas Verlags und Buchhandels AG. 2001 Wien.

Island Refuge. Britain and Refugees from the Third Reich 1933-1939. AJ Sherman. University of California Press. Berkley. 1973.

The Jews of Czechoslovakia Historical Studies and Surveys, volume 3. Eds. Avigdor Dagan, Gertrude Hirschler and Lewis Weiner 1984. The Jewish Publication Society of America, Philadelphia.

Society for the History of Czechoslovak Jews, Ansonia Station. PO Box 230255. New York, NY 10023

Memoirs of a Volunteer. Henry Baumgarten. The Book Guild Ltd. Lewes, Sussex, UK. 1990.

Escape to England. Karel A. Machachek. The Book Guild Ltd. Lewes, Sussex, UK. 1988

Ten Days to D-Day: Countdown to the Liberation of Europe. David Stafford. Thistle Publishing. 2015. London. UK

Praise for the Kohut Trilogy

The Dragontail Buttonhole: After losing their home and possessions, Willy and Sophie Kohut and their small son flee Nazi-occupied Prague in the summer of 1939. They arrive in Paris after a chaotic and desperate journey.

… at once a moving portrait of a marriage, a brilliant evocation of a frightening period of history and a spell-binding tale of survival.
   David Laskin, Author

Café Budapest: penniless in Paris, the Kohut family struggles to survive. Overcoming illness and befriended by a kindly baker and his wife, Willy, Sophie and Pavel head south to join up with the Czechoslovak Army–in Exile, just as the German armies invade from the north.

The Kohut's year-long sojourn in France includes the warmth of the Café Budapest, the shock of their son's illness, the rigors of army life and the chaotic sea evacuation by thousands as France surrenders to the Germans … Curtis vividly evokes the atmosphere and stresses of those times assisted by a firm grasp of historical facts.
   Jaroslav Bouček Ph Dr.CSc. Historian

Pavel's War: Seeking refuge in wartime Britain, the Kohut family, reunited with Willy's parents in London, are caught up in the Blitz After their apartment is destroyed by an incendiary, they are forced to separate. Willy joins the British Army. Sophie finds work as a maid and begins to assert her independence. Pavel, like so many other British children, is sent to live with strangers on a farm. Gradually each family member begins to carve out their own path in wartime Britain.

…Curtis continues to artfully braid literary poignancy with potent historical witness in this achingly realistic tale. A heartbreakingly beautiful drama about the wages of survival …
   Kirkus Reviews May 2019

CPSIA information can be obtained
at www.ICGtesting.com
Printed in the USA
FSHW012146091119
63881FS